PERFECT

PERFECT

CECELIA AHERN

SQUARE
FISH

FEIWEL AND FRIENDS
NEW YORK

SQUARE FISH

An imprint of Macmillan Publishing Group, LLC
175 Fifth Avenue, New York, NY 10010
fiercereads.com

Square Fish and the Square Fish logo are trademarks of Macmillan and
are used by Feiwel and Friends under license from Macmillan.

Our books may be purchased in bulk for promotional, educational, or business use. Please
contact your local bookseller or the Macmillan Corporate and Premium Sales Department
at (800) 221-7945 ext. 5442 or by e-mail at MacmillanSpecialMarkets@macmillan.com.

Library of Congress Cataloging-in-Publication Data

Names: Ahern, Cecelia, 1981– author.
Title: Perfect / Cecelia Ahern.
Description: New York : Feiwel and Friends, 2017. | Sequel to: Flawed. | Summary:
  Since Celestine, eighteen, was declared a public menace, she has been on the run
  with Carrick, the one person she can trust, but she has a secret that may save all of
  those branded Flawed.
Identifiers: LCCN 2016024481 | ISBN 978-1-250-14414-0 (paperback) |
  ISBN 978-1-250-13561-2 (ebook)
Subjects: | CYAC: Science fiction. | Prejudices—Fiction. | Fugitives from justice—Fiction. |
  Government, Resistance to—Fiction.
Classification: LCC PZ7.1.A33 Per 2017 | DDC [Fic]—dc23
LC record available at https://lccn.loc.gov/2016024481

Originally published in the United States by Feiwel and Friends
First Square Fish edition, 2018
Book design by Liz Dresner
Square Fish logo designed by Filomena Tuosto

10 9 8 7 6 5 4 3 2 1

LEXILE: HL730L

For Yvonne Connolly, the perfect friend

PERFECT: *ideal, model, faultless, flawless, consummate, quintessential, exemplary, best, ultimate;* (of a person) having all the required or desirable elements, qualities, or characteristics; as good as it is possible to be.

PART ONE

ONE

THERE'S THE PERSON who you think you should be and there's the person who you really are. I've lost a sense of both.

TWO

A WEED IS just a flower growing in the wrong place.

They're not my words, they're my granddad's.

He sees the beauty in everything, or perhaps it's more that he thinks things that are unconventional and out of place are more beautiful than anything else. I see this trait in him every day: favoring the old farmhouse instead of the modernized gatehouse, brewing coffee in the ancient cast-iron pot over the open flames of the Aga instead of using the gleaming new espresso machine Mom bought him three birthdays ago that sits untouched, gathering dust, on the countertop. It's not that he's afraid of progress—in fact he is the first person to fight for change—but he likes authenticity, everything in its truest form. Including weeds: He admires their audacity, growing in places they haven't been planted. It is this trait of his that has drawn me to him in my time of need, and why he is putting his own safety on the line to harbor me.

Harbor.

That's the word the Guild has used: *Anybody who is aiding or harboring Celestine North will face severe punishment.* They don't state the punishment, but the Guild's reputation allows us to imagine. The danger of keeping me on his land doesn't appear to scare Granddad; it makes him even more convinced of his duty to protect me.

"A weed is simply a plant that wants to grow where people want something else," he adds now, stooping low to pluck the intruder from the soil with his strong hands.

He has fighting hands, big and thick like shovels, but then in contradiction to that, they're nurturing hands, too. They've sewn and grown, from his own land, and held and protected his own daughter and grandchildren. These hands that could choke a man are the same hands that reared a woman, that have cultivated the land. Maybe the strongest fighters are the nurturers because they're connected to something deep in their core, they've got something to fight for, they've got something worth saving.

Granddad owns one hundred acres, not all strawberry fields like the one we're in now, but he opens this part of the land up to the public in the summer months. Families pay to pick their own strawberries; he says the income helps him to keep things ticking over. He can't stop it this year, not just for monetary reasons but because the Guild will know he's hiding me. They're watching him. He must keep going as he does every year, and I try not to think how it will feel to hear the sounds of children happily plucking and playing, or how much more dangerous it will be with strangers on the land who might unearth me in the process.

I used to love coming here as a child with my sister, Juniper, in the strawberry-picking season. At the end of a long day we would have more berries in our bellies than in our baskets, but it doesn't feel like the same magical place anymore. Now I'm de-weeding the soil where I once played make-believe.

I know that when Granddad talks about plants growing where they're not wanted, he's talking about me, like he's invented his own unique brand of farmer therapy, but though he means well, it just succeeds in highlighting the facts to me.

I'm the weed.

Branded Flawed in five areas on my body and a secret sixth for good measure, for aiding a Flawed and lying to the Guild, I was given a clear message: Society didn't want me. They tore me from my terra firma, dangled me by my roots, shook me around, and tossed me aside.

"But *who* called these weeds?" Granddad continues as we work our way through the beds. "Not nature. It's *people* who did that. Nature *allows* them to grow. Nature gives them their place. It is *people* who brand them and toss them aside."

"But this one is strangling the flowers," I finally say, looking up from my work, back sore, nails filthy with soil.

Granddad fixes me with a look, tweed cap low over his bright blue eyes, always alert, always on the lookout, like a hawk. "They're survivors, that's why. They're fighting for their place."

I swallow my sadness and look away.

I'm a weed. I'm a survivor. I'm Flawed.

I'm eighteen years old today.

THREE

THE PERSON I think I should be: Celestine North, daughter of Summer and Cutter, sister of Juniper and Ewan, girlfriend of Art. I should have recently finished my final exams, been preparing for college, where I'd study mathematics.

Today is my eighteenth birthday.

Today I should be celebrating on Art's father's yacht with twenty of my closest friends and family, maybe even a fireworks display. Bosco Crevan promised to lend me the yacht for my big day as a personal gift. A gushing chocolate fountain on board for people to dip their marshmallows and strawberries. I imagine my friend Marlena with a chocolate mustache and a serious expression; I hear her boyfriend, as crass as usual, threatening to stick parts of himself in. Marlena rolling her eyes. Me laughing. A pretend fight, they always do that, enjoy the drama, just so they can make up.

Dad should be trying to show off in front of my friends on the dance floor, with his body-popping and Michael Jackson impressions. I see my model mom standing out on deck in a loose floral summer dress, her long blond hair blowing in the breeze like there's a perfectly positioned wind machine. She'd be calm on the surface but all the time her mind racing, considering what is going on around her, what needs to be better, whose drink needs topping off, who appears left out of a conversation, and with a click of her fingers she'd float along in her dress and fix it.

My brother, Ewan, should be overdosing on marshmallows and chocolate, running around with his best friend, Mike, red-faced and sweating, finishing ends of beer bottles, needing to go home early with a stomachache. I see my sister, Juniper, in the corner with a friend, her eye on it all, always in the corner, analyzing everything with a content, quiet smile, always watching and understanding everything better than anyone else.

I see me. I should be dancing with Art. I should be happy. But it doesn't feel right. I look up at him and he's not the same. He's thinner; he looks older, tired, unwashed, and scruffy. He's looking at me, eyes on me, but his head is somewhere else. His touch is limp—a whisper of a touch—and his hands are clammy. It feels like the last time I saw him. It's not how it's supposed to be, not how it ever was, which was perfect, but I can't even summon up those old feelings in my daydreams anymore. That time of my life feels so far away from now. I left perfection behind a long time ago.

I open my eyes and I'm back in Granddad's house. There's a store-bought cold apple tart in a foil tin sitting before me with a single candle in it. There's the person I think I should be, though I can't even dream about it properly without reality's interruptions, and there's the person I really am now.

This girl, on the run but frozen still, staring at the cold apple tart. Neither Granddad nor I are pretending things can continue like this. Granddad's real; there's no smoke and mirrors with him. He's looking at me, sadly. He knows not to avoid the subject. Things are too serious for that now. We talk daily of a plan, and that plan changes daily. I have escaped my home; escaped my Whistleblower Mary May, a guard of the Guild, whose job it is to monitor my every move and assure that I'm complying with Flawed rules; and I'm now off the radar. I'm officially an "evader." But the longer I stay here, the higher the chance I will eventually be found.

My mom told me to run away two weeks ago, an urgent whispered command in my ear that still gives me goose bumps when I recall it. The head of the Guild, Bosco Crevan, was sitting in our home, demanding my parents hand me over. Bosco is my ex-boyfriend's dad, and we have been neighbors for a decade. Only a few weeks previously we'd been enjoying dinner together in our home. Now my mom would rather I disappear than be in his care again.

It can take a lifetime to build up a friendship—it can take a second to make an enemy.

There was only one important item that I needed with me when I ran: a note that had been given to my sister, Juniper, for me. The note was from Carrick. Carrick had been my holding-cell neighbor at Highland Castle, the home of the Guild. He watched my trial while he awaited his; he witnessed my brandings. *All* of my brandings, including the secret sixth on my spine. He is the only person who can possibly understand how I feel right now, because he's going through the same thing.

My desire to find Carrick is immense, but it has been difficult. He managed to evade his Whistleblower as soon as he was released from the castle, and I'm guessing my profile didn't make it easy for him to seek me out, either. Just before I ran away, he found me, rescued me from a riot in a supermarket. He brought me home—I was out cold at the time, our long-wished-for reunion not exactly what I'd imagined. He left me the note and vanished.

But I couldn't get to him. Afraid of being recognized, I'd no way of finding my way around the city. So I called Granddad. I knew that his farm would be the Guild's first port of call in finding me. I should be hiding somewhere else, somewhere safer, but on this land Granddad has the upper hand.

At least, that was the theory. I don't think either of us thought that the Whistleblowers would be so relentless in their search for me. Since I arrived at the farm, there have been countless searches. So far they've failed to uncover my hiding place, but they come again and again, and I know my luck will eventually run out.

Each time, the Whistleblowers come so close to my hiding place I can barely breathe. I hear their footsteps, sometimes their breaths, as I'm crammed, jammed, into spaces, above and below, sometimes in places so obvious they don't even look, sometimes so dangerous they wouldn't dare to look.

I blink away my thoughts of them.

I look at the single flame flickering in the cold apple tart.

"Make a wish," Granddad says.

I close my eyes and think hard. I have too many wishes and feel that none of them are within my reach. But I also believe that the moment we're beyond *making* wishes is either the moment we're truly happy, or the moment to give up.

Well, I'm not happy. But I'm not about to give up.

I don't believe in magic, yet I see making wishes as a nod to hope, an acknowledgment of the power of will, the recognition of a goal. Maybe saying what you want to yourself makes it real, gives you a target to aim for, can help you make it happen. Channel your positive thoughts: Think it, wish it, then make it happen.

I blow out the flame.

I've barely opened my eyes when we hear footsteps in the hallway.

Dahy, Granddad's trusted farm manager, appears in the kitchen.

"Whistleblowers are here. Move."

FOUR

GRANDDAD JUMPS UP from the table so fast his chair falls backward to the stone floor. Nobody picks it up. We're not ready for this visit. Just yesterday the Whistleblowers searched the farm from top to bottom; we thought we'd be safe at least for today. Where is the siren that usually calls out in warning? The sound that freezes every soul in every home until the vehicles have passed by, leaving the lucky ones drenched with relief.

There is no discussion. The three of us hurry from the house. We instinctively know we have run out of luck with hiding me inside. We turn right, away from the driveway lined with cherry blossom trees. I don't know where we're going, but it's away, as far from the entrance as possible.

Dahy talks as we run. "Arlene saw them from the tower. She called me. No sirens. Element of surprise."

There's a ruined Norman tower on the land, which serves Granddad well as a lookout tower for Whistleblowers. Ever since I arrived he's had somebody on duty day and night, each of the farmworkers taking shifts.

"And they're definitely coming here?" Granddad asks, looking around fast, thinking hard. Plotting, planning. And I regret to admit I detect panic in his movements. I've never seen it in Granddad before.

Dahy nods.

I step up my pace to keep up with them. "Where are we going?"

They're silent. Granddad is still looking around as he strides through his land. Dahy watches Granddad, trying to read him. Their expressions make me panic. I feel it in the pit of my stomach, the alarming rate of my heartbeat. We're moving at top speed to the farthest point of Granddad's land, not because he has a plan but because he *doesn't*. He needs time to think of one.

We rush through the fields, through the strawberry beds that we were working in only hours ago.

We hear the Whistleblowers approach. For previous searches there has been only one vehicle, but now I think I hear more. Louder engines than usual, perhaps vans instead of cars. There are usually two Whistleblowers to a car, four to a van. Do I hear three vans? Twelve possible Whistleblowers.

I start to tremor: This is a full-scale search. They've found me; I'm caught. I breathe in the fresh air, feeling my freedom slipping away from me. I don't know what they will do to me, but under their care last month I received painful brands on my skin, the red letter *F* seared on six parts of my body. I don't want to stick around to discover what else they're capable of.

Dahy looks at Granddad. "The barn."

"They're onto that."

They look far out to the land, as if the soil will provide an answer. *The soil.*

"The pit," I say suddenly.

Dahy looks uncertain. "I don't think that's a—"

"It'll do," Granddad says with an air of finality, and charges off in the direction of the pit.

It was my idea, but the thought of it makes me want to cry. I feel dizzy at the prospect of hiding there. Dahy holds out his arm to allow me to walk ahead of him, and I see sympathy and sadness in his eyes.

I also see *good-bye.*

We follow Granddad to the clearing near the black forest that meets his land. He and Dahy spent this morning digging a hole in the ground, while I lay on the soil beside them, lazily twirling a dandelion clock between my fingers and watching it slowly dismantle in the breeze.

"You're like gravediggers," I'd said sarcastically.

Little did I know how true my words would become.

FIVE

THE COOKING PIT, according to Granddad, is the simplest and most ancient cooking structure. Also called an earth oven, it's a hole in the ground used to trap heat to bake, smoke, or steam food.

To bake the food, the fire is allowed to burn to a smolder. The food is placed in the pit and covered. The earth is filled back over everything—potatoes, pumpkins, meat, anything you want—and the food is left for a full day to cook. Granddad carries out this tradition every year with the workers on his farm, but usually at harvest time, not in May. He'd decided to do it now for "team building," he called it, at a time when we all needed reinforcement, to come together. All of Granddad's farmworkers are Flawed, and after facing the relentless searches from Whistleblowers and with each of his workers under the eye of the Guild more than ever, he felt everybody needed a morale boost.

I never knew Granddad employed Flawed, not until I got here two weeks ago. I don't remember seeing his farmworkers when we visited the farm, and Mom and Dad never mentioned them. Perhaps they'd been asked to stay out of our view; perhaps they were always there and, like most Flawed to me before I became one, seemed invisible.

I understand now that this helped drive a wedge between Granddad and Mom, her disapproving of his criticism of the Guild, the government-supported tribunal that puts people on trial for their unethical, immoral acts. We thought his rants were nothing but conspiracy theories, bitter about how his taxpayer's money was being spent. Turns out he was right. I also see now that Granddad was like Mom's dirty little secret. As a high-profile model, she represented perfection, on the outside at least, and while she was hugely successful around the world, she couldn't let her reputation in Humming be damaged. Having such an outspoken father who was on the Flawed side was a threat to her image. I understand that now.

There are some employers who treat Flawed like slaves. Long hours and on the minimum wage, if they're lucky. Many Flawed are just happy to be employed and work for accommodation and food. The majority of Flawed are educated, upstanding citizens. They aren't criminals; they haven't carried out any illegal acts. They made moral or ethical decisions that were frowned upon by society and they were branded for it. An organized public-shaming, I suppose. The judges of the Guild like to call themselves the "Purveyors of Perfection."

Dahy was a teacher. He was caught on security cameras in school grabbing a child roughly.

I've also learned that reporting people as Flawed to the Guild is a weapon that people use against one another. They wipe out the competition, leaving a space for themselves to step into, or they use it as a form of revenge. People abuse the system. The Guild is one gaping loophole for opportunists and hunters.

I broke a fundamental rule: Do not aid the Flawed. This act actually carries a prison sentence, but I was found Flawed instead. Before my trial, Crevan was trying to find a way to help me. The plan was that I was supposed to lie and say that I didn't help the old man. But I couldn't lie; I admitted the truth. I told them all that the Flawed man was a human being who needed and deserved to be helped. I humiliated Crevan, made a mockery of his court, or that's how he saw it anyway.

As a result, I was seen to have lied to the Guild. I brought them on a journey of deceit, grabbed people's attention, and then admitted the truth publicly. They had to make an example of me. I understand now that my brandings were really for misleading the Guild, for embarrassing them and causing people to question their validity.

One of the strengths of the Guild is that they feed the media. They work alongside each other, feeding each other, and the media feeds the people. We are told that the judges are right, the branded are wrong. The story is obscured, never fully heard, the voice of reason lost through the foghorn of a Whistleblower siren.

Among the long list of anti-Flawed decrees, Flawed are not allowed to have positions of power in the workplace, such as managerial roles or any functions where they have influence over people's thinking. In theory, nonmanagement jobs are open to the Flawed, but despite that, most Flawed *are* discriminated against in the workplace. Granddad isn't one of those employers. He goes out of his way to find Flawed workers, to treat them exactly as he'd treat anyone else.

Dahy is his longest-standing employee. With Granddad for thirty years, he has an ugly scar on his temple for his bad decision to grab the child. His brand was seared before the Guild managed to finesse the branding chamber and its tools. Still, it is nothing in comparison to the sixth brand on my spine, the secret one that Judge Crevan gave me. That's a personal message, and it was done in anger, without practice and without anesthetic. It's a raw, shocking scar.

Dahy is making another bad decision right now, colluding with Granddad in hiding me. Granddad could get a minimum of six months' prison time for aiding a Flawed, but as a Flawed man, helping another Flawed, I dread to think of what Dahy's punishment could be. As a Flawed person you think life couldn't be any worse for you until the Guild turns on your family and uses them to inflict further punishment and pain.

The three of us stare down into the rectangular pit in the ground. I hear doors slam—multiple doors—and I imagine a Whistleblower army in their red combat gear and black boots. They will be with us in a matter of minutes. I lower myself into the pit and lie down.

"Cover me," I say.

Granddad pauses, but Dahy tugs at the sheet and puts it in motion. Granddad's hesitancy could cost me.

Once the sheet is over me, they start adding the wood and moss that I gathered from the forest this morning. Never mind digging my own grave: I prepared the coffin, too.

The footsteps draw near.

"We need to get to Carrick immediately," Granddad says quietly, and I agree silently.

I hear the crunching of boots on soil.

"Cornelius," Mary May says suddenly, and my heart pounds. Everything about her terrifies me, a woman so heartless she reported her entire family to the Guild for immoral practices in their family business, in retaliation for her sister stealing her boyfriend. She has always been present for the searches of the farmhouse, but now it seems she has returned with an army. Or at least twelve others.

"Mary May," Granddad says gruffly. "Siren run out of batteries today?"

Another stick lands on top of me, hard. Thrown into the pit casually to throw her off the scent, no doubt. It lands right on my stomach and I fight the urge to groan and move.

Mary May doesn't do banter, or humor, or conversation. What she says goes. "What's that?"

"A food pit," Granddad says.

The two of them are standing over me, on my left-hand side. I feel logs land on me from the other side, which means Dahy is still here.

"Which is?"

"Have you never heard of a food pit? I thought a country girl from the yellow meadows like you would know all about it."

"No. I don't." Her words are clipped. She doesn't like that he knows where she's from. Granddad enjoys doing that, putting her off, showing her he knows things about her. It's subtle, and it's jolly in tone, but the undertones are threatening.

"Well, I dig a hole, put a sheet on the base. Cover it with logs. Light them. Then when it's smoldering, I add the food and cover it with soil. Twenty-four hours later the food is cooked in the ground it grew from. Absolutely delicious. No food like it. Learned it from my pops, who learned it from his."

"That's a coincidence," Mary May says. "Digging a hole just before we arrive. You wouldn't be hiding anything in there, would you?"

"No coincidence when I wasn't expecting you today. And it's an annual ritual—ask anyone on the farm. Isn't that right, Dahy?" Another bunch of logs and moss land on my body.

Ow.

"That's right, boss," Dahy says.

"You expect me to believe a Flawed?" The disgust at even being spoken to by one is clear in her voice.

There's a long silence. I concentrate on my breathing. The sheet hasn't been flattened on all sides, so air creeps in, but not enough. This hiding place was a ridiculous idea, but it was *my* ridiculous idea. I'm regretting it now. I could have taken my chances hiding in the forest—maybe Mary May could have gotten lost in there forever, too, the two of us hunting and hiding from each other for the rest of our lives.

I hear Mary May slowly walking around the pit; perhaps she can see my body shape, perhaps not. Perhaps she is about to pull it all off me and reveal me right now. I concentrate on my breathing, everything is too heavy on me, I wish they'd stop piling on the wood.

"That wood's for burning, then?" she asks.

"Yes," says Granddad.

"So set it on fire," she says.

SIX

"WHAT?" SAYS GRANDDAD.

"You heard me."

On top of me is the white sheet. Above it, firewood and moss. Suddenly, something shifts and the sheet, which has been rucked up, giving me space to breathe, collapses to my skin. I try to blow it away but I can't move it. And now Mary May wants to set me on fire. She knows I'm here. I'm the mouse caught in the trap.

Granddad tries to talk her out of it. He wasn't intending to light it quite yet. The food isn't ready, it needs to be wrapped up. It will all take time. She tells him she has time. She tells Dahy to prepare the food, but she doesn't care about the food: She is more intent on setting me alight. She tells Granddad to concentrate on the fire. She's not asking him—she's telling him. She knows there's nobody on this farm to share the food other than a bunch of Flawed, and she has no respect for their plans.

It's happening *now*.

I feel another bundle land on my legs. Granddad is taking his time, chatting, dillydallying, doing his old-man-persona trick.

"Put one there," she says.

It lands on my chest.

I can't breathe. I can't breathe. I close my eyes, try to return to the yacht. My eighteenth birthday, the chocolate fountain, the music, the breeze, the person I should be, not the person I am. I try to go far away, but I can't disappear. I'm here and now. The logs are heavy on my body, the air is close.

Mary May wants him to hurry. If I'm discovered, then Granddad will be punished, too. I take deep breaths, not wanting my chest to visibly rise and fall beneath the sheet and logs.

"I have a lighter," Mary May says.

Granddad laughs at that. A big hearty boom. "Well, that won't do. My tools are in the barn. You stay here with Dahy, watch how he prepares the food. I'll be back."

It's the way he says it. So untrustworthy, it's obvious that he's lying. He's so clever. She thinks he's trying to get away from her, that there's something or someone in the barn that he needs to hide from her. He's so insistent on her staying here with Dahy that, of course, her attention leaves the pit and she insists on going to the barn with him. Dahy can help me out of here, lift some of the wood off.

But of course she then contacts her fellow Whistleblowers and tells them to accompany Dahy, to help him gather all the Flawed workers and line them up at the cooking pit.

She's going to burn me out for everyone to see.

SEVEN

AS SOON AS I hear their footsteps die away and their voices fade, I try to come up for air. Terrified it's a trick and that Mary May will be standing beside me with a swarm of Whistleblowers, I fight my way out from under the sheet and timber. It's more difficult than I thought; it's heavy— Granddad has really piled on the wood.

No longer concerned about the possible trap, I don't want to suffocate, so I use both legs to kick up. The timber goes flying. I do the same with my arms, pushing the wood up and out. Some of it lands on my legs and shins, and I gasp with pain. I pull the sheet away and feel the air on my face. I gulp it in hungrily. I climb out of my grave and run toward the woods. As soon as I'm at the edge of the farm that leads into blackness, and safety, I look back. The pit is a mess. If I leave it like that it will be obvious that Granddad hid me and led Mary May away for my escape. He will suffer for my carelessness. They'll know I'm here and they'll find me in seconds. I will have no hope escaping from so many Whistleblowers in this wood.

I hear Granddad's and Mary May's voices in the distance as they return from the barn. Granddad is speaking loudly, perhaps deliberately, to warn me.

I look to the pit and then back to the woods, to possible freedom. I have no choice.

I sprint back to the pit, fix the sheet and the strewn timber and moss as quickly and neatly as I can, hearing their footsteps, so close now. My heart thumps wildly, I feel the throbbing in my neck and head. It's as though I'm moving in slow motion, like this is a nightmare that I can only hope to wake from. But it's not. It's happening for real. I see the flash of red of Mary May's uniform, then I run again. I've barely entered the woods and hidden behind the first tree when they come fully into sight. I'm sure they've seen me. Terrified, I push my back flat against the trunk, heart pounding, chest heaving.

"I don't see why you couldn't just use my lighter," Mary May says, irritated. She's annoyed she didn't find me in the barn.

Granddad laughs, mockingly, which I know will anger her further. "No, no. You've got to be authentic. This tradition is thousands of years old. It's one thing, you forcing me to do this before I'd intended to, but if I'm lighting it, I'm lighting it my way."

He sounds adamant and I know none of it is for real. Though he does like authenticity, he isn't averse to matchsticks or lighters; he simply went to the barn to give me a chance to escape.

He starts to light a fire using flint and his penknife. I've seen Granddad do this numerous times—he can light a fire in a matter of seconds, but he messes around now, playing the part of a confused old man. He's buying time, either because he knows I've escaped and is giving me time to hide or because he's afraid I'm still under the pile of stones and he doesn't want to set me on fire. I want to shout to him that it's okay, that I'm not in the pit, but I can't, so instead I listen to his agonizing wait and steal a glimpse of his face. He's not so confident now.

"What's wrong, Cornelius?" Mary May asks slyly. "Afraid to set it on fire?"

Granddad looks lost. Torn. Tortured.

Dahy arrives with more Whistleblowers, not the huge army I'd expected. Two men and one woman, and a line of the eight Flawed farmworkers. They look haggard, as though Dahy has told them what's about to happen.

"His papers and all the others' are in order," a female Whistleblower says to Mary May.

"Still in order since you checked them yesterday," Granddad says. "And two days before that, and two days before that, and the three days before that. You know I might report you to the police for intimidation."

"And we might take you in for aiding a Flawed," the Whistleblower replies.

"On what grounds?" Granddad demands.

"On the grounds that the only people you seem to hire are Flawed workers, and you house them right here on your land."

"I'm only doing what's legal."

"You're going beyond what's legal. Most Flawed get minimum wage. All your workers are on more. They get paid more than some Whistleblowers."

"What do you think, Flawed?" A male Whistleblower takes over, while Mary May is silent. "Is the old man giving you special treatment? Think you're able to escape us here?"

Dahy is wise enough to not say anything.

"I don't let anything get past me here," says Dan, the Whistleblower in charge of the Flawed farmworkers. This is his patch, and his colleague's suggestions that he lets them have free rein is an insult.

"Light the fire," Mary May says, ending the feud.

Finally the fire sparks. There are so many Whistleblowers I'm afraid to move in case they hear me. The forest floor is covered in branches, twigs, leaves, everything that can give me away in seconds.

Granddad takes the flame to the moss and I'm afraid that he won't do it, that he'll give the game away, that they'll find me. *Have faith in me, Granddad. I'm your flesh and blood; have faith that I got away.*

"What are you hiding, old man? Celestine? Is she under there? If she is, don't you worry, we'll smoke her out," Mary May says.

"I told you she's not here," Granddad says suddenly, and he throws the flame into the pit. The moss lights quickly and fire spreads to the twigs and logs. Dahy looks at Granddad, head hanging weakly; Granddad and the Whistleblowers watch the fire spread, waiting for the sounds of my screams. I watch them thinking that I'm under there, the smugness and satisfaction on the Whistleblowers' faces. This fills me with so much anger and hatred for them that any thoughts I had of turning myself in, of giving up on my freedom, dissolve immediately. I will not give up; I can't let them win.

"So what now?" a male Whistleblower asks, disappointed that the show hasn't delivered.

"Well." Granddad clears his throat, trying to keep his cool, but I know that he's rattled. He has either set fire to his granddaughter, or he hasn't. I could have passed out from lack of air, I could still be under there. The fire is spreading.

"We let it burn until it smolders, then we pile the food in and cover it with soil."

"Do it."

Granddad looks at Mary May, lost, old, hope seeming to be gone. But the hate in him is clearly greater than ever. "Waiting for it to burn to a smolder will take hours."

"We have time," she says.

EIGHT

THEY STAY THERE for three hours.

My muscles burn, my feet ache, but I'm afraid to move.

When the fire has reduced to a smolder, Granddad and Dahy are ordered to place the bundles of food onto the coals. The farmworkers watch from their orderly line, their *F* brand armbands all visible on their right arms, just above their elbows.

This was supposed to be a celebration, a coming together to show that the Guild couldn't beat them down. Now the Whistleblowers themselves are here. Hiding behind the tree, huddled on the ground, hugging my legs, shivering from the damp forest, I can't say that I feel empowered. This feels like a defeat.

Granddad and Dahy cover the food with the soil so it will cook under the ground in the heat. Granddad looks at the ground, his work finished, as though he's buried me alive. Again I want to call out to him that I'm okay, I made it out, but I can't.

A phone rings and the female Whistleblower takes it. She steps aside, walks away from the others, so she can talk in private. She moves closer to me in the woods. I tense up again.

"Judge Crevan, hello. It's Kate. No, Judge, Celestine isn't here. We've checked everywhere."

Silence as she listens and I hear Crevan's voice from where I stand. Kate walks farther and stops by my tree.

I press my back to the tree, squeeze my eyes shut, and hold my breath.

"With all due respect, Judge, this is the Guild's sixth visit to the property and I believe Mary May was meticulous in her search. We've checked everywhere you can imagine. I don't believe she's here. I think the grandfather is telling the truth."

I can hear the frustration in her voice. They're all under pressure to find me, pressure placed on them by Judge Crevan. Kate takes a few more steps, right into my eyeline.

She slowly scans the forest, her eyes searching the distance.

Then she looks right at me.

NINE

I EXPECT HER to tell Crevan that she's found me, hang up, call to the others, blow the large red whistle that hangs on a gold chain around her neck, but she stays calm, her voice not changing. She is looking right through me, as though she can't see me at all. Has it come to this? Have I been hiding so long that I'm no longer visible? I actually look down at my hands to make sure I can see myself.

"You'd like us to take the grandfather to Highland Castle," Kate says, looking me up and down, continuing the conversation as if I'm not there.

Why isn't she telling him I'm here?

The news that they're going to take Granddad to Highland Castle, to Judge Crevan, the man who personally branded me and destroyed my life, causes panic to well in my chest. It's quickly followed by a large wave of anger. They can't take my granddad.

"We'll bring him in now," she says, eyes still on me, and I'm waiting for the bombshell, for the moment she tells Mary May and Judge Crevan that I'm right here, beside her. "We'll be with you in two hours."

I'm about to scream at her, punch her, kick her, yell that she cannot take me and my granddad, but I stop myself. There is something peculiar about the way she is looking at me.

She puts the phone in her pocket, fixes me with a long stare as if she's trying to think of something to say, then decides against it, and turns and leaves.

"Right, old man," she calls to Granddad. "We're taking you in. Judge Crevan needs words with you."

Even after I hear the vehicles drive away, I stay where I am. I sit in the cramped and damp conditions of a hollowed-out tree, trying to understand what exactly has happened.

Why didn't she take me?

TEN

IT'S BEEN ONE hour since Mary May left with my beloved granddad in tow, carting him off as if he's some kind of criminal. I'm still huddling behind the tree, exhausted, hungry, cold, and very afraid. I can smell the smoke from the pit, smoldering under the earth, cooking the food that probably no one will eat now that Granddad is gone. I feel an overwhelming guilt at his being in this position, and I'm scared of what they'll do to him in Highland Castle.

I'm scared, too, of what he might be thinking. Does he fear he burned me alive? I wish there was a way to tell him I wasn't there, in the pit.

When all the vehicles left, initially I was afraid to move, thinking it was a test or a tease, that as soon as I came out of the woodwork they'd grab me. Then I waited, thinking perhaps the farmworkers would come for me, but they didn't, in lockdown at this hour by their Whistleblower, Dan.

It's after the 11:00 PM curfew, the time when checkpoints and searches on individuals increase. It's not a good time to be roaming alone, though at least I can move around under the cover of darkness. I've decided that going back to the farmhouse is out of the question, despite its warmth and the welcoming light on the porch.

Perhaps I can make it to Granddad's nearest neighbor. Can I trust them for help?

But then what did Granddad tell me? Rule number one: *Don't trust anybody.*

Suddenly I hear a vehicle return. A door slams. Followed by two more. They're back. I feel so stupid now. Why didn't I run? Why did I allow them to return to get me?

I hear footsteps nearby. Male voices I don't recognize, and then one that I do, clear as anything.

"Here's the pit," Dahy says. "She was in here."

Can I trust Dahy? Or is he the one who called the Whistleblowers in the first place? Has he sold me out, or has he been forced to help another Whistleblower team find me? I don't know who to believe. I'm cold; I'm scared; I can either jump up and yell "Save me!" and ruin everything I've done to get to this point, or I can sit tight. Sit tight. Sit tight.

"She must have gone into the forest," another man says.

I see the light from a flashlight stretch in front of me, illuminating the black forest for what seems like hundreds of miles. Tall, thick tree trunks for as far as the eye can see. Even if I run that way and the Whistle-blowers don't see me, I'll be lost in no time.

It's over, Celestine; it's over.

And even though I tell myself that, I'll never give up. I think of Crevan's face as he hissed at me in the branding chamber, asking me to repent; I think of Carrick's hand pressed up against the glass as he watched it all unfold, the offer of friendship. The anger burns through me; I hear the footsteps near my tree and I unfold myself from my cramped position. I stretch my arms and legs, and on one, two . . . I fire myself out of the hole, catapulting into the woods, startling whatever is living nearby, and sprint with stiff legs.

The men jump into action straightaway.

"There!"

The flashlight moves to find me; I dodge its line of fire and instead use it to see what's in front of me. I dodge trees' long, thin pine needles; duck and dive; and hear them closing in fast behind me.

"Celestine," a voice hisses angrily, coming close. I keep running, I smack my head against a low branch and feel momentarily dizzy, but I don't have time to stop and center myself. They're closing in on me, three of them. Three frenzied flashlights as they run.

"Celestine!" a voice calls louder, and another hushes him.

Why are they hushing? I'm dizzy, I think I've cut my head, all I know is that I need to keep running, it's what my mom told me to do. Granddad said don't trust anyone. Dad said to trust Granddad. I need to keep moving.

The flashlights suddenly go off and I'm running in pitch blackness. I stop still, my breathing all I can hear. I don't know which way is forward or which is back the way I came; I am utterly disoriented in the dense forest. Panic descends again, then I take control. I close my eyes, allowing calm to encapsulate me. I can do this. I turn around, trying to see light from the farmhouse in the distance, or any clues. As I move, twigs snap beneath my feet.

Then I feel strong arms around my waist, a smell of sweat.

"Got her," he says.

I fight against his grip, but it's no use: There's no room to move. I keep trying anyway, wriggling with all my energy to hopefully exhaust him, hit him, scratch him, kick him.

A flashlight goes on, someone is shining it in my face. Both my captor and I look away from the harsh light.

"Let her go, Lennox," says the man holding the flashlight, and I stop wriggling immediately.

The arms release me, and the flashlight is passed to Dahy, who holds it so that the speaker is illuminated.

The man is amused.

The man is Carrick.

ELEVEN

I'M BUZZING AS I follow Dahy back to the farmhouse. Carrick and his friend Lennox are behind me. I want to keep turning around to get a look at Carrick, but with Lennox there, I can't. I've done it twice already, and Lennox caught me both times. I feel nervous, happy, surprisingly giddy at being reunited with Carrick. Finally something is going my way. My birthday wish came true.

I bite my lip to hide my smile as we walk single file back to the farmhouse; now is not a time for smiling, though they couldn't possibly understand my relief.

"Any word from Granddad?" I ask Dahy quietly.

"No," he says, turning around briefly so I can catch the worried look on his face. "But Dan is doing everything he can to find out."

I'm skeptical of trusting Dan. His arrangement with Granddad to loosen the reins on the Flawed workers was based on feeding his alcohol addiction through gifts from Granddad's home whiskey distillery rather than common decency.

"You'll let me know when you hear something?" I ask Dahy.

"You'll be the first to know."

"You'll make sure Granddad knows that I'm safe?"

Dan never knew I was here at the farmhouse—their arrangement was never that sweet—and so he can't possibly relay the message to Granddad that I'm alive. Maybe the Whistleblower Kate told Granddad, but placing my faith in any Whistleblower is the last possible move, regardless of whether she let me go or not. I reach out to grab Dahy's arm so that he stops walking, and my hand grips his Flawed armband. Lennox and Carrick stall behind me.

"Dahy, can you contact my family? Tell them Granddad's at the castle? Tell my parents that I'm okay?"

"They already know he's at the castle, but it's too risky to tell them about you over the phone, Celestine. You know the Guild is probably listening in on the phone lines."

Members of the Guild aren't super spies, but if Juniper and I figured out a way to overhear our neighbors' phone conversations through Ewan's baby monitor years ago, and a journalist can tap phones, then the Guild certainly can.

"You have to find a way to tell them. And you have to tell him I'm okay."

"Celestine—"

"No, Dahy, listen." I raise my voice and I hear the tremor in it. "I cannot have Granddad sitting in a cell, or wherever they've put him, thinking that he has just burned his granddaughter alive." My voice cracks. "You need to get word to him."

Dahy finally understands. He softens. "Of course. I'll find a way to tell him."

I let go of his arm.

"He'll be okay, Celestine, you know he's made of tough stuff." Dahy adds, "If anything, they'll want to let him go quickly, before he conspiracy theories them to death."

I smile weakly at his attempt at humor and nod my thanks. I try to ignore the tears that are welling, try not to picture the terrible scenarios for Granddad that my mind keeps wanting to create. Granddad being booed and heckled as he walks across the cobblestoned courtyard of Highland Castle. People looking at him and shouting at him like he's scum, throwing and spitting while he tries to keep his chin up. Granddad locked in a cell. Granddad having to answer to Crevan in the Guild court. Granddad in the branding chamber. Granddad being put through all the things that happened to me. When it's yourself, you can take it; when it's happening to the people you love, it can break you.

What Crevan did to me was rare, at least I think it was; it was a moment of stress, of his utter loss of control. All I can do is hope that he won't treat Granddad as he's treated me.

We walk back to the Jeep they parked at the farmhouse. There is no time for catching up on old times; I sense that the three of them are all anxious to get back to safety. It's after 11:00 PM, we're all Flawed and should be indoors. Three of us are "evaders" who have disobeyed the Guild.

I have time to very quickly gather some of my things from the house, the small amount of clothes Granddad managed to successfully retrieve from Mom on a recent visit to her, the longest day of my life when he left me at the farm alone. It's not much, a small backpack, and I suppose it's all I need, but I think of all my clothes in my wardrobe at home, each item that meant so much to me, every one a part of me, a way of expressing who I was. I'm stripped of those now, realize I have nothing but my own words and actions to truly show who I am.

We say good-bye to Dahy, he wishes us luck, and I beg him again to get word to me about Granddad as quickly as possible, and vice versa.

Carrick holds the door open for me. Our eyes meet and my heart pounds.

"We need to see to that cut," he says, focusing on my forehead, the small wound from where I slammed into a branch moments ago. With the surge of adrenaline I didn't feel the pain, but now I feel it sting in the breeze. As Carrick studies my forehead, I'm able to take in his face. This is the closest I've ever been to him, in the flesh; every other time was behind glass, or when I was comatose after the supermarket riot. It's like I know him so well, and yet we're perfect strangers at the same time.

Feeling flustered, I step into the Jeep and bang the top of my head on the doorframe.

"I'm okay," I mumble, hiding my flushed face in the darkness of the Jeep.

Carrick drives and I sit behind him, our eyes meeting often in the rearview mirror. Lennox sits beside him in the passenger seat, equally large in stature. Both of them looking like soldiers.

"Where are we going?" I finally ask.

Carrick's eyes meet mine in the mirror and my stomach flips. "Home."

TWELVE

"HOME" TAKES US through back roads and trails, away from towns and main roads. Every lamppost and billboard is covered in election campaign posters. I see Enya Sleepwell from the Vital Party, a politician who attended my trial. I didn't know it at the time, but she was there to support me. I didn't even know who she was until journalist Pia Wang questioned me about her. Enya Sleepwell recently became leader of the Vital Party and one of the main items on her campaign agenda is to discuss rights for the Flawed. It's a risky topic for a politician: The Guild and the government go hand in hand. But despite her choice of issues, her popularity is growing week by week.

On the poster, her cropped hair and reassuring smile stand above the slogan COMPASSION AND LOGIC. These are my words from the trial, when explaining why I aided the old Flawed man on the bus.

Why did I help him? All the confused faces kept asking me during the trial. It was beyond belief, incomprehensible, that anyone would want to aid a Flawed, a second-class citizen.

I helped him because I had compassion and logic. I felt for him, and helping him made sense. They were the first words that came to me in the court, I hadn't planned them. The only story that had been planned was the lie that Crevan had wanted me to tell. It feels so peculiar to me to see those words in big, bold writing on posters, like they've been stolen from me, and have been bent to someone else's purpose.

I want to ask Carrick and Lennox a million questions, but I know not to ask anything. The atmosphere is tense in the car, even between Carrick and Lennox as they decide which way to traverse.

The Guild has increased the number of Whistleblowers on the ground. Judge Crevan is in a panic trying to find me; the most Flawed person in the history of the Guild is not allowed to just disappear. Crevan has widened searches to all public and private properties, the hope being that there will be less support for me when members of the public are made to look like Flawed aiders in front of their neighbors.

Crevan has even started delaying the Flawed curfew buses. Designed to bring the Flawed population home in time for their 11:00 PM curfew, people are now missing their curfews at the hands of the Guild, and they're being punished. This is all in my name. Crevan is playing a game with me. *I will continue to punish the innocent until you come out of your hiding place.*

Riots have begun to break out in the city. The Guild is characterizing them as random outbursts from Flawed groups, but Granddad believes it's not just Flawed who are feeling angry about the Guild. He believes regular people are feeling uncomfortable about Flawed rules, too, and that they're starting to speak out. I know now that there *is* sense in what I once considered Granddad's nonsensical rants. Whatever excuses the Guild gave to the public, I know that Crevan's real reason for this surge in Whistleblower activity is to find me.

There are times when I've wanted to give myself up, for the sake of others, but Granddad always stops me. He tells me that I can do more for people over time and they will appreciate it then. It just takes patience.

We see a Whistleblowers' checkpoint up ahead, and take a sharp left down the back of a cluster of shops, an alley so narrow we have to squeeze by the Dumpsters. Carrick stops the car and they pore over the map some more in search of a new route. This happens a few times. The relief that I experienced on seeing Carrick has now dissipated as I realize I'm still not safe. I yearn for that feeling of not having to constantly look over my shoulder.

Beads of sweat glisten on Carrick's brow. I take the opportunity of sitting behind him to study him. His black hair is closely shaven; his neck, shoulders, everything wide, muscular, and strong. Soldier is what I named him in the castle cells before I knew his real name. His cheekbones and jaw are perfectly defined, all hard edges. His eyes, a color I've never been able to work out, still look black in the rearview mirror. I study them: hard, intense, quick, always analyzing, looking for new angles. He catches my stare and, embarrassed, I quickly avert my eyes. When I finally glimpse back I catch him looking at me.

"Home, sweet home," Lennox says, and I can see them both visibly relax. But I look out the window at our destination and I tense even more. This is not the "home" I was expecting. Or hoping for.

We drive toward a compound surrounded by twenty-foot-high fences with rows of barbed wire. It looks like a prison. Carrick looks back at me again, to gauge my reaction, his black eyes fixed on me.

I have broken the most basic rule that Granddad taught me. Don't trust anyone.

And for the first time ever, I doubt Carrick.

THIRTEEN

FLOODLIGHTS LIGHT THE SKY, I can barely see past the front window they're so bright, and a man with a machine gun charges angrily to the door of the car.

"Uh-oh," Lennox says. He throws a blanket at me and tells me to cover up and lie down. I do it immediately.

Carrick lowers the window. "Good evening, boss."

"Good evening?" he splutters. "It's midnight. What the hell are you thinking? The city is crawling with Whistleblowers, and my guys here are loyal, but they'll start to ask questions if we have too many comings and goings between shift hours. Do you have any idea how much trouble you could have caused being out here at this hour?"

"Could have, but didn't," Lennox says.

"Sorry, Eddie. You know we wouldn't have been out unless it was extremely important."

He curses under his breath. "You're good workers, but not that good. I could find replacements for you at a moment's notice."

"Yes, us Flawed should always be grateful for every opportunity," Lennox says sarcastically.

"Len." Carrick silences him. "It won't happen again," Carrick says. "And you know that if anything did happen out there we would never be linked back to here. You have both our words."

"Scout's honor," Lennox adds. "How about you let us in now? I don't know if you heard, but it's dangerous out here with Whistleblowers sniffing around the place."

There's a long silence as Eddie thinks it over and I feel the tension again. If he cuts us loose, we won't survive one night out here, off the radar, three Flawed. No more than two Flawed are allowed to travel or be together, *and* it's after curfew, *and* we're evaders.

"Okay. Don't think I can't see a body under the blanket. I just hope it's alive. I don't know what you're up to, but I'm not running a refugee camp here; he just better be a good worker."

"The best," Carrick says, and I smile under the blanket.

"What is this place?" I ask after we've driven through the front gates and they tell me it's safe to remove the blanket. I look out the window and strain my neck to take in the height of what looks like a nuclear plant.

"This is a CCU plant. Next door is a CDU plant. They're sister companies."

"What do they do?" I ask as Lennox jumps out of the Jeep before it stops and disappears into the shadows. Carrick parks the Jeep.

"Carbon capture utilization and carbon dioxide utilization," he replies.

I look at him with even more confusion.

"I thought you were the whiz kid."

"In math, not in whatever this is."

"Come on, I'll give you a tour."

Carrick holds the car door open for me and his manners remind me of how he was raised in a Flawed At Birth institution. F.A.B. institutions are for children of Flawed parentage. The Guild's reasoning for taking these children is to dilute the Flawed gene pool, and these special schools retrain their Flawed brains. Carrick was taken from his Flawed parents at the age of five and was raised in a state school boasting the best facilities, education, and standards. The Guild, the state, raised him to be strong, to be one of them, to be perfect, but when he graduated, he turned on them by doing the one thing F.A.B. children are told not to do: He sought out his parents. He was branded on his chest for disloyalty to society.

Carrick is eighteen years old and a giant of a man; his only flaw was wanting to find his parents. He walks me around the compound explaining, using a key card to access the doors.

There are a dozen metal containers that look like shuttles side by side, the kind of thing you'd see at a brewery plant, or at a NASA facility, looking like they're about to lift off.

"As you know, the earth produces more carbon dioxide than can be absorbed. Carbon points have risen to the highest levels for eight hundred thousand years. Most of it comes from oil or coal, fossil fuels buried underground for millions of years. It's a polluting waste product, so this CCU facility harnesses it and puts it to better use as a resource, reusing the carbon to create new products."

"How does it do that?"

"It captures the carbon dioxide from power plants, steel, and cement works, or collects it from the air. It extracts the carbon, which provides the raw material for new products like green fuels, methanol, plastics, pharmaceuticals, building materials."

"This is government owned?" I ask, wondering why on earth he's brought us here. How can we be safe in a state-owned factory when they're the very people we're running from?

"It's private. This is a pilot plant, everything here is research, just testing, nothing is on the market yet. Whistleblowers can't carry out surprise searches for Flawed without prior warning, which is, at minimum, usually twenty-four hours' notice."

"That's why you chose here?"

"I didn't choose it. I followed the others."

"The others?"

"I'll introduce you later. First, I'll give you the tour. There are four units. This is the capture regeneration section." He swipes his card and the red light on the security panel turns green. He pulls the door open and lets me walk in first. Once inside, I see that the enormous plant is like an airport hangar, with more containers and pipes stretching in every direction, ladders climbing up the walls and ceilings to access them. Carrick hands me a high-visibility jacket and hard hat.

"This is where I work. Don't worry, I don't do anything important, just drive the forklift, so you're going to get this in layman's terms."

"I won't notice the difference," I say, looking around, completely overwhelmed by the futuristic metal facility.

"This container here is where the flue gas is routed to a pretreatment section. It cools, then the flue gas is sent to the absorber column, to remove the carbon dioxide. The flue gas enters the bottom of the absorber and flows upward." He walks as he talks, pointing at the equipment, and I follow. "It reacts with the solvent solution, where a bunch of stuff happens."

I smile.

"The treated flue gas is sent here to what's called the stack so it can be released to the atmosphere. The carbon dioxide liquid leaves the absorber and is pumped to the regeneration section, where the CO_2 chemical absorption process is reversed. The CO_2 liquid leaves the bottom of the absorber and is sent to heat exchangers where the temperature rises. More stuff happens. Then the carbon dioxide vapor is sent to the carbon dioxide product compressor. Which is over here." We stop at the product compressor. "And there it is. Want to know anything else?"

"Yes. Who are the others you followed here?"

He nods. "We're getting to that."

FOURTEEN

WE LEAVE THE factory behind us and take quite a walk in the enormous compound to a less futuristic side of the facility. This new section feels more residential, contains rows and rows of white portacabins, all layered on top of one another, five levels high, ten boxes across, steel balconies and staircases connecting them. We enter a simple one-story concrete building with a reception area, with a desk that's empty at this late hour, a few chairs, and technological and scientific magazines scattered on the coffee table. A beefy security guard is asleep in an armchair in the corner.

"One hundred employees live on-site," Carrick explains. "This place is out of the way—the closest village or town is too far for a daily commute—so the owners thought it best to house them here."

"Owners?"

"Private company, *Vigor*." He shrugs. "I've been here only two weeks, but I haven't seen them around. Whoever they are, they're sympathetic to the Flawed. They've allowed a gang of evaders to work and live here. He's one of them." He nods at the security guard, who's snoring quietly.

He points at the poster on the wall behind the reception desk and I see the same red *V* logo I've been seeing all around the plant. The *V* in "Vigor" is designed as a mathematical square root sign, and I've seen it before somewhere, though I can't place it.

√IGOR. TURNING A PROBLEM INTO A SOLUTION.

"There are four different recreational areas, depending on which unit you're in. Flawed are all employed in the same unit; it's this way."

He pushes open a door and we're back in the night air and walking across to a collection of portacabins. Despite the late hour I can hear voices and activity coming from one of them and I know that our time alone is running out for now. There's something important on my mind that I need to discuss first.

"Carrick, I need to know something." I swallow. "Have you told anybody about . . ." I indicate my back.

"No one."

I feel relieved, but awkward for bringing up the sixth brand. Things have been easy between us, but thinking about the branding chamber has caused me to tense up again.

"Apart from the guards and Crevan, Mr. Berry and I are the only two who know," Carrick assures me. "I've been trying to contact Mr. Berry, but I haven't had any luck so far," he explains. "It's been hard, trying to do things while I'm off the grid."

"The guards are all missing, Carrick," I say urgently. "Mr. Berry is missing. I was afraid Crevan had gotten to you, too. We have so much to talk about."

"What?" His eyes widen.

At the end of the corridor, the door opens and I hear voices, laughter, a gang of people. I'm not ready to meet them yet; I need to talk to Carrick first. I speak quickly. "I told Pia Wang about my sixth brand."

He raises his eyebrows, surprised that I would share this information with a Flawed TV and Crevan Media journalist. It had been Pia's duty to tell my story, and after the trial she had set out to destroy my character, as was the norm with all her Flawed interviewees, but something happened with me. She believed me. She doubted my trial from the beginning and she couldn't justify her one-sided reporting any longer. She sensed something was amiss.

"I know it's hard to believe, but we *can* trust her. She was doing all she could to gather information to write a revealing story about Crevan. I haven't heard from her in over two weeks. It's not just our communication that has been broken: I've been checking online and she hasn't written an article under Pia Wang . . . or under her pseudonym."

"Her pseudonym?"

"Lisa Life."

Carrick whistles. "Wow. *She's* Lisa Life? Okay. Now I get why you told her."

Lisa Life is a notorious blogger, writing stories critical of the Flawed system. The authorities have been trying to find her and shut her down for months, but she just keeps changing servers.

"You can't tell anyone," I say. "She swore me to secrecy."

"My lips are sealed."

"Anyway," I say, "she hasn't posted anything for weeks. I hope she's being quiet because she's in the thick of writing her big, juicy Crevan reveal that will tear him apart," I continue, "but . . . Pia isn't the type of person to ever be quiet. The last I heard from her she was going to speak to the guards' families."

He frowns, still back at square one. "Have their families reported them? Are the police looking for them?"

"I think they're afraid to. Mr. Berry's husband said he just disappeared. I was worried about you this whole time, afraid that Crevan would make you disappear, too. Crevan has no idea that you were in the viewing room, he never saw you and I didn't tell Pia about you, so I think

45

you're safe. Also Crevan had no idea that Mr. Berry was filming the brand-ing until he overheard a phone conversation between me and Mr. Berry's husband. He told me that *I* have the footage," I whisper.

"So that's why Crevan wants you so badly? He wants the Branding Chamber footage?"

I nod.

"He's afraid you'll reveal the video."

"I think so."

He looks at me with the utmost respect. "Then we've got him. I knew it, but I didn't know why. He's afraid of you, Celestine. We've got him."

FIFTEEN

"YOU TWO HAVE plenty of time to talk," a woman calls suddenly, startling me. She's standing at the open door of the cabin that the noise was flowing from. "Come join us, Celestine." She has an enormous welcoming smile on her face.

I blink. Then I realize: My face has been in the news for two weeks now; of course this stranger knows who I am.

"Um, thanks," I say.

"Celestine North," she says as I reach her. She opens her arms and embraces me. "It is an honor to meet you." She wraps me up and I'm stiff at first but slowly relax into it. When was the last time I received a hug? I think of my mom and dad and fight the emotion that follows. "I'm Kelly. Come inside and I'll introduce you to everyone."

I look back at Carrick for help, but Kelly takes me by the hand and brings me along with her. Once inside the cabin, I see a roomful of strangers staring at me. Carrick follows us into the room and disappears into a corner somewhere.

"This is my husband, Adam," Kelly introduces me.

Adam hugs me warmly. "Welcome."

"Come and meet Rogan," Kelly says, dragging me away.

In a darkened corner, a younger teen lurks.

"Say hi to Celestine, Rogan," Kelly coaxes him, as a parent would do with a much younger child.

He gives me a weak wave, like the effort to care is too great.

"Oh, come on," Kelly says to him, and he slowly stands, shuffles over to me with feet too big for his body, trousers too big for his waist, and reaches out to shake my hand. It's limp. It's damp. He doesn't look me in the eye and quickly scampers back to his beanbag. If I were on the outside I would say he was disgusted by a Flawed, but in here, in the company of so many Flawed and assuming he's one of us himself, I put it down to shyness. Kelly talks a mile a minute, introducing me to the rest of the group.

There's Cordelia and her little girl, six-year-old Evelyn, who shows me that her top teeth fell out, pushing her tongue through the holes. I'm surprised to recognize the two men I was standing beside at the cash register when the entire drama started at the supermarket riot two weeks ago. Now I know their names are Fergus and Lorcan. Fergus has stitches across his forehead, and Lorcan is covered in bruises. I meet Mona, a girl around my age, with a smile so bright and sizzling energy that would light up the darkest day. I immediately like her. There's an older man named Bahee, a chilled-out dude wearing circular blue-tinted glasses and a long gray ponytail, who'd look comfortable sitting around a campfire and singing "Kumbaya."

"And you already know our eldest son, Carrick." Kelly smiles. Carrick comes a bit closer. "I'm so glad you were with him in the castle." She takes my hands, her eyes filled with tears. "We know how horrific the experience is. I'm glad you were there with my boy." She reaches out to him, but he recoils slightly. It's as though his actions have surprised himself, but it's too late—the damage is done. Kelly pulls her hand away from him, trying to hide her hurt expression.

"You found your parents?" I ask in surprise.

I look from Adam to Kate, finally and suddenly seeing a resemblance between Carrick and his dad. But he's nothing like his mother; she's tiny, birdlike. Carrick towers over her, though he does with most people. She's more like Rogan, who would barely shake my hand. I look to Rogan then and realize that he's her son.

"That means you two are . . ."

I wait for them to say something but nobody speaks. They don't even look at one another. There's such an awkward atmosphere, so much tension. But of course being reunited with loved ones after thirteen years was never going to be easy.

"They're brothers!" Mona suddenly announces. "Yay! Do I get a point for that?" she asks sarcastically, punching the air. "It's just one big happy family around here, isn't it, guys?"

"Mona," Adam says, annoyed, as Kelly turns away. It doesn't seem to bother Mona in the slightest.

"You didn't tell her you found us, Carrick?" Kelly asks, confused and hurt.

There's a long silence as Carrick pulls at his earlobe self-consciously, trying to search for an answer that will help his situation.

"Hey, has Carrick showed you the sleepboxes yet?" Mona jumps in at just the right time.

While I deal with the shock of Carrick finding his parents, I'm dragged away by a chirping Mona, who talks so fast I can barely keep up.

"Doesn't matter, I'll show you. You can share with me."

The accommodation is a series of portacabins piled on top of one another, but not just regular cubic cabins with basic beds inside—these are modern, state-of-the-art. I steal a glimpse inside one of them as we pass and see an entire living space cleverly built in the pod. There's a bunk bed—single on top and double beneath—built-in shelves, drawers beside the beds. There's even a toilet and shower. Everything is glossy white.

"Each sleepbox has an en suite bathroom, air-conditioning, a flat-screen TV, and a personal safe," Mona says in a funny accent, as though she's my hotel guide. "The rooms all include a double bed and a single bunk bed."

I laugh. "I've never seen anything like these before."

"Nothing but the best for CCU workers." She lowers her voice, though the section of non-Flawed living space is so far away nobody could possibly hear us. "The owner of Vigor is sympathetic to the Flawed. None of us have ever met him; he's a secret shadowy figure," she says sarcastically, eyes wide and fingers moving spookily.

"Is that Eddie?"

She laughs. "No. Eddie runs the place. I'm talking about the *big* boss: the owner, creator, inventor, whatever, of Vigor. Bahee claims to know him, but I'm not so sure. Bahee is a scientist; he can sometimes be a little bit . . ." She whistles to finish the sentence. "Anyway, Eddie knows about us. He keeps us living away from the others, manages shifts to keep us apart most of the time. Nobody but him and us knows that we're Flawed, and it has to stay that way. Obviously here we're all *evaders*." She rolls her eyes at the term. "So you won't see any armbands on us. If you have a brand on your hand, you get a job that requires gloves; if you have a brand on your temple, you get a job that requires a hard hat or you find a fancy way of keeping your hair down. Don't trust makeup to cover it. It gets hot here; it can melt off your face faster than you know. If the brand is on your tongue, you don't talk too much. Get it?"

I nod emphatically. I have a brand in every place she's mentioned, and more.

"Cool." She studies me to make sure she believes me and seems happy with what she finds. "Had a girl in here who fell in love with a scientist. Lizzie. She shared my room. She kept talking about telling him. Needing to share with him her true self because she was so in love." She rolls her eyes. "Honestly, I had to hear this crap every night. As you'll see, that didn't work out too well for her. She told him what she was, he was grossed out, and so she ran off. Could have got us into a whole lot of trouble," she says angrily, unlocking the door to her cabin and pushing the door open.

It's identical to the cabin I stole a glimpse of. The single bed above is clearly Mona's, with posters and possessions, a teddy bear on the bed. Beneath it is the double bed. It's just a naked mattress, where Lizzie once slept, where she thought this place was her home, where she was in love with a scientist, and then abandoned it. How replaceable we all are.

I understand how this girl Lizzie must have felt when she wasn't wanted by her boyfriend as soon as she revealed that she was Flawed. I recall the way Art looked at me in the school library after my brandings, how he couldn't bring himself to kiss me. I suppose that is the point of a tongue branding. They say it's the worst of them all. In fact, it turned out to be the second worst. Crevan himself held the hot weld to my spine to show that I was Flawed to my very backbone. But no one here will ever know about that, no one but Carrick, who witnessed it.

"When did Lizzie leave?" I ask, looking at her empty double bed.

"Two weeks ago. No good-bye," she says angrily. "She left most of her stuff here, too. You spend every day with someone and you think they're your friend. . . . Anyway—" She changes the subject, pretends not to care, though it's clear she's hurt. "So, ground rules. You sleep here, wash there, and do your thing in there. Depending on your job, you can go to bed and get up whenever you want. There are night shifts and day shifts. You can help yourself to the food in the kitchen in our rec room. The plant has a better cafeteria—more options, tastier food—but it's harder to avoid people getting too close there. Kelly and Adam work in the kitchen; Bahee is a scientist; Cordelia a computer whiz; I'm a cleaner. You can talk to the other staff, but don't get too close. No one knows we're Flawed, but some people ask too many questions, you know? Best thing is to keep to yourself, but not too much, or you'll stand out. Whatever you do, stay away from Fergus and Lorcan; they're only after one thing." She looks at me knowingly.

"Oh, right, sex."

"No." She bursts out laughing. "I wish. No"—she turns serious—"revolution. I mean, Carrick probably is, too; he hangs out with them, but he's a quiet kind of guy, you never know what he's thinking." She leaves a silence, while she studies me with a smile. "I see you've already caught his attention." She raises her eyebrows.

"It's not like that with me and Carrick," I say, unable to explain how it really is.

Our connection goes deeper than that. We shared something that will link us forever, something I'll never have with anybody else. Though I don't know if it's a good thing, to look at him and always remember that he was the person there in the Branding Chamber during the toughest moment of my life. It causes me to remember it, over and over again. Maybe being away from him would help me to forget.

Mona is looking at me for juicy details, but I'm uncomfortable. To tell her what bonded us would be to tell her what happened, and nobody can ever know what happened.

"How long have you lived here?" I ask, looking around.

"Oh, you're as bad as Carrick, deflecting the questions. Whatever. Don't tell me, but watch out, those Institution boys are famous for only wanting one thing." She steps on my double bed with her big black leather boot and climbs up to her bed. She sits on the edge, her legs dangling over my bed.

I think about it. "Revolution?"

She grins. "Nope. Mostly, they want sex."

I have to laugh.

"I've been here one year. To answer your question."

"You've been Flawed for one year?"

"Two years." She looks away, reaches to a glossy cabinet on the wall with no handle, pushes it to pop it open. She takes bedsheets from the shelves and drops them onto my new bed. Then she stamps on my bed with her big leather boots again and jumps to the floor, where she busies herself with the sheets. I try to help her, but she waves me off, talking as she goes. I can sense it's easier for her to be busy while telling me her story.

"My family threw me out of the house when I was branded Flawed. Dad said, 'You're no daughter of mine.'" She puts on a deep voice and pretends to make fun of the situation, but it's no laughing matter. "He had my bags packed when I got home from school one day. He walked me out to the taxi while Mom watched from the window. He gave me enough cash for a week and that was it." Her eyes are distant. "I lived on the street for one year as a fully fledged Flawed. Then I started to hear about these evaders, these magical people who were able to live without having to report to Whistleblowers, without the Guild breathing down their necks. I always thought it was a myth, that evaders were like fairies, but they turned out to be true. I came here finally. Best thing that ever happened to me."

My eyes widen and I realize how lucky I am to have a family that supported me all the way through. And what my poor granddad is going through now to protect me.

"What did you do?" I ask.

"I spent a year doing this and that, following the rules, doing what I was told by my Whistleblower, but then I got tired of that—it wasn't for me. I couldn't get a job; I couldn't get work, so I couldn't pay rent. Moved around some homeless shelters. I can tell you it's bad being Flawed with a roof over your head; you can imagine what it's like without one." Her eyes glisten. "So I made a decision and came here," she replies, eyes back to me.

"What did you do to become Flawed?"

Her tears disappear immediately, her eyes darken, and I learn the first rule of being Flawed. Never ask a Flawed person how they became Flawed.

SIXTEEN

I WAKE UP in the cabin to a nightmare, as usual. They haunt me. I'm always on the run from Crevan. Sprinting, leaping over walls, but I'm never fast enough, it's like I'm on a treadmill, running and running but not getting anywhere. It's exhausting and it continues all night, like it's on a loop. The only difference between this nightmare and every other night is a new addition: my granddad being tortured in the Branding Chamber.

Sweating and panting in the early hours of the morning, I sit bolt upright. I need to speak to Dahy. Even more urgently, I need to call home; I need to know what's going on.

Morning light streams in through the window of the cabin, and when I look up I see that Mona has left her bed. Probably gone to work. I check my watch and can't believe that it's midday.

There's a knock on the door.

I wrap myself in the bedsheet, lifting it to cover the brand over my heart, and open the door.

"Hi," Carrick says, swiftly looking me up and down, and his eyes on me send goose bumps rising on my skin. "Brought you this." He hands me a steaming mug of coffee and a chocolate muffin. "I'm on a break from my shift."

"I can't believe I've slept this long."

"You needed it." He looks at me intensely. "You've had a tough time."

I cup my hand around the mug and feel the warmth. "Thank you."

"The others wanted me to tell you to come to the rec room when you're ready. Most of them are on a lunch break; they want to show you something. Don't look so worried." He offers a rare smile.

"Okay, I'll be there soon. Carrick . . . you found your parents!" I grin at him, in celebration.

"I know," he says awkwardly, face scrunched up in thought. "It's weird. It's new. It's been only a few weeks. I barely know them. But they know me—my mom, more so; it's like she knows everything about me and I know nothing about her."

"It's bound to be weird. I was only in the castle for a few days, and when I went back home it felt different."

It was odd with my sister, Juniper, the entire time; we didn't get along at all and made up moments before I escaped from the house. She admitted to feeling guilty for not standing beside me on the bus, for not speaking out in court. Bizarrely, she felt jealous because, despite my punishment, she felt I'd done the right thing and she hadn't. I also discovered she was Art's accomplice in helping him to hide, when I desperately wanted to see him more than anything in the world. So much of what happened between us during those weeks was all due to lack of communication.

"I think when things happen to you, it can . . . alienate you from people," I say quietly. I think of my experience of going back to school and having no friends, being excluded from classes by teachers, being captured and locked in a shed by school kids, the end of my relationship with Art. Everything shifted; everything changed, nothing for the better.

He looks at me intensely. "But what happened to us didn't alienate us from each other, did it?" he asks.

I don't even need to think about it. "No."

"It brought us together," he says.

"Yes." I smile shyly.

He nods. "See you in the rec room. Make sure you come the route Mona showed you; we don't want anyone else seeing you here."

I close the door, my body brimming with energy just from standing next to him, though I feel a little shot down by his parting comment. I use the shower in the cabin and dress quickly, knowing everybody is waiting for me. As I open the door, I come face-to-face with a knuckle, which at first I think is aiming to punch me and so I squeal and duck.

When nothing happens and the feet haven't kicked me or run away and are just shuffling in my eyeline, I uncover my head from my hands and slowly look up.

A young man stands there, his fist still in the air, and he's looking at me, startled. "I was just about to knock on the door."

"Oh! *Oh.* Right." I clamber to my feet, feeling mortified.

"Sorry for scaring you," he says, embarrassed, as his cheeks start to go the brightest red I've ever seen on a human being. "I'm Leonard," he says, eyes on the floor, on the wall, on the door, flitting everywhere but on me. "I work here." He fumbles with the pass around his neck and offers it through the gap in the door. *Leonard Ambrosio, Lab Technician.* He looks like a choirboy.

"Hi, Leonard," I say, widening the gap a bit.

I'm afraid he recognizes me, but because he's in this unit, does that mean he's Flawed, too? Can I trust him? Do his eyes narrow a little as he processes me? My name and face are all over the media. Is it the end for me?

"I'm sorry to disturb you; I know you're new here. My girlfriend used to sleep in this room." He looks around as though he's more nervous to be here than me. "Her name is Lizzie."

I tense up. This is the boyfriend who doesn't like Flawed.

He looks at me expectantly.

"I just arrived. I don't know anything about her," I say defensively, thinking just because *she's* Flawed, doesn't mean that *I* am.

"No? Okay. Here's a photo of her." He studies my face as I take it, hoping a memory has stirred. "And here's my number." He hands me a piece of paper with his name and number. "If you hear anything about her, or if anyone else mentions her or where she might have gone, please call me. I really want to find her."

"For what?" I say, my voice cold.

He seems taken aback by my tone. "What do you mean?"

"Why do you want to find her?" I'm not going to offer up her whereabouts just so he can call the Whistleblowers on her.

"Because I love her," he says, eyes pleading. "I'm so worried about her." He looks up and down the corridor before lowering his voice even more. "I know who she is . . . *what* she is . . . you know?" He looks at me intently. "I think she was afraid to tell me, but I wouldn't have cared, I always knew and never cared. I mean, of course I cared, but it didn't stop me from loving her; if anything, it made me love her more." His cheeks pink at that again, as he becomes embarrassed. "I think it's important that *you* know that I don't have a problem with Flawed people. . . ." His eyes dart around the place again. "But mostly I just need Lizzie to know that. Okay?"

"Okay." I frown, thinking this is the complete opposite to what I've heard, but I don't want to get lost in somebody else's drama. And in the back of my mind I'm wondering, *Is this a setup?* Use me to get her and she gets in trouble? "But I told you, I don't know her."

A door bangs shut around the corner. We both look nervously down the hall.

"Don't, um, please don't tell Mona, or anyone, that I was here. I shouldn't be in this section. Lizzie gave me a key card so we could meet. This is just, um, between me and you," he says.

He looks so earnest, so concerned, so nervous, that I almost believe him. I understand his words to mean: I tell nobody about him, he tells nobody about me. I close the door quickly, unsure whether I should tell Mona. His story clashes with hers, but I've just arrived—I really don't want to be getting involved in a war of words with anyone, especially when it's none of my business.

Finally, I shrug and make my way to the recreational room, deciding not to give it any more thought.

My first mistake.

SEVENTEEN

"YOU TOOK YOUR TIME!" Mona says loudly when I enter the rec room. "Our lunch break is almost over."

"Sorry," I say. "It's just been a while since I showered without having to worry about a Whistleblower walking in on me."

They laugh and welcome me into the room. There are more Flawed here who I didn't meet last night, and they greet me. Evelyn wants to show me her cartwheels, which she does all around the room while her mother, Cordelia, tries to stop her.

"I'm sorry." Cordelia sits beside me. "Evelyn's been here since she was two years old. She's always excited by new people. It's a rare thing."

"It's okay. She's sweet." I smile, feeling sad for the little girl.

"Welcome." Bahee takes my hands; his are warm. "I hope you slept well."

"Much better." I smile again. Despite the nightmares, it was an improvement to sleeping in the farmhouse, where the fear and anxiety kept me awake most of the night. I feel guilty for sleeping when Granddad is being held in the castle because of me.

"Good. I'm sure you needed it after your recent journey. We've all been in your shoes, remember, we all understand how difficult the adjustment is. It takes time, but we'll help you. You're welcome to stay here as long as you want," he says, smiling warmly.

"Thank you," I say.

Bahee claps his hands suddenly. "Okay, my friends. Thank you for gathering on your break, and to those of you who took unofficial breaks: Eddie will kill you, but don't blame me." He throws a warning look at Mona, who laughs in her cleaner's uniform. "Let's show Celestine North what we do here."

The couches are moved to form a circle. I sit beside Mona. Carrick hangs back, standing outside the circle, arms folded, leaning against the wall, serious expression, always on alert.

Kelly sits beside me. "You and I need to have a chat," she says excitedly with a wink. She holds my hand and squeezes it. I can understand Carrick's discomfort with his mother wanting so much so soon. She is so eager to be back in his life she's grabbing at everything that's connected to him. Adam sits beside her and taps her thigh with a hand, a gesture that I read as an instruction to calm herself. She apologizes to me and lets go of my hand.

Rogan stays in the same dark corner I met him in last night, on a beanbag, near the computer games. He comes closer to the edge, to see what's happening, and he ends up glaring at Carrick for most of the time, studying his every move.

"Many people have come and gone from our tribe; all of them have been welcomed in with open arms and love," Bahee begins. "Before I became Flawed, in my previous life as a scientist I went on many travels, had laboratories and factories all around the world, which took me far and wide," he says, and it feels as though he's talking directly to me, that this is all for me. "It's what I miss most, stepping off a plane, breathing in and smelling the air of a new country, or feeling the heat of the African sun hit me." He seems frozen in a memory momentarily and everyone waits patiently, possibly remembering those moments of freedom, before, when we took them for granted. "But I consider myself lucky to be able to share news of my travels with those who haven't." He directs this at Evelyn.

"On my travels I came across the Babemba tribe of Africa, who could teach this nation a thing or two. The tribe believes that each human being comes into the world as good, that each person only desires safety, love, peace, and happiness. But sometimes in the pursuit of these things, people make mistakes. When a person makes a mistake, he or she is placed alone in the center of the village. All work stops and everyone gathers around the individual to take part in a beautiful ceremony where each person of the village shares all the good things that the individual ever did in his or her lifetime. Every positive story, their good deeds and strengths are recounted. At the end, a celebration takes place and the person is symbolically and literally welcomed back into the tribe."

"That's beautiful," I say dreamily. If only.

"These are my favorite days," Mona says.

"So, Lennox, as a new arrival to our home. Stand up," Bahee says, and Lorcan, Fergus, and Carrick cheer him on. Lennox grins and sits in a chair in the center of the room, acting as though he's a rock star taking the stage, waving as though there are thousands of us in his audience.

Evelyn jumps up and down with excitement, wanting to start it off.

"When Lennox first came here he was so nice to me. He used to carry me around on his back and pretend that he was the daddy monkey and I was the baby." Lennox becomes embarrassed. "And he was the first person I ever heard burp the alphabet."

Everyone laughs.

Evelyn continues. "Lennox is always happy and makes jokes and I love that about him because he makes everybody else happy. But then Lennox was sad one day. I found him crying in his room and asked him what was wrong. He was looking at photographs of him and his wife surfing. He said that he missed the sea. I told him that at least he'd seen the sea. I've never ever seen the sea. I've been here most of my life. The next time Lennox went out when he wasn't supposed to, he came back with a shell for me. He told me to put it to my ear and whenever I wanted to hear the sound of the sea then all I had to do was listen. And always, when I feel a bit sad, I put the shell to my ear and I close my eyes and even though I'm just in my cabin with Mom, I imagine I'm on the beach, my toes in the sand, and the waves are crashing and I'm in my swimsuit and I've made dozens of castles and Lennox is surfing with his wife. So thank you, Lennox, for giving me the sea."

Cordelia wipes her eyes, tears for her little girl, who has missed so many experiences while living here in the facility.

Kelly starts clapping and everybody else joins in.

Lennox clears his throat. "Man, this is going to be hard."

And it is, but it is the most beautiful thing I've ever witnessed, a room of people heaping praise on somebody, and through their stories I receive a huge insight into Lennox's character. Sure, he's a wisecracking smart-ass, but he has a kind soul. It also teaches me more. Lennox is married, or was, so where is his wife? What happened? What did he do to become Flawed? I know now after Mona's reaction last night not to ask that question so easily. Yet I can't help but wonder what everybody in here did to become Flawed, especially Carrick's parents.

Eventually everyone but Carrick and I have spoken about Lennox.

"That's it," Bahee says. "Celestine, you are new here—we don't expect you to say anything about Lennox; you have yet to discover his charming ways." Everyone laughs.

"Carrick never speaks," Mona whispers to me, as though Carrick has been there for longer than his two weeks.

"Uh, wait," Carrick speaks up, and everyone falls silent, in surprise. He unfolds his arms and steps away from the wall, a rare glimpse of awkwardness from him as he fidgets and cracks his fingers.

"Nice," Mona mutters.

He glares at her and shoves his hands into his pockets instead.

"Right, Lennox," he says awkwardly, his voice deep and serious. "We met around two weeks ago and I didn't know much about you. Still really don't."

"Well, this is moving," Lennox says, to chuckles.

"But I needed your help with something. And you were there. I got a call from Dahy, and we had to move fast. Because these two idiots' faces are posted everywhere in the city"—he refers to Fergus and Lorcan—"I needed you. You rose to the occasion. You were there. You didn't ask many questions. You helped me find someone"—he looks at me and my heart pounds and my stomach flutters—"who is incredibly important to . . ."

Thud, thud, thud.

". . . the Flawed cause."

Mona tuts.

"And I'll never be able to thank you enough for that."

While I melt under Carrick's intense gaze, Lennox interrupts, "Cash money will do just fine," and everyone laughs.

"Let's not get into a discussion about any 'causes,'" Bahee interjects nervously. "The only cause we should be discussing is the cause for celebration yesterday that we only learned about today."

Suddenly the lights dim and there's an outbreak of "Happy Birthday" and Kelly, who was beside me and disappeared without my noticing, is exiting the kitchen holding an enormous cake with eighteen candles in it. Evelyn skips alongside, excitedly singing and licking her lips. When the cake reaches me, Evelyn sits on my knee and helps me blow out the candles.

I said I would never wish again, but twenty-four hours later, I do.

"Thank you so much, everybody." I beam.

They give me a very generous portion, one that is far beyond what a Flawed is allowed to take in, with our rules on weekly luxury intakes.

"Do you like it?" Evelyn asks. "What's your favorite part?"

I laugh to cover my awkwardness and look at the sponge cake, cream oozing from the layers.

"The vanilla," I say easily, taking another bite.

Evelyn frowns. "But it's lemon sponge."

I feel my cheeks pink and I heap another spoon into my mouth to avoid having to say anything else. From the corner of my eye I feel Carrick watching me.

Kelly sits beside me, puts her arm around my shoulders, and speaks quietly into my ear, "Your taste will come back eventually. Trust me."

As I swallow the next tasteless piece of cake, I can't help but wonder what lie Carrick's mother told.

EIGHTEEN

AT NIGHT, WHEN everybody has finally gone to bed, or to work, Carrick comes for me in the cabin. Mona raises her eyebrows at me suggestively, and I laugh as I leave. It's not what she thinks it is; Carrick and I desperately need to talk. Even though I understand why she's doing it, Kelly constantly trying to be near Carrick and fussing around him has prevented us from being able to talk. And then I had to wait for him to finish his shift, and when he finally did there was a group dinner, where Kelly sat between us, thinking she was bringing us all together when, really, Carrick sat by stiffly, giving one-word answers, and I was too tired to speak.

It's been an exhausting two weeks, a terrifying twenty-four hours, and now that I have finally stopped, and the adrenaline has worn off, I am sore and stiff, my head aches, and I feel like I could sleep forever.

Carrick takes me to the kitchen, the farthest room from everybody's sleeping quarters, and closes the door. We sit at the kitchen table.

"Did you hear anything from Dahy about my granddad?"

It is the tenth time, at least, that I've asked him and Lennox today, though at one point Lennox fixed me with a dangerous look and said, "North, I like you, but I will swat you like a fly."

"Yes. Just a few minutes ago. Your parents went to see him today. He's in a holding cell; they're treating him well. They're questioning him and holding him for another twenty-four hours on suspicion of aiding the Flawed. They're trying to say he's been giving his employees privileges."

I'm both relieved and not, at the same time. He hasn't been charged, or hurt. Yet.

"They have no proof against him, or they would have charged him by now. They're just holding him to smoke you out."

I wince.

"Sorry." He backtracks. "I didn't mean to use that expression. But on the positive side, the fact that they're holding on to him means he knows you're still alive."

"You're sure?"

"Certain. He's not stupid."

I smile. "No, he's not."

"So . . . I've been formulating a plan to get us out of this mess."

"What mess?"

He makes a general gesture, indicating the room around us, the factory.

"You want to leave Vigor?" I ask, surprised.

"You don't?"

Would it be stupid to say that I like it here? That for the first time in weeks I feel safe? Surrounded by steel, metal, enormous structures, card keys to get through doors, heightened security, all to keep the outsiders from getting in. I don't feel locked inside, I feel protected, as if for the first time it's me who is being guarded.

"I feel safe here," I admit. "And you've found your family, and your brother—did you even know you had a brother? Why would you want to give up being with them?"

"I understand, Celestine, I do. But this place isn't real life. This isn't freedom. Poor Evelyn is six years old and hasn't been outside of these walls since the day she arrived. She has no friends her age, probably has never *met* anyone her own age. Bahee doesn't want us to fight for freedom. If he hears us speak about it, he tells us to stop, so nothing around here is ever going to change."

"But I got ten hours of sleep last night," I whine, and he laughs gently.

"I felt the same for about a day, but you've just arrived. You'll see."

"You sure you're not just trying to run away?" I ask gently. "It's going to take some time to get to know your family again, Carrick. It's normal for it to be . . . awkward."

"You noticed," he says sarcastically. "When I left the institution, the worst thing I could have done to the Guild was to find my parents. I didn't think the Guild would really be watching me. Of all the students, I was the person to least suspect; I thought I'd fooled them. I thought they trusted me. It just taught me that no matter how good a relationship I thought I'd built up with them, they didn't trust me anyway. The dean came to see me at the castle."

"I remember that." I recall the well-dressed gentleman visiting his cell. He looked like a lawyer, but Carrick had chosen to represent himself.

"He said he'd never felt so betrayed by someone in all his life. He'd kind of taken me under his wing." He shakes his head. "He'd watched me grow up, come to all my games, celebrated all my exam results. He has kids himself. And yet he still couldn't understand my wanting to find my parents. And then I'm branded Flawed, and I'm allowed to search for my parents. There's no rule to stop me now. It's so twisted."

"Illogical," I agree. "How did you find your family?"

"I was tipped off that they were here. They moved here when I was brought to Highland Castle."

"They've been here less than two months?" I ask, surprised.

"Seems longer, doesn't it?" he asks. "That's the weird thing about this place"—he looks around the walls—"it's as though time doesn't exist.

People come here and they never leave. There are more Flawed who you haven't met yet, I dread to think of how long they've been here."

"Apart from Lizzie," I say.

She's been playing on my mind. One of the reasons my friends considered me perfect before I became Flawed was because of my perfect grades, always As, particularly in math. I just have the head for it. The theorems, equations—they always made sense to me. A problem that could easily be solved. If anything tested me, I'd stick with it until I got my solution. I feel the same way now. Something doesn't feel right. There's a problem. It's lingering, like a ghost with unfinished business, waiting for somebody to figure it out. You'd think after what happened to me, I'd be able to change, but I can't. When the Guild brands you, they can't change the person, not really; they just change peoples' perception of the person.

"Lizzie?" He seems confused by the change in direction.

"What do you know about her?"

"She was a Flawed girl who worked and lived here. She left a few days after I arrived. She shared a cabin with Mona, they were pretty close. I didn't pay much attention. The rumor is she told her boyfriend that she was Flawed and he wasn't interested anymore, so she left. I didn't bother with the gossip, that's Mona's territory. Why?"

"Do you know her boyfriend?"

"I know what he looks like. Kind of a nerdy computer guy. Why?"

"Is he trustworthy?"

"Celestine," he warns. "Why?"

"Just wondering. Humor me: I'm worried about her, you said when people come in here they never leave. She left. She disappeared."

"I don't think her boyfriend chopped her up into little pieces, if that's what you're worried about," he teases. "Don't worry, people here are mostly good. I'm sure a few of them suspect us, might even have seen a brand or two, but they don't say anything; they let us keep to ourselves."

He stops talking, but he looks like he wants to say more.

"What?" I urge. "Tell me."

"I can understand why you want to stay. There's goodness in here, yes, but there's something you need to think about. What exactly do you think you can do here?" he asks gently. "What's your role?"

I have romantic visions of me making cakes with Adam and Kelly in the kitchen. Skating around suds-soaked floors on brush-skates with Mona, cleaning the floors at night while everyone sleeps, Pippi Longstocking–style. Teaching Evelyn math. Becoming Bahee's side-kick, donning a white lab coat and sensible glasses and studying things on petri dishes. Wearing night-vision goggles and sitting with the security team, scanning the horizon. For a few hours at least, this factory was my oyster.

Carrick goes on. "After Fergus and Lorcan escaped the supermarket riot, their faces were plastered all over the news. They're on the Guild Wanted list. They have to work night duty from now on so nobody recognizes them by day and gives them up. Night duty falls to the Flawed mostly. You have one of the most recognized faces in the country right now; maybe that will calm down after a while, maybe not. And people here are good, but I'm sure they're not *that* good. They won't want their lives in danger, because if the Guild discovers that they were working with you day in and day out but never reported you, they'd all be in trouble. They wouldn't take that risk. You'll have to be kept away from everyone, for a while."

The way he says *while*, he drags it out and makes it sound like a long time.

He shrugs. "For the record, my wanting to leave has nothing to do with how things are going with my family. It's about me. I'm not settling for this life and neither should you."

He leaves a silence, gives me time to think.

I want to see my family, my heart hurts when I think of them, of the home that I've left behind, of the life I'm missing, but I said good-bye to that life as soon as I was taken to Highland Castle. I'm dreaming of Mom, Dad, Juniper, and Ewan visiting me here, transported through the gates hidden in the back of a food truck or something. Special Sundays where we hang around the rec room together, playing soccer or whatever Ewan wants to do outside. But I know this is ridiculous thinking. Bahee and the others would never allow it. Carrick is right: I'm tired, and feeling safe is a rarity, something so beautiful I should want to fight for it outside these walls.

"This life isn't good enough for me, either," I admit.

He grins. "Good. Because when I said I wanted us to get out of this mess I didn't just mean leave the plant, I meant I wanted out of this entire Flawed *life*. I've got a plan."

NINETEEN

CARRICK LEANS FORWARD, brimming with excitement. "I've been thinking about what you told me last night. About Crevan, about his searching for the footage of the branding. Do you have any idea the power that it gives you?"

I ponder that. Mr. Berry and Pia Wang knew about the footage and they've since disappeared. Crevan thinking that it's in my possession fills me with fear; it puts me in a vulnerable situation, and I doubt that telling him I *don't* have it will be believed. If anything, it makes me feel like the most hunted person in the universe.

Carrick can tell I'm not seeing this the same way he is. "Celestine, you can use that footage to *reverse* your branding. And not only that, if the public sees that Crevan has made a mistake with his rulings once, then who knows how many mistakes he's made in the past? It calls the entire Guild system into question."

My heart starts to pound. I think there's something in what he's saying. It's the first light I've seen through all of this. It's better than revenge: It's a way out. He *has* convinced me, I *do* think it's worth trying, but . . .

"What's wrong, Celestine? You should use this. You should show the video to every single person you can."

I don't have the footage.

Tell him, Celestine. Tell him you don't have it. Say it. I open my mouth. I think how to phrase it. It should be simple. *I don't have the footage. I don't know where it is. Somebody just thinks that I have it. Because the person who apparently gave it to me told him so.*

Carrick's waiting. I close my mouth again. I can't break his enthusiasm; he's holding on to this plan like it's his only chance to undo all of this. And who knows—I *might* have the footage. If I could gain access to my house, it *could* be there. My mind races. Can I get back to my house without the Whistleblowers seeing me? Can I contact my family and ask them to search for it instead? Can I really do this?

"It's okay," he says, like the wind has been taken out of him, backing down. "It's a lot to ask of you, I understand. You've just arrived, you're tired, I shouldn't have . . . Anyway"—he perks up—"I brought you in here for a reason." He stands up, opening the fridge, turning off the lights, and placing two cushions on the floor in front of the open fridge. "Take a seat, please."

I look at him in utter confusion. The moment has passed, I'm relieved, but I don't like that I'm keeping something from him. I should tell him.

"It's okay, Celestine, really. It's something for you to think about. For now, just sit, please."

I sit down on a cushion on the floor, the light of the fridge the only thing illuminating the room.

He sits opposite me. "We're going to have a lesson. Are you ready to begin?"

"Yes, Master Vane."

He fights a smile, and I wonder what he'd look like if he let himself go, if those facial muscles untensed and a real smile took over, or even better, a full-blown laugh, how it would transform him.

"Of all our senses, smell is one of the most important. Animals need sense of smell to survive. A *blind* rat might survive, but a rat without a sense of smell can't taste, therefore can't mate or find food."

I realize what this is about. "Your mom told you I couldn't taste the birthday cake."

"She may have said something," he says softly.

"You're comparing me to a rat." I pout.

His mouth twitches as he tries to hide his smile. "Listen. You might have lost your sense of taste, but you haven't lost your sense of smell. Seventy percent of what we perceive as taste actually comes from scent."

"I did not know that."

I could barely eat in the weeks after my tongue branding, as my tongue swelled and scabbed from the sear. It's been a month and everything tastes like nothing. I'm assuming I'll never taste again for the rest of my life, which is fine, because the Flawed diet doesn't allow for luxuries. I might be saved from tasting the endless grains and pulses we have to eat.

Carrick continues the lesson. "When you put food in your mouth, odor molecules from that food travel through the passage between your nose and mouth to olfactory receptor cells at the top of your nasal cavity, just beneath the brain and behind the bridge of the nose."

I raise an eyebrow. "And when you swallowed the encyclopedia, what did it taste like?"

"This is my good schooling talking," he says sarcastically. "You can't taste but you *can* smell, *and* you can feel the texture and temperature of the food. You need to use all these things to your advantage."

I nod along.

"In school we had to do a taste test. We had five items: a pinecone, a cinnamon stick, lemon, baby powder on a cloth, and a mothball. We were told to sniff each one until a memory came to mind. Up to the age of eight, I hated my parents. The institution made me hate them. Between what we were told about Flawed, and the fact they never came to get me, never rescued me from that place, I hated them more than anyone. But then we did this test, and it brought back some memories I'd forgotten. Good memories, happy memories. It made me wonder about how bad my parents were after all. I wrote the memories down and then I couldn't stop, as soon as I wrote one, it would lead to another, and then another. I was afraid if I didn't write them down then I would forget everything forever, so every day, I wrote in my secret diary, all the things I remembered about my parents. I wouldn't give my diary to anyone, I had to hide it in my room. They like to know everything you're thinking in there."

I think of catching Mary May reading my diary in my bedroom, of her wanting to be in my head.

"And everything changed for me after this test. I knew that everything they were telling me about my parents was a lie."

I want to reach out to him, hug him, tell him I'm sorry he was taken away from his parents at such a young age, but there's something about Carrick that stops me each time. He's so contained. It's like he has a force field around him, like the glass that was between us in the castle cells is still between us now. He's there, but I can't reach him.

He clears his throat. "You have nerve endings on the surface of your eyes, nose, mouth, and throat. They detect the coolness of mint, the burning of chili peppers. Use them. You're not alone in this, you know."

"Your mom had the same thing after her branding?" I guess. *What was her lie?* I want to ask.

"It's not just Flawed people who experience this. Not being able to taste is called ageusia."

"So it's a thing?" I ask, surprised.

"It's an actual thing."

I feel happy about that.

"So here is a taste bag." He places a bag down. "And here is a smell bag." I laugh.

"Let's use"—he scans the shelves in the large refrigerator—"Bahee's jelly beans."

"Jelly beans?" I laugh. "In the fridge?"

"He's an odd man. Consumes more sugar in one day than Evelyn does in a week, and he never shares, which is what makes this all the sweeter." He takes the bag of jelly beans out, tells me to look away.

"What are you doing?"

"Crushing the jelly beans, so the odor is released in the smell bag. Now." He reaches into the back pocket of his jeans and pulls out a bandanna. "Close your eyes."

He moves behind me and gently ties the bandanna around my eyes, his fingers brushing against my skin at one point, and I feel my skin tingle and the hairs stand up on my arms. The last time I was blindfolded, it was by some kids from school, playing a cruel joke on me. They stripped me and examined my scars with ghoulish curiosity like I was in some freak show at a circus. I felt terrified then, broken, had lost all faith in people and my new life. But now, I'm completely relaxed, excited even. Despite the terrifying feeling I had when we approached the gates of the CCU plant, I realize I completely and utterly trust Carrick. He feels like my partner in all this. If my sixth brand is as powerful as Carrick says it is, he could have used his knowledge of it for his own purposes. He could have threatened Crevan himself, but he didn't; in fact, he didn't tell anybody. He wants to help me reverse my own branding.

"Okay." He's back in front of me. "Taste this."

"You better not slip a chili pepper in." I laugh.

I open my mouth and feel him place a jelly bean on my tongue. I close my lips and self-consciously chew. I don't taste anything, unsurprisingly. I feel the texture, though I don't think I would have known it was a jelly bean had he not told me.

"Take a sip of water."

I suck through a straw.

"Now smell." He holds the bag up to my nose and I breathe in the crushed jelly bean.

"Strawberry," I say easily. Nothing wrong with my sense of smell at least.

"Now taste." He places the jelly bean on my tongue.

I expect it to be strawberry again but I frown. "That's not strawberry," I say confused. "I know it's not strawberry but I don't know what it is."

"Aha," he says happily. "Progress."

"Yay," I cheer myself.

"Smell."

I sniff. "Orange."

"Now taste."

I feel his fingers brush my lips as I open my mouth. I'm so distracted by everything around the jelly bean, everything that's happening, I can barely concentrate on what I'm doing. All of my other senses are on fire. I try to focus. I smell as I chew, waiting for my nerve endings to recognize whether it's bitter, salty, sweet, or sour flavor. I recognize the taste as being the same as the previous taste. Bitter. "Orange."

"Yes," he says happily. "Now let's go again."

Carrick is nothing if not efficient, and persistent. Over and over again, we try the test until I think I get the hang of using my gift of smell. He's practically emptied out the fridge of flavors. I have correctly identified most without needing to smell the bag first.

"Right, last one." He places it on my lips and I concentrate, I concentrate so hard. He said there are taste buds in my throat—I never knew that. I can also smell as I chew. I feel like an animal, zoned in on my food, sniffing as I chew in the dark, hoping for scents and clues.

"Mint?" I ask hopefully.

"Perfect," he replies.

I smile. It's been a while since I've heard that word, or felt anything close to it.

TWENTY

ART AND I never had sex. We had been dating for six months and we were close to it happening but we never got there before the branding, before both our lives changed. In the few days before I left, he told me that he'd been in love with me. Not that he was in love with me *now,* but that he *had been* in love with me. It took me only a few seconds of silent celebration before I distinguished the difference, and then the party inside me died.

When Art and I were alone, we explored each other's bodies, but shyly, clumsily. I don't feel that way with Carrick. He shattered that transparent glass between us as soon as we began the taste test. I feel so connected to him, feel that our bodies went through so much together already that it links us tighter. We have a physical bond. And that was never Crevan's plan. Instead, it was to mutilate us, make us appear ugly, dangerous, different, not to be touched. He said it himself, at the ruling. A tongue brand so that everyone who talks to me or kisses me knows that I'm a liar. I remember how repelled Art was by it, whether he noticed it himself or not. How I feel when I'm with Carrick is not what Crevan intended, for the people who are punished to find harmony and safety together.

I don't know where Art is now. I don't know if he's gone back to his dad or if he has run away. I asked Granddad about him once and he quickly shot me down, but not cruelly; I suppose he was just being realistic.

"Why do you want to know about that boy?" he asked.

"Just because . . ." I'd mumbled something incoherently, embarrassed to be talking about feelings with my granddad, particularly when I knew he was never a fan of the Crevans anyway.

He stopped what he was doing and fixed me with a hard look. "He cut you loose, girl, I suggest you do the same."

So I never asked again.

I take off the blindfold and Carrick is looking at me intensely, his eyes on mine. The light from the fridge dances from his dark pupils, like cat eyes.

To his surprise, I reach out and open the top buttons of his denim shirt. Three buttons it takes me to see the contrast between the color of his neck and the skin hidden below his collar. I see his *F* brand, only a month old, still new and fresh like mine, healing over, trying to settle, to find its place on his body.

His breathing is heavy; his chest rises up and down; he looks almost nervously from my face to my fingers as they hover above his scar. I press them to his skin and with my forefinger I trace the sign of the *F* and the curve of the surrounding circle. I feel his heart beating beneath my fingers. It was supposed to be a branding to symbolize his disloyalty to society, to the Guild, for seeking out his parents after thirteen years in an institution that tried to teach the Flaws out of him. He turned his back on the Guild. But his dishonor to them only proves his loyalty to what's good and right, and proper and honest.

I move my body closer and press my lips to his scar, and I hear him breathe out. I look up to see if I've hurt him, but his eyes are closed, and his hand moves to my hair, to my right temple. His thumb rubs my temple. My brand.

For your bad judgment, your right temple. I hear Crevan's courtroom voice boom as though he's in the kitchen with us right now.

Carrick lifts my right hand, and I feel his thumb circle my palm.

For stealing from society, you will you branded on your right hand. Whenever you go to shake the hands of any decent people in society, they will know of your theft.

He kisses the palm of my hand, gently.

Then he reaches out, pushes the refrigerator door closed, and we're plunged into darkness.

"Carrick?" I whisper.

"I didn't want it to defrost."

I smirk, then start laughing.

"Let's go to my cabin," he whispers.

TWENTY-ONE

"WHERE IS LENNOX?" I ask as we enter the cabin, and I pick up on a distinctively male smell to the room.

Carrick kicks a pile of dirty clothes under the bed and I pretend not to notice.

"Not here."

I laugh.

His cabin is exactly the same as mine and Mona's, but messier. He sits down on the double bed. "I can't believe you're here."

"Should I have played more hard to get?" I tease.

"I mean I can't believe I found you. I told you at the castle that I'd find you, but it was harder than I thought. You were well guarded. I wanted to meet my parents, of course I did, but now . . . but now that we have you, we're moving out of here. It's finally time to move," he says, pumped.

"Who's the 'we' you keep referring to?"

"Fergus, Lorcan, Lennox, you, and me. Maybe Mona. I haven't discussed it with my parents. Bahee has a fit if people can't agree on what to watch on TV, never mind the Flawed movement."

"So you, me, Fergus, Lorcan, and Lennox are going to change the world, are we?"

"Not the world. Just the country. And to change the country you only have to change a few minds."

I stare at him in surprise.

"Celestine." He takes my hands and pulls me to sit beside him on the bed. "To most people, Crevan seems all powerful. He has control over the Guild, and the Guild has somehow found a way to manipulate the government—probably because they've branded most of them and those people now live in fear of the monster they created. Much of the public supports Crevan, *but not everyone.* You got people listening who never listened before. I always knew you were special. And now, I realize that you have something even more powerful against him."

The sixth brand. And the footage of it occurring. My chest tightens that I haven't told him I don't have it.

"The video will expose Crevan. He'll lose credibility, he'll lose his power. You'll be able to force him to undo the charges against you. You know you can. If he has made a mistake with one Flawed, then perhaps he's made a mistake with more. It will call the entire thing into question. Then we can all be free. But it's you who has the key to unlock it."

"That's all?" I ask him, terrified by the prospect. "I just make Crevan change his mind?"

"You can do it, Celestine," he says softly.

"But I'm exhausted, Carrick." I finally break down. I sit on the bed beside him. "I can't do it anymore." And that's all I can say, because the tears take my words away and the exhaustion sweeps in and takes over.

Carrick removes my hands from where they're hiding my face and pulls me to him. I rest my head on his chest; his shirt is still open and my tears fall on his scar. He lets me cry for a moment, holding me perfectly still.

"Whenever I think I can't do something, do you know what I think of?" he asks.

"Raindrops and roses?" I say weepily.

He doesn't laugh. He's not really the laughing type. "You."

I pull away from him, confused.

"What you did on the bus, in the courtroom, and in the chamber," he says quietly, as we both remember, "was the strongest, bravest thing I've ever seen anyone do. You are my inspiration, Celestine. Every time I think I can't get through this, that there's no way out, I think of you. There's no one like you. Courageous, so damn stubborn, and you have all the power now. You're like Superman to Crevan's Lex Luthor."

Despite my fear and sadness I laugh. "That's a terrible comparison."

Embarrassed, he says, "I was trying to be serious."

"Oh."

"When I was watching you in the chamber I saw awesome power. When I was in there myself, I was terrified. I just thought of you the entire time. I wanted to be brave like you were. I didn't make a sound, just like you. I've told Lorcan, Fergus, and Lennox about you, that you have . . . *something*, that they just have to wait and see. Because even though you don't know it, Celestine, it comes out of you, when you're least expecting it, when the timing's right."

"They'll be terribly disappointed if you've built me up to be Superman."

"They already believe me. They saw you in action at the supermarket, standing up to that policeman. But they don't know about the—"

"Shh . . ." I hold my finger to his lips.

I see a shadow beneath the door.

TWENTY-TWO

CARRICK FOLLOWS MY GAZE. As if sensing our attention on it, the shadow quickly moves. Carrick jumps up and pulls the door open. He charges down the balcony, his boots clattering on the metal.

I lie back on his bed.

He returns, out of breath. "Couldn't see anyone."

"It doesn't matter. You didn't say it out loud," I say blankly, staring at the ceiling, feeling everything positive I felt about this place this morning further draining away. Of course Carrick is right: I can't stay here forever. I miss my parents, Juniper, and Ewan. I miss life. But it's not just that: This place has layers I didn't see on arrival last night, and today. Now it doesn't feel safe.

Carrick finishes checking the corridor and closes the door. "Are you okay?"

"My new happy, peaceful world has been officially deflated. So, no."

He comes toward me, lies on the bed, above me, on his elbows to take his weight off. He gives me a long kiss. Long, slow, beautiful. Soft despite his strength. Then he pulls away and asks me again. "Now are you okay?"

"Almost," I whisper.

He smiles. "So where was I?" He lifts up the palm of my hand and kisses it. "One." He kisses my right temple. "Two." Then next is my mouth. He kisses my tongue. "Three." He reaches for the hem of my T-shirt and lifts it over my head, revealing my chest scar, between my bra cups. He does what I did, makes the shape of it with his finger before kissing it gently. "Four." Then he moves down slowly, kissing my belly button, which isn't branded, but I'm not complaining, and he removes my shoes and socks. The sole of my right foot *for your collusion with the Flawed, for walking alongside them, and for stepping away from society.* He kisses my foot, I feel him whisper, "Five," with his lips on my skin, and I hear the voices, the shouts, the fury, the pounding of the hammer of the court-room all in my head. I'm almost dizzy from reliving it.

He kneels and looks at me.

I'm nervous. My heart is pounding. I vowed to never let anyone see this.

"Turn over," he says.

I shake my head, swallow hard.

His enormous hands take my hips and turn me. I move with him so that I'm lying on my side. He lies down beside me, behind me, hand on my waist. If he's disgusted by what he sees he doesn't show it. The sixth brand wasn't planned, it was carried out without anesthetic by a furious and out-of-control Crevan. I jerked when it happened, as I felt it burn through my skin. The *F* is gaudy and unclear, it's as brutal-looking as it felt.

He starts at the nape of my neck with his tongue and he traces my spine all the way down to my lower back. There, he kisses my most pain-ful brand—yet the one he believes to be my most powerful of all.

I hear Crevan amid all the branding chamber panic. *Brand her spine! We have never seen anyone so Flawed to their very backbone. . . .* Until his voice dies out and I can't hear him anymore. He's gone from my head. Cleansed.

"Six," Carrick and I whisper in unison.

TWENTY-THREE

IT'S CLOSE IN THE CABIN, the small window doesn't allow any air in on the still, hot night. We're tangled in the covers, my leg draped over Carrick's, my head against his chest. My left hand is resting on his chest, guarding his brand, and his left hand is holding mine, his finger circling my palm. I don't know if he notices that this is the natural position we've both adopted.

"So I guess two Flawed make a perfect," Carrick says, and I giggle. "I don't do jokes well," he says with a small smile.

"You don't need to. You just be serious and mean and sexy." I kiss his jaw.

Art was funny, it was what I adored most about him. He always made me laugh; he lightened every tense atmosphere with his well-timed obser-vations. He also managed to be appropriately inappropriate, which is a feat. Guilt envelops my mind, and I stiffen.

"Okay?" Carrick asks.

"Mmm-hmm."

But it's as if he can read my mind. "I was thinking, we do have a way to get to Crevan. You have more power over him than you know. Apparently he's close to his son, particularly now. Crevan would do anything for him."

I freeze. Use Art?

I'm so disgusted by the suggestion, by the tactless timing and the way it was raised, that I clamber off Carrick, clumsily, trying to untie my body from his, but he's so strong and it's tricky. I eventually get away from him and off the bed, but only because he gives up the fight, and I hurriedly start putting my clothes back on.

"Come on, Celestine." He sits up, bedsheets low on his hips, revealing the tattoo of a weather vane on his hip, the one he says he got when he was sixteen on a school trip away and won't tell me why.

"Is that why you slept with me?" I snap. "To make me fall for your plan? So you could use me to get to Art, to get to Crevan?"

"No," he says, annoyed but calm. He doesn't raise his voice, doesn't get dramatic like me. He just says steadily, "Anything we can do to get our lives back, we should do."

"*Without* hurting the people we love."

Pause.

"You love him?" he asks, revealing nothing.

"No! I mean, no."

"You're still wearing the anklet he gave you."

"How do you know he gave me that?"

"The chamber."

I remember now. I'd refused to take it off. The guard who branded me was the very same blacksmith who had made it. It had shaken him to see it on me, branding a girl Flawed who he had only days previously thought was perfect, even if he didn't know me.

"So you'll protect Art no matter what he's done to you?" he asks.

"What exactly do you think he's *done* to me?"

Art ran away after the branding, he hid out, only letting Juniper know where he was, which hurt me deeply. But I've since realized he wasn't trying to hide from me, he didn't want to hurt me. He was trying to stay away from his dad, whom he hated for what he'd done to me, and anyway, Carrick wouldn't know anything about that. He wasn't around, and I didn't tell him. "Carrick, what are you talking about? What do you think Art has done to me?"

"Nothing," he says, his face unreadable.

"Carrick, no secrets, tell me everything." I'm aware of my hypocrisy, seeing as I haven't told him about not actually possessing the footage.

Deadpan face again, revealing nothing, but then it breaks. "If I were him, I wouldn't have left you like that on the bus. He let them take you away from him. I wouldn't have let them take you without a fight. I would have made them take me, too. I would have stood beside you on the bus *and* in court. I would have told the media the truth. Everybody wanted to hear from him, and he chose not to say anything."

"He did try to speak for me in court . . ." I say quietly.

"His last-minute hissy fit? It was too late. It was more of a tantrum against his dad than anything else. I just wouldn't have let it happen," he says simply.

I start to realize what exactly Granddad meant when he said Art had cut me loose. I never thought about it the way Carrick phrased it. I kept understanding Art's perspective; his fear, his situation, but maybe Carrick's right—perhaps Art could have spoken up for me more.

"You were there for me in court every day," I say, remembering. Carrick was loyal to me; Carrick showed the support that my boyfriend at the time didn't. "But you hated me when you first saw me." I smile, sitting back down on the bed.

"*Hated* you," he agrees.

"Hey!" I slap him playfully on his arm. He catches my hand and pulls me close.

"You were hugging Crevan," he says. "I remember you all, huddled around the table with your parents and him, trying to come up with a way out of it, your fancy clothes all laid out like they were going to fix it all."

I picture my story from his angle, and I don't blame him for hating me. It was pathetic.

"When did you stop hating me?" I ask.

He fixes me with an intense stare. "Approximately fifteen minutes ago."

I shake my head, trying to hide my smile. "You're right, you don't do jokes very well."

"It was when I saw you in court for the first time."

"Judge Sanchez announced they weren't letting me home for the trial. You realized the Guild wasn't on my side then."

"No. It was before that. The minute you stepped inside the courtroom you looked so terrified—I don't think I've ever seen anyone look so scared. I wanted to be glad. I wanted to be pleased by what everyone shouted at you in the courtyard; I wanted to feel like you deserved it, but as soon as I saw you in court I thought to myself, *This girl doesn't think that it will be all handed to her on a plate.* You were afraid from the start, which makes your bravery all the more striking."

I feel shy all of a sudden, from his compliments.

"Sorry for losing my temper." I sigh.

"I understand," Carrick says. "My timing sucked."

"Can we just rewind five minutes?"

"Let's rewind more." He smiles. "Thirty minutes? I want to try the combination code again if I can remember it. What was it? One, two, three . . . ? I should have written it down," he murmurs as he kisses my branded skin again.

His head disappears up my T-shirt.

"Found one," he says, voice muffled.

I can't help but laugh.

And then an alarm rings out.

TWENTY-FOUR

CARRICK'S HEAD APPEARS from under my T-shirt and he leaps out of the bed at top speed to dress. Thankfully I'm already dressed, so I search for my sneakers.

"What's that?"

"I don't know. Nothing good."

The door to the cabin bursts open. It's Lennox, who takes no heed of the fact I'm in Carrick's cabin at this hour and he's half-naked. "Whistle-blowers at the gate."

"Oh my God." My stomach sinks. My haven has been sprung.

The east wing, which houses the Flawed, is in pandemonium. Everyone is running around in a panic, half-asleep, trying to gather themselves. The Flawed workers who were on shift are running toward the cabins, terror in their eyes. There are at least a dozen more Flawed whom I haven't met yet.

Eddie arrives, the stress crawling up from his neck to his face in a red rash.

"What's going on, Eddie?" Carrick asks.

"I don't know, but let's be clear about one thing: I never knew anything about you guys, okay?"

Mona looks disgusted. "Your ass is safe, Eddie, don't worry, now come on—help us save ours."

Cordelia clings to Evelyn, the terror clear on her face. If the Whistle-blowers find us, not only will they take us away, but they'll also separate Evelyn from Cordelia because she's F.A.B.

"What's the routine? What's the drill? For these types of situations?" I ask, hearing the shake in my voice.

Eddie won't meet my eye; he paces the room.

"Surely you have some sort of emergency plan?" I look around at everybody.

"We never needed one," Bahee says anxiously. "They've come here twice in all the years I've been here, and each time we were warned."

"Well, they knew exactly when to come tonight. Somebody told them," Carrick says accusingly.

I look at Carrick in panic: His face is clouded over.

"Which one of you told them?" he shouts.

"Carrick!" Kelly says gently. "Nobody here would do that." She reaches out for him and he pulls back from her, an insult of the worst kind. It's not just a rejection of his mother, it's almost an accusation, a show of distrust.

"Where's Rogan?" Carrick asks.

We look around for his brother, but there's no sign of him, even in the darkened corners.

"How convenient," Carrick says angrily. "Someone alerts the Whistle-blowers and Rogan disappears."

"How dare you." His mom slaps him across the face, then pulls her hand away in surprise, as if the slap hurt her more.

I gasp as Adam jumps in between them. "Carrick, you need to check yourself now, and calm down. We're all under pressure. I'm sure Rogan is hiding somewhere safely. He wouldn't do this."

"No?" Carrick challenges him. "I guess I don't know him as well as you do."

Uncomfortable, Bahee tries to calm everyone down. "I have my passes to the lab. The Whistleblowers won't be allowed access without the correct paperwork. They'll have to wait until morning to get it, and the bureaucracy will kill them. Everyone will be safe with me."

Carrick eyes him suspiciously. "Okay, you all go with Bahee. Lennox, Fergus, Lorcan, and I will break away. Celestine, you stay with me."

I can tell that Carrick has a plan, so I don't bother asking him what it is. I trust him.

"Celestine can stay with us," Bahee says, placing a protective arm around me. "It's too risky out there. I'll keep her safe in the lab. You have my word."

Carrick shakes his head. "We've got a route out of here. We can get straight to the Jeep. If anyone wants to come, come, but we have to go now." He grabs my hand and leads me out of the cabin.

"And lead her straight out to *them*?" Bahee pipes up. "Whistleblowers will be blocking every street leading from here. *Think*, Carrick."

Carrick looks doubtful.

"You have to trust us," Kelly says tearfully.

I can see Carrick's guilt, for how he made his mother feel. He looks at me. Bahee's plan sounds better than Carrick's. Hiding gives me more of a chance than running straight into their arms.

"Maybe we should stay," I whisper to him.

"We shouldn't all stay together," he says. "I'm going to take my chances this way. You hide with the others. I'll get the Jeep ready. I'll make a plan; I'll come back and get you when the time is right. Trust me."

"I do." I smile.

He kisses me quickly.

Bahee pats Carrick on his back. "She's in safe hands. Follow me, everyone," Bahee says urgently, hand on my arm.

We follow Bahee. Through the east wing, down the steps, and outside to the night air. The sun is about to rise, I can see light on the horizon. I wonder what state we'll all be in when the sun is up. We run at high speed, keeping low, following Bahee across the compound, avoiding the main routes. Though he said otherwise, I'm betting Bahee has this escape route mapped out in his head and takes it every night just in case.

There's still no sign of Rogan, and I wonder about Carrick's accusation. Rogan clearly had dark thoughts about his brother joining their lives, but I'm not sure if he would orchestrate all this and risk being found and having his family broken up. But perhaps Carrick is right about it being someone within these walls. I fear that it was Leonard, that this is all my fault. If I'd told Carrick about him coming to see me in my cabin, asking about Lizzie, then maybe we would have had time to plan an escape just in case.

Who was listening to Carrick and me outside the cabin door tonight?

We run up six flights of stairs, trying to be quiet as our shoes hit the metal, and reach the rooftop. Bahee is ahead of us all, standing at the high-security door entrance, holding it open. Everyone runs inside and down a corridor. I start to relax at seeing the size of the door, a big steel shield from the Whistleblowers, and the wall beside it covered with all kinds of security keypads and locks. Safety is in sight.

Evelyn runs in ahead of me. When it's my turn, Bahee blocks the entrance.

His smile has vanished, his eyes are cold behind the tinted glasses. He holds on to the door handle tightly.

"Bahee?" I say, a nervous tremor in my voice.

"Remember, *you* brought this on us. You should never have come here." And he slams the door in my face.

TWENTY-FIVE

I'M LEFT STANDING on the rooftop in absolute shock, while an army of Whistleblowers streams into the compound below. Their red suits are gaudy and warn of danger; it's like they bleed into the courtyard. They're dressed in their riot gear, with their black helmets and shields. What do they think is going to happen? A shoot-out? And then I realize it's all for the media. To show the public just how dangerous Celestine North is.

It's too late for me to hide anywhere now; I'm completely exposed on the rooftop, all they need to do is look up. I'm surrounded. There's no way of getting down off this roof, not alive anyway.

The Whistleblowers climb the metal fire escape, and the first feeling of panic consumes me. It's over. After all this, it's over. But then a hatch opens in the ground beside me and a head pops up. I leap away and retreat to the corner, thinking it's a Whistleblower.

"Come on!" Leonard says impatiently, nervously.

I have one second to judge his honesty. I curse myself for not going with Carrick when I had the chance. He's the only person I trust. I hear the Whistleblowers' boots on the metal stairs. Leonard's face is open and honest; Carrick said I could trust Leonard. I trust Carrick. Granddad said don't trust anybody. I trust Granddad. My head spins.

With no other options open to me, I take a leap of faith and hurry toward him. He's standing on a ladder and offers me his hand. I take it and lower myself inside while Leonard shuts the hatch quickly and silently above us. We are in a narrow passage, I'm not sure if it's for ventilation or heating, but the air is tight and it's close. We're crouched down, hunched over.

Leonard holds his fingers to his lips to keep me quiet, but he doesn't need to tell me that—I'm terrified, and I know he is, too, from the sound of our short breaths in the tight space. We hear the Whistleblowers' boots clambering around above us trying to figure out the magic act: How did Celestine North disappear?

My heart pounds, and sweat glistens on Leonard's brow; I can smell the fear emanating from him. People I love have surprised me by hurting me, and it's been the people I've least expected who have redeemed and restored my faith. It never ceases to both break my heart and amaze me. Juniper could probably have predicted this, she always understood people and situations so much better than I did. If she was watching me from anywhere she'd probably be saying, "*Now* you're getting it, Celestine!"

The heavy footsteps above us are circling, scurrying around in panic, all order lost, like a trail of ants that have lost their scent. I didn't know the hatch was here until it opened, the outline faint and flush with the surface. I'm hoping they won't see it, but they're Whistleblowers—they're trained to see everything; they don't miss a trick.

"They won't be able to open it from up there," Leonard whispers, his hot breath on my neck. "They can't gain access from outside." He points to the panel on the ceiling, which opens with the swipe of a security key card. "But it's only a matter of time until they try to find their way to us from another angle."

The stomping on the hatch ends and we begin to hear pounding on

Bahee's door instead. I think of Carrick's parents, Cordelia, little Evelyn, and Mona, all huddled inside, thinking they were safe.

You brought this on yourself. I direct Bahee's words back at him angrily. Bahee, the peace-loving leader. If he has orchestrated this search to get rid of me, then it's his fear of change that brought greater change than I ever would have, and will inevitably hurt the people he loves the most.

"Bahee locked me out of the room," I whisper to Leonard. "Could he have called the Whistleblowers? I don't get why he'd risk his own safety."

"I'm not surprised." He shakes his head angrily. "Lizzie always thought Bahee was a creep. She couldn't stand him. I'm sure it was him."

And at that, I am surprised by how little I have learned after all. I fell for Bahee's nice-guy act.

I feel that I owe Leonard something.

"I asked Mona about Lizzie," I whisper, and despite what's happening above us I have his full attention. "She said that Lizzie told you she was Flawed, that you didn't want anything to do with her, and she ran away heartbroken."

"That never happened," he says, hurt, angry.

He says it too loudly. I push my hand to his mouth. His eyes are wide and he nods quickly, understanding, keen to continue our conversation.

"I told you," he whispers, "I knew she was Flawed all along. Or I suspected. Her brand was on her chest. She was funny about me touching her . . ." His face goes beet red. "I wouldn't have cared; I would never have let her go. I wanted her to confide in me; I kept bringing up the fact that I'm against the Guild, trying to make it easy for her to tell me. Why would Lizzie tell Mona that?"

I frown, trying to work it all out, but I can't. Was Mona lying to me? I don't know her well enough—I don't know anybody here well enough, but even so, that idea of her feels wrong.

I shake my head. "I don't know. But we'll find out," I say, determined.

The Whistleblowers' footsteps retreat back down the fire escape.

"Thanks for your help, Leonard. I appreciate what you've risked."

"I'm just following your lead. During the trial you said you helped the old man because it was the right thing to do. Compassion and logic," he says. "I'm voting the Vital Party."

I smile.

"We'd better move, in case they try to find another way in here. This way." He moves and I follow him through a maze that traverses the plant.

Leonard guides me to a safe position where we can see the Whistleblowers gathering in the entrance courtyard. On one side are a dozen Flawed people who work in the factory legitimately, all of them displaying their F armbands on their sleeves. They have been called to witness whatever is about to happen. On the other side a team of Whistleblowers surrounds the discovered evaders: Carrick's parents, Cordelia and Evelyn, Bahee, and Mona, who thought they were safe in the laboratory. My heart thuds: If they're here for me, I should give myself up. Me instead of them would be the right thing to do.

Thud, thud, thud.

I move forward.

"What are you doing?" Leonard asks, panic in his voice.

"I can't let them be taken away. They're here for me."

"You don't know that!" he says. "Celestine! Come back!"

Suddenly Evelyn screams as a Whistleblower grabs her, and I stand up tall and quicken my step. If anyone looks up now they'll see me. A hand grips me from the darkness and pulls me close. I go to fight it but as soon as our bodies touch I sense it's Carrick. I can smell him. I squeeze my body tightly to his, and he wraps his arms around me.

"Don't even think about it," he says, voice low.

"I can't let them be taken away."

"So they'll take you *and* them, what good will that do? Think about it, Celestine."

He's always calm; even under these circumstances, his sentences are slow, as if he is able to process everything in proper time, unlike me, whose head is jumping around with images and thoughts, panic and fear.

"How did you get away?" he asks.

I quickly tell him, Lennox, Fergus, and Lorcan about what happened with Bahee. Apart from Leonard and Carrick, they're surprised to hear this, perhaps even doubtful. And they have a point: Bahee locking me out may have been just to save his own skin; we don't know for sure that he alerted the Whistleblowers. And if he didn't, there is still a traitor among us. I wonder again about Rogan, who is the only person not present. Or Mona, who may have lied to me about why Lizzie left.

I duck down, staying tight to Carrick as a Whistleblower starts to drag away a kicking and screaming Evelyn. Cordelia is howling with grief as they take her child away and is being held back by two Whistleblowers.

"Oh my God," I whimper, hands in front of my face. I don't want to watch but I have to.

"This was not the deal!" Bahee shouts, and everyone, on the ground and in hiding, turns to stare at him in utter shock.

"It *was* him," I whisper, shocked, even though I suspected him.

"*You* arranged this, Bahee?" Mona shouts.

The dozen Whistleblowers clear the way for their leader, a woman, I think, who walks toward Bahee. He quickly backs off, the fight in him gone. The Whistleblower removes her helmet, and to my absolute shock I see it's Mary May.

I gasp and Carrick blocks my mouth.

"The deal was," says Mary May, "we leave you all here and we take Celestine. There's no sign of Celestine and no one mentioned anything about an F.A.B. child on the premises. We must remove her immediately. We must give her the care and treatment she needs, though it may be too late already." She looks at Evelyn with disgust.

I feel Carrick tense beside me. He knows all about that special-institution care.

97

"What have you done?" Cordelia screeches at Bahee, who cowers away from her, looking so weak that a light breeze could blow him over.

"You're lucky I'm not removing you all. Take her away," Mary May says, waving her hand.

I've never seen Mary May in combat uniform. Usually she's in her Mary Poppins Whistleblower persona, the one who does house calls, who checks to make sure I've made my curfews and stuck to my diet and followed all of the daily anti-Flawed decrees. Even the Mary May who came looking for me on Granddad's farm wasn't this woman; it tells me that she's stepped it up a level. It's as though she has mentally walked onto the battlefield. Riot gear, helmet and all, she will do anything to find me. What chance have I got?

Evelyn puts up a good fight. She kicks a Whistleblower between the legs, and he curses loudly, hunches over, and loses his helmet. My heart stops. I feel Carrick's grip on me tighten and his hand blocks my mouth for the second time, because he knows that I want to shout out.

The Whistleblower is Art.

TWENTY-SIX

ART'S UNRULY BLOND hair collapses in curls around his face as he holds on tight to Evelyn's arm, his face an angry mush of pain and irritation.

Cordelia howls for her child.

Some of the other Whistleblowers seem to look at Art and Evelyn in amusement, though they are all human and I hope, behind those helmets, some are finding it heart-wrenching.

"Look, can't we just take them both together?" Art asks, and his voice breaks my heart. "The mother and the child?"

"Yes! Yes!" Cordelia leaps up from her knees, eager to be taken away, ready to be taken to the ends of the earth if it means staying with her child.

I'd longed to hear his voice for so long and now it's here, under these circumstances. He looks strange in the uniform. Like a young boy dressing up as a soldier; no wonder the helmet fell off, even with the huge mop of hair I don't think it fits him. He's the same age as Carrick but he's no soldier, he's baby-faced, never serious about anything. The only time he ever truly concentrated was when he played his guitar, and even then he made up ridiculous songs, his favorite being about the polka-dot zebra. The elephant with no trunk, the tiger that got a manicure, the giraffe that couldn't find a turtleneck to fit, the broccoli that wouldn't eat its vegetables. That kind of thing.

This situation isn't suited to Art, this is too real-life for him. No awkward jokes can get him out of this. He's ripping a child from her mother. He's been in that position: He lost his mother. He can't do it. He won't do it.

"Take me instead," a voice suddenly booms from the opposite side of the gate. Rogan appears. He was out; he was free. What is he doing?

The Whistleblowers turn to stare at him.

"I'm an F.A.B. child, too," he says, voice cracking with fear, but he's trying to appear strong.

"Rogan! No!" Carrick's mother screeches.

"What the hell is he doing?" Carrick says, moving from his position, and it's my turn to pull him down. It takes Lennox to hold him down as well.

"Leave Evelyn here. Take me," Rogan says, pleading with them all. "I'm fourteen years old. My parents are Flawed. I've been living outside the system all my life. Take me!"

Mary May barely glances at him. She gives a signal and the Whistleblowers all move out, ignoring Rogan as they pass him by, some bumping against his shoulders, knocking him about, teasing him as they pass.

"Take me!" he shrieks now in a high-pitched, desperate voice, arms out in surrender.

They move by him and load themselves into the vans.

"Am I not good enough for you?" he yells. "My brother was good enough, but I'm not?"

I look at Carrick, who is shaking his head angrily, eyes black as coal.

Kelly runs to her youngest son and wraps her arms around him, both of them barely able to stand with the tears. Rogan is exhausted from the shouting.

Evelyn is taken into the van, her screams still audible from outside.

Cordelia sobs uncontrollably, back on her knees on the ground. It reminds me of when my neighbor Angelina was torn away from her family in front of my very eyes. The sound of children screaming for their mother, the anguished sound of a mother's heart being ripped apart. Angelina's detainment had been the first moment with Whistleblowers that I'd witnessed. I'm going to make sure this is my last.

The red vans drive away, taking Evelyn with them.

TWENTY-SEVEN

"WHAT THE HELL did you do?" Back in the recreation room, Carrick pushes Bahee up against the wall. We've gathered here, wild and angry with one another, nobody trusting anybody, to try to make some sense of this. Bahee yelps as his tiny frame is crushed.

"Please." Bahee holds up his hands in self-defense as Lennox, Fergus, Lorcan, and Mona gather around him, like scavengers eyeing their dinner. I hover in the background, too stunned to say or do anything. I'm feeling so guilty to have brought this upon everyone, even if it was Bahee who pulled the trigger. He would never have done it if I wasn't here.

"I can't breathe . . . I can't . . ." he squeals.

"Carrick," his dad says, warning.

Carrick loosens his grip around Bahee's neck and the blood drains from Bahee's face as he fights to catch his breath.

"I didn't know it would work out this way; this wasn't the arrangement," he says nervously, and Cordelia cries to herself, hugging Evelyn's pink bunny rabbit close to her body. "You know I adore Evelyn. I would never have arranged for this to happen. Please believe that I did it for the right reasons." He hardens. "*She* shouldn't be here." He points a finger at me, and they look at me. "I know you all agree. Nobody wanted to say it, but I will. She shouldn't be here. We've been safe for *years*, and she was about to ruin everything."

"No, *you* ruined everything," Carrick says, through gritted teeth, giving Bahee one last hard shove against the wall before releasing his grip and charging away.

"They would have found her eventually," Bahee says, trying to get everyone on his side, growing in confidence as he's given the chance to defend himself. "Of course they would have. Celestine has the most recognizable face in the country, someone would have seen her and told the Guild. I just did it in a way that protected this family forever."

"Family," Mona spits out. "You're living in cuckoo land."

"You should have consulted us on a decision like that," Adam says, and I'm surprised that Carrick's dad isn't immediately defending my presence. "And I'm afraid, son"—he turns to Carrick—"that *you* should have consulted us in bringing Celestine here."

Carrick is stunned, then very quickly becomes angry. "Consulted *you*?" He steps forward, fists clenched.

"Son," Adam warns, looking at Carrick's fists.

"He's not your son," Rogan says quietly, back in his darkened corner, sitting on the bean bag.

Carrick turns to him. "Say that again and you'll be sorry."

"You're. Not. His. Son," Rogan says, slower and louder. He stands up. "*I'm* his son. You showed up, what, two weeks ago? I've been by their side *all* my life. Do you know what I sacrificed to be his son? School, friends, a normal life. I've had a lifetime of hiding underground. Moving every few weeks, months if we were lucky. While you got to live like a king. I've seen those institutions on TV: swimming pools, restaurants, holidays, skiing. What did you have to give up?" he shouts.

Kelly lets out a pained sound and covers her ears as her sons argue.

"What did I give up?" Carrick asks, as if Rogan's stupid. "My parents," he yells so loudly that even Cordelia stops crying and looks up. "People who loved me. I was five years old, alone and afraid. You think that was fun for me? I waited for my mom and dad to come get me, and they never did. I was told every day that my parents were monsters. You think I was treated like a king? I had *no one*. I didn't trust anyone. Every day I was fed so many lies I didn't know who to believe. So forgive me if I have no sympathy for you. I gave up my freedom to find you all, and I get here to discover that *my parents already have a son*. That the whole time I thought they were missing me, they'd already started again. That's what *I* sacrificed." He turns to his dad. "And for that, I expected some trust, for you to believe that I was bringing someone important here." The veins in Carrick's neck pulsate, his fists tightly clenched. Everyone gives him space, like he's a monster about to explode.

"I understand your feelings for Celestine," his dad says quietly, patiently, as if everyone has forgotten that I'm still in the room.

"Forget about my *feelings*. This is not about me having some *crush*. You've no idea the power Celestine holds over Crevan, the importance she has in the Flawed movement."

I see a few eyeball rolls at his mention of the movement.

"Oh yes, this *power*." Bahee actually laughs. "You talk about this power a lot, but I don't see it. She doesn't even want to leave this compound, she said so herself."

All eyes on me. I shift my feet nervously.

"That was before," I say.

"Before what?" Bahee sneers. "Before the sweet nothings he was whispering in your ear this morning? Celestine, don't let people push you out front and hide behind you for their beliefs."

It was him outside Carrick's door listening to us. He heard me admit I didn't want to leave; he heard Carrick trying to convince me to join him. I'm not sure what Bahee is more afraid of: me staying, or me leaving.

"This is ridiculous," Carrick says, fed up. "Talking to you is a waste of time. We have to get moving. We have things to do, whether you lot are with us or not. Whether Celestine has power over Crevan or not, it doesn't matter, people are behind her, and the numbers are growing. It's not just Flawed people. To everyone she is a symbol. Compassion and logic, that's the Vital Party's new campaign slogan. A political party quoting a Flawed, when has that ever happened?"

"Oh, please," Bahee says dismissively. "That's a gamble Enya Sleepwell will lose. She is offering false hope to the Flawed. When has anybody ever done anything to help us? Remember Lizzie! She told her boyfriend she was Flawed and he left her! Right here in our own community. And she was so in love!" He laughs mockingly. "You're all delusional if you think you have the slightest support out there."

"Lizzie didn't tell Leonard she was Flawed," I speak up on Leonard's behalf. For his own safety he couldn't come with us to the east wing. "Leonard knew that Lizzie was Flawed, and he didn't care."

Everyone turns to me. Even Rogan, who looks at me in surprise.

"How do you know that?" Mona asks, confused.

"Exactly. You've been here twenty-four hours, Celestine, what do you know?" Bahee says dismissively.

"Celestine's right," Rogan says quietly.

We all turn to him.

"What do you mean?" Adam asks.

"It's not true that Lizzie left because of Leonard," Rogan says, his voice trembling. He won't look up, like he's afraid.

"I wouldn't listen to anything that comes out of his mouth," Bahee says.

"Shut up," Carrick snaps, and then says more gently: "Rogan, tell us what you know."

He briefly looks at Bahee and then away, eyes back down to the ground. He closes up again.

Mona goes to him. "You can tell us the truth. Don't worry about Bahee."

"I saw him taking her."

"Who? You saw who?"

"Bahee," he says, tears filling his eyes. "He made Lizzie get in the Jeep. She didn't want to. She was crying. I heard him telling her that he wasn't going to let her ruin our life here. She was going to tell Leonard that she was Flawed. She was on her way. Bahee wouldn't let her. He took her away. I saw them."

Everyone looks at Bahee.

"Only moments ago, his own brother thought he was a traitor, so I wouldn't pay much heed to what he says. He's young. Confused. I haven't left this compound for years, everyone knows that."

Carrick fires himself at Bahee and lashes out, punching him in the jaw.

Bahee screams in pain. "You've broken it," he groans, rolling around. Nobody goes to his aid.

"Where did you take Lizzie?" Mona stands over him.

Bahee whines about needing a doctor. Mona ignores him.

"Where did you take Lizzie?" she screams, and he finally looks at her coldly.

"Not far. Into the city. I told her to get out, to find somewhere else to live." He says it so devoid of emotion, so unlike the man who called the meeting to welcome Lennox to the tribe, as though he has two personalities, one so warm and the other so cold. The perfect and flawed man all in one, like two sides of a coin. "But I did it to protect you all. None of you have any idea what I've done to protect you in the past. We've all lived here happily and safely, until Celestine came along. You were happy for me to lead you, but if you want to follow *her*, then you're digging your own grave."

There's a long silence.

"I met Celestine only yesterday," Mona speaks out. "I haven't seen any sign of her leadership or of this 'power' that Carrick speaks about, yet. But has nobody else questioned who else has had *twelve* Whistleblowers search for them at a high-security government-funded laboratory? She's got something on the Guild." She views me curiously. "And whatever that is, I'm in."

"Still in," Lorcan says.

"Me too," Fergus says.

"I was never out." Lennox grins.

TWENTY-EIGHT

THE DOOR BURSTS open and Eddie enters.

"Glad to see you're still alive, boss," Lennox jokes, lightening the atmosphere.

"I'm not your boss anymore," he says, red-faced and looking like he's about to keel over with a heart attack at any moment.

"They let you go?" Bahee asks, holding his jaw.

"No," Eddie barks, looking the sorry sight up and down. "They're letting *you* all go. The owner of this company let evaders work here in good faith, under the agreement you would keep it secret. You broke that agreement."

"But he can't do this," Bahee says, his face going even paler. "I've kept his identity a secret; I've kept my word. He promised me safety."

"You break your promise; he breaks his. He wants you out by noon. It's not safe anymore. You've placed him and his plant under too much suspicion. How's he going to explain all this?"

"But where will we go?" Bahee asks, his whole life crumbling.

"I don't know and I don't want to know. Less I know the better. You will all have *escaped* my security by noon today. And by that I mean we're going to let you leave." At the door he gives me a sidelong look. "Good luck to you."

Cordelia starts weeping again, and then, as if she's had enough already, she stands up angrily and shouts at me, "All you had to do was give yourself up, Celestine."

I freeze.

"They would have given Evelyn back if you had just surrendered. But you didn't. I waited for you. And you *didn't*. I know that you're young, but Evelyn is *six years old*. What kind of leader sacrifices others for their own gain? You and him." She looks from me to Bahee angrily. "You're both the same."

This insult I cannot take, because I fear that she's right. While Carrick tries to reach out to me, I storm out of the room, straight to my cabin. I power up a bill-free mobile that Granddad gave me, and I dial one of the numbers I saved into the phone. I didn't think I would ever be calling this person, but it's an emergency.

One hour later, the twenty Flawed evaders line up at Vigor's front gate. Carrick, Lennox, Fergus, Lorcan, and I are hidden from view. Nobody knows what to expect, not even Carrick. I just told them to wait here with me. That it would be worth it.

This is my chance to prove myself to anybody who doesn't believe in me.

A black town car appears in the distance. Eddie looks at me uncertainly; I give him a nod and step farther back into the shadows with Carrick.

"What's happening?" Carrick asks.

I ignore him, arms folded. I watch the gate slowly opening, hoping this will go to plan. The car, its windows blacked out, stops at the gates and doesn't drive in. The others look in my direction nervously. I remain strong. Chin up. This has to work. The car door opens.

Evelyn steps out. She closes the door behind her and runs to her mother, who falls to her knees sobbing. Cordelia calls out so that I will hear her.

"You got her. You got her back," Cordelia says, through heaving cries. "Thank you, thank you, thank you."

The town car reverses and drives back the way it came. The gates to the facility close again. There are no tricks; everyone is safe.

"How did you do that?" Lennox asks.

"Yeah, how did you do that?" Carrick repeats.

They're all looking at me, stunned. Unsure. In awe.

I like it.

TWENTY-NINE

"I'M IN," ROGAN says suddenly, shouting up from the courtyard.

"Us too," Adam says, firmly nodding at Carrick in apology.

"Right, let's get this started," I say, adrenaline surging. "Let's all pack up and get out of here. It's time to move on."

———

Back in my cabin, my hands are trembling as I throw my few possessions into my backpack. I throw it over one shoulder and reach out to the door handle. Instead of turning it, I lock the door and huddle down in the corner of the room. Head down on my knees, I cry as it all sinks in.

Art is a Whistleblower. Mary May is training him. He came here to capture *me*. My head pounds with all the thoughts racing through my mind. There could be no greater betrayal. Carrick knew about Art being a Whistleblower the entire time. That's what he'd meant when he suggested using Art to get to Crevan, *after what Art had done to me*. He wasn't trying to use me; if anything, he kept the truth from me so I wouldn't be hurt.

"How did you do that?" Carrick asked me over and over after Evelyn's release. They were all looking at me like I was some kind of god, and some kind of freak. I didn't tell him how. I will when we are alone. I think the shrouded mystery is on my side at the moment, when inside I feel like a bag of rattling bones.

The truth is, I was terrified when I made the phone call that led to Evelyn's release.

The truth is, I'm still shaking with nerves now.

THIRTY

ONE HOUR EARLIER

"HELLO?" I PACE the small cabin. "Judge Sanchez?"

Sanchez is one of the three judges who sit alongside Judge Crevan in the Guild. She was responsible for my Flawed verdict, too, but spent the entire trial trying to undermine Crevan. I just happened to get caught in the middle. Sanchez caught me on the run and tried to make a deal with me to help her bring down Crevan. I didn't trust her, but she let me go, to prove that I could. I told Granddad about her and he told me to tread carefully. Getting involved with her could get me in more trouble.

"Sanchez speaking."

"Celestine North."

Pause. "Well, well, well. She surfaces. I hear you escaped him again. I must say I'm enjoying this little game of cat and mouse. Can't say the same for Crevan."

"You told me two weeks ago that you'd help me."

"In return for something else, I recall."

She has no idea what exactly I have against Crevan, she just knows that he is panicking about something and is sending Whistleblowers out left, right, and center to find me. She drew her own conclusions.

"I'll work with you on that. But first do something to show that I can trust you."

"I believe I already did. I let you go, don't you remember?"

"But things have changed. You're holding my granddad in your cells. That doesn't seem very trustworthy to me."

"My, you've learned fast. What can I do for you?"

"A little F.A.B. girl was taken from the CCU facility an hour ago. They need her back."

"That's impossible."

"Then so is my helping you. Good-bye."

"Wait." She pauses. "Give me an hour."

THIRTY-ONE

NOW, AFTER MY magic trick, they all await my next move, believing in me, trusting me. I can't tell any of them that the weapon Carrick thinks I have, which is the footage of Crevan losing control and in a psychotic episode illegally branding me for the sixth time, is not in my possession. Nobody can know that I don't have it. It's the only power I have. It's the only thing that any of us Flawed have—without it we have nothing.

For now, people believing in me is all I have to go on. And I'm lying to them all.

But what else can you expect from a Flawed?

THIRTY-TWO

MY NEXT MOVE is to search for an angel. Naturally.

Raphael Angelo.

The only defense lawyer to *ever* have a Flawed verdict overturned.

The first time I heard that name was when my granddad mentioned him during the trial when he visited me in Highland Castle. I dismissed his ramblings as nothing but hopeless conspiracy theories. At that time I thought it was all a big misunderstanding, that Crevan would get me out of the mess. I didn't know that I would now be basing my only hope on that conversation.

After hunkering down in the corner of my cabin feeling like the world is too great for me, that everything is too large, overbearing, and over-whelming for me, I refocus, wipe my eyes roughly, and formulate my plan. I have people waiting for me.

I call Judge Sanchez again.

"Thank you," I say as soon as she answers.

"Pound for a pound, Celestine. Now let's meet."

"Not yet. I need an address from you."

"Another favor?"

"I'm helping *you*, remember?" I say, trying to keep the tremor from my voice. "The next time we meet will be in the Guild courtroom, and you'll know exactly what to do. I intend to get my conviction overturned. I intend for everything to be undone so that I can return to my life, return to my school, return to my family, and everything can be as it once was." My voice cracks.

"Oh, Celestine." She sighs. "I was hoping for so much more from you. You know the odds are not on your side. A Flawed verdict has never been overturned."

"That's not true," I say. "Jessica Taylor."

She goes quiet.

"How did you know about her? That information wasn't made public."

"I know lots of things that you don't think I know." I find my confidence again, almost to the point of cockiness. "I also know lots of things that *you* don't know. Why do you think Crevan is so worried?"

"Who will be your representative in court?" she asks.

"Not Mr. Berry, considering he's missing. Along with all the guards who were present in the Branding Chamber, and Pia Wang, who started asking questions."

She's silent for a moment. She knows this already. "Yes. What did happen in that Branding Chamber, Celestine? I'm eager to know."

"Maybe they're all on a team-building trip. Feel bad you were left out?"

"Crevan can never know that we're talking. It can't look like we've planned anything. I'm protecting you, but you need to protect me, too."

"We haven't planned anything. You'll know when it happens, and I'll need you on my side."

"Whose address do you need?"

"Raphael Angelo."

She chuckles. "Now this just got interesting. But unfortunately I can't help you, Celestine. That would be aiding a Flawed, which, as a leading judge in the Guild, would be an unspeakable act. You'll have to do the next part on your own. Call me when you've got something for me to work with."

Considering she has just helped me to release an F.A.B. child, the hypocrisy drips from her every word.

I immediately want to return to huddling in the corner of the cabin again—it worked so well for me the first time—but I don't. Instead, I curse, throw my phone on the bed, and pace. Outside I hear everybody waiting for me, voices on the balcony. Their bags are packed, they're ready to go, prepared to follow my next instruction. Which is what?

Think, think, think, Celestine. Use what you have. Use what you have. There is a problem, find the solution. I go back to my mathematics skills. What have I got on my side? *Who* have I got on my side? Boom. I grab my phone again and search the Highland Castle website. I don't need to move far; right on the homepage is the flashing hotline number for people to call with information and sightings on the most wanted evader, Celestine North.

I call the number.

"Highland Castle Hotline," a woman answers.

I roll my eyes at the name, and I alter my voice, assuming these calls are recorded.

"I'd like to speak with Whistleblower Kate, please. I have information that I would like to share only with her."

"Connecting you now."

It couldn't be that easy.

The phone rings and she answers, out and about, probably searching for me.

"Kate speaking."

I'm assuming the Whistleblowers' cell phones are also being monitored.

"It's the girl from the tree."

She's silent. I hear her move away from wherever she was. The background noise changes. "I'm sorry, I can't hear you. This is a bad line—let me call you back from a landline. Can I have your number?"

I pause. "No."

"Fine. Call me on this number in two minutes."

I rummage through Mona's things, looking for a pen. I can't find anything but makeup. I use a red lipstick and write on the wall.

Kate hangs up and I pace. Two minutes.

Agitated, confused, I don't know why I do it, but I put the red lipstick to the white wall again and draw the red *V* from the Vigor logo that equals a square root sign.

$$\sqrt{}$$

I study it for a moment, wondering for the thousandth time where I've seen it before.

Someone knocks on the door.

"Just a minute." I hear the tremor in my voice and take a deep breath.

The door opens anyway. Mona, Carrick, Lennox, Kelly, Adam, Rogan, Cordelia, and Evelyn are lined up in the corridor, bags in their hands, ready to go. Bahee, squeezed tightly between Fergus and Lorcan, looks like he's not there by choice. The tension is thick. Even Carrick looks nervous, and I'm sure his relying on somebody else to take control isn't easy for him. I fear he's losing his faith in me already. I fear that he might be right to.

"The other evaders are all gone; they scattered. We need to move, Celestine," says Mona. "Eddie is about to kick us out any second. We have one chance to get away with their help, or that's it."

Everybody stares at me with expectancy, such hope, such reliance. I can't function like this. I can't lead a team.

I clear my throat and will myself to be more authoritative. Problem, solution—this is the stuff I should be good at.

"We need to split up," I say. "Fergus, Lorcan, and I can't travel together. Our faces are too recognizable."

Everyone agrees instantly.

"Carrick and I will take the next step alone. The rest of you will wait somewhere safe until we give you further instruction."

They look at one another uncertainly.

"Where do you suggest we wait?" Mona asks, the doubt in my leadership already growing.

Think, think, Celestine. Problem-solve, that's what you're good at.

"What the hell did you do to my wall?" she says, eyes narrow.

"Who cares, Mona? It's not your wall anymore," Carrick says, but I can hear the impatience in his voice. They're all getting tired of standing around and waiting . . . for me to make a decision.

I turn around and see the phone number scrawled in red lipstick, with the Vigor logo beside it, and suddenly something clicks into place so clearly, my heart starts pounding.

I recall a conversation from a couple of weeks ago with Professor Lambert. His wife, Alpha, who was my math teacher, brought me to their home for a meeting disguised as a support group for families affected by Flawed issues. It was more of a rally, an attempt to raise support for the Flawed cause, and it was raided by Whistleblowers. In hiding, I met her husband, Professor Lambert, who is Flawed. He'd been a prominent scientist; he had photographs of himself with important people in gold-framed photographs all over his wood-paneled walls. He even had a photo of himself with Crevan in happier times. They'd been old acquaintances, until Crevan branded him. I knew he was an intelligent man, but he'd also had a few too many whiskeys and so hadn't thought any further of his parting advice. It's only now, as I struggle to find a solution, that his words mean something to me.

"Are you familiar with George Pólya?" he'd asked.

"Of course," I'd replied. He was a mathematician; my mom had bought me a book of his for my birthday. Strange gift for most kids, but I'd loved it.

"I liked his philosophies. Pólya advised, if you can't solve a problem, then there is an easier problem you can solve: You just have to find it. . . . Like I say, look to your strengths, look to your heroes for guidance. I'm a scientist."

Professor Lambert gave me that advice, and now he can help me in more ways than one. I never thought to ask how he was using his being a scientist in his own favor, but I know the answer now because the Vigor logo is the very logo I saw in Professor Lambert's secret office in his home, stamped on his work, on the backs of his photographs, on stationery, on plaques. It's Professor Lambert who's in charge of this facility.

"The owner of this facility will help us; he'll take you in," I say, the adrenaline kicking in again as my plan comes together.

Bahee snorts. "You don't even know the owner. Nobody does, apart from me, and Eddie just told us that the owner is no longer interested in helping us."

"I know him personally," I say confidently. "His name is Professor Bill Lambert."

Carrick looks at me in surprise.

"He may not want you to stay here anymore, but he didn't say he wouldn't help. He and his wife, Alpha, are awaiting your arrival at their home as we speak." Or they will be a few minutes from now. Alpha will be more than happy to do this, especially if there are two F.A.B. children in the group.

"But how did you know about Professor Lambert . . . ?" Bahee splutters. "He is anonymous . . . he . . ." Bahee looks at me, surprised, confused, angry, impressed. It all flashes across his bruised face as he looks from Carrick to me in surprise.

"How does she know this?"

"I told you: She's powerful," Carrick says smugly.

"Now excuse me for one more minute, I have to make an important phone call," I say, and close the door in their faces.

I press my back up against the door and take a deep breath before dialing the number I wrote on the wall.

Kate picks up on the first ring.

"It's me," I say.

"Our conversations are being listened to on our mobiles. This is a secure line. How can I help you?"

I almost want to cry with relief. "Are you on my side?"

"I should have reported you as soon as I saw you; why else would I leave you there?"

"I don't know what to think anymore."

"You got away, didn't you? You're a tough cookie; I knew you'd be fine."

Which is apparently the message I give out to most people when, in fact, the opposite is true.

"Two things. There's another Whistleblower on our side. His name is Marcus—he's Professor Bill Lambert's Whistleblower." Marcus helped Granddad hide from the Whistleblowers at the Lamberts' house; he made sure we weren't seen. "I have to get in touch with him. There are some people here who need hiding in a safe place."

Kate is silent.

"Hello?"

"He's my husband," she says quietly.

I smile with surprise and punch the air, grateful for life's wonderful coincidences.

"So he can get my people to the right place?"

"Yes, I'll call him right away."

"There's another thing. I need an address for someone called Raphael Angelo."

"Raphael's your next move?"

"Yes."

"I can get it, but no one has seen him for years. Crevan scared him off a long time ago."

"Well, then we already have something in common."

THIRTY-THREE

RAPHAEL ANGELO LIVES in the mountains, a two-hour drive from Vigor, deep in the forests, on mountainous terrain. He is more than off the beaten track: I wouldn't have found him in a million years. Even finding our way there *with* Kate's specific directions is difficult.

While the others use the Jeep from Vigor to get to Alpha and Bill Lambert, Leonard gives Carrick and me the use of his car. I will never be able to repay him for his help, especially as this is aiding a Flawed and carries a prison sentence, but I plan to try to do all that I can for him.

This drive through the mountains is the first time Carrick and I have been alone since the early morning hours. I've barely had time to think about it, but now that we're away from the city and safely in the mountains, mostly Whistleblower-free, we both relax. He rolls down the windows, puts the music on low, avoiding the radio stations that are announcing to the country how I once again evaded the Whistleblowers.

If it's a Crevan-owned station, the story is that I'm a fugitive to be feared and avoided. If it's regular stations, then the discussion is why an eighteen-year-old woman is so hunted, and is it that easy to evade the system? Is the system itself flawed? Is there any reason at all for Flawed to be so monitored, if I'm living quietly and not causing trouble? What is the Guild trying to prove? All good questions.

Except that each discussion is shot down by the Crevan media, who pinpoint me as the cause of every single riot that has broken out around the city, using footage of the supermarket riot where I stood up to the police officer as proof.

"Are you okay?" Carrick asks, reaching across and holding my hand in my lap.

"Yes."

"I mean, after last night . . . are you okay?"

It was my first time and I'd told him; he was gentle and understanding, constantly making sure I was okay. And though he never said, I know it wasn't his. Those institution boys have a reputation, at least that's what Mona told me. And I've a feeling she'd known—that she was at least a part of creating that reputation. Not with Carrick, though, I'm sure that nothing ever happened between them.

"Oh, *that*. Yes, I'm fine, thanks." I blush and he smiles.

The smile transforms his face. I'm so used to seeing him tense and stern, but his smile makes him look younger.

"How did you know that Professor Lambert owns Vigor?" he asks, studying me curiously.

I laugh. "Carrick, you're the one who keeps telling people that I have magical powers, and then when I get something right, it surprises you?"

"Yes, exactly."

"I recognized the company logo. I couldn't remember where I'd seen it when I first arrived, but then it clicked. I'd seen it in his office. And it's typical of his sense of humor, too, to invest in that kind of company." I laugh.

He frowns. "What do you mean?"

"Carbon is a waste that pollutes. So Vigor finds a way to use it as a resource."

"Yes," he says, still confused.

"And they're using Flawed to do that. *We are* the carbon." I chuckle. "The thing that nobody wants. *Turning a problem into a solution.* It is textbook Professor Lambert. He gave me some advice, and I didn't understand it at the time, but I do now." I change my tone. "Bill and Alpha told me that you were placed with them after you left the institute."

"Neighboring homes, the Institution calls them," he says angrily. "More like halfway houses where they monitor your every move. Out of one prison, into another. Their job is to help you slide into society under their care. But really it's to keep an eye on you so they can report back to the institution. If I'd known that Professor Lambert had anything to do with the plant, I would never have gone there."

"You think that *Bill* reported you to the Guild?" I ask, surprised.

"I'm not on as close terms with him as you are, obviously," he says, removing his hand from mine and gripping the steering wheel, face closing back up again.

"I only met Bill once," I say quietly. "Alpha was my math teacher, the only teacher willing to homeschool me after my school politely asked me to leave for the good of their reputation." I can't be bothered to hide the bitterness in my voice.

He looks at me, gentleness back on his face, concern for all I went through after we parted ways.

"Carrick, tell me what happened to make you not trust them," I say softly.

He takes his time, the anger evident as he retells the story. "I was in their care when I was searching for my parents, it had only been a day, I'd barely started looking around for Mom and Dad, then all of a sudden I was hauled into Highland Castle. There were photographs of me visiting the last place I'd been taken."

"Photos? That's all? That doesn't prove that you were trying to find your parents," I say, annoyed. "Since when does taking a trip down memory lane make you Flawed?"

"The guy I spoke to at the house, who'd rented us a room thirteen years ago, made a statement to the Guild," he says, resigned.

"Still, Carrick, that's *nothing*. Since when is asking questions—"

"I wasn't going to deny it, Celestine," he says angrily, then takes a moment to calm down. "Besides, I enjoyed admitting exactly what I was doing. I didn't find my parents, but it was as damn close to a success as I could get, just to see the look on their faces when they'd realized they'd failed."

I examine his profile, adoring his commitment, his strength, even his stubbornness, even if all of those traits got him into trouble. He'd rather be right than safe, and for that we have much in common. "But I don't see why you blame Bill," I probe.

"Alpha practically works for the Guild, running her charity to help counsel Flawed people's families, so it wasn't difficult to draw my conclusions."

"That's what the charity is on the outside; she's actually using it to gain support for the Flawed cause. She uses it as a way to gather everyone together. She is trying to end F.A.B. institutions. She was trying to get me on her side, and bring you with me," I explain.

Carrick absorbs this. I see that he is having the same crisis of trust I am. Nothing is simple when you're Flawed, you become a pawn in many peoples' games. As much as I feel for him, I'm comforted that what I'm experiencing is not unique to me.

"Bill told me that if you'd stayed with them longer they would have helped you to find your parents. That was their intention all along, but you were with them less than twenty-four hours. You never gave them a chance to prove themselves to you." I say this as delicately to him as possible, trying to judge his mood before continuing. He doesn't respond, two hands tight on the wheel, looking straight ahead, an intense look on his face.

"After you were taken to Highland Castle, your parents were brought to Vigor to live safely. Then on your release, you were given a tip as to their whereabouts. When you think about it, I'm sure Alpha and Bill were the ones who orchestrated your being reunited with your parents. I mean, how did you find out about Vigor in the first place?"

He still doesn't answer me: He's silent and lost in thought as he tries to figure it all out, moves the pieces in his mind that he was once so sure of. Carrick ran away from Alpha and Bill to find his parents. If he'd just stayed with them, he could have found them and not have been branded. It's quite possible that his loss of freedom was all for nothing. I don't push the conversation about his parents any further, but there is something I can't avoid anymore.

"You knew about Art becoming a Whistleblower, didn't you?"

He shifts uncomfortably in his seat, concentrates on the winding road inclining up the steep hill.

"I thought *you* knew," he explains. "It's been in the news."

My granddad must have known and kept it from me.

"When we were in bed," he continues, "and I mentioned him, I thought that you knew he was a Whistleblower. But then you defended him. I realized you had no idea."

And I'd accused Carrick of sleeping with me to get to Art. Why can't anybody trust anybody? I sigh.

"Sorry if I should have told you then," he says gently. "I'd timed mentioning him so badly in the first place, I didn't want to do any more damage."

"It's okay. I'm not angry." I pause. "Actually I don't think I've ever felt more angry, but I'm not angry with *you*."

Now that I've opened the doors, the anger suddenly pulsates through me. The image of Art wearing the Whistleblower uniform makes me feel ill. It was never a career Art would have pursued; he wanted to study science. A job in the labs of the very facility he just raided would have been his dream. Becoming some eccentric scientist with his big mop of hair, he who would try to find a cure for the cancer that took his mom away.

We had a plan. A very specific, much-talked-about plan. Humming University for his science degree and my mathematics degree. Art and I were supposed to be together. But instead, I'm Flawed and he's a Whistleblower. The hunted and the hunter.

His decision to become a Whistleblower is personal. It's a slap in the face, a kick in the stomach; it's telling me that he supports his dad, that he agrees with the Guild's decision. It's him saying, *I believe that you're Flawed, Celestine. Flawed to the backbone, just like my dad believes. I support the pain he put you through, you deserve everything you got. And when I find you . . .* What then? What's he going to do to me?

Carrick is looking at me anxiously.

But as angry as I feel, I just can't suddenly hate the person I once cared for so much. I can't switch it off that quickly. I'm not a robot; I want to try to understand. What is Art thinking? Why is he doing this?

"Maybe he's pretending," I say suddenly. "Maybe he became a Whistleblower to help me."

"How would he do that?" Carrick's voice is flat.

"I don't know." I rack my brain. "Maybe he's just using it as a way to find me. Maybe he's like Marcus and Kate, one of the good guys."

As soon as I say it, I believe it. I sit up in my seat, full of hope. I look at Carrick, though, and his soldier face is back. He's angry, closed off.

Juniper and I got mood rings as gifts one year from our parents. They worked through the measurement of your temperature. If you were hot, they were red; if you were cold, they turned purple or blue. When they were sitting on our bedside tables at night, they were black. Carrick's eyes remind me of those mood rings. I've spent so long trying to figure out what color they are, and now I know why. Their color seems to represent whatever mood he's in, which is why they appeared black when we were in the Highland Castle cells, why they were hazel with green speckles when we slept together, and now . . . well, now he won't even look at me.

He pulls the car over, stops it right on a dangerous curve, as if he doesn't notice or doesn't care. Anyone coming around the corner won't have enough time to see us, will hit us. He gives me a fright. He looks at me angrily, dark brown eyes now, no green, no light.

"You're deluding yourself if you think he's *pretending*. Today we watched him take Evelyn away from her mother. Your granddad is still sitting in a cell in Highland Castle; don't you think Art knows someone who could pull a few strings? He was part of a team that was searching for you in a state-sponsored facility. You want him to rescue you, Celestine? Is that what it is?"

"No!" I snap.

"Because *I'm* right here, *actually* putting my life on the line, helping you."

"So am I!" I yell back.

He glares at me, anger steaming from him, and I match his stare, feeling the heat rising inside me and burning. He looks like he's going to say something else, but he thinks better of it, pulls the car off the curve, and continues to drive up the mountain. We don't say a word to each other for the remaining forty-five minutes. In fact my neck gets sore just from looking out my window, away from him.

I'm fuming. It takes a long time for the rage to slowly simmer, and when it does, it's not him that the anger is directed at—it's myself. Because I know he's right. Art isn't trying to help me. If he was trying to he would have by now.

PART TWO

THIRTY-FOUR

THE ENTRANCE TO Raphael Angelo's house is a good five-minute drive from the front gate. With an engraved wooden plaque announcing it as THE GRAVEYARD, my hopes aren't exactly high. The house suddenly comes into view. It's an enormous wood cabin with large panes of glass that reflect the forest behind us. It's almost as if the few bricks we can see are a mirage, floating in the center of the forest, as though the house is trying to camouflage itself. I get out of the car and stretch my legs, feeling anxious. I don't know what to say; I need help, but after the argument with Carrick, I can't ask.

"So who's going to talk?" I ask quietly. "We need to make a plan."

"Bit late for that now," he snaps, avoiding my gaze. He walks straight to the door and presses the doorbell. Stubborn as anything. I rush to catch up and the door opens before I get there.

The man who answers is a little over four feet tall.

He looks from me to Carrick and back to me again. "Well, my life just got interesting. Come in."

He opens the door wider and leads the way farther into his house.

We walk through a large entry with a wooden staircase to an open-plan kitchen with floor-to-ceiling windows overlooking a rambling garden and the forest beyond. The interiors—walls, floors—are timber, all of varying types, colors, and grains. The cabin is light and bright, modern and classy. It is also manic. Everywhere I look I see children. From teenagers all the way down to a baby in a high chair, some with dwarfism, some not. They scatter when we walk in and gather at a long timber table beside more floor-to-ceiling tinted windows. They're covered in paint.

"Ash, I told you not to eat the paint," Raphael says. "Aspen, share the brushes with Elm. Hazel, the paint water is not for drinking. Little Myrtle is working on a masterpiece." To us, "Myrtle makes everything look brown. I think it's a skill."

I look to the wall he's pointing at, a section for each child. Ash, Aspen, Elm, Hazel, Cedar, and Myrtle. Myrtle's are entirely brown.

"They're all named after trees," I say.

"Ding!" He makes the sound of a game show bell.

A woman laughs and makes her way past us and to the table to restore order.

"This is my wife, Susan. She is a saint." She bends down to give him a long kiss as she passes. "A genius and the reason for my success. Susan, kids, this is Celestine and Carrick. Say hi."

"Hi," they say in unison.

Carrick and I glance at each other, noting he knows both our names.

Susan grins and waves us off.

We follow Raphael. Carrick's eyes are more green than brown now, his innocence shining through as he studies the place with curiosity. We enter a room with a desk, and we both look around in awe. It's no regular home office. Everything has been built for Raphael's height, apart from the couch for us. Raphael sits in his chair; we sit on a couch opposite him.

On the floor is a rug made from the sewn-together outfit of a cowboy, a flattened rubber face, and a cowboy hat. I step over the boots, trying not to trip on the spurs. Over the fireplace is a human head, fake I hope, with antlers. It's of a gray-haired old man who's smiling with a gold tooth. The couch we're sitting on, I realize, has been made to look like white skin with freckles.

"Nothing animal here," he says, watching our reactions. "Irony. Go on, take it in. I'm vegan. Don't believe in the murder of animals for food, fashion, or interior design. Everything here is faux, including the leather chaps on the rug. I call it Wayne." He pauses. "I know, I know, a vegan little person. Dining out is difficult, but more so for my sister. She's a celiac. That's a joke," he says, not breaking a smile or taking a breath. "I don't have a sister." He stands and goes to a cabinet for a whiskey. "I'd offer you both one, but you're Flawed and the rules say you cannot drink alcohol. Here's some water." He throws us each a plastic bottle from a fridge and we catch them.

Carrick views the water suspiciously.

"Don't worry. It's not a trick: No animals were harmed in the packaging of that water. So here's the thing. I love movies." He reaches over and pulls out a drawer displaying hundreds of DVDs. "I watch around three a day and I know the score. Aged cop is about to retire, but he solves one last case and gets shot. Aged thief takes on one last job before retirement. Goes wrong and he gets caught. It's inevitable. You attract your fears, art imitates life, life imitates art, and so on, and even though it will concern my wife, Susan, greatly—"

"Do it or I'll leave you," she shouts from the room next door.

"*Even though* it will concern my loving wife, Susan, greatly, I will *consider* taking you on. In my story I won't get shot or caught. I'm a lawyer who has never lost a case, so for me, the movie is that I come out of retirement, and then I lose."

I look at Carrick finally.

"But that's the worst-case scenario. I never lose, don't intend on doing so now. I assume you have no money; you're on the run, which makes it difficult for you to hold down a job and pay me, and even if you were working, no Flawed job could afford you my fees. It also puts me in a precarious position and makes this even more difficult than it would have been had you not become evaders, but that's okay. I'm used to complications. I suggest representing you both separately, no offense, Carrick, and I noticed you were surprised I knew your name, but I read the news, follow the court proceedings, and while you didn't get anything close to the publicity of your neighbor here, I managed to read a few sentences about your little debacle. An honorable if stupid one.

"Celestine's the star here. Every power couple has one member who's less successful—it always causes cracks, but suck it up, some people figure out ways to work it out. I'm assuming you're here because I am the only lawyer in the history of the world who has had a Flawed verdict overturned. I don't know how you found that out, it was strictly confidential, no paper trail whatsoever, but you can tell me that later. It was an outcome that didn't even benefit your dear friend Mr. Crevan. So how did I do it?"

He pauses, then smiles.

"I was *right*. And right wins every time. Along with hard work, perseverance, ridiculous amounts of money, threats, trickery, and somebody leading the case who has the time to be bothered to care. When I care, I care.

"Every week I receive dozens of requests from Flawed to take on their cases, and I don't. I am the fantasy, dream lawyer of many, not because they know of my verdict overturn, but because of my reputation in the courtroom. I am the *giant* of the Flawed litigation world. Ironic, isn't it?

"That's why I'm here; retired, young, and safe in the mountains away from it all. I'm not quite sure how you found me, but I'm impressed. I can see from your face, Celestine, that you don't believe me about being safe in the mountains, you frowned when I said it. Well, you're right, there's the issue of your friend Crevan. I've decided it would be best for us if he and I keep our distance. He's a sore loser to say the least. But he knows where I am if he wants me. He makes sure to let me know of that."

Raphael leans forward and looks at me properly for the first time since I arrived. "As for you, you've managed to evade him. Which is a curious thing, for two reasons. How you're doing it, and why he wants you. And I want to know why, of course, but I can't let that be the deciding factor in whether I take this case. I can deal with not knowing."

He sits back and taps his chin in thought.

"If I ask you why you have Crevan's fullest attention, Celestine, will you tell me?"

I sense Carrick about to speak, but I jump in. "Only if you agree to represent me first. In writing," I add.

He smiles. "The problem is, no matter what is going on with you and Judge Crevan, I'm not sure that I can win your case. It was a curious one from the start. You're Flawed, not for aiding a Flawed, which should have carried a prison sentence, but instead for lying about it. You admitted it yourself in court. *After* lying about it, which puts a stain on your character already. But the fact is, *I want to know* what has gotten Crevan so anxious. And I'm wondering if knowing is worth losing for." He looks at me and thinks. "Currently, I'm swaying toward yes."

He stands up and paces, walking back and forth over Wayne the cowboy rug.

"Ah, yes."

He stops and smiles as if he's listened to my silent rebuttal.

"I understand now. What you want to do is argue the Flawed case entirely, which is a human rights issue that would ordinarily be taken to the high court, which would defeat your case because no lawyer of any quality has represented a Flawed outside of the Guild for fear of being seen to be aiding a Flawed, even if money changes hands, which I'm guessing it won't because you don't have any. No, what you need is someone like Enya Sleepwell from the Vital Party fighting in your corner, but your boyfriend would know all about her, being entrenched so deeply in her campaign."

At first I think he's talking about Art but I notice he's looking at Carrick. I'm confused.

"Oh, no, Mr. Angelo, you're mistaken, Carrick doesn't have anything to do with Enya Sleepwell," I explain.

"Ah. Oh dear. She doesn't know about you and Enya Sleepwell, does she, Carrick? Are you going to enlighten her, or shall I?"

Carrick swallows.

THIRTY-FIVE

"ENLIGHTEN ME ... PLEASE," I say, feeling fear and anger rising, as I look from Raphael to Carrick and back again.

"Your boyfriend's mission, should he choose to accept it, and let's face it, he already has, was to get you in his care and carry out this plan of action, so that Enya Sleepwell could use you in her campaign. She's aiming for the Flawed vote, and no politician has ever tried that before. As you may know, the Flawed traditionally *don't* vote in elections, despite it being one of the few rights they have left. What's the point in a Flawed voting for a politician who controls a society they are not technically part of?

"Going for the Flawed vote is a clever but risky tactic. Enya needs more than just the Flawed on her side, and in order to do that she needs people to believe in the Flawed. How can people believe in the Flawed? Celestine the hero to save the day. It's a vicious circle. How much of her campaign rests on your shoulders alone, Celestine?" He's looking at Carrick. "I bet a lot."

"How do you . . . That's not exactly how it . . ." Carrick stumbles.

"Hmm." Raphael looks at me again. "Think for yourself, Celestine."

I'm so shocked by what I've just heard, the idea of Carrick being in cahoots with Enya Sleepwell, that I can't tear my eyes off Carrick. He won't meet my gaze; he's looking down, uncomfortable, fingers toying with the frayed knees of his jeans.

"Hair pulling, name-calling, and catfighting later. Eyes back on me, eyes back on me," Raphael says with a smile. He makes his way to his desk, slides open a drawer, and takes out a piece of paper. He fills it out, hands it to me.

"This is a standard agreement binding us as lawyer and client, but it will do."

I take my time reading it. It is a short and simple contract, worded to say that Raphael Angelo represents the interests of Celestine North. No obvious tricks.

"So tell me"—he sits on a footstool and leans toward me—"what do you know that's so bad that Crevan the fox is hunting down poor little Celestine?"

"Don't tell him," Carrick says as I stand up. "We don't know if we can trust him."

"Trust?" I spit angrily. "So you *do* know the word?"

Carrick looks away, annoyed, with a shake of his head.

"And we're off," Raphael says with a sigh, and folds his arms.

I turn my back to Raphael, lift my T-shirt, and lower the waist of my trousers.

Silence.

Then Raphael sucks in air. "A sixth brand. On your spine." He stands closer to me, inspects it. "It's not in the Guild paperwork. They're illustrious for their paperwork. It's your word against his."

"There's footage of Crevan ordering the extra brand on me," I say, measuring my words. "That's what he's looking for."

He leans forward, raises his eyebrows. "Footage? Well, now, that changes things."

"Well, there's more," I say. "The guard wouldn't carry out the brand,"

I explain. "The spine is not an official branding zone and there was no anesthetic; it's outside of Guild guidelines, so Crevan branded me himself."

Raphael's eyes almost pop out of his head. He stands and paces while he thinks. I can see the excitement in him, though he's trying to hide it, and it's confirmed to me that I've got something here. I've really got something against Crevan.

He stops pacing. He looks at me sympathetically, suddenly very sad. Genuinely.

"I must apologize, Celestine. I'm afraid I've let you down. I've fallen for the oldest trick in the film, which is to jump the gun, assume I'd heard and seen everything in my time. I missed the fact there could be a twist. I'm afraid I'm a man of black and white, of right and wrong. Just as I wouldn't offer a Flawed alcohol, I couldn't aid a Flawed who is on the run, in my home. I have seven children and too much to lose."

Carrick stiffens beside me.

"We have an exceptional camera system around this house. Our friend Crevan has given us plenty of reason to have them. I saw you arriving from quite a distance away. As soon as I saw you, I instructed my dear wife, Susan, to alert the Whistleblowers."

Carrick lets out an angry curse and he jumps to his feet, hands making fists. He towers over Raphael.

"*But*"—Raphael holds a finger up to Carrick—"we're living out here for a reason. The nearest Whistleblower is one hour away, at best, which gives us forty-five minutes to devise our plan. So"—Raphael looks at Carrick nervously, curiously, slightly amused—"let's get devising."

THIRTY-SIX

"COME ON, CELESTINE, let's get the hell out of here," Carrick says angrily, giving up on his very visible desire to beat Raphael to a bloody pulp.

"How macho of you," Raphael says, amused.

"Stop it, the both of you." I raise my voice. "Carrick, we need his help."

"His *help*?" he asks, appalled. "He just called the Whistleblowers on us."

"Just on Celestine, actually. I didn't think they'd come any quicker if I mentioned you."

I look from Carrick to Raphael, feeling torn. We've come all this way. This is the only plan I've got. Raphael Angelo is the only lawyer ever to overturn a Flawed ruling. *I need him.* Without him, what do I do? How do I take my case to Judge Sanchez?

"Fine. You stay," Carrick says. "I'm not sticking around. I don't trust this guy. One more second here and we'll land ourselves back in Highland Castle."

"Carrick, wait." I turn to Raphael. "Can he and I talk privately?"

"Sure. Tick, tick, tick," Raphael says, watching the clock over the fireplace, which I notice for the first time is a pair of "human hands" in the pointing position wearing marigold gloves. Raphael leaves the room.

Carrick faces me, arms folded, jaw square. Black eyes. "We can't trust him."

"What was he talking about when he mentioned Enya Sleepwell?" I ask shakily.

And even though he's trying to be cool about it, his body language changes.

"Look, Celestine." He comes to me, takes my hands gently. "Now is not the time to talk about that."

"Now is exactly the time. I need to know the truth."

He sighs, annoyed that I'm killing time. "Enya Sleepwell approached me during your trial—she wanted to contact you. She wanted to help you. She's running a campaign entirely based on your principles, *compassion and logic*, those were your words, you've seen them on every lamppost and billboard in the city. I told her I'd help her find you, but it was difficult. The press was at your house, your school. I couldn't get to you. Pia Wang was on your case."

"You came to find me because Enya Sleepwell asked you to?" I ask, feeling the tremor in my voice. I hear him say those words to me when I was walking down the corridor to the Branding Chamber. *I'll find you.* I waited for him in those weeks afterward, thinking it was something else, a connection or a bond of some sort, but it wasn't. It was a favor to a politician.

"Wait, Celestine, listen," he says impatiently. "Enya was the one who was at the castle for me when my trial was over and I was allowed to leave."

"She helped you become an evader?"

He looks around and lowers his voice. "I can't say that. She guided me. Gave me tips. Who I could trust and who I couldn't. She received information that my parents were at Vigor, which we now know came from Alpha and the Professor. I didn't know it then, but he must be funding her campaign. She has a lot of resources. It was through Enya that I met Fergus, Lorcan, and Lennox. She has plans for the Flawed, she puts like-minded people together. There's strength in numbers. Her campaign just needs *you*. You're the key to all this. She wants to meet with you but she can't, given that you're wanted. She's not the enemy, Celestine, she's trying to help us."

"Does she know about my sixth brand?"

"No," he says firmly, and I believe him.

"She was at the supermarket riot. I remember seeing her."

He freezes.

"Lorcan and Fergus were there, too. You were there. I never thought about it before, but why were you all there?" My eyes narrow suspiciously.

He doesn't say a word.

"Carrick. Talk."

"We were told you were going to be at Alpha's house."

The revelation leaves me feeling like I've been punched in the stomach. Alpha invited me to a gathering at her house, and I felt that she'd tricked me. I was called up to the stage in front of hundreds of people, placed in front of the microphone, and expected to tell my story. Something rousing. Something inspiring. I couldn't get a word out of my mouth. I choked. I had nothing at all to say to those people who wanted so much from me. The arrival of the Whistleblowers was what ironically rescued me.

"We went there to find you," Carrick explains. "I thought it was the best chance of me getting to you. Obviously when the raid occurred we couldn't go inside. After the raid, we followed you and your granddad from the house. We saw you go into the supermarket."

"You *set me up* in the supermarket," I say suddenly, and from the look on his face, I know that's exactly what happened.

He stutters and stammers his version of events, but it doesn't matter how much he tries to twist it.

"You set me up," I say louder.

"I needed to find you, Celestine."

"You could have tapped me on the shoulder and said, *Hi, Celestine, it's me, Carrick. Remember me?*" I say sarcastically, voice trembling. "You didn't have to start a riot."

"I needed Enya and everybody else to see how good you are, how brave you are. Under pressure, you're a real hero, Celestine."

"I'm not a hero! I'm just a normal girl who did the right thing! There is nothing heroic about anything I did!" I say with frustration.

"We have become so lost in the fear of making mistakes that nobody is acting on gut instinct. You are rare. Celestine, believe me, we need Enya, and she needs you. She needed to see that you're worth getting behind, that people can believe in you. Fergus and Lorcan believed in you straightaway at the supermarket; they've backed you all the way since then. Nobody expected it to turn out the way it did. Nobody expected the police officer to behave the way he did. I just wanted people to see your strength, how you stand up for yourself. It doesn't change how I feel about you."

My head is racing.

"You set me up," I roar now, and he falls silent. "Because of you, because of what happened in that supermarket, I had to leave my family." My voice cracks. "I had to run away from the people I love. *You* got me into this mess."

"No, Celestine, no," he says, hands out at me like he's trying to tame a wild horse.

"You're just as bad as Art," I spit out, the anger and hurt coursing through my veins. All that I've been through since that moment, and it's because of Carrick. I was following the rules until Lorcan and Fergus stood beside me in line. Three or more Flawed are not allowed to gather together. And for the second time, my life changed forever. "So if Enya Sleepwell is going to help me, why don't we sit tight until the election is over? When she's in power, she can put an end to the Guild herself; she can free the Flawed or whatever it is she is intent on doing."

"Enya needs *you* to convince the people that the Guild is worth disbanding. You're the only Flawed person the public has ever really rooted for. You're allowing them to see that we're human; it's because of you that they're hearing our stories, and only through sharing our stories can we make changes. The more Crevan chases you, the more people are questioning his motives. But most important, you have the tool to do so. You have the footage. It's what everybody needs to see."

But I don't have it. A secret that I've kept from him. I feel the blood rush to my face. I'm accusing him of being a liar but I am one, too. But isn't his lie worse?

"Enya Sleepwell is just another person who needs me for her cause," I say. "I can't trust her. She's trying to get the Flawed vote so that she can climb the ladder to her own success. If she's elected as prime minister who knows what she'll do then? A U-turn on every promise she made? And where will that leave me? You're right, Carrick. I am on my own. Everybody is in this for themselves, and I have to start thinking of me. I don't need anybody. I don't need you."

He blinks in surprise, obviously hurt. His eyes go from black to brown, brown to hazel, green flecks appear.

And before I change my mind, I say, "Please go. I can do this on my own."

I leave the room in search of Raphael, who is no doubt listening to everything transpiring between me and Carrick. He's in the kitchen feeding mushed banana to the baby.

"Thirty-five minutes until the Whistleblowers get here," he says. "Tick, tick, tick. You're staying?"

I nod.

"You're alone?"

The front door bangs and the car engine revs. I truly am alone now.

THIRTY-SEVEN

"WELL, THAT ANSWERS THAT," Raphael says jovially, giving the spoon back to the baby for her to finish, but the food is sent flying around her face, the table, and the room like a catapult. "Well done, Maple," Raphael congratulates his daughter on her eating talents. "Don't worry, Celestine, you're not completely stranded. I have a car you can take. One that you stole, after you threatened the life of my child and forced me to hand over the key." He turns to his children. "Ash, isn't that right, dear?"

She nods, big blue eyes serious. "She was so scary, Daddy, I thought I was going to die!" she says dramatically, disturbingly credible, and the others laugh.

"Good enough," he says. "Now, let's get to work."

We sit outside in his back garden on wooden benches at a table, the trees our only counsel.

"Who knows about the sixth brand?" he asks.

"The guards—"

"Names, please."

"Tina, June, Funar, Bark, Tony. Crevan. Then there was Mr. Berry." I pause. "And Carrick."

He looks at me to see if I'm serious.

Nobody knew that part about Carrick.

"If I'd known that then . . ."

"What?"

"Well, it's just that . . . he has a purpose. He's important. He's a *witness*, Celestine. I would never have let him go if I'd known."

I close my eyes, groan, and rest my forehead on the table.

"And Mr. Berry was filming this," he continues.

"Yes." I speak to the table. "From the viewing room." I sit up again. "And now he's missing. As are all the guards."

Raphael looks up from his notepad in surprise.

"Pia Wang also knows about the sixth brand. She'd started asking some questions, but she's missing, too."

He takes off his glasses. "You trusted Pia Wang?" he asks, as though I'm a fool.

"She also writes as Lisa Life."

His mouth falls open.

"She was looking for the guards, to question them," I say. "She was building a story against Crevan. I haven't heard from her in over two weeks. My mom and dad know about the brand, but they didn't witness it and they don't know that Crevan did it. I didn't tell them. I'm not sure if my sister knows; we never discussed it. The Guild has been leaving my family alone. Kind of. But they took my granddad in for questioning two days ago. He knows about the brand and that Crevan did it."

Has it been only two days?

"They're trying to get him for aiding a Flawed," I continue. "Then there are some students I went to school with who know. They kidnapped me and locked me in a shed, stripped me, and photographed me." I say this all without emotion, and he stares at me in shock. "They are Logan Trilby, Natasha Benson, Gavin Lee, and Colleen Tinder."

At that, he drops his glasses on the table and his eyes go even wider. "Come inside."

146

I follow him into the kitchen and he switches the TV to Flawed TV, which the children groan at. There is a Pia replacement reporting. A beautiful blond with icy pink lips and cheeks like the Good Witch, who smiles through every hate-filled word she says. Photos of Logan, Colleen, Natasha, and Gavin appear. Natasha's is a selfie after her lip injections. She looks ridiculous, like a blowfish. I'm not sure why I'm looking at their photographs, at all their silly, smiling faces. Like butter wouldn't melt. I know the truth.

But then I realize why. One word pops up beneath their pictures. MISSING.

THIRTY-EIGHT

THEY'VE BEEN MISSING for two days. Logan's religious parents are pointing the finger at me for their son's disappearance. They give Flawed TV the exclusive interview.

Raphael switches off the TV. "Everything is stacked against you. How exactly do you think I should move forward, bearing in mind that everybody who knows about this is now missing, and you had a lovers' tiff with your only remaining witness?" He looks around at his kids and for the first time I see nerves.

Susan ushers us back outside so we can continue, muttering, "I don't wanna know. I don't wanna know."

I need to win him back over. I need to give him more. "Judge Sanchez is on my side. Don't ask how or why, she just is. My plan was to find you and reopen the case. When faced with the footage, Crevan would have to take back the wrongful sixth brand, and if he has made one mistake, then he's made more. That would make him Flawed himself. He'll have to apologize, and the entire Flawed system will be questioned. Crevan will be humiliated, will have to step down, which is what Sanchez wants."

Raphael smiles and looks at me with what I think is admiration. "You want to accuse Crevan of being Flawed?"

I chew on my lip nervously. "I know it's not conventional. . . ."

"I'm not a conventional kind of man. But I'd have to see the footage first."

Ah. "There's one problem." I swallow. "One *big* problem. I don't have it." Silence.

"Mr. Berry's husband *says* that I have it. He told me over the phone. Crevan overheard the conversation; our phone lines must have been tapped. But I don't have it. I have no idea where it is."

He looks quite close to wanting to wrap his fingers around my neck and squeeze tightly, but thankfully he doesn't. He breathes in and out a few times.

"Did Mr. Berry visit you at your house after the trial?" he asks.

"No." Those early days were difficult, my coming in and out of painkiller-induced sleep, but I know that he didn't visit me. I could count on one hand the number of people who did. The doctor. Angelina Tinder.

"Tina visited," I remember suddenly. "She was one of the guards. A nice guard."

"Then *she* must have given you the footage."

My mind races. I think back to four weeks ago. It feels like a lifetime. "No. She brought cupcakes. Her daughter had made them. I remember thinking it was selfish because I couldn't eat them. Only one luxury a week, and one cupcake alone was over the permitted calorie intake."

"There was something in the cupcake," he says.

"No. I gave them to my little brother to eat." I stand up and pace. "I think we'd have noticed if he swallowed a . . . a . . . I don't know, Mr. Angelo, what are we even looking for? A file? A disk? A chip?"

"I'd imagine it's a USB," he guesses. "Or the memory card from Mr. Berry's phone."

Fifteen minutes until I have to leave.

149

"She must have given you something else," he says.

"I didn't even see her." I rack my brain. "I wasn't well. My mom wouldn't let her in to see me. She didn't think it was appropriate."

"It wasn't really, was it?" he says, thinking about it. "No, it was a completely inappropriate visit, and a risky one for her. There must have been a purpose. She must have given the footage to your mother."

"There was a snow globe," I remember suddenly. "A Highland Castle snow globe. When you shook it, red glitter fell down, like blood. I thought it was the most horrific, disgusting gift anybody could give me after what happened to me in there. I wondered why she would give it to me."

"It's in there," he says, standing. "It must be in the globe. Where is it?"

I view him suspiciously now, wondering if I can trust him. I have told him everything, but have I told him too much? If I lose the footage, I lose all the power.

I feign disappointment. I lay my head on the table, and it's not difficult to make the tears come; they were already close to the surface anyway.

"I threw it away," I lie. "I threw it against the wall. It smashed. Mom put it in the trash. That was weeks ago. It's gone."

Raphael seems angry, but I think he believes me. All the time, my mind is racing over how I can get the snow globe back. If I call my house, I'm sure they'll be monitoring the calls. That's how Crevan learned about the footage in the first place, through my conversation with Mr. Berry's husband. How foolish I was then!

Ten minutes left until I must leave.

Raphael seems anxious. He slowly sits down. "Unconventionality is my way of thinking, of being. That is my strength, Celestine. You don't get to my age looking as I do without having had to toughen up and fight. When you're a teenager, what makes you different can be the worst thing in the world. The older you get, the more you realize that it's your weapon, your armor, your strength. Your gift. For me it is thinking in a nonlinear way, which means doing the very thing you think you must *not* do."

"And what's that?"

"What have you been doing for the past two weeks?"

I frown, mulling his question over. Running, hiding, crying, feeling sorry for myself. Losing my virginity, but I'm sure he doesn't mean that. I look at him suddenly, fearing what he is going to say. "Avoiding Crevan."

"Exactly. Now you and Crevan must meet."

THIRTY-NINE

PLAN MADE, RAPHAEL goes back into the house to get me the car keys. He's left his phone on the table. I grab it. After calling Judge Sanchez and Whistleblower Kate on my secret mobile, I don't want to call Juniper on it, too. It might not be safe any longer. Through Granddad I learned that Juniper was working in a café in the city. It's weird how other people's lives move on, how they have to move on, while mine stands still.

When someone is accused of being Flawed, that person must hire a lawyer to help represent them. If they're found not guilty, the Guild pays the court fees; if they are found guilty, the Flawed must pay the fees. Mr. Berry was the best and most expensive lawyer in the Guild, and I know that paying for his services depleted all of Mom and Dad's savings.

As well as that, since Mom is a top fashion model, she lost some contracts, and left some of her own accord, no longer happy having to live up to the perfect standards that the products advertised. I doubt she has any money coming in. Dad works as an editor at TV network News 24, but I'm sure he is completely under the thumb of the new management, Candy Crevan, Bosco's sister. She won't want Dad deciding the direction of the news, particularly when his daughter is much of the story.

So Juniper is working. It is summertime, we both would have had to get summer jobs anyway, before college started, but I know things must be tight at home. Despite Juniper's being older than I am, we are less than a year apart, and people always think we are twins. During the weeks when the media was swarming our house, we often used Juniper as a decoy, sending her outside to be trampled on by photographers while I made a swift exit out the other side. We may look alike, but we're poles apart in personality.

I loved school, excelled at it; Juniper hated it and always had to work harder because of her dyslexia. But while I got better grades, Juniper was always smarter than me. She is more savvy and has a greater understanding of people and situations, as though sitting back and observing was teaching her a whole lot more than me, who was always involved.

Juniper was the more vocal one whenever Crevan visited; I thought she had the same conspiracy theory brain as Granddad. It is like we switched roles on the bus that day: It should have been her to help the Flawed old man. I think, in a way, she would be happier if she was Flawed, because she has always felt on the fringes of society anyway. Being Flawed would almost be a badge of honor to Juniper. There is a multitude I should learn from her. I miss her so much.

I called Juniper at the café twice from Granddad's house. She picked up only once. I just wanted to hear her voice—I never spoke; I couldn't get her in trouble, but I knew that if the Guild was looking at Granddad's phone records, it wouldn't seem odd that he calls his granddaughter at work.

Now I dial the number again.

"Coffee House," a man answers.

"Glory, please." I'd also learned she'd changed her name. No one wants to hire someone whose sister is on the Guild's Wanted list. Glory and Tori were the fake names we used to give each other when playing as children. We used to stick cushions up our T-shirts and pretend to be two overweight ladies who owned a cake shop. We'd spend hours making cakes from mud in the back garden, sprinkling them with petals and grass, and serving them to our imaginary customers, usually Ewan, who attempted to eat them much to our amusement and Mom's panic.

"No personal calls," he says.

"Her grandmother died," I snap, and he quickly gets off the phone.

"Hello?" She sounds nervous.

"Glory. It's Tori, from the cake shop."

She pauses. "Is that you?" she whispers.

"Yes," I say, and I want to cry. There is so much I want to say to my sister, but I'm afraid to give too much away. I'm running out of time and I need to leave now, before Raphael gets back and before the Whistle-blowers get here.

"Oh my God, are you okay?"

"Yes. I need your help, though. I need something from the house. Can you get it to me?"

"I'll try." She lowers her voice. "It's difficult. They keep coming to the house. For searches. And she took everything from your room. I'm so sorry. We couldn't stop her."

Instantly I know exactly who she's talking about. Mary May.

"The day after you left she came and trashed your bedroom, then after Granddad . . . well she *took* everything. All your stuff. They're looking for something, and most of the time I don't think it's you."

"You're right," I say simply. "Where did she take it?"

"I don't know, but she wasn't in her uniform and she drove her own car. She just packed away everything in garbage bags and left."

She did this when Granddad was taken away, when they couldn't find me at the farm. So this was only two days ago. But they're still looking for me, which means they're still looking for the footage. I just hope she hasn't discarded the snow globe. Knowing Mary May, she hasn't.

I hear Raphael returning and I wrap it up.

"That was a great help," I say hurriedly. "I love you." I end the call and place the phone back on the table.

"I've left a message with Crevan's secretary for him to call me urgently on his return," Raphael says, placing a glass of water down on the table for me. "I'm sure he'll know what it's about, he will have been alerted to your presence here. And any phone call from me is deemed urgent."

He seems nervous by what he's just taken on. Or who: Judge Crevan.

I'm not waiting around for Crevan to call me back, to be a sitting duck for the Whistleblowers. It is impossible to know who to trust anymore. Instead of thinking of the uncertainties, I need to deal with the facts.

I know who I *can't* trust.

I know exactly how to get to Crevan in one swift phone call.

FORTY

"ART, IT'S ME," I say, phone to my ear as I rattle down the bumpy mountains in Raphael's Mini Cooper. My heart is banging in my chest, I feel it thudding in my ears, the hot anger. I want to scream at him, *I know who you've become!*

"Celestine?" he asks, surprised.

I put him on speakerphone and place two hands on the wheel to concentrate as the Mini steams down the mountainside.

"Where are you?" His voice crackles.

"I need to meet you," I say firmly. "I have something to show you."

"What is it?"

"Video. Of your dad and me."

"What? What are you talking about?"

"I'll meet you in two hours. Our usual place."

He's silent as he thinks about it, then, "Okay."

I end the call.

Carrick was right about one thing. Art *is* bait.

FORTY-ONE

I HIDE AT the top of the hill, under the cover of darkness, feeling sick to my stomach. Susan insisted on feeding me something I still couldn't taste before I left the house, to give me some energy, but now it's threatening to revolt. I wait on the summit that overlooks the city, my old nightly meeting place with Art. It's the first time I've ever been earlier than him; he was always here waiting for me—just another telltale sign that our situations have reversed.

The moon is high in the sky, not a perfect full moon like that last moment I was here with Art, the night he gave me the anklet with the three circles signifying geometric harmony, perfection, the night before my life changed forever. Maybe the moon wasn't perfectly full, maybe I just thought it was, because I can see now that I thought a lot of things that weren't true. I think back to who I was then and see how naive I was, thinking I knew it all, thinking I could plan it all, thinking that I could have every solution to every problem. Thinking I could trust people.

I'm still wearing the anklet that Art gave me. There was only one occasion when I thought about ripping it off and throwing it away: the moment I saw him dressed as a Whistleblower. But just like the sixth brand that is seared into my lower spine, the anklet gives me power. Now I know it was given to me by a Whistleblower, the son of the man who branded me. It labels me as Perfect. They're all hypocrites.

I hear the crunch of footsteps on the gravel and I pull back. Jeans, a dark hoodie, that mop of playful blond curls, the soft face, the gentle eyes, the lips that sit as if every word that passes them is a joke. Art. I wait to see if he's alone. I leave him waiting one minute, then two. Nobody else is in sight, for now.

I step out from the shadows.

"Hi," he says, like he's afraid of me. He looks me up and down. And then he looks around, nervous he'll be found. I wonder if Crevan will jump out and catch me now, or if he'll wait until after our conversation. If Art's task has been to get the information from me, or if he even knows he's being used at all. Poor Art, I feel a flash of sympathy for him, trapped in the middle of all this. But then the sympathy dies, because he chose the wrong side.

"Hi," I reply, sounding much softer than I'd intended to.

I hear footsteps behind Art and I prepare myself. I'm surprised to find that I'm disappointed Art and I didn't get any time together. There's no big crew, no SWAT team of Whistleblowers in their riot gear. It's just Crevan, as I suspected. I knew he wouldn't bring an army to listen to me talk about the footage. He doesn't want anybody to know about that. He's wearing jeans, a hoodie—an older version of Art, on an unofficial visit.

"Dad!" Art says, spinning around, and I'm glad to see that Art is genuinely surprised. "What are you doing here?" Then he asks angrily, "Did you follow me?"

"I got your message," Crevan says to me, ignoring Art, smug as if he got one up on me. He places his hand on Art's shoulder. "Son, you go back to the house now. I'll take it from here."

"What's going on? What do you mean you got the message?"

"I'm sorry, but now that you're a Whistleblower, the castle has access to your calls. The phone call from Celestine was flagged straightaway. We can talk about it later," he says firmly, and then turns to me. "Art can't stay up too late, not like he used to, not with the new job," he says, smiling, eyes crinkling at the sides.

I look at Art angrily, then back at Crevan. "You must be so proud of your son. He's just like you now."

Art looks down at the ground. He's happy to get away from me now that he knows I know he's a Whistleblower. He takes a last glance at the two of us, then quickly disappears.

"Ironic, how your misdemeanors did me a favor, bringing my son back to me. We're closer than ever now," Crevan says, taking a few steps forward.

The breeze carries a familiar smell of mint. Peppermint. Or an antiseptic smell. I can't place it. Maybe he's chewing gum. Perhaps it's a familiar smell of Crevan from my previous life, when we were friends, almost family.

"He would never have gone into the family business if it weren't for you betraying him, going on the run, becoming an evader."

I want to run at him and punch him, kick him, I want to scream so loudly at him, vent all the most disgusting words I can think of, but I know it will have no effect. He is impenetrable. Any emotion or affection he had for me died a long time ago. Now I think he sits for hours thinking of ways he can simply destroy me and the connection his son has with me.

"So you wanted to show Art something." He enjoys seeing the look on my face. "I assume this is the so-called secret footage. Hand it over." He tries to act cool, but I can tell that he is nervous. He has searched the width and breadth of the country for two weeks for this.

I smile. "You actually think I'd bring it with me?"

His smile fades.

"I called Art *presuming* he'd tell you we were meeting. Do you think

I didn't know he was a Whistleblower? Of course I know. But I didn't think Art would actually keep us meeting from you. That father-son bond isn't as strong as you think it is," I say, enjoying hurting him. "I've changed a lot since you branded me. I got smarter. Ironic, how you've done me a favor, too."

His face darkens as he realizes that he's fallen into my plan.

"I'm not here to show Art the footage. I'm here to talk to you. I'm here to tell you that you've made a mistake. I think you know that already. You're trying to cover your steps, but you can't. The guards, the students, a journalist, a lawyer . . . don't you think you're going a bit too far? Do you think nobody's going to notice? That nobody will eventually put it all together? You can't brand everybody, Bosco."

"You think a piece of video holds that much power?" He laughs.

"I know it does. Because I know what's on it. I was there, remember? And because you're going out of your way to find me, hunting me down. You're panicking. You know you can't talk yourself out of this one. When people see this footage, they'll see what an animal you are. A monster who's out of control, who can't be trusted with the power he's been given."

He swallows, pretending not to be bothered by my words, but I know that he is. Nobody in his life speaks to him like this.

I take a deep breath. "I can make it all go away. I'll give you the footage if you admit that I'm not Flawed. That what I did on the bus wasn't wrong. *Repent*, Crevan," I say, repeating the word he said to me in the chamber.

He looks surprised. "I'd never do that. If I do that, then every Flawed will demand the same thing."

"That's the deal." I shrug.

He sighs. His shoulders slump, and he pushes one hand in his pocket while the other rubs his face tiredly.

"Fine. I'll do it."

I'm taken aback by the haste of his agreement—Raphael's advice worked, but I need to continue while the going is good. "There's one other person you need to do the same for. Carrick Vane." Carrick may have lied to me about his involvement with Enya Sleepwell, but it doesn't change what happened between me and him, what we shared in the castle and what we shared in his cabin last night. He may owe me an apology, but he is the one who believed in me more than anyone, which has led me to this point right now, and I owe him this.

He looks at me and narrows his eyes, and I try to stay strong. A part of me is panicking that I've given up Carrick's name, that I've linked us together.

"You give me the footage, *all copies*, and I'll do that for you and your friend. But here's my part of the bargain. You must both leave the country. I don't want to ever hear from either of you again. If you set one foot back in Humming, then you'll find yourself in the same situation."

I'm so shocked that it has worked. Leave the country? No problem. Be free? Yes, please.

"But the deal remains private," he continues, explaining the terms. "Nobody can know that your verdicts have been reversed. You live in freedom, and the powers that be here will be aware, but the public won't. We keep this quiet."

This is exactly what happened with Raphael Angelo's winning case. Agreeing to not being able to speak about the overturned verdict publicly would mean that I could never truly clear my name and nobody else could use my case to fight for their own freedom. We couldn't accuse Crevan of being Flawed. Enya Sleepwell couldn't use me for her campaign, and Flawed rights would suffer. Sanchez wouldn't be able to remove Crevan from power.

But I'd be free. And so would Carrick.

I think of what Cordelia said to me in Vigor. *What kind of leader sacrifices others for their own gain?*

"No," I say shakily. "I can't agree to that."

Crevan tuts. "And you were so close, Celestine."

I'm not alert enough. I'm too lost in the repercussions of the decision I've made that I'm slow to react. I thought I was smart, but I'm not smart enough. When he takes his hand from his pocket, he reaches out and sticks a needle in my thigh.

I crumple to the ground.

FORTY-TWO

I WAKE UP in a hospital bed. I'm surrounded by a white curtain, white walls, white ceiling, white bedding, bright strip lighting. I wince against the light. I'm wearing a red gown.

I try to sit up but I'm stuck. My upper body is stiff but it moves, my arms and upper torso will do what they're told, but from the waist down, absolutely nothing happens. There's no movement. I'm paralyzed.

Feeling trapped, I start to whimper with the effort. I throw off the covers and try to lift my legs with my hands. They're heavy and I can move them, but I can't feel a thing. I thump them, slap them, try to wake them up, force them to obey.

The curtain is pulled back and I jump, startled. Tina appears.

Tina. The guard who was with me during the branding, the guard who disappeared. The guard who I *thought* had disappeared, along with all the others. She's wearing her Whistleblower uniform and everything I thought I knew dismantles in my mind. The neat little theory that she had been on my side, that she'd smuggled the footage to me, that Crevan had hidden her away, all disintegrates. She is the enemy.

She holds her finger to her lips conspiratorially.

"He gave you some kind of injection to paralyze you," she whispers. "They plan to do a skin graft to remove the sixth brand."

"What?" I hiss.

"Shh," she says loudly. "Dr. Greene has been brought in by the Guild to carry out the surgery. I'm sorry, Celestine, this is a mess."

"I thought you were missing. I was actually worried about you."

She comes closer, takes my hand. "He threatened me and my daughter. I saw what he did to the others. I couldn't . . ." Her eyes fill. "I tried to help you as best I could. Did you find the USB I gave you?"

"In the snow globe?" I ask.

She brightens with relief. "Bark added a fake base. I wasn't sure you'd figure it out, but he thought you would. *She's a clever girl*, he said." She smiles sadly at the memory of him. "I thought I should write it down but then I didn't want a paper trail, or for it to fall into the wrong hands. I couldn't contact you; I wasn't sure if you would find it."

"I didn't realize it was there until too late. Mary May removed everything from my bedroom. I don't think she knows it's in the snow globe, though, otherwise I wouldn't be here. Where would she have put it?"

"I don't know." She thinks, eyes panicking. If they find the footage in the globe, it will land her in a lot of trouble.

"Please, Tina, I need to know. Please find out for me."

The door opens.

She reaches out and I think she's going to slap me but she pushes my head back down on the pillow and places her hand over my eyes so that I instantly close them.

"She's still sleeping, Dr. Greene," Tina says quietly.

"Goodness, I've never known somebody to sleep so heavily."

"I suppose she has been on the run for quite some time. I imagine she's exhausted," Tina says, and I hear the pity in her voice.

"Hmm." Dr. Greene doesn't sound so certain. "Are you sure she's not on any medication?"

"I wouldn't know, Doctor," Tina says carefully. "I've just been asked to keep an eye on her."

"Usually I prepare for weeks in advance, to make sure the medication doesn't interfere with the blood's ability to form clots." She talks to Tina like she distrusts her, like she is giving her a chance to fess up to drugging me.

There's an awkward silence. They're watching me.

"I'm afraid Judge Crevan is the person to ask about that."

"I already did."

And they both know that they can't ask him twice.

I try to keep my breathing steady. I'm reminded of being under the ground in the cooking pit. At least now I can breathe. Things are looking up. Though the paralysis is a new one.

"Have you seen the brand?" Dr. Greene asks in a hush.

"I was there at the time, Doctor."

"I can't believe that the girl would do this to herself. How did she get the branding tool from the guard in a moment like that? Aren't the Flawed supposed to be restrained in the chair?"

"Excuse me?" Tina asks, surprised.

"Judge Crevan tells me you were all unable to stop Celestine from branding herself."

Silence.

"It's important that we remove it immediately. Her accusations against Judge Crevan would have serious repercussions. You know she's telling people that *he* did it to her? No wonder he's been going out of his mind to find her."

Tina is completely silent.

"It is what happened, isn't it?" Dr. Greene asks uncertainly.

"Is she awake?" Crevan's voice booms as he bursts into the room.

"Not yet, Judge," Dr. Greene says, startled.

"Call me as soon as she is. I don't want her talking to anyone, spreading more of her lies."

"Yes, sir," Tina says quickly.

"All is in order? The operating room is to your satisfaction, Dr. Greene?"

"Yes, Judge, thank you. May I ask, what is this facility? I wasn't aware of its existence."

"This section is new. Secret government stuff, Dr. Greene." I hear the smile in his voice and imagine his face. I used to think he was handsome, too, before the mask came off.

"I'd like to take a look at the scar before surgery, if I may," Dr. Greene says firmly.

Tina and Dr. Greene roll me to my side. I hope that Crevan isn't standing by and watching. Dr. Greene sucks in air.

"Gosh, that looks painful. Like torture. Why would a young girl do that to herself?" she asks.

"Who knows what goes through the mind of a Flawed? We'll reconvene after surgery, Dr. Greene," Crevan says. "I'm afraid I must prepare for this dreaded interview that the prime minister has asked me do ahead of the election. I must prove to the public I'm not the big bad wolf the Vital Party is making me out to be," he jokes again, trying to play it down.

If the government has asked him to do this interview, then he is in a lot of trouble indeed. Damage control.

"Oh, indeed, a sit-down with Erica Edelman. She's"—the doctor stalls—"an efficient interviewer. I wish you luck."

"Luck indeed," he says. "She's out for my blood, I think, but I'll get around her."

His footsteps die away as he leaves the room.

"What is entailed in the surgery?" Tina asks in a small voice.

"When Celestine wakes we'll place an IV in her arm, to administer the general anesthetic and fluids. I'll inject medicine into the IV and she'll go to sleep; she won't feel any pain. I'll be doing a split-level thickness graft; I'll remove skin from her inner thigh, then I'll fix it to the brand with stitches. I'll cover the donor area with a dressing. We'll take her back here to recovery, where we'll administer her pain relief, anything to

166

make her feel comfortable. I'll need to observe her for a few days to make sure both the donor site and the graft are healing well. She'll have to avoid strenuous activities for three to four weeks and the donor site should heal within two to three weeks."

"She's been there before, treating her wounds," Tina says quietly.

"You seem . . . forgive me for saying this, but you seem concerned about her. Fond of her, perhaps?"

"My daughter is her age," Tina says.

"Interesting," Dr. Greene says. "You sound just like her."

"What do you mean?"

"I watched Celestine's trial. She said the reason she helped the old man on the bus was because he reminded her of her granddad."

"I believe it's called empathy," Tina says gently. "We may have lost that as a society."

"Not all of us," Dr. Greene says.

Her footsteps squeak on the linoleum and then it's just me and Tina.

"You've got one hour at most to get yourself out of here," Tina says quickly in my ear. "Any longer and Dr. Greene will start asking Crevan questions and then she'll be in a world of trouble. I'm going to take a coffee break. I've left my car keys beside my bag on the chair in the corner of the room. My car is outside in the parking lot. I'll distract the others. But that's all I can do for you, Celestine," she says, almost apologetically. She leaves quickly, before I beg for more. Which I would.

I don't waste any time. I use my elbows to sit up. I reach for the curtain to use it to ease myself to the floor but I'm too heavy and it comes away from the rings on the rail. I topple to the floor with a grunt, hurting my side, and doing who knows what to my legs, but I can't feel them as they bang to the ground. I roll onto my belly, trying to ignore the pain, and pull myself on my front, using my elbows, dragging my legs behind me.

My body feels heavy and sluggish, like it's dead; it won't listen or obey my commands. Sweat breaks out on my skin immediately from the effort and my skin slides along the polished floor. I can't feel the floor against

167

my legs. It's as though my body has been halved, I've no feeling at all below my waist. I have no idea where I am; I'm wearing just my underwear beneath the red gown; I can barely make it to the door of my hospital room, never mind attempting to escape the building. I know that I'm not in Highland Castle anyway.

I get to the chair with Tina's black leather bag and reach up to grab the set of car keys.

I have visions of Crevan walking in on me, finding me sprawled on the floor, moving like a slug at his feet. Helpless and at his mercy, right where he wants me. This thought gives me more strength and I increase my pace, pulling myself along faster.

The door has been left ajar, enough of a gap for me to reach my hand in and pull, thankful I don't have to stretch to the handle, which would have been impossible. Tina has given me more of a chance than I'd thought. I look outside to the corridor. It's empty. I hear voices down the hall, from a staff room.

"Jason, can you come over here? Judge Crevan instructed me to go through this security manual with you all," Tina says, and I see a Whistleblower at the end of the hall monitoring the security cameras abandon his station.

"We received that weeks ago," he says, pulling up his trousers over his gut as he makes his way to the small group of Whistleblowers.

"Yes, well, apparently he's not happy with how we've been following it," she says, to groans from the others. "Let's just get it over with. Why don't we brew some coffee?"

"Good idea," Jason agrees.

"Page one," Tina begins.

I'm about to pull myself out to the corridor and turn right toward the exit stairwell when I hear Flawed TV blaring from the room across the way. It's the much-talked-about live debate between all the party leaders.

"Compassion and logic is the Vital Party's campaign logo, proving

168

that 'a good head and a good heart are always a formidable combination,'"
Enya Sleepwell says from her podium.

"Which are words straight from the mouth of a Flawed, proving that
Enya Sleepwell is in bed with the Flawed population," Prime Minister
Percy says.

"Interesting you should say that, Prime Minister. I was quoting Nelson
Mandela."

Score one to Enya.

I crawl across the hall to the room opposite and see armchairs. More
people, patients, all in red gowns. More Flawed. They'll be able to help me.

"Excuse me," I whisper, pulling myself into the room. "I need help."

Everyone has their backs to me, they don't turn around. Perhaps I
should leave, but if, as Carrick said, all you have to do is change one mind,
then maybe we can help one another out of here. I don't imagine I'm
going to have much success driving with my legs as they are, though I'll
try if I have to, but assistance would be safer and quicker. I call to them
again, louder this time, but they either can't hear me or are ignoring me
and don't want to help. I pull myself up to the nearest armchair, the sweat
from the effort trickling down my face and back.

"Excuse me, I need your—" I stop immediately.

The hairs stand up all over my body.

The man in the chair is Mr. Berry.

FORTY-THREE

"MR. BERRY." I shake his arm lightly, trying to get his attention. His dead eyes don't move from the television and I don't think it's because he's engrossed in the live debate. He has that drugged look about him. He looks old; his face is younger than the rest of his body, but less so without his usual blush and concealer, and it's like his neck can barely hold it up.

I look to the chair beside him and I see Pia Wang. Beautiful Pia Wang who was trying to help me, she has the same distant look, hair tied back and greasy, as if it hasn't been washed in weeks. I'm afraid to look around any more, but I have to. I pull myself up to the next row, and I see the guards. Bark, who branded me; Funar, June, and the security guard Tony, who all witnessed it.

In the front row are the kids from school, Natasha, Logan, Gavin, and Colleen. I watch them in their red gowns, powerless, not at all like the last time I saw them, when they tied me up and stripped me to inspect my brands. The smell of peppermint in the air makes me queasy, that same smell that came from Crevan.

I'm ashamed of myself for the sense of satisfaction I feel looking at the kids who bullied me not so long ago and took photographs of my brands. It was that evil act that sealed their fate. I do feel something for Colleen, who I grew up with. She lived across the road from me all my life and was a family friend, someone I have memories of playing with as a child, up until the fateful day her mom, Angelina Tinder, was taken away and branded Flawed. On the last Earth Day gathering that changed all our lives. It doesn't make what she did to me right, but Colleen targeted me from a place of hurt, not from pure menace, like the others. I'm grateful not to see Granddad, any other members of my family, or Raphael Angelo in this room.

None of these people can help me—they can't even see me. I've stayed here too long. I hear the Whistleblowers' voices in the corridor, telling Tina they refuse to listen to any more.

"He won't know, Tina. We'll tell him we read it again," says one, while Tina desperately tries to win their attention back. She loses the battle, their coffee cups have been drained, the guards start to disperse.

I've run out of time.

FORTY-FOUR

THE DOOR TO this bizarre television recreational room opens and a guard steps in. I keep my eyes firmly fixed on the television, trying to mimic the others. My heart is pounding from the effort of climbing up onto the spare armchair, the sweat rolls from my temple and down my back, I'm not sure if I imagine it, but I think I feel it drip past my waist, tickling. Is the injection wearing off? I can't test my legs to see, but I feel the beginning of pins and needles in my thighs. I'm out of breath from the effort it took to sit here and I hope they can't see my chest heaving up and down beneath the red gown. I try to control my breathing and what I imagine is the wild look in my eyes, a stark contrast to the others, who are like couch potato zombies. What has Crevan done to them? How long have they been here, and what does he intend to do with them?

The guard gasps suddenly, perhaps seeing me, and she runs from the room.

"Stacey!" she calls down the corridor, keeping the door open with her body so that I still can't move.

I quickly take a risk and wipe the rolling sweat from my brow, that single movement a danger. She returns with another guard. They're whispering, heads close together.

"That's her. Celestine North."

"It's not her, Linda," Stacey says.

They come close to me, and I try to keep staring straight ahead as if I don't notice them.

"She's so young."

"She's prettier in person."

"Probably lost weight, on the run."

"The fugitive diet. I could do with a bit of that."

One snorts and they laugh, then quickly shush themselves.

"I knew Tina was hiding someone in that room. And the arrival of that uppity doctor. And having to read through all those rules. I wonder what they're up to."

"Not our job to know or ask."

"Take a photo of me with her, will you?"

"Stacey!"

"What? Just for me. No one will know."

They giggle as Stacey fluffs her hair and crouches down beside me, arm across my shoulder as if we're best friends on a night out.

Linda holds the phone up in front of us; I can feel Stacey's breath on my skin, can smell her sweet perfume. I try to focus on the television, but . . .

"One, two, three . . . Goodness!" Linda says, taking a step back.

"What?" Stacey jumps away from me as though I'm a bomb about to explode.

"She looked at me."

"She can't have," Stacey says. "They've enough drugs in them to last them a week. Look at her, from the TV." She clicks her fingers in front of Pia's face. "Pia Wang reporting live," she imitates. "Not so peachy perfect now, is she?" She chuckles.

Linda isn't quite so sure. I scared her, and I'm quite enjoying the power.

There are voices in the corridor. Official-sounding, lots of boots on the ground. Another gang of Whistleblowers. They arrive at the door, push it open. Five of them appear. All wearing helmets. Two guard the door; three come inside.

My time is up, they've noticed I'm missing.

They file into the room and one lifts her helmet. It's Kate. I try not to react.

"We're here under order of Highland Castle. I have a document for Celestine North's custody officer." Kate looks from one woman to the other.

"That's Tina," Stacey says quickly, eager to get out of there, after their unprofessional acts with me only moments ago. "I'll get her."

Linda clears her throat nervously. "I'll come, too."

Kate follows them. As soon as the three have left the room, the second Whistleblower lifts his helmet and I see Carrick. My stomach leaps. Then the last Whistleblower reveals herself. Juniper.

I gasp.

"Rescue squad is here," Juniper says, jumping into action. "We have to be fast. If anyone contacts the castle we'll be in trouble. Quickly, put this uniform on." She starts to strip off.

Carrick looks away.

"Juniper! What the hell are you doing?" I ask.

"Taking your place."

"What? You—"

"No time to talk," she says urgently. "I'm doing this, no discussion. You disagree, you get us all into trouble. Stick to the plan."

I can't believe it. I can't let this happen. I can't abandon my sister in this place, not with what they're about to do to me in the operating room.

"I'll delay them. It will give you time to do what you have to do. Stand up. Take off the gown," she says, annoyed now.

"I can't!" I say.

"Of course you can!" She raises her voice.

"Shh!" Carrick says.

"No, I mean, *I physically can't*. Crevan injected me with something. I can't move my legs."

They both look at me then, and I see the fear in their eyes. The plan must be abandoned. How can we all walk out of here if I can't walk?

FORTY-FIVE

"WE'LL CARRY YOU OUT," Carrick says. "Keep going."

"Carrick, don't be stupid, they'll ask questions. It won't work," I argue.

Juniper lifts the gown over my head.

"Please don't do this, Juniper."

"Stop, Celestine," she snaps, annoyed. "It's the only way."

"But Mom and Dad will never forgive me."

"It was Mom's idea. She would have taken your place herself if she could."

Juniper removes her clothes and helps me dress. I can put the jacket on, as I can control my upper body, but the combat pants are awkward because I can't lift myself. Carrick rushes over to help. I think of yesterday, when his eyes and hands were on my body. Perhaps he's thinking the same thing because our eyes meet. Green eyes, hazel flecks. He didn't abandon me after all. Juniper looks from him to me, then smiles happily, and I know she knows about us. They slide the red combat trousers over my legs, the boots on my feet, no time for socks.

The pins and needles are spreading down to my knee.

I see the *F* brands on Juniper's temple and palm.

"Mom did it," Juniper says, out of breath, nervously as she moves. Then she looks at me softly. "All six of them."

She knows; it's the first time we've ever discussed the six brands.

Trust Mom and her makeup skills to pull off such authentic scars. As a famous model, Mom has been exposed to the best makeup artists, particularly for her wilder shoots. She's managed to make Juniper's brands look authentic, bubbling wounds newly scabbed over.

Carrick pulls me up, but I can't stand on my own. I'm numb from the knees down now.

Juniper sees Gavin, Logan, Natasha, and Colleen in the front row. "Good," she says, a hardness in her eyes.

"Thank you," I whisper, leaning in to kiss her.

She wraps her arms around me tightly and hangs on. "I owed you, now go save the world, baby sister," she says, and I see tears filling her eyes when we pull apart.

When I returned home after my branding, I waited every day for Art to visit or contact me. He didn't. I noticed that Juniper was disappearing from her room late at night, and one night I discovered them together, in our secret place on the summit. I jumped to the wrong conclusions. I believe now that it was entirely platonic. Neither of them had wanted to get me into any further trouble, but it took me a while to realize that. I thought they had both betrayed me. Juniper and I already made up over this, but I know she feels she needs to redeem herself. This act of love is way beyond what I thought she'd ever do. This is dangerous.

Juniper places the helmet on my head while Carrick holds me up under the arms.

Kate returns with Tina, who looks nervous. Stacey and Linda tag along, watching it all unfold, curiously. I hope Carrick and Juniper have a plan. I hope that Tina can protect my sister. I discreetly pass Tina her car keys and she quickly pockets them. Tina hands me a slip of paper.

"A message for Highland Castle," she says firmly.

"We're ready to move out," Kate says, moving to the door.

Carrick pulls me up beside him. The guards view me suspiciously.

"Stupid bitch kicked me," I say, disguising my voice as best I can, leaning all my weight on Carrick.

They immediately look away from me to Juniper, in the chair, staring lifelessly at the TV. They ignore us as we exit and instead study Juniper.

"*Kicked* her," Linda says. "I *told* you she looked at me."

"Does she look different to you?" Stacey asks.

"Famous people always look different in the flesh," Linda replies.

"I better get her to the bed for her operation," Tina says. "Help me lift her into the wheelchair." She lifts Juniper under the arms and the others hold the wheelchair in place. Juniper does a good job of looking like a rag doll as she's lifted.

We march together down the corridor toward freedom, and I feel the greatest pain in my heart at leaving Juniper behind. Carrick holds me up and I attempt to move my legs to look like I'm walking. I know he's using all his strength to keep me upright. The two Whistleblowers who were guarding the door follow us, and I try to guess who they are. Fergus and Lorcan would be too risky to bring to a place like this; perhaps it's Mona and Lennox. One is definitely female. We all walk together out of the facility. I feel fresh air on my skin. We can't be getting away with this, we just can't.

We reach a Whistleblower van and I recognize the driver: Marcus, Professor Lambert's Whistleblower and Kate's husband.

Inside the van we all sit tight as we approach the security gates. I realize that we're at Creed Barracks, the Whistleblower training college that is the national center for Whistleblower training and education. Set on ten acres and named after the town in which it's located, Crevan has created his own facility away from the main headquarters, to hide the people who threaten him. He won't be able to keep this up for too long— my sister is in there, people who tried to help me are all in there. My heart pounds as we slow at the gates, as Marcus lowers the window.

He holds out his arm and waves confidently to the guard in the security hut.

Everybody is silent. A collective intake of breath.

The guard leaves the security hut and makes his way to Marcus.

"Can you open up the van? I just need to take a look. New rules." He looks at Marcus like he appreciates these rules as much as a hole in the head.

"Sure." Marcus unlocks the doors. "What are you looking for?"

"Extra bodies."

"Not a bad idea. We need them. It's getting wild out there," Marcus says.

"Tell me about it." The guard slides open the door and takes us all in, like he's doing more than just counting us. I feel like I'm going to vomit.

Kate lifts her helmet off. "Hi, Ryan," she says casually.

He nods at her. "Hey. Okay. Thanks." He slides the door shut, gives it two bangs with his hand.

The gates open. I will Marcus to drive away at top speed, but he can't raise suspicion. He takes his time.

Far enough away from Creed Barracks, the two mystery Whistle-blowers remove their helmets and Mona and Lennox grin at me.

"Thanks, guys." I hug them, and Mona squeezes me tightly.

"Did everyone from Vigor make it to Professor Lambert's safely?" I ask.

"Everyone except Bahee," Lennox explains. "We decided to take a detour and abandoned him on a road somewhere in town."

"We left him exactly where he dumped Lizzie," Mona explains, fire in her eyes, payback for her friend Lizzie. "We asked around for her, but it wasn't the safest area in the world. We had to get out of there fast."

I can tell she feels guilty for not searching for her friend sooner, for not realizing that her disappearance was sinister.

"We'll find her," I say encouragingly.

"Even after all he's done, Bahee actually thought we were going to bring him to Professor Lambert's with us," she says angrily. "I give him one week max on his own before the Whistleblowers find him. He's got no idea how to survive out there."

"What if he talks to the Guild?" I ask.

Carrick shrugs, nonplussed. "I doubt he'll tell anybody about Alpha and Professor Lambert. They've been his only lifeline all this time. He hasn't a clue of any of our plans anyway."

"And what a house the Lamberts have," Lennox wades in. "Good call, Celestine." He holds his hand up for a high five, and I laugh as our hands meet in the air.

"You were right, Celestine, they're good people," Carrick says, and I hear the apology in his tone.

Everyone apart from Kate and Marcus starts taking off their uniforms in the van as Marcus speeds away, no time for discretion.

"Anyone stops us now, we're taking you guys in, okay?" Kate warns, and we all agree.

Carrick hands me a bag of clothes. Juniper must have brought them. I'm gaining feeling in my legs but nowhere near enough to take off the trousers. Carrick doesn't say a word and starts untying my bootlaces. The simple act brings tears to my eyes.

"Thank you, everybody," I say again.

"We can get you out of a whole lot of little messes as long as you get us out of the big one," Lennox says, and I get it. I finally get it. We're in this together; it's not all on me. Every person here is taking a massive risk, too.

"How did you find me here?"

"Carrick followed you," Mona says.

I look at Carrick, but his eyes are down, taking off my boots.

"How did you get in touch with Juniper?"

"Last number dialed on Raphael Angelo's phone," Carrick says, with an unimpressed raise of his eyebrow. Not one of my smartest moves. Always pulling other people into my trouble.

That thought leads to another, horrible one. "What's going to happen to Juniper?" I suddenly panic. "They're planning on doing a skin graft."

"A skin graft!" Mona says, confused. "For what?"

She doesn't know about the sixth brand.

I look at Carrick, worried.

"Don't worry. There's a plan in action. Your mom is going to charge in there, with a solicitor and a police officer, as soon as we give her the word, and she's going to accuse them of taking the wrong daughter."

My mouth falls open. "Do you think it will work?"

"It will work," Whistleblower Kate says confidently, and I wonder at what point she changed sides and why, or if she was always against the Guild and just found a better way of fighting them, from within. I'd love to talk to her more, but now isn't the time.

"Maybe my mom should charge in there with Bob Tinder, too," I add.

"Bob Tinder?" Carrick's brow furrows, looking up at me as he slides a boot off my foot. "He's the new editor of *The Voice*."

"He used to be head of Crevan Media's newspaper," I explain. "He's my neighbor. His wife, Angelina, was branded. Before us. Something to do with a disagreement between Crevan and Bob, it was Crevan's way of punishing Bob. His daughter, Colleen, is in there. She's one of the missing students."

"Are all the students in there?" Kate asks suddenly, leaning forward. I nod.

"Logan Trilby?" she asks, and I cringe at the sound of his name. Just thinking of what he put me through still hurts, and he was the worst, the most malicious of them all.

"Then perhaps the famous married Trilby priests should storm in there and find their son, too," Kate says thoughtfully.

I shake my head. "His parents would go straight to the Guild with that kind of information. They're the Guild's biggest supporters; they blame me for everything. They'd never believe you." I recall their interview on Flawed TV when they blamed me for Logan's disappearance.

"They'd listen to anything if it meant finding their precious son," Kate says, sharing a knowing look with Marcus, an unspoken plan brewing between them.

"An idolized model, a respected religious duo, an angry newspaper editor. They've annoyed the wrong parents." Mona smiles, almost gleefully. "What about the other kids' parents?"

"Natasha and Gavin," I say quietly, remembering how they stripped me in the shed and examined my body's scars. Then I picture them from only moments ago, eyes glazed, practically drooling on their red hospital gowns. I'm so conflicted. I hate them and I pity them. I'm relieved they've been punished, and feel guilty at the same time.

"I say leave them in there," Carrick says angrily. I can't meet his eyes. He must know what happened to me; Pia Wang as Lisa Life documented the entire event in its awful detail.

While Marcus and Kate excitedly discuss their plans, inside I tremor, because I know exactly the place my mother will be entering and the kinds of people she will be accusing.

It won't be easy. When it comes to the Guild, nobody is untouchable.

FORTY-SIX

MARCUS DRIVES KATE, Mona, and Lennox back to Professor Lambert and Alpha's mansion, where they are all hiding. I have visions of Evelyn in a pink bedroom of her own, brushing a doll's hair, and even if it's not true, I want her to be somewhere where she feels free. I know Alpha will give her the best life she can. But Carrick and I aren't safe yet. The van stops in what seems to be the middle of nowhere, at a row of shops. It's late and they're all shut, apart from a Chinese takeout.

"Just me and you," Carrick says, sliding the van door open, checking left and right before hopping out.

I would quite happily go back to Alpha's house, have a bath, eat, sleep, and pretend none of this has happened, but it's gone too far for that. Juniper has taken my place. The clock is ticking. I have to do as much as I can before they realize she's not me.

"Good luck," Kate says, before sliding the door shut.

And as quickly as that, Carrick and I are on our own again. Creed Barracks was out of the city; Marcus and Kate brought us to the outskirts, the suburbs. Carrick is holding me up again. I look around for someplace to hide, not that it matters much at the moment, as we're on a relatively quiet backstreet and the sun is down. It is easier to hide under the cover of darkness, but harder after curfew, when checkpoints are raised, and curfew is not far off.

"What now?" I ask.

He looks at the palm of his hand as if he's reading something. "Rescue Celestine North, the most beautiful woman in the world. Tick."

I laugh in surprise, not expecting this from him.

"Next. Say sorry." He looks at me, swallows his pride. "Sorry. I'm sorry that I didn't tell you about Enya Sleepwell, but please know that my intentions were good. Everything that I've done has been for the good of the Flawed cause, for you and for me. I never wanted to hurt you. None of this has been a trick. I'm just doing all that I can."

His heart is true. I know this and I don't want to fight with him anymore. Still, no harm in letting him stew in it for a while. I wait for more from him.

"I thought that saving your life would show you how sorry I am, you know, so we wouldn't have to do the talking thing," he says, biting his lip to hide his cheeky smile.

"Um, you actually didn't *save* my life. They were going to do a skin graft, not kill me. But I appreciate being rescued all the same."

"Nothing's good enough for you," he says, amused.

I hold my hand out to his chest, palm against his brand. "*You* are. I wanted to blame somebody for all this. Someone other than my stupid self. I love my family, I never wanted to leave them. I'm not used to being by myself; it's easier when it's somebody else's fault."

I think of Juniper alone in the hospital and I shudder. Have they discovered that she's not me yet? I hope the plan holds firm and that Tina can help to make it work. I know I won't be able to relax until I know that both my mom and Juniper are safe.

"And I'm only ever used to being by myself," he says. "I'm sorry," he whispers, holding me tighter, "for what happened at the supermarket, for leaving you in the mountains. But if it's any consolation, I followed you the whole way. And you were driving way too fast down the mountain in that Mini, by the way."

"I was on a mission."

"I saw you with Art," he says, studying me.

I don't say anything.

"I heard you with Crevan."

I look down, embarrassed that my rogue plan didn't work. "Crevan knows about you. I'm sure he's guessed that you're helping me. I'm sorry. I tried to bargain with him for our freedom, which he was willing to give us, but I couldn't leave everybody else behind. I couldn't do it."

I wait for him to yell at me *What a stupid thing to do, Celestine*, but he doesn't.

"Go on, tell me I'm an idiot."

"You're brave to have tried."

"Stupid."

"A little bit stupid." Except I hear the smile in his voice. "But you were right not to take the deal. As much as I want to run away to another country and live completely freely, I couldn't do it knowing that everybody else was left behind."

I'm relieved that I made the right decision. "The other night, in your cabin, was one of the best nights of my life," I say.

He reaches down to my face, lifts my chin, and kisses me tenderly.

I close my eyes and savor the moment—who knows when we'll get to do this again?

"So why have you taken us here?" I ask as we pull away and gather ourselves.

"I want you to meet someone."

"Who?"

"Enya Sleepwell."

FORTY-SEVEN

IT USED TO be a cell phone shop. It's closed down, there's a FOR SALE sign in the window, and the glass has been painted over so no one can see in.

"She's in here?" I ask, confused. I'd have thought the possible future leader of our country would be somewhere more refined.

"When you have as many Flawed supporters as she does, you can't just meet them anywhere. She has to be careful."

He rings the bell and the door opens immediately. Carrick still has to assist me in my walking, but my strength has grown, and I limp along with him.

As soon as we're inside, I'm surprised by the setup. Desks and chairs everywhere, whiteboards showing stats and opinion poll results. Laptops hooked up to every socket around, and because it was an electronics shop, there are plenty. No one even bats an eye at me and Carrick, they're so busy watching a large plasma on the wall.

On-screen is the interview with Judge Crevan and Erica Edelman. He's wearing a sharp suit, a blue shirt and tie that make his blue eyes shine and glisten under the lights. Someone you can trust. Erica is in a neat skirt and blouse, toned legs, perfectly blow-dried hair. One of our most famous anchorwomen, she has her own show, and every politician fears her because she reduces them to schoolchildren.

I look around for Enya Sleepwell but I can't find her. I don't even know what I'll say to her. Carrick and the others show such loyalty to her, but all I've ever felt from others like Alpha and Raphael is that she hasn't quite earned her place yet to be trusted. Some accuse her of using the Flawed cause to climb her way up, which is fine if she sticks to her guns once she gets to the top.

We stand at the back of the crowd and watch the interview. I lean against the wall to prop me up.

Crevan and Erica Edelman walk around the place where he grew up, recorded footage from days earlier. He shows her the house he grew up in, his football trophies, photographs of his grandparents, things to make us think he's a human with a bloodline. And then back to the studio. Only it's not the studio. It's his living room. The grand living room that is rarely used. The beautiful fireplace, bookshelves, the walls filled with photographs of Art as a baby, moved closer together to be caught on Crevan's close-ups. I note that the photos of me have been removed.

"Mr. Crevan, starting off, let's get to know a little about you. Even the name is unusual. Where did Bosco come from?"

I like that Erica calls him Mr. Crevan and not Judge; it immediately removes him of his weaponry, makes him human again, and I know each time she addresses him as such it will bother him, hammer him down an inch or two into the ground.

"From my grandmother. She was Italian, Maria Bosco, a good Italian name, and so my parents wanted to honor her, a great woman."

"Maria Bosco, wife of Mitch Crevan, whose idea it was to begin the Guild."

"Indeed. It was him and the great prime minister Dunbar who brought in the first Guild, the tribunal, which was initially a temporary measure to look into wrongdoing within the government."

"And it was your father who brought it further."

"It was my father who upgraded it to permanent status and, along with others who played important roles, brought it to what it is today, yes."

Erica looks at him deeply, her brown eyes probing into his soul. "Tell me, Bosco, what was your childhood like?"

"We had a very happy childhood, two brothers and one sister, Candy. . . ." And he explains the story of a happy family who worked hard but reaped the rewards.

"You paint quite the glossy picture, Mr. Crevan," Erica says. "Let's go back to your younger years. Tell me about the punishments you endured at the hands of your father and grandfather."

Crevan laughs. "You make it seem so . . . draconian. It was the same disciplinary action that my father received from his father, and indeed my grandfather at the hands of his father. It wasn't . . ." He shrugs. "There were worse styles of disciplining around at that time, believe me." He smiles, trying to get off the subject.

"Tell me about it," she pushes.

He sits back, sits straighter, casting his mind back. "It was a method of discipline based on the seven main character flaws. Whatever our mis-behavior or misdemeanor was, we had to wear a sign around our neck that displayed what our flaw was."

"You wore this sign around the house?"

"No, no." He smiles as if it's a humorous memory. "We had to wear it everywhere. Soccer practice, school, you name it. I remember Candy going out on a first date with 'Greed' hanging around her neck." He laughs. "And Damon wearing 'Stubborn' around his neck during a soccer tournament. But we quickly learned. And what I mean by that is that we quickly learned how to identify our behavior, we learned what our 'chief features' were at an early age and how to control them."

"At thirteen years of age, you learned this?"

"At thirteen it was introduced to us. I think it took some time for us to learn it." He laughs again.

"Tell me about these character flaws, the chief features that you mentioned, and the purpose of the punishment."

"In brief . . . everybody, every single one of us, has a 'chief feature,' which is a negative trait. It takes control at times, resulting in a grotesque character flaw. We must learn to identify it so that we can handle it and improve our personal growth."

"Tell us the seven flaws; are they like the seven deadly sins?"

"My childhood discipline isn't part of the Guild practice." He smiles pleasantly, but his eyes are hard. "I thought we were here to talk about the Guild and dispel some of the myths the Vital Party and others are spreading, which is what I'd really like to do."

"This disciplinary action is part of your childhood. It's the roots of the Guild, if you like, so I'm interested," Erica reasons.

He inhales slowly through his nose. I can tell he's angry but he's trying to hide it. "There are seven character flaws. Self-deprecation is belittling and undervaluing oneself. Someone who does this has an inferiority complex. Self-destruction is sabotaging, punishing, and harming. Someone who does this has constant inner turmoil that makes them want to get away from themselves.

"Martyrdom is someone who denies responsibility, blames others.

"Stubbornness, resisting change, even a positive one.

"Greed is selfishness, overindulgence, overconsumption.

"Arrogance, a superiority complex, a need to be seen as better than others because being ordinary is intolerable.

"Impatience, intolerance of obstruction and delay."

"Do you use this disciplinary method with your son, Art?"

My heart pounds at the sound of Art's name. At first I feel defensive of him, a natural response to somebody I thought I loved, and then the anger sets in as I remember who he now is. But still I hold my breath while they talk about him.

He visibly tenses. "My son is eighteen years old."

"But when he was growing up?"

"No," he says simply. He shifts in his chair.

"Did that sit well with your father and grandfather? This appears to be the traditional way of doing things in the Crevan household."

He frowns at the seemingly ridiculous question. "My son didn't require this method of discipline, and it furthers my theory that people are changing. This is a new generation of cleansed people. Year after year the number of accused Flawed is falling."

"Or it could be said you placed your parental disciplinary action on an entire nation instead."

He laughs, pretending to be amused by this analysis. "I would say that is not true at all."

"Enya Sleepwell says she believes people in this country are living in fear. Is what you consider a people *changing* actually a people frozen by fear, afraid to make any mistake, any decision, take any risk in case they are punished, cast out from society?"

"No, I disagree with Enya. Again. People are now thinking *before* they act."

"And if it is through fear, is that okay? Have we overstepped the line of democracy?"

"Oh, please," he says, getting annoyed. "We live in a democratic country, the people of this great nation will have the opportunity in two days' time to take to the ballot boxes to have their voices heard."

"And if the people vote for the Vital Party, whose main policy is to abolish the Guild?"

"I don't believe that will happen," he says confidently. "The Vital Party is inexperienced. We know little about where Enya Sleepwell and her party stand on any issues other than 'not agreeing with the Guild.' This makes me wonder what Enya Sleepwell has to hide. Why does the Guild scare her so much?"

"I think it's because she finds the Guild *inhumane*," Erica says.

That gets a cheer in the room.

Erica moves on, turns a page. "I received information that there is an inquiry beginning, into you."

Crevan looks confused but manages to deal with what's been revealed to him on live television.

"There have often been inquiries into the Guild's cases. Cases have needed further clarification or detail. There are always watchdogs who keep things in line, and rightly so," he explains.

"But this inquiry is specifically looking into *you*, Mr. Crevan. One would assume it will look into some of your most controversial cases, particularly the recent, infamous Celestine North case. There are people who feel she was unfairly branded, that the case itself is flawed."

My heart pounds at hearing my name being mentioned.

"It's a private government inquiry; we've seen the documents," a voice says close to my ear, and I look around to see Enya Sleepwell standing right beside me.

I blink. Maybe things really are changing.

On-screen, Judge Crevan pauses. "I'll be happy to provide the inquiry with any information regarding the Celestine North case, but I have no knowledge of this inquiry and I'm not going to discuss any of the details of that case with you. I can assure people I am a man intent on seeing justice being done."

Crevan grinds his teeth as he waits for the next question, trying to hide his anger.

"Final question. If your grandfather and your father were alive today, which label do you think they would place around your neck *now*? What is, to quote you, your 'grotesque character flaw'?"

He thinks about it, an amused smile on his face.

"Greed," he says finally. "I want a lot, possibly *too* much for my country, for my fellow people. I want the best for us, and I suppose people may see me as I saw my father, when I was a teenager, which I do understand. If I have to be the big bad wolf in order to make our society better, so be it, but the people will thank me for it just as I thanked my father. The number of accused Flawed are falling. People are changing. People can recognize what is right and wrong immediately, they don't have the same moral codes as in my grandfather's time, when the country was in financial ruin and the place was, frankly, a disaster."

"Or you might say," Erica replies, "that our current leaders learned from their predecessors' experiences, from their *mistakes*. And for that, they can thank them."

This isn't something that appears to have occurred to Crevan, or that pleases him, but he smiles anyway, a kind of a snarl.

"I spoke to Mark Houston before this interview, in my preparation. . . ." Erica leafs through some papers on her lap.

Crevan's face lights up. "Mark. Yes, he was my friend at school. I haven't seen Mark for years." Then he frowns as he awaits what's coming next, while Erica consults her notes.

"I asked Mark if he remembered the character flaw disciplinary action that your family used. If he remembered you showing up to school, to soccer, to the movies, nights out, wherever you went, with the label around your neck. And he said yes, he did. I was curious to know which flaw was your most common one. And do you know what he said?"

"I don't, but if he remembers all the way back to a small detail like that, then Mark's memory is far better than mine." Big smile.

"He said it was easy to remember because it was always the same one. What I guess you would call your *chief feature*." She looks down to read. "It was *arrogance*, which, by your earlier explanation, would mean a superiority complex. Inflating, overvaluing oneself, *a need to be seen as better than others because being ordinary is intolerable*."

The anger on his face is penetrable.

"Mr. Crevan, thank you for joining me tonight, it has been very insightful." Erica smiles at the camera.

Everybody in the room cheers when the interview ends. The lights remain low as people turn to one another and analyze it, as others take to the Internet to garner the reaction from the public. As surveys and opinion polls and tactics are devised.

"You don't look very pleased," Enya says to me.

I shake my head. "He's going to be very angry."

And I know what Crevan is like when he's angry.

FORTY-EIGHT

"IT'S NICE TO finally meet you," Enya says.

She holds out her hand and I take it. Her grip is firm, her skin warm.

"You too," I say, hearing the uncertainty in my own voice. "Are you going to abolish the Guild if you get into power?"

She smiles. "You get right to it, don't you? Well, around here we use the word *when*, not *if*."

I note that she doesn't answer the question.

"Come with me. Let's talk in private," she says, leading me away.

Carrick watches me go, a little nervously, probably afraid I'll further insult the woman everybody here is hailing as their hero.

I'm able to stand unaided now, but my legs feel like jelly. I concentrate on trying to walk normally. Enya places a hand on my back and guides me into a small office away from the action. A group of people huddled around a computer see her and quickly shuffle outside.

Enya half sits on the table and gives me her complete attention. "You don't trust me. Why?"

"I don't trust anyone," I say simply.

"That's understandable."

"I know that Carrick trusts you. He believes in you, and so do all the people in this room, and the thousands around the country who are supporting you. I just haven't had any cause to yet." I swallow. "I just hope that you won't do a U-turn if you're voted into power."

"*When* I'm in power, I won't do a U-turn. I will do my best to uphold my promises."

"What are your promises?"

"Fair treatment for Flawed. An overhaul of the Guild," she continues.

"An overhaul? Fair treatment?" I say. "It's not enough. We need to get rid of it."

"You want it to be abolished completely?" she asks, concerned. "We can't do that straightaway, Celestine. Baby steps are required."

"Baby steps are not effective when you're living in a country that needs big leaps."

She ponders that. "You can trust me that I will keep my word to the Flawed. And if you keep doing what you're doing, being a strong role model, showing the entire population that Flawed are people and not monsters, then you're not just helping me. You're helping yourself. You're an inspiring young woman, Celestine. The country has needed somebody like you for quite some time, to start the conversation about Flawed. You've inspired me, I'm sure you can tell that from the campaign logo."

I nod. "It's . . . flattering."

"So, what now can I do for you?"

I look at her in surprise.

"I think it's time somebody helped you, don't you?"

"You would be aiding a Flawed. You would be aiding an evader," I tell her.

"Look around, Celestine."

I look through the window to everybody outside and notice the *F* armbands on the majority of her supporters, some obvious scars, some in places that can't be seen.

"I'm not aiding anybody in here," she explains. "The way I see it is everybody here is aiding me."

I smile. "Good defense." My legs feel weak and I suddenly have to sit down.

"Are you okay?"

"Crevan injected me with something to paralyze me, captured me, brought me to a private Guild facility on Creed Barracks property. I escaped."

She looks at me in shock. It takes her a while to wrap her head around the words. "What is going on with you and him, Celestine? What has got him so obsessed with you?"

"I can't tell you."

"But it's something."

I nod.

"Something big."

"Huge."

Her eyes widen.

I make a decision to trust her. "I'm working on getting the truth about Crevan out there. Will you help me?"

"Anything I can do."

––––––––––

We leave the office and Enya brings me to a man who's away from all the madness, in a quiet corner. He's hunched over a computer with the largest screen I've ever seen, surrounded by three laptops and endless wires. He wears headphones and is concentrating hard on the video on the monitor, which is footage of Enya Sleepwell on the campaign trail.

"He's editing the party political broadcast," Enya explains. "It's due to go out tomorrow night." She places a hand on his shoulder and he removes his headphones. "Pete, I have a girl here who needs your help. Give her whatever she wants."

Fired up, I take whatever I can from Pete, squeezing a laptop, a phone, and chargers into my bag. I sense Carrick behind me.

"I just spoke to Tina," he says. "Dr. Greene decided not to carry out the skin graft until first thing in the morning. So we have the night. Your mom will go in at first light."

I feel sick at the thought of Juniper spending the entire night in that horrific place. With Crevan lurking, and no doubt in a temper after that car-crash interview with Erica Edelman, anything could happen. I also feel fearful of Mom standing up to the Whistleblowers, bursting in there and accusing them of taking the wrong daughter. Will it really work? Will they really just apologize and let them both walk out of there? Will they allow any of the parents to leave with their children? I move with ferociousness now.

"Do you have permission to take this stuff?" Carrick asks in a low voice.

"Enya said I could take whatever I want."

He raises his eyebrow.

"She's nice," I finally admit.

"What are you planning?"

"We're going to visit somebody."

"Who?"

I think of the advice Raphael Angelo gave me. Instead of running from something forever, the only way to deal with it is to face it head-on.

The note Tina passed to me as I escaped contained a home address, there was nothing else attached, no name, no explanations, but I don't need it. I know exactly whose address it is.

"We're going to visit Mary May."

FORTY-NINE

WHENEVER I'M CONFUSED, I look at what I *know*: Who is against me; who is on my side. Who can I trust; who can't I trust, and how do I utilize them both. In a massive generalization: Who is against me? Non-Flawed. Who is with me? Flawed.

We can't risk making our way to either Leonard's car or Raphael's Mini so late at night, and using any of Enya Sleepwell's vehicles is a definite no. Having her implicated in helping me will destroy everything she has done to build up trust with people. We need to be among our own people, and the only transport we can safely use to get to Mary May's house is the Flawed curfew bus.

Mary May lives out of the city, past the suburbs, near the lake. I imagined her as a farmhouse type of person, maybe with horses, but perhaps animals don't like her, either. They have extra senses for people like her. I never would have suspected the lake. The lake is beautiful, magical, surrounded by rolling mountains decorated by the shadows of clouds and mountain mist. My friend Marlena's family have a second house there. She used to go most weekends, and sometimes they brought me. Mom used to take us on drives all around the lake, she used to like to watch the sunrise. Until Juniper and I started complaining about it being boring and then she just went on her own. I feel guilty about that now.

Carrick and I don't know if the footage is in Mary May's possession for sure, but it's all we've got to go on. Juniper told me that Mary May removed everything from my room and put it in her own personal car, while wearing her civilian clothes. I can't even imagine what kind of clothes they would be, or believe that she would possess an item of clothing that wasn't some kind of Whistleblower uniform. But I do know that Mary May must be under immense pressure from Crevan to find me and the footage. She was responsible for both, and she let them slip through her fingers. If she's taken my things anywhere, it must be to her own home, where she can search on her own time. They're only objects, but I think of all my possessions sitting in her house. Teddies, photographs, books, clothes, the only things that *I* own, all taken away from me.

Juniper has provided me with a cap, and I keep it low over my head and let my hair down to cover my branded temple. We wear *F* armbands that we were given at Enya's office, to make sure we don't stand out. A Flawed person on a Flawed bus without an armband would cause alarm bells to ring. It has been weeks since I've worn the armband, and sliding it up my arm feels like a weight being added to my body. I can tell Carrick is feeling the same, as his demeanor completely changes once it's on. But I suppose that is the entire point, for us to feel harassed, humiliated, and isolated from society.

At least Carrick was spared having to reveal his scar every day, though when it seemed the brandings were unfair to those whose brands could be seen, the *F* armbands were brought in to eliminate that little loophole.

We join the crowded curfew bus stop, filled with Flawed. Our own people. Carrick wears a cap low and stays close to me, head down. I keep my back to everybody.

Once on the bus, each Flawed swipes his or her identity card and takes a seat.

"We don't have identity cards," Carrick whispers.

"Yes, we do," I say, reaching into my backpack and handing him the two cards I borrowed from Enya's team. If she does care about them so much, she can help them get new identity cards.

Carrick looks down at them with surprise, and laughs with admiration at my resourcefulness. Though I am Harlan Murphy, thirty-year-old computer analyst, and he is Trina Overbye, a fortysomething-year-old librarian.

When we get on the bus we keep our eyes down and sit in the back row. I don't know if anybody is looking at me because I'm not looking at them.

I should feel safe in a bus full of Flawed, these are my people, but I'm afraid. A message appears on the screen at the head of the bus. It's a Guild-sponsored piece, as all the pieces are on Flawed transport. It's a photo of Carrick. My heart drums and I elbow him roughly to get his attention.

The photograph was taken at Highland Castle when he was brought in by the Whistleblowers. I recognize the backdrop, like a mug shot. He stares down the lens with pure hatred and venom, looking like a total badass, his neck thick, the muscles in his shoulders all pumped up.

Beneath the photo is the word EVADER.

And the voice-over, Pia Wang's perky replacement.

"Carrick Vane is on the run with Celestine North. He is her accomplice. If anybody finds them, call this number and you will be rewarded."

For a Flawed, to be offered a reward is like letting a child loose in a candy shop.

"Juniper," I say to Carrick. "They know she's not me. We're out of time."

"No, it doesn't mention you," he says. "Look."

And he's right. This piece is just about Carrick. Crevan still thinks that he has me in the hospital, and now he needs to silence Carrick. In the morning my mom and her team will swoop in on Crevan's hospital and he'll know that I have escaped him again. He'll want my head on a plate.

The woman in the seat in front of us turns around to stare at us. I look up and see a few more heads turn.

"It's okay," Carrick says, keeping his head down.

But it's not okay, at some point every single person on the bus has turned around to look at us. I see some tapping on their phones.

Suddenly the bus pulls over to the side of the road and my heart thuds. Carrick and I are holding hands—I'm at the window; he's at the aisle—his thumb circles the brand on my palm. I don't know if he even notices that he's doing it. It's like he's guarding my wounds, like whatever the world thinks is ugly, he cherishes.

The driver stands and leaves the wheel. He addresses us all. "I'll need everybody to get off the bus for a moment. Go shelter in the café, have a coffee, take a pee break, whatever you want."

There are groans, some worried faces.

"What's going on?" I whisper.

Carrick shrugs.

"No, no, no, I will not accept this," a man stands up and shouts. "This is the *third* time this week that my bus has been delayed. I won't hear of it. We get off the bus, we suddenly can't get back on. Problem with the engine, problem with the tires. And then what? I miss the curfew again, another punishment. I'm not getting off this bus." He folds his arms.

Some others cheer him on.

"This is a setup," somebody else shouts, and there are louder cheers.

Most people don't want any trouble at all and just get straight off the bus. A half-dozen people remain.

"Look." The driver sighs. "I'm under orders. They just radioed it in. I have to pull the bus over and wait for a mechanic. I'm just doing what I'm told."

The passengers all shout at him, waving their hands dismissively. Nobody moves from their seats.

"We should get off," Carrick says, making a move, but I pull him back down.

"Wait."

The problem for the Guild is that with a Flawed bus, everyone on it is Flawed. For people who are not usually allowed to gather in more than twos, there was no getting around the rule when they created the curfew bus. At the beginning there was a Whistleblower on each bus, but then it proved too costly, so it was a Whistleblower as the driver. But then leading up to an election campaign, the bus drivers went on strike, said their jobs were being taken from them. The government wanted to create new employment and opened the bus jobs back up to civilians. Surveillance cameras were installed in the buses instead to make sure of no uprising plans.

An old woman turns around and addresses me and Carrick. "Can't you two do something about this?"

Everyone twists around to look at us. The driver included.

"Shit," Carrick whispers.

"What are you two up to?" the driver asks, recognizing us immediately.

"As if they're going to tell you," the old woman barks at him. "They're young; they've time on their side; they're doing exactly what the rest of us should have done from the beginning."

I smile at her gratefully.

"Look." The driver holds his hands up. "I got a grandson who's Flawed. Couldn't stand the sight of you all until that happened to him. Guess you could say it opened my eyes."

Silence.

"I don't want to be on this bus with these two," another woman shouts. "I'll get into trouble for just having seen you. You've made us suffer enough. Why don't you just keep your head down and do what you're told, Celestine North? Stop getting the rest of us into trouble."

I stand up and address the bus, my legs shaky.

"I'm on your side, remember? I'm trying to prove that we're *not* Flawed. Or if we are, that there's nothing wrong with that. We've made our mistakes, we've learned from them. I just need some time to make it all come together."

"She's the only one who's speaking up for us," one woman says. "The only person who's not using violence, at least. Those hooligans behind the riots aren't doing anything to help our cause, at least Celestine is doing it peacefully."

"Yes, she's right. The people like her, you know, I've overheard them talking. They're confused about it, but they *like* her. They're talking about whether she had a fair trial. Can you believe they're talking about a Flawed like that?"

"Nothing will come of it," a man says. "It will die down like talk always has."

"What talk?" the old woman snaps. "There's *never* been this amount of support for Flawed. We need to help it grow."

"The support won't die down," I say firmly to the man. "I won't let it."

The bus driver seems to take all this in, considers the arguments thoughtfully, as though he's judge and jury on his own bus.

"Are you going to make my grandson free again?" he asks.

"I'm trying my best."

He nods again. Looks at Carrick. "Are you helping her?"

"She's helping us all."

"Where are you going?"

I hand him the address. He studies it. "I'm guessing this is important."

I nod.

"Everyone else is getting off, and I'm taking these two wherever they need to go—does anybody have anything to say about it?"

The doubters don't say a word.

"Any word to anyone about this and I'll tell them you're a bunch of liars, do you hear?" the driver threatens.

The women in front of me shake our hands and wish us luck.

"I want you to know I'm only getting off this bus for them," says the man who started the protest in the first place. He looks at me. "Do it for us, Celestine. You can do it." He points a finger in the driver's face as he passes. "You better get them where they need to go."

My eyes fill with tears, in gratitude for the gesture. I have to do this for them, for everyone.

The driver sits down behind the wheel and closes the door, stopping any of the others from boarding again. They all glare at the bus angrily. He starts the engine and drives off.

It was on a bus that I lost my faith in humanity. It was on a bus that it was restored.

FIFTY

THE DRIVER DROPS us as near to Mary May's address as possible, but it's difficult to get too close, as a Flawed curfew bus off the beaten track would attract too much attention.

Mary May's cottage, with its thatched roof, sits alone by a fishing pier. There is a sharp turn right into her driveway before the end of the pier, and her garden juts out into the lake. Fishing paraphernalia bobs gently on the shore. The lights are off in her house. I hope that she's not home, which would make this all the easier, but so far nothing has been easy.

We make our way down the pier and climb the wall attached to her garden, a long lawn of luscious exotic flowers, well tended, with a pretty bridge across a stream. Such a picturesque place for a monster to reside.

We keep low and I follow Carrick, hiding behind Mary May's shrubbery to get in a good position to view the house. It's the back of the house that faces out to the lake, the back of the house that does all the living. The plan had been so simple—go to Mary May's house and grab the snow globe—but now that we're here I see the gaping holes in my idea. How we are going to get in being the biggest problem.

"How are we going to do this?" I whisper.

"We ring the bell, tie her up, I punch her if I have to, punch her even if I don't have to. You grab the snow globe."

I look at him, certain that is the lamest idea I've ever heard.

"If we hurt her, it will get us into more trouble. The police will be after us, too. Mary May is the most prized Whistleblower."

"So I won't hurt her. I'll just tie her up. Really tight."

"Carrick," I say, frustrated, "we need to think of something other than brute force."

He looks at me blankly.

I curse, knowing I'm alone on the plan-making front. I can understand his nerves, just the very idea of what we're risking by being here. I study the house, trying to figure out a way to break in. A figure appears at the door. The back door opens suddenly and we duck.

"Crap. It's her." I'm sure she's seen us; who goes out to their garden for a leisurely stroll after 11:00 PM?

An old lady in a nightdress wanders outside barefoot onto the grass. She has long gray hair, plaited to one side, and appears like a kind of ghostly vision, in her floating white gown in the dark night.

She has left the back door open, I can see Carrick looking at it. I know what he's thinking, but my gut instinct says he's wrong to make a run for it.

The old woman looks like Mary May, and I know instantly that it's her mother, the only member of her family other than Mary May not to be branded. Mary May must have had a soft spot for her mother. The old woman picks up a watering can by the back door and proceeds to water the hanging baskets. No water comes out.

"Tsk, tsk, tsk." She sighs. She looks out to the lake and makes her way down the garden.

"Okay. I run into the house, you keep a lookout," Carrick says, getting ready to run.

"Wait." I grab him. It takes my two hands around his biceps to hold him back. "We can't just leave her. She's dangerously close to the water. She'll fall in."

"What is it with you helping old people?" he asks, but his voice is soft and his touch on my hand is warm.

She's lying on the grass, leaning over the edge, trying to reach down to the lake with her watering can. I make my way over to her. I take the can from her, and without saying a word, I scoop it full with water and hand it back to her.

She eyes me warily, not coldly but curiously, as if trying to place me.

"Is he coming for me tonight?" she asks with a sweet voice, almost childlike.

I don't say a word, unsure as to what she means.

"Our Lord. He's sent you to take me. It's all right." She straightens up. "I'm ready. I'll see my Andy again." She looks back at the house. "I should make my peace with her. I hope the Lord will be kind to her." She looks at me hopefully. "She has done things for reasons she thinks are right. I'm her mother, I'll go before him and speak for her. But the others . . . they'll never forgive her. I hope they forgive me. It's because of her they're Flawed." She hardens again. "I know that I don't remember much but I remember that. She's looking for something. Do you know what it is she's looking for?"

I nod.

"Every night, she goes to the garage. Does he know where it is? If he does, I think she'd find peace. It's driving her . . ." A light goes on in the cottage and we both look up.

"She's coming," she whispers. "How much time do I have before he takes me?"

My heart is banging in my chest at the sight of Mary May stepping outside and breaking out into a run across the grass.

"Mother!" she screams angrily.

I hold my finger over my lips, hoping Carrick's frantic waving won't catch her eye. Mary May's mother nods. "You'll come for me?"

I nod.

At peace with that, she takes the watering can and I quickly duck out of view in the darkness, behind a bush. Carrick throws me a warning look, but we don't move, there's nowhere for us to move to now, except into the lake. If we have to, we will. He places a protective arm around my waist, he holds me tightly.

Mary May's mother is looking out over the lake like it's for the last time, drinking it in with an air of finality, not sadness. Contentment, satisfaction, acceptance. I feel guilty for this misunderstanding, but she does seem happy with it.

"Mother!" Mary May's voice has an edge to it, a growl. She's in her nightdress, too, and unhappily traipses across the grass to her mother.

"I was collecting water for the flowers," her mother says distantly. "There has been no rain for days."

"How many times have I told you not to lean over the edge? It's dangerous! You could fall in. How did you . . . Mother, where did this water come from?"

"The angel, the kind angel. She's here for me."

"Angel?" Carrick whispers, covering his face with his hands.

I don't want to explain myself out of fear Mary May will hear me speak. With her supersonic Whistleblower senses, I'm surprised she hasn't sniffed us out already. She takes the watering can from her mother. "No more angel nonsense, Mother. It's after eleven; you should be in bed. I'm going to have to get an alarm system if you keep this up."

Carrick and I look at each other. No alarm system.

"Andy likes to have the flowers watered, he insists."

"Daddy is gone, Mommy, remember?"

"Alice likes to pick the petals and use them for her art."

Mary May sucks in air. "Don't you dare say her name in my company," she hisses. She empties the water back into the lake, takes her mother's elbow, and guides her back to the house.

"Where are they all?" her mother asks, in a desperate childish way.

208

"Why won't you ever tell me? I want to see my children. I want to know that they're all safe. I want to say good-bye."

"You don't need to say good-bye, you're safe here with me, remember? Just you and me, Mother, we don't need the others."

Carrick and I watch them go back inside the house.

"She's even more messed up than I thought," he whispers.

She's training the future Whistleblowers. I think of Art and of how much she's poisoning his mind. Who knows what she has told him about me. She could tell him any lie and he'd probably believe it. And am I trying to make excuses for Art again? I shake him out of my head.

A light goes on in the front room.

"Mother's bedroom," Carrick says. "Where the hell do we find this snow globe? It could be anywhere."

"The garage," I say, looking to the connected building.

"How do you know?"

"Her mother said she's looking for something in the garage. It must be in there."

We see Mary May pass by the back door again, then another light goes on and reveals the kitchen. She keeps walking and goes into the connected garage. A light goes on in the two high windows. The only way into the garage is through the house, or through the car entrance at the other side.

We hear thrashing sounds, boxes being moved, crashing, then screaming, demented screeching. It's disturbing, like a witch being burned at the stake, a tortured scream of anguish and frustration.

It sounds as though she's trashing the place, and I'm afraid she will smash the globe and find the footage hidden inside, or damage it. It's chilly outside, the breeze coming from the lake. I shudder in my thin T-shirt; Carrick takes me in his arms and kisses my neck, and I'm warmed instantly by his body heat.

Mary May searches for twenty minutes, then there's silence. She's exhausted from her frenzy. The light goes out in the garage. She appears in the kitchen, haggard, her hair standing up crazily, loose from its usual pristine bun. She goes to the sink, takes a drink of water, stares outside almost as if she's seeing us. I shiver again and Carrick tightens his grip on me.

The light goes out and she disappears. Her bedroom is in the front of the cottage, her mother's facing us in the back.

"I say give her forty-five minutes, then we'll move," Carrick says. "It's going to take her a while to settle after that frustration."

I sigh impatiently. So close yet so very far.

"We can't wait that long, Carrick. If Crevan discovers that I'm free, who do you think he'll call? She'll be the first one."

"I told you, we have time," he says, looking at his watch. "They've delayed the surgery until the morning. Your mom isn't going in for at least another seven hours. She won't be going in alone. Tina is guarding Juniper. Crevan isn't there. Everything is okay. If Crevan arrives, Tina will let me know."

"Seven hours is too much time." I shake my head, thinking of all the things that can go wrong in that time. I settle down to watch the house, with a sick feeling in my stomach.

Granddad locked up in Highland Castle while they build a case against him, their line about holding him for twenty-four hours an unsurprising lie; Juniper in a dodgy makeshift hospital, my mom about to barge in there declaring injustice and criminality; Carrick on the Wanted list. We're all in danger now. I can't drag them down with me. This plan needs to work.

FIFTY-ONE

WE WATCH MARY May's house like hawks. Forty minutes later, when it is still and she hasn't stirred for some time, we make our move. Carrick ducks down and moves quickly across the yard, to the garage, to see if he can gain access without needing to go through the house. There's no door, no lock to fiddle with, no glass to break, and the two windows high up are too narrow to slide through. We have no option but to gain entry through the house.

I go to the mother's bedroom window, heart pounding, and gently rap on the window, praying Mary May isn't inside.

Her mother appears at the window, which startles me. A bright white gown, skin and gray hair more eerie than angelic in this light. I put my finger across my lips. I motion to the front door and she moves quietly. The door opens and I step inside, leaving the door open for Carrick, and follow her to her room. The house is so quiet and I tiptoe, while Carrick and his boots are so heavy it's harder for him to be nimble through the house, so I almost have a heart attack each time he bumps something or the floor creaks. The house smells of baking, mixed with a stale musty stench.

Across the narrow hall is Mary May's bedroom. The door is ajar, presumably so she can be on the lookout for her mother's wanderings. I go inside her mother's room and close the door gently.

"Sit, sit," she says, holding her hand out.

I sit in the chair beside her. She is sitting up in her bed, propped up by pillows.

"I'm ready for him," she says, lifting her chin bravely.

I freeze, not knowing quite what to say, hoping Carrick will locate the snow globe before this all unravels.

"Do you know what it is that Mary's searching for?" she asks again. I nod.

"You will find it for her?"

"I'm trying," I whisper.

"And will it make it right again?"

I nod.

"All I want is to see my children again," she says, her eyes filling with tears, her voice sounding childlike. "She took them away from me."

I reach out and hold her hand to comfort her.

"She was always a little . . . peculiar. As a child, she wanted things so much, *too* much. She loved Henry so much; she was . . . obsessed with him. When Henry fell in love with her little sister, Alice, Mary couldn't bear it. She turned on Alice, turned on everyone in the family who hid it from her. She tore us all apart." Her tears fall; even after all this time, the pain is raw. "But despite what she has done, I'm her mother. I just ask that the Lord is kind to her," she says, pleading at me with her eyes. "She has hurt so many, but it is because she is hurting."

I offer her a tissue, and she wipes away the tears.

She gathers herself, as if preparing for what's about to come. "I'm not scared. I think it means that I'm ready."

There's a rap on the bedroom window and we both jump with fright. I'm sure it's all over now; Mary May has called the Whistleblowers. They'll be outside surrounding the house, a helicopter hovering above with a spotlight on me. Flawed TV capturing the live arrest. Heart pounding, I pull back the curtains and it's Carrick, shaking the snow globe at me.

"Who is it?" she asks fearfully, pulling the blankets tight around her.

I feel giddy, the adrenaline pumping. I take her hands and squeeze them warmly. "It's not your time to go," I whisper.

"No?" she asks, surprised.

I shake my head and smile. "Go back to sleep. You will see your family soon. I'll make sure of it."

I help her lie down, wrapping the blankets tightly around her tiny frame. She closes her eyes and relaxes, a smile on her face at the very thought of her reunion.

FIFTY-TWO

SIX HOURS LATER, Raphael Angelo and I are in Judge Sanchez's home. A glass-and-marble penthouse apartment in the tallest building in the city, it's a stark contrast to Raphael's mountain retreat. There is big money in being a Guild judge, branding citizens and looking down on others, from the bench in the courtroom to the penthouse apartment in the city. People are mere specks in the park below her window, almost nonexistent, decisions are made without a connection to humanity.

But reality has been brought into Judge Sanchez's home now. She's barely awake, the sleep still in her eyes, thanks to us bursting into her home at the crack of dawn.

She is almost unrecognizable without the red lipstick and matching red-framed glasses for which she is known. She wears no makeup, her hair is scraped back in a clip, and she wraps her body in a black cashmere cardigan as if she's cold, but it's not cold in here at all.

We stand in an open-plan kitchen/living/dining room; it's enormous, with floor-to-ceiling windows and a glass ceiling. She catches me looking at it.

"My son, Tobias, is a stargazer," she says. "The reason we bought here."

"I believe the professional word is astronomer," a teenager says, appearing in the kitchen, looking sleepy-eyed and messy-haired, tightening his robe belt. He looks around the same age as me: He's handsome, stands tall, with an air of arrogance.

"Only if you're *paid* to look at them," she says, focusing on the laptop computer Raphael is placing down before her.

Her son looks at me, registers me, then looks to his mom in surprise. Celestine North is in his home.

"Coffee, Mom?" he asks.

I find it hard to believe that she could be anybody's mother. That she would have a heart big enough to love and care for somebody. The mirror has two faces. Though, I suppose Sanchez is trying to help me, even if it's for her own gain.

She shakes her head to the coffee.

"Yes, please," Raphael calls to him.

"My mom likes to look down, I like to look up," he says, brewing the coffee. "Would you like to come upstairs and have a look?" he asks me. "I have a telescope in the atrium."

I don't want to see what Raphael and Judge Sanchez are about to watch, but I know I should be here. It's too important to miss.

"No, thanks," I say politely.

He runs his eyes over me. I see that his robe bears the crest of the most prestigious boarding school in the country.

"They shouldn't have found you Flawed," he says loudly, as if he's deliberately trying to annoy his mom. "I told her that. It was a preposterous verdict. Something sinister at play, I'm guessing."

The USB was found, just as Tina said, in the base of the snow globe. The snow globe had been set aside from all my other belongings in the garage; Carrick hadn't taken long to find it. It was as though Mary May's allegiance to the Guild had stopped her from even considering that the proof that would destroy her leader could lie in something so close to her heart. The USB was sitting inside the false bottom, which was easily found after unscrewing it. After finding it, we called Raphael from the burner phone we took from Enya's campaign office, and he collected us from the lake. I didn't want to view the footage. I left the car while Raphael and Carrick watched it. From their faces afterward I could tell what needed to be seen had been captured. Raphael couldn't look at me, and Carrick couldn't stop.

I'd thought it was best not to bring Carrick here with us. Someone like Sanchez uses what she needs and discards the rest. Carrick has no value to Sanchez and could very easily have been sent straight to Highland Castle on first sight. And besides, right about now my mom and Bob Tinder are storming the Whistleblowers' training center, and soon Crevan will know I'm free. Carrick is safer away from me, and I need him to help my mom and Juniper.

I check the burner for an update from Carrick. There's nothing.

I look into the kitchen at the television, wanting to see if there's any news. No surprise Sanchez watches News 24, Crevan media. But there don't seem to be any breaking news reports about my mom and Juniper, only of course there wouldn't be, not on News 24. They would bury that detail. Bob Tinder won't.

Tobias hands me a cup of coffee even though I didn't ask for one, and one to Raphael, too. I need it, though—I haven't slept all night and I'm exhausted, running only on adrenaline.

"Thank you." I take it from him, touched by the simple act of kindness. I smell coffee, I know it's coffee. I taste. Nothing.

"Tobias, out," Sanchez says sternly, and her son strolls away, chin up, shoulders back, newspaper rolled in his hand, off somewhere to read it.

I position myself behind Sanchez so I have a view of the screen. Now that I'm with Judge Sanchez I need to see what she sees, and I need to see how she sees it.

"Who else has a copy of this?" Sanchez asks before Raphael plays it.

"This is the original," Raphael says. "We haven't shown it to anyone."

"This was filmed on Mr. Berry's mobile phone. He must have transferred it to a computer in order to save it to the USB," she says.

"We believe Judge Crevan found the laptop and memory card when he found Mr. Berry. This is the only footage remaining. The footage he has been searching for," Raphael explains.

"And you expect me to believe you didn't make another copy before you got here?" She raises her eyebrows.

Raphael looks at me. "Give it to her."

My mouth falls open in surprise. "Raphael."

"Absolute honesty," he says. "It's the only way for this to work, Celestine."

Annoyed, I take the copy we made and put it on the table in front of Judge Sanchez. She pockets it immediately.

They press play and Raphael sits back in his chair, knowing what's about to come. Sanchez sits forward.

I hover in the back, chew all my fingernails down.

The picture begins. The image is shaky. I see a floor, then it bumps around, blurry, loud voices and commotion. A glimpse of my mom's shoes, moving away, my dad yelling, the mess as they're all removed from the viewing room. Sanchez looks at Raphael, annoyed, as if this is a waste of her time.

The camera lifts and the Branding Chamber comes into view. You can see the back of Crevan, in his bloodred gown. He blocks me in the chair.

The phone lowers again, more shouting, more commotion, a blurry picture.

"Oh, come on," Sanchez snaps impatiently. "So Crevan is in the chamber at the time of the branding, this proves nothing."

"Keep watching," Raphael says calmly.

Mr. Berry moves to get a better view. He's standing outside the door, which is why I never saw him. Crevan moves and I'm in view. I'm strapped in the chair, and seeing myself like that is upsetting enough. My mouth is clamped open. I feel sick at the memory of that horrendous moment.

Mr. Berry seems to get shoved away at this point and his camera drops. We watch his feet. Then Whistleblowers' boots, a third pair of shoes. Carrick's sneakers.

"Keep filming," Carrick says, his voice clear on the tape.

Judge Sanchez's head snaps up to me. "Whose voice is that?"

We both ignore her. The phone is lifted just in time to see my tongue being branded. And then Crevan starts shouting.

"Repent, Celestine."

He paces before me in the chair, the picture perfectly clear. "Repent!"

The guards are unstrapping me from the chair. They all appear shaken, including Bark, who branded me, and Funar, who hated me. They are helping me into a wheelchair.

"Brand her spine," Crevan says suddenly. It's loud and clear, and I'm so relieved that we've got him.

I move away from the computer not because I can't bear to see it but because I want to see Judge Sanchez's face. I need to see her witness what happened to me under her power.

Her face is blank, unreadable, controlled. Not a sign of any emotion, no pity, no sympathy, nothing. Her eyes move across the images, processing them all like a robot.

As I hear Crevan shout, the guards putting up a fight, Crevan grabbing the branding rod, and then my own guttural sounds, she doesn't blink once. Raphael scratches his head, his nose, fidgets in his chair, uncomfortable, and as my spine is branded without anesthetic and I scream out in utter anguish, so loudly that Tobias returns to see what's going on, she doesn't even blink.

The video finishes.

She looks up at me, cool as a cucumber. But it's too cool; it's too calm; it's too obvious that it's a mask to hide how she really feels.

"He'll argue that it's a reenactment."

"Baloney," Raphael says.

"Was that . . . ?" Tobias asks, in shock.

"All you have to do is go on YouTube and you'll find hundreds more like it." Sanchez ignores her son.

"This is clearly authentic," Raphael says.

"Did Crevan . . . ?" Tobias asks again. Nobody pays attention.

"Her Flawed character, his power and persuasion, he could convince people this isn't real," Judge Sanchez continues.

"There's this." I turn around and show her the brand on my body.

"Oh my God," Tobias says, hands going to his head, his coolness gone.

"Tobias! Out!" she shouts. "This is none of your business!" He looks at her with shock and then anger. He storms back to his bedroom.

Sanchez turns back to us. "This spine brand doesn't appear to take the same shape as the other brands."

"She wasn't strapped down, there wasn't any anesthetic, Judge Crevan did it to her himself, the girl screamed bloody murder with the agony—you saw it yourself. Her brand is perfect, in keeping with the events we just viewed." Raphael looks at her incredulously, trying to stay calm, but his anger is obvious. "What's going on here? I thought you wanted to remove Crevan from the Guild. Have you lost your nerve?"

"No, I haven't lost my nerve, and removing Judge Crevan as head judge *is* my plan."

"You told me to bring you the proof to take Crevan down and I did," I say, anger rising because I can sense her backing out.

She looks at me then and for the first time her expression changes.

"You brought me too much, Celestine. What you have here is enough to bring down the entire Guild. Now I know why Crevan wants you so much."

FIFTY-THREE

I LOOK AT Raphael nervously. He shares a similar look. We just went from advantage to disadvantage. We are in a precarious position. Sanchez wanted Crevan out, not to bring an end to the Guild. This gives her reason to be the cat and me the mouse once again.

Raphael clears his throat. "So this gives us the opportunity to make a deal."

Sanchez's head snaps around to him so fast. "Are you threatening me?"

"Are you threatening my client?" he replies coolly.

Her forehead wrinkles a little.

"Judge Sanchez, the game hasn't changed here. We brought you what you wanted, but this doesn't have to go public. You can use the video in any way you want to discredit Crevan. You're still in control here. All that needs to happen is that Crevan's actions are found to be not in keeping with Guild rules and he is discharged. And my client's verdict is therefore overturned."

She's thinking hard. "But Crevan will know I won't want anyone to see this. I have nothing on him. I was part of the judging committee that allowed this to happen. Whether I knew about it or not, I am also responsible. It will fall to all three Guild judges—me, Jackson, and Crevan—to take responsibility."

"Not if you bring it to light. You get to make the first move," Raphael says.

"We have him," I say, hearing the tremor in my voice.

"What I have, Celestine"—she looks at me—"is *you*. And Crevan is looking for you."

"You're going to use me to get what you want," I say.

"This is preposterous," Raphael yells, jumping down from his seat. "This is unethical, immoral, unprincipled, and below the very laws that the Guild practices. I'll fight you on this all the way," Raphael says. "There is an inquiry into Crevan already. This is the beginning of the end for the Guild. You need to choose whose side you're on. That of the survivors, or the sinking ship."

"You're right. I'm a survivor."

Raphael looks relieved.

"It's just a shame I see your cause as the sinking ship. It will be very difficult for you to fight this all the way, Raphael, when you're being held by the Guild for aiding a Flawed."

"He's my lawyer. We signed a contract."

"Representing an evader."

Raphael is shaking his head, a big smile on his face, as though finding the dismal situation hilarious.

He looks at me. "Come on, Celestine, let's get out of here."

"I'm afraid I'm not going to let you leave." She picks up the phone. "Grace, it's me. Get Crevan on the phone immediately."

I rush for the USB, which is still in the laptop, but she grabs it from me and shoves me away. She's stronger than I thought and I fall back against the coffee table, which shatters as my elbow whacks the glass. Raphael runs to my side.

"Are you okay?"

"Tobias!" she calls.

Her son appears, dressed now in his boarding school tracksuit, assesses the situation, me on the floor lying on broken glass, his mom on the phone. He knows her well.

"What did you do?" he asks his mother.

"Stop them from leaving." She rushes to her bedroom with her mobile to her ear. "Damn it, Grace, keep calling him. I need to speak to him immediately. *Tobias*, lock the door *now*!" she yells as she closes the bedroom door behind her.

Tobias rushes to the front door and locks it, then keys a number into a control panel. A robotic voice announces the apartment is in lockdown. Someone in Sanchez's position needs high security. Tobias looks at us uncertainly.

Raphael is strong, but not enough of a match for Tobias.

"Let us out," Raphael says. "You can't hold us here against our will. You saw the video, you know what Crevan did. You know who's right and who's wrong here."

Tobias, panicking, can't make a decision. The sweat breaks out on his brow.

Raphael shakes his head, disgusted. "The problem with people who are always gazing at the stars is that they often miss what's going on around them. You seem like a nice boy. Your mother doesn't. Seem like a nice woman, that is."

Tobias looks worriedly from him to me, where Raphael is pulling me up from the shattered glass. Thankfully none of it has punctured my skin.

"I can't do this," Tobias mutters, his upper lip breaking out in sweat. "Mom!" he yells at the top of his voice so that she comes running out of her bedroom, half-dressed. "You're on your own. I can't do this anymore. You say you're right, you say it all the time, but . . ." His voice catches. "You should hear how they talk about you at school. They're talking about marching on the castle. *Protesting* the Guild. I'm embarrassed to say who you are, and what you do, to my own friends."

"It's *Crevan*, Tobias," she says, in a tone that I'm not used to hearing from her, her mom voice. "He's brought our reputation down, but I'm doing *this* to fix it. People will believe in the Guild again. I promise you. I want you to be proud of me, but you have to trust me."

"No." He shakes his head. "You're just as bad as him. I'm beginning to wonder who the Flawed really are. It's not them. . . ." He takes a deep breath, summoning the courage. "It's you." He spits it at her. He enters the alarm code, unlocks the front door, and storms out, leaving it wide open.

FIFTY-FOUR

RAPHAEL AND I both stare at the open door in surprise.

Judge Sanchez is momentarily stunned by her son's leaving her alone in this situation, but then she recovers. Instead of chasing after him, she slams the door and fires the code into the keypad. We are once again in lockdown. She has one heel on, the other foot in a stocking. She's wearing a burgundy pencil skirt and a red silk blouse. The red lips and red-framed glasses are back on.

Her phone rings from her bedroom and she slowly backs away from us, torn between answering her phone and afraid of leaving us alone. She runs to her room. The ringing stops on her way and we hear her curse.

I check my own phone to see if there's a message from Carrick.

Juniper out. Everybody safe. You?

The relief floods through me. The good news fires me up and I get an idea. It's okay for Crevan to now know that I'm no longer in his control. Juniper is safe; Mom is safe; Carrick is safe.

"What are you doing?" Raphael asks as I pick up the phone on Judge Sanchez's desk.

"Connect me to Highland Castle, please," I say quickly.

"*What* are you doing?" Raphael hurries over to me.

I block the cradle, afraid he'll end the call, and mouth, "Trust me."

He backs off a little.

"Hello, my name is Celestine North, and I'd like to turn myself in," I say quickly, while Raphael practically rolls around in horror. He stretches to try to reach the phone but I stand on a chair to get farther from him.

"I'm at Judge Sanchez's apartment in Grimes Tower, and I would like to be taken away from here immediately. Thank you." I hang up the phone, my heart pounding.

"Why did you do that?" he asks.

"Judge Sanchez is phoning Crevan. She wants to make a deal with him. Do you think either of them is going to allow us to be officially taken into the Guild's custody, knowing what we know about them? We would actually be safer if the Whistleblowers take us in."

Raphael suddenly turns around and sits up. "I hadn't thought of that. You know what, that might be one of your cleverest ideas yet. It's my intelligence—it's rubbing off on you."

"We just have to hope the Whistleblowers get here first."

Judge Sanchez checks on us now and then, while desperately trying to make contact with Crevan, dialing every number she can think of. She doesn't want us to hear her make a deal using my freedom for her own gain, and so she talks in a low voice in another room. Raphael and I sit in the living room awaiting our fate. Within minutes there's banging on the door. I look out the spyhole and I've never been so happy to see red helmets.

"Whistleblowers," I say.

We high-five.

FIFTY-FIVE

"WHISTLEBLOWERS!" THEY SHOUT. "Open the door!"

"I'm afraid I can't," Raphael says, cool as anything, through the door. "We're locked in and we can't open it. I think you'll have to break down the door."

Despite what's going on, Whistleblowers about to break down the door to take me away, it's so easy to be sucked into Raphael's blasé view of the world. I feel as cool as he is acting. Though I know that is only for appearance's sake; a man who is vegan and decorates his entire office in faux human trophies just to make a point, and spends his life fighting for justice for others, isn't blasé about anything. Perhaps that's why I'm smiling, because I know that beneath all the jokes, he means business.

"Stand back, we're going to breach the door," one shouts, and we do.

I expect to hear a mechanical lock pick but instead there's a bang on the door.

"A sledgehammer," Raphael says, leaning against the wall, arms folded. "They came prepared."

There's a second bang against the door.

"What's going on?" Judge Sanchez says, firing herself out of her bedroom, and in a flap. I wonder if she got to negotiate with Crevan yet. If my life has been traded for her power.

"Whistleblowers are here," I explain calmly.

"What?" She looks from me to Raphael in horror. Our calm demeanors are no doubt rattling her even more. "No. They can't be."

BANG.

"They are," Raphael backs me up, and pops a mint into his mouth. "I daresay we wouldn't hear the whistles from all the way up here."

Her face crinkles up. *"What?"*

She is so unsettled, it is amusing.

BANG.

"What are they doing?"

"Breaching the door," Raphael explains.

"What? Why? Hello! Helloo! Please stop!"

"Because we're locked in," I explain.

She attempts her authoritative voice but she can't be heard from the other side of the door, where the Whistleblowers are concentrating hard on knocking it down with a sledgehammer.

The door finally caves in.

Judge Sanchez jumps back as sawdust, wood, and part of a sledgehammer come flying in on her plush carpet. There are a dozen Whistleblowers outside.

"Judge Sanchez," one young man says, breaking through the door and stepping in. "We received information that Celestine North is here. Are you okay?"

Judge Sanchez looks at him in disgust, at her carpet, at her silk shirt covered in woodchips and sawdust.

"You broke my door."

He suddenly looks nervous. "We were told that it couldn't be opened."

"That's right, because *I* locked them in."

He reddens.

A Whistleblower behind him bites his lip to stop himself from laughing.

"We'll arrange to have a new door fitted immediately, Judge."

"Of course you will," she snaps, then pinches the bridge of her nose. "Now tell me, why . . . How . . . What are you doing here? This is a private matter for Judge Crevan. I was waiting for him to call me back."

They look at one another, obviously confused. "Somebody called us from this address, and I believe Judge Crevan is preoccupied at the moment with arrangements for the gathering."

"Gathering?" Raphael asks. "What gathering?"

"All Flawed have been asked to report to their Whistleblowers immediately, where they will be brought to a central location. We have been informed we must take *all* Flawed to this location, no exceptions."

"No, but you can't take Celestine. She's an Evader. I must speak to Judge Crevan first," Judge Sanchez says.

"We are following Judge Crevan's instructions, Judge Sanchez," another Whistleblower speaks up, stepping closer to me. "*All* Flawed, no exceptions, are to be brought to this location. Judge Crevan will be informed of Celestine's capture and we'll ensure she receives appropriate punishment for her evasion."

Before he takes me by the elbow, he lifts the red whistle that's hanging on a gold chain around his neck.

"Block your ears," I say to Raphael.

He does so just in time, because all twelve Whistleblowers blow their whistle to signal the arrest of another Flawed. Again.

PART THREE

FIFTY-SIX

JUDGE SANCHEZ ORDERS them to take custody of Raphael, too. Despite his profession and our contract, he is seen as aiding an evader.

We're brought to a warehouse along the docklands where Flawed curfew buses line up.

"What's going on?" I ask Raphael, who doesn't answer. He's too busy looking out the window, trying to figure it all out.

"Were you informed that you were to report to your Whistleblower today?" he asks me finally.

"I wouldn't know. I'm an evader. I've been with people who never report to Whistleblowers."

"Could someone please tell me what's going on?" Raphael sits forward and asks a Whistleblower.

"All Flawed are to gather at this address at nine AM sharp."

"Why?"

"Guild's orders."

"And tell me, what do you plan to do with me? I'm not Flawed."

"We're bringing you to the castle."

"Judge Crevan is going to address the Flawed," a more helpful Whistle-blower adds.

"In person?" Raphael frowns. "All the Flawed in the whole of Humming?"

"Not all at once. Everyone has designated areas. Have you not heard any of this?" a Whistleblower asks, twisting around in his seat and look-ing at me as if he thinks I've been living on another planet.

"Fugitive." Raphael points at me. "Not much use for this kind of thing when you're on the run. Though it would have helped to know."

"I'm sorry about this, Raphael," I say.

"Don't apologize. I knew the ending, remember? I feel strangely free. Perhaps my house in the mountains was my self-imposed imprisonment. This is the stuff I was made to do. Are you okay?"

I nod, then shake my head, then shrug. I tried to beat them, I tried to stay one step ahead of them, but now I'm here and I don't know what this is.

"I'll take that as a yes, only because I'm not good at reassurance."

The car stalls in traffic and I look out at the warehouses that line the docks. Down a narrow alley that separates two warehouses I see two women on a cigarette break. They're wearing white overalls covered in red stains, and the stains mark their arms, too, splattered all the way to their elbows.

"Raphael," I say, hearing the tremor in my voice.

"Fish guts," he says too quickly. "They use these warehouses to gut and pack fish."

I'd like to believe that's what's happening in there now, but I don't.

Raphael's door opens and a Whistleblower orders him out. We barely even get to say good-bye, he just yells, "Good luck, kiddo," before the door slams.

Then mine opens and I'm taken outside. I'm accompanied on either side by two Whistleblowers. Raphael is taken to another Whistleblower car, to be brought to Highland Castle.

The door slides open on the warehouse. The entrance has a security

X-ray machine that I pass through safely, an ID machine that identifies me immediately. Men are taken right; women are taken left. I want to retch from the smell of fish in the building. As I'm entering the women's quarters, another worker appears, her apron covered in red, like she's just butchered a body. Our eyes meet and her eyes soften.

"Sorry," she says softly, and hurries on to meet a friend, another worker in a bloodied apron, as if they're late for something.

I step into the women's quarters and I'm faced with hell.

FIFTY-SEVEN

HUNDREDS OF PEOPLE, my fellow Flawed women, turn to look at me. Some cheer, some come to me and shake my hand, pat me wherever they can reach me. One woman cries because she believes I can rescue her; another cries because my capture means that now all hope is lost.

I look around the warehouse and take in the scene. It is indeed a fish-processing facility, where fish are taken in fresh from the boats, gutted, and sent to the local market and businesses. Long lines of what look like rectangular sinks fill the space so that employees can work in a comfortable standing position. The floor is made of light clay tiles, for easy cleaning, and sloped so that the blood can easily flow to the drainage outlets. Why are we here? My imagination works overtime and the scene makes me shudder.

In the crowd I see one familiar face. A blond girl. I know her from a photograph I was given recently by her boyfriend, Leonard.

"Lizzie?" I ask.

She looks up at me, confused.

"Celestine North? How do you know me?"

"From your boyfriend, Leonard. He's looking for you. He always knew you were Flawed. He helped me. I promised him I'd try to find you."

She stands up, confused. "But Bahee told me that Leonard found out I was Flawed. That he didn't want anything to do with me. He told me I had to leave. That I'd put them all in danger. I didn't want to go, but he made me."

I shake my head. "Bahee was lying all along, to a lot of people. Leonard loves you; he's been looking for you since you left."

"Oh." Her eyes open in surprise at probably the best thing to have happened to her in the weeks since Bahee dumped her in the worst part of town. She smiles. "Thank you."

"He rescued me from the Whistleblowers; he's a good person," I say.

A whistle is blown and everyone is silenced.

A projector lights up on the warehouse wall.

Flawed TV. Many groan to show their discontent and disapproval.

"We have Judge Crevan live on Flawed TV to tell us what's happening today," Pia Wang's replacement says, bubbly, like she's on an entertainment channel.

Crevan appears on-screen, sitting in a brown leather armchair in the Guild study, wearing his red robe. "It is the fortieth anniversary of the Guild, which my grandfather founded. I feel we have come a long way since then. If we can cast our minds back to the state of the country then, politically and economically, and the pandemonium which emerged from the careless, ruthless decisions for our leaders and then look at where we are now . . .

"We are on our way to becoming almost cleansed of all Flaws, of irrational, immoral, unethical, and downright irresponsible decisions. Our businesses are led with competence; we are recognized on the world stage as a country that is trustworthy, and one to do business with.

"Recently there have been a series of riots in the city and across small towns in the country; we appear to be losing our way, losing our focus.

Today is a day to refocus. Today there will be a display of those we are protecting our society from. A parade of the poisonous few who do not think and act like us. Of course we love our family members—branding them does not make us love them less, but it *helps us*, sends a signal to the rest of the world that *we* are an organized, decent society."

He looks straight down the camera lens, his blue eyes searing into all of us. "What you will see today is the reason why the Guild is in place. The people you will see are the population that you will join if you do not wish to live in our organized, decent society. I invite—I *implore* the public to get outside, line the streets, and support us."

The picture disappears and all the women in the warehouse immediately start talking, debating, some keeping their cool, but mostly an air of panic is rising.

A whistle blows and it needs to be blown four times before the chatter dies.

A head Whistleblower stands above the rest and yells, "Flawed! Take off your clothes and dress in the outfits laid out in the piles at the top of the room. Do it without questions, and do it now!"

I stand on tiptoe to see what's at the top of the room. I see red items; some look tie-dyed, as though they've been just stained, and suddenly the women I saw outside with the red stains on their white aprons make sense to me. They've been dying clothes red—red for Flawed.

At first the movement is slow. Women discuss it among themselves, before slowly shuffling up the sloped floor to the displayed clothes, but it's when there's a realization that the amount of each size is limited that everyone starts grabbing, some pushing others aside to fight for the red rags.

Small, medium, large, extra-large. An old woman beside me whimpers. I go to the table, grab an extra-large for her, hoping that that size will be enough for her. There are no other small sizes left. A woman to my left hands me hers and reaches for the medium pile.

"Thank you," I say, confused.

Nobody tackles me, to my surprise. The old woman accepts the extra-large I hand to her, in tears.

When I shake the garment out from its crumpled pile and hold it up before me, I am appalled, as is everyone else, judging by the howls and the shrieks and the shouts. It's a red string slip that leaves little to the imagination.

"I'm not wearing this," a woman shouts. "I am *not* wearing this."

The line quickly works its way across the crowd until everybody agrees to take the same stance, some confidently, some timidly, and the red slips are thrown to the floor of the warehouse.

A group of Whistleblowers make their way to the woman who began the protest. "By order of the Guild you must put on these clothes."

Everyone quiets down to watch.

The woman picks up the slip and then tosses it on the floor at the Whistleblowers' feet.

There's a pause, then the baton is whipped out and it takes the woman down by the backs of her legs. She falls forward and bangs her face; her lip bursts open, blood gushing, and she yells out in pain. This causes two things to happen. Some women retreat and immediately dress, others attack. I'm away from it all, at the back of the circle, stunned, terrified by what is happening. We are crammed in here, being treated like animals.

Suddenly the Whistleblowers start whistling. We look around at one another, confused. They're not asking for silence, they're whistling as if they've caught somebody. But everybody here is Flawed and so we look around in confusion—can a Flawed be caught twice? It would be unheard of.

Most of the Whistleblowers leave their stations as if it has already been rehearsed, blowing their whistles and pushing through the crowd of Flawed. Instead of surrounding a Flawed woman, they stop at a Whistle-blower, who is looking around at them, terrified. She is completely surrounded by her colleagues. The sounds of the whistles are so loud in the echoey warehouse that she and all of us have to block our ears. They gather around her, huddle around her in a circle, and start prodding their fellow Whistleblower with their batons. And they're not joking, either.

"Take your clothes off, Karen."

"It's an insult for someone like you to wear our uniform. Get it off," another one yells.

"You know what you did, Karen," one jeers.

"We heard what you did," another sings.

They continue to heckle her, poking her, prodding her, until she screams at them all to stop. She screams for help, but none of us do. Moments ago she was forcing us to remove our clothes, and now she is suffering at the hands of her colleagues, a punishment for something she did that we'll never know of. A mistake at work? Something in her personal life? Whatever it is, they know, they found out. Karen is not safe. They planned this attack on her, even worse for her this way because she's been taken down in front of hundreds of Flawed.

The Whistleblowers push her to the floor and start to remove her clothes, through much kicking and yelling. They succeed in removing the uniform and putting the slip over her head. She tries to get her uniform back, but it's useless. She can't get out of the warehouse: They won't let her out; it's locked and she's trapped among us now. She is completely powerless, just like the rest of us. She retreats from all of us, to the corner to cry.

This stops any further fights from breaking out for a moment. I move to the wall, back against it so that no one can see my sixth scar, and I dress in the red slip. I'm looking down at myself, feeling the emotion bubbling up inside me, when a scrap starts between two women on the far side of the room and brings me out of my self-pity. It sounds vicious, and they start lashing out at each other.

"She took my slip!" one shrieks.

"I did not," another snarls. "I had it first. I put it down for a second, and *you* grabbed it!"

People stand by uncertainly, not wanting to get involved. I look at the Whistleblowers and see the lead Whistleblower laugh, the delight on her face is obvious, and I literally see red. I charge through the crowd, push through the women standing around the fight, and launch myself at the two women fighting. I pull them apart and break them up immediately. They're bigger than me, older than me, stronger and tougher than me. They look at me in surprise.

"They. Are. Laughing. At. Us," I say. I meant to whisper it so the Whistleblowers couldn't hear, but instead it comes out as an angry menacing hiss.

One woman isn't listening to me, still ranting about the dress, but I have the attention of the other. She looks at the Whistleblowers, sees a group of them chuckling together at us arguing over scraps of clothes. Her fists clench.

"Do you want them to laugh at us?"

She shakes her head.

"You are giving them exactly what they want," I say, feeling the anger surging through me.

"You're Celestine North," the woman says.

This grabs the attention of the larger woman, who finally turns to me.

"But this," the bigger woman growls, clenching her hand around the slip, "doesn't fit me. It fits her."

"It's too tight, you can see what I ate for *breakfast*."

"This thing won't even go over my head. And that is two sizes too big for you. Use your common sense!"

"Tough! I got it first!"

The Whistleblowers have a right old giggle again at the argument over the dismal scraps of material, the only things to hide our modesty. The arguing women glare at them, argument paused. I sense their rage. Now they're on the same side.

"Work together." I keep my voice low.

"No whispering, North!" the lead Whistleblower yells, stepping closer.

I ignore her, keeping my voice low. "The minute they put us in this room together, we became friends. We are all on the same side in here. We are against *them*, not one another."

I take the slip from the bigger woman's hands. "Look, stretch the fabric like this." I put my arms into the slip and widen my arms, the cotton stretching. Then I lift my knee and push it with my knee, stretching it further. The red turns a pinkish color as the fabric stretches. I hand it to the leaner woman. "Give her the bigger size."

She thinks about it, then sighs and hands over the larger slip. They look at the slips in their hands, like two petulant children.

"Now, smile." I lighten my tone.

"What?" They look at me in confusion.

"Smile," I say perkily, through gritted teeth.

They attempt to smile.

"Chins up, let's get through this with some dignity."

They lift their chins, and it has the effect of working its way through the crowd. Our show of togetherness wipes the smirks off the Whistleblowers' faces.

The Whistleblowers blow their whistles so loudly, together, that we have to block our ears. We're moved like cattle into a series of single files, broken up only by the long fish-gutting tables. I stand behind Lizzie. Even Whistleblower Karen must embark on the next journey, whatever that is, and she knows what's coming and looks pale, lost, as though she's going to vomit.

The old lady continues to cry in the line beside me. She stands in her tight red slip, stripped of all her modesty, her pride, her aged flesh sagging, her varicose veins on display. Bodies burst out of the slips, boobs too big, butts and hips straining the fabric. Others are too tiny, having to pull up the strings and tie bows at the top to protect their bodies. All of our shapes are on show. A girl who looks younger than sixteen but can't be, due to Flawed rules, tries to hide her changing body with her hands and arms, red-faced.

As women, we dress to please ourselves, to hide our imperfections, to accentuate our best features. Our clothing is an extension of who we are, a reflection of what we are thinking and feeling. This is ripped from us now, we are laid practically bare, all the parts of us, the parts we want to hide, the parts we are ashamed of, or the versions of ourselves we don't want anybody to see. And even if anybody isn't self-conscious of their bodies, the wearing of a uniform is simply demeaning. They have stripped us of our individuality, our uniqueness. They have told us we are not to be differentiated, we do not matter, we are insignificant. We are just numbers, a weakened army of imperfections.

And we all wonder the same thing: What is this in aid of? What's going to happen next?

We're each handed a pair of flip-flops, the soles so thin I can still feel the cold of the clay tiles through them once I put them on. The lead Whistleblower patrols the line, inspecting us. She stops at me, looks me up and down, with a face like she's smelling raw sewage.

"You. Celestine North. You like to play at being a leader, don't you?"

I don't answer.

"Well, now's your time to shine," she says nastily. "Front of the line."

I walk through the single files, all eyes on me.

"Go on, Celestine," one woman says.

Another person claps, like they're gearing me up for something, like I'm about to walk into a boxing ring. I feel pats on my shoulder, on my back, receive encouraging winks and nervous smiles. The entire room starts to support me, and I feel the tears come to my eyes, tears of appreciation and pride to be so propped up.

The Whistleblowers blow their whistles to stop the rising support, which the lead Whistleblower hadn't counted on. I take my place in the front of my single file. We will be the first line to move, and I will be the first in line, though I don't know where we're going.

The warehouse door slides open and light fills the space, and we're told to walk.

FIFTY-EIGHT

AT EXACTLY THE same time as we exit, the men exit their quarters beside us. They wear red tank tops and boxer shorts. From the look of some fresh bleeding noses and shiners it's clear their uprising was lost, too. Some women start to cry as they see the men. Some men start to cry, and others look away out of respect, when they see us.

The man who leads the Flawed line looks at me and curses when he sees what we have to wear. The male lead Whistleblower immediately clatters him across the head, which silences him. We meet in the middle and are ordered to walk alongside each other. I lead the women; he leads the men. I wonder what he's done to be picked to go first; I'm sure men weren't fighting over their boxer shorts. I scan the men's line to see if I can find any familiar faces, but a whistle is blown loudly in my face, signaling that I must keep my head straight.

"You're Celestine North?" the man beside me asks, lips not moving.

"Yes."

"What's going on here?"

I look around. "I don't know."

"Well, I hope you have a plan of some sort," he says.

We step onto the docklands and the streets are lined with people, members of the public who have come out from their houses and workplaces to see the Flawed parade through the streets. The walk of shame. The walk of blame. Dotted along the sidewalks are Whistleblowers dressed in their riot gear, shields in their hands.

We are in the old part of the town. On the other side of the river is the urban, vibrant, modern city, which rises from the once-derelict docklands. On this side, the old cobblestoned roads have been maintained, home to the market traders, wholesale and retail, from fruit and vegetables to meat and fish—a thriving, busy, colorful world filled with people and life. And so this is where we begin our journey, from the warehouses, past the stallholders in the market, and I feel it's fitting. I feel like cattle about to be traded, sold, gawked at, and valued.

Then the laneways widen and bring us by cafés and restaurants, stories of apartments above, people out on their balconies, watching us with steaming cups in their hands. The cobblestones are difficult to walk over in our flimsy flip-flops, and more than once I stub my toe on the sharp edges of the pitched paving and am not alone in stumbling. A few people fall to the ground, cutting their knees, and are helped up by their fellow Flawed.

Through the city speakers we hear Crevan's voice, a recorded version of what he said earlier. Snippets of phrases that have been cut, edited, now replay over and over again.

"Today is the day we say *thank you* to the Flawed population for helping us cleanse our society of imperfection and for allowing us to have an organized, decent society." This one statement is popular and plays over and over like a broken record.

Big, small, skinny, fat, black, white, old, and young, there is nothing left to the imagination, as we're paraded through narrow cobblestoned streets in front of the audience. There are some wolf whistles from childish groups of teenage boys, but mostly the looks are of horror and embarrassment that this is happening. It is one thing to know that Flawed are branded and must live as second-class citizens, it is another to have to watch them parade the scars of these punishments. Out of sight, out of mind. It is easy for people to live their lives when they are not faced with the reality in such a harsh way as this.

This parade was designed to be cruel, to put fear into people's hearts; the public is *supposed* to be horrified. It is a message being sent out to the country: Don't believe in the country's ideals and this will happen to you. But nobody can do anything about it; speaking out would be to aid a Flawed, and they would end up walking alongside us, so everyone keeps their mouths shut, the fear of joining us too great.

Despite all the eyes on my near-naked body, I feel invisible. Nobody can truly see me. It feels the more they have lumped us together, the less human we have become, no longer individuals. I walk, the tears spilling from my eyes, down my cheeks. Head straight, focused on the path before me. Our tears are pointless and worthless—they can do no good. No one but ourselves can wipe them.

My eyes meet with those of the other Flawed men and women. What can we do? Have we stopped even seeing one another? They look as powerless as me, as though they've given up, some heads down so low, they're tripping up when the person in front slows, some with their heads so high they're defiant. Others crying. Others showing nothing, unreadable. Living the moment until it's over. Putting up with it.

I look out for Carrick but know he would be crazy to risk coming here. I wonder if he's watching this on television, and that makes me smile. I hope so. I picture him on a couch, in a safe house, free.

"Leonard!" Lizzie suddenly screams from behind me.

Leonard is at the side of the road, among the crowd.

He reaches his arms out to her and they embrace before the nearest Whistleblower manages to pull them apart.

"Let him hug her!" I hear one woman shout out and the crowd in that section begin to all call out against the Whistleblowers.

"Flawed scum!" someone else shouts at us.

244

I keep walking.

I turn around to see how long the line is and I catch a glimpse of Mona, way in the back. I gasp. Cordelia is behind her. There's no sign of Evelyn, and I hope that she is safe with Alpha and Professor Lambert and not in one of the F.A.B. institutions, though I fear the worst. I suddenly see Carrick's mother, Kelly, and across from her I see Professor Bill Lambert. My heart breaks; they've all been caught. I fear for Juniper and my mom, and Carrick. I feel weak.

We emerge from the cobblestoned roads and enter the old town square, surrounded by colorful ornate buildings built in the eighteenth century. What these buildings have seen in their lifetimes, and now this cruelty.

"We must be going to the castle," I say to the man beside me, my heart pounding. The castle holds nothing but terrifying memories for me, but I think of Granddad. At least there is a part of me that wants to go there, perhaps I'll be reunited with him. Then I wonder if Granddad is among the men and I turn around and study them again. I'm looking behind me too much and I fall to the ground and cut my knee.

A man stops to help but a whistle blows for him to continue. He apologizes and keeps walking. A woman along the side of the square gasps and reaches out her hand to help me. A Whistleblower glares at her and she backs away.

"I'm sorry, dear," she says, bottom lip trembling. "I'm so sorry."

Everyone keeps marching right on by me while I stay on the ground, knee bleeding, pretending I've been more badly injured than I have. I must time this correctly.

"Back in line," the Whistleblower orders.

I take my time standing, until I see Mona nearing me, then I get up and jump in line in front of her. Her face lights up at the sight of me.

"Hey, girl, fancy meeting you here. Nice work in the warehouse."

I look to the men beside us and see Lennox, Fergus, and Lorcan.

"Looking good, Celestine," Lennox says good-naturedly.

I smile, feeling energized to be back in the company of my tribe.

"I hate it when I go to a party and everyone else is wearing the same thing," Lorcan says, and, despite everything, we laugh.

"So, Celestine, everything going to plan?" Lennox asks.

We all laugh at that again.

"Stop talking," a Whistleblower orders as we pass.

"Where's Carrick? Are Juniper and my mom safe?" I ask quickly, knowledge of their safety more important than finding out how these guys were captured.

"Juniper is out of the facility; she's safe with your mom," Lennox says. "You'd be proud of her, she raised quite the stink at the Whistleblower base. She showed up with a lawyer, a cop, and the newspaper editor. They had a look around at everybody who's being held there: the guards, Pia Wang, the missing schoolkids. The cop is kicking up big-time, especially seeing as they've been doing an official search for the kids for the past few days. Crevan has a lot to answer for about that. I think it's all about to be blown wide open."

I smile with relief, so proud of my mom and Juniper, but there's a long way to go yet, and I have no idea what lies in store for us.

"What about Carrick? Where is he?" I ask.

Lorcan looks at Lennox anxiously.

"Tell me," I plead.

"We don't know," he says. "That's the honest truth."

I swallow hard, fight the tears that start to come again. I just hope Crevan hasn't got his hands on him.

"How did you end up here?" I ask.

"Bad luck," Lennox replies.

"Professor Lambert's house got raided," Mona says. "They discovered his secret basement."

I gasp. I feel like it's all my fault. I told them to go there; I promised them they'd be safe.

"It's not your fault," Lennox says, sensing my guilt. "Whistleblowers were becoming suspicious of Marcus and Kate. We all agreed he should alert them to us to stay on their side. Better to have Whistleblowers on our side than none. It was Lambert's decision. Evelyn is still safe."

I agree, having Marcus and Kate's help is invaluable. But what a sacrifice. And I'm so relieved about Evelyn. I knew Alpha would cherish her.

"I ran away with my English teacher," Mona says suddenly, out of nowhere.

"What?" I turn around.

"Head straight," another Whistleblower orders.

I turn back around.

"You asked me what I did to become Flawed when we first met. I didn't tell you. When I was fifteen, I ran away with my English teacher. He was twenty-nine. And married. It was my idea. I thought it would be okay. But it wasn't. It was all over the news. As if I was missing. We got caught. He was sent to jail. I was under eighteen, so I got branded."

"I couldn't give up smoking when I was pregnant," Cordelia says suddenly, loudly so that others listen in, too. "The suburban moms of Madison Meadows were disgusted. They held their own little Flawed court, after which they gave me a warning. But I couldn't stop. I was caught, eight months pregnant, with my head out the bathroom window of the charity bake sale, and they all decided to report me. I pleaded with them to wait until after my baby was born to report me so that she wouldn't be born F.A.B. and taken away from me. A single Flawed mother can't keep her child. They all agreed, bar one woman."

"I used to wear my grandmother's clothes," Lennox says, serious, then starts laughing. "Just kidding. I set up and managed a dating website that assisted people in cheating on their wives."

We all look at him, disgusted.

"That was you?" Mona asks, her face scrunched up. "You jerk."

"One million customers. Perfectly legal. I had a Ferrari and everything."

"The Guild took it?" Fergus asks, more moved by the loss of a Ferrari than anything else.

"Nope. Wife got it in the divorce."

We all laugh.

"Well, you deserve your brand," Mona says, but we know she doesn't mean it.

Fergus speaks up, serious for once. "I was a police officer. I swapped 'intimate images' with my girlfriend on my work phone. I was suspended on full pay for fifteen months. It wasn't anything illegal and I was cleared of gross misconduct, but the force reported me, found me Flawed."

I look at them all in surprise. As each person confesses, it's like it gives the next person the confidence to tell their story, too, their secrets all coming out as we walk together.

Carrick's mother speaks up. "I got a brand on my tongue for speaking out against society. Adam and I weren't always bakers at plants," she says almost sarcastically. "We were doctors. We had our own general practice. We wrote anti-vaccination papers, speaking out about the dangers of vaccinations. The medical profession and the government didn't like our professional opinions."

"I didn't do anything," an older man I don't know joins in. "I was set up. The Guild told me I was lying and branded me."

We all fall silent after that.

FIFTY-NINE

AS WE WALK over the bridge that connects the city to the castle, I start thinking about capacities and then I can't stop. There is a space that people hold for you, within themselves. Every person has a space for every person they meet—sometimes the capacity is deep, sometimes it is shallow. The streets are lined with people and Whistleblowers, all this for us. The capacity these people hold for us is enormous, in each of them.

People who are loved can eventually be hated in equal amounts. How Art loved me before I was caught versus his anger with me now, the rage that led him to join the Whistleblowers. How guilty Juniper felt for not telling me about helping to hide Art, which led her to take my place in the hospital, risking her own freedom to make it up to me. Switching one with another.

If the space is there for us, all we have to do is alter the feelings. As I look at the faces of those who watch us parade through the streets, with our flaws on display, our weaknesses, our imperfections, I feel hopeful, I sense that the tide could change. If they hate us this much, they could love us equally.

We turn the corner and start to walk up the steep cobblestoned road to Highland Castle, and as if the people lining the streets could read my thoughts I suddenly hear cheering. Great, big, loud, happy cheering. It jars with the sounds that have led us here. I look around and up ahead on the right-hand side, my side, I see my mom, Juniper, and Ewan jumping up and down on the edge of the road, cheering everyone on, thumping their fists in the air.

"Whoooo!" Mom screams happily, tears in her eyes. "That's my daughter; that's my girl!"

"Mom!" I yell. "Mom!" I can't believe it, I start jumping up and down. "That's my mom!" I tell the others who start to wave at her as we near.

As they gather as much attention as they can, Juniper, Mom, and even little Ewan open their shirts, lift their sweaters over their heads, and reveal T-shirts that read ABOLISH THE GUILD in red print.

The Flawed who see grin and cheer, applaud my family's bravery in showing their support, and I'm so proud of them. Everybody who passes them smiles and wipes their tears as my family, and the surrounding people Mom has managed to muster together, applaud us. I realize it's not just the family and friends of the Flawed who have gathered at the gates of Highland Castle but also the students from Tobias's school who have carried out their plans to protest. I see Tobias among the crowd, too, protesting his own mother's organization. As we pass, Mom reaches out her hand and I grab it. A Whistleblower immediately tries to pull us apart, but we hold on, looking deep into each other's eyes, tears flowing.

"I love you, baby. I'm so proud of you," she says, barely able to keep it together. "Chin up, Celestine." She raises her voice. "Chins up, all of you. We're here to support you."

I lift my chin and I intend to keep it up. Then we let go.

And there are the very special people in our lives who have the endless capacity to love us for all of our flaws.

SIXTY

THE SINGLE FILES of men and women merge together as we enter the courtyard of Highland Castle, familiar territory for all who took steps from our normal lives to Flawed lives. We are wedged together, thousands of us; it's hard to breathe. A temporary stage has been set up beneath the Clock Tower, the headquarters of the Guild.

Crevan's red robe blows in the light breeze as he makes his way from the offices to the stage. Art stands beside the stage, guarding, eyes running over the crowd. Seeing him like this doesn't have the same punch-in-the-stomach effect it had before. I've had time to relive the sight of him, think about it and picture it often. Now I study him curiously, trying to analyze what's going through his mind. As Crevan passes Art he places an affectionate hand on his shoulder and grins broadly, proud to have his son by his side. Someone tuts beside me. Art is embarrassed by this public display of affection and lowers his head, cheeks rosy.

Crevan takes to the podium and looks around. Eyes searching. At first I think he's taking it all in and then I realize he's looking for someone. For me. He knows that I'm here.

I'm too far away from the stage.

"Celestine," Mona hisses. "What are you doing?"

"I need to get closer."

I push my way through people who are happy to let me pass; nobody is vying for the front row. Nobody here is present out of choice.

Crevan sees me moving through the crowd, which was the point, and I appear to distract him from his speech.

He pauses, put out for a moment, then continues. Art sees me, too, looks me up and down in my red slip, identical to everybody else's. I don't know what he sees when he looks at me—I don't have time to wait, and my eyes are back on Crevan.

"Ladies and gentlemen, I gather you here today to thank you for taking part in the parade through our city. I appreciate your time. All across the country, similar parades are happening in towns and cities, as Flawed show their communities how we are being cleansed. I've brought you all here today to share a new strategy with you."

It's the look in his eyes, the way he does something with his mouth— I feel a slow dread beginning to crawl up my body.

"Yesterday I met with Prime Minister Percy to discuss a new plan, called the Reduction of the Flawed."

Murmurs.

"The Guild felt that it was our duty to allow Flawed to live among the rest of society, to show society what can happen if they give in to their weaknesses, their imperfections, but in recent weeks, due to the rising danger and violence"—he looks at me—"it is clear that this two-tiered society is dangerous. It is for the best interests of *everybody* that a new system be implemented.

"The Reduction of the Flawed is an initiative to house the Flawed in their own community, to give Flawed the freedom to live as Flawed *together*, under Guild rules."

There is an uproar as people start shouting up at him. It doesn't matter how he tries to phrase it, how he tries to sugarcoat it as freedom for Flawed: It doesn't sound good. My body starts to shake.

"You're putting us in a prison!" someone shouts.

"Ghettos!"

"Camps!"

"This will not be a prison, a ghetto, or a camp," he assures everyone calmly. "But it is clear that Flawed cannot live side by side with the rest of society." Over the shouts from the crowd he continues for the purposes of the television cameras. "The proposal has been drawn up, and it will be put into action with the new government." He's looking into the camera now with that calm, reassuring smile, and I see him giving me that same look in another life. *It's going to be okay, Celestine.* Before I got on water skis for the first time, when Art was driving us for the first time. Before I tasted oysters for the first time. After Art's mom's funeral, when Crevan caught Art crying in my arms, and he watched us from the doorway. His look always said, *It's going to be okay, Celestine.*

The tears are streaming down my cheeks as the crowd erupts in anger around me, as Crevan marches off the stage with his cloak swinging, as he whips it behind him, as a stunned Art is pulled along with him, as the Whistleblowers move in with their riot shields raised and their batons out, expecting revolt.

But it's not okay; none of this is okay.

I see the large old woman from the warehouse, arms still wrapped around her body in humiliation, crying and crying all alone in the center of madness. Another lady joins her and they hold hands. A younger teenage boy stands by her, all gangly, skin and bones and not a fighter. The woman takes his hand and the three of them stand together, as if in prayer. Some clusters of people are trying to talk to the Whistleblowers rationally. I can sense that sections of Flawed are starting to get so angry that it may become physical.

I rush to Mona, who's arguing with a Whistleblower, telling her exactly what she thinks of her in a way only Mona could. I grab her by the arm and pull her away from the Whistleblower.

"Stop, Mona."

"What? Celestine, get off me!" She tries to pull away from me but I dig my nails into her skin.

"Ow! What the . . . ?"

"Stop it," I say through gritted teeth. "You're giving Crevan exactly what he wants. Look."

She finally pauses and looks around.

"The eyes of the world are on us now and they want us to behave like animals. Crevan marched us through the streets and then gave us the speech about the Reduction of the Flawed, with cameras on every angle. We need to be locked away because we're troublemakers. He's set us up."

Everyone watching at home will want us to be segregated, they'll fear us and agree with his plans. Mona finally sees what I see. She taps Fergus. Then she kicks him when he doesn't respond.

"What?" he replies, annoyed.

As she relays my words I leave their side and stand with the small group of people who are the calm in the center of the storm. I take the old woman's hand. I grip it tight. She's trembling.

"Everyone," I say, loud but not shouting. "Everyone hold hands."

"What the hell is she doing?" I hear Lennox ask.

"Carrick would want us to follow her lead. Enya would, too."

They make their way over to us. Mona holds my hand, and Lennox holds hers on the other side. Fergus and Lorcan wrap their arms across one another's shoulders, like brothers-in-arms. More people join us. It doesn't take long, but soon we all stand in rows in the courtyard hand in hand, shoulder to shoulder, united.

We are all silent. And yet I feel a power build inside me that I've never felt before, a sense of place stronger than anything. I cling to the old woman's and Mona's hands even tighter. I see the tears glistening in everybody's eyes and the way Fergus's jaw hardens as he struggles to compose himself.

The TV cameras capture it all, while the Whistleblowers look to one another, confused, waiting for something to happen. They were prepared for a riot. We won't give them one. I study them. I want to take their power away from them. I feel so strong, stronger than ever before. I don't know how I think about it, it just comes, but I start to whistle. A long, high-pitched whistle as close to their sound as I can make it. Mona catches on immediately and does the same. It spreads. Then three thousand people join in. Three thousand voices, three thousand whistles. The Whistleblowers are confused, how could they ever stop this when it's not violent? We're standing peacefully, mimicking their sound but making it our own.

A Whistleblower removes his shield, takes off his helmet and drops it to the ground.

"I can't," he says, looking dizzy, as though he's about to faint.

"Riley," one says. "Get back in line!"

"No, I can't. I can't," he repeats.

"It's working," the old lady says joyously beside me. I feel her stand taller beside me. "They were right about you."

The whistling intensifies as another Whistleblower drops out. A woman. It's Kate. She drops her shield, takes off her helmet, and walks away from the line of Whistleblowers standing guard, to join us. She stands between me and the old lady and takes my hand. She blows her whistle from our side, and we all erupt in cheers.

From a window beside the Clock Tower I see Art watching me. He looks worried.

Good.

Because I'm just getting started.

SIXTY-ONE

"SAY SOMETHING," Kate says to me. Her hand is clammy, and I can smell her nervous sweat. I can tell she is terrified by the move she has made but is sticking with it, such is the strength of her conviction.

"What?"

"You should say something, address the people."

"Yes, do it." Mona overhears and lets go of my hand. She shoves me gently out of line.

I'm standing alone, the broken link in the chain.

"No," I protest, my stomach filling with butterflies and my throat tightening at the very thought. I try to step back in line, but they push me forward again. "I don't know what to say."

I think back to weeks ago in Alpha and Professor Lambert's house, when Alpha invited me up to the stage to speak. All the eager faces looking at me expectantly, hoping for something great to come out of my mouth after their rapturous applause. I had their complete attention, they were on my side, and I couldn't think of one thing to say. The Whistle-blowers, ironically, saved me that day by breaking up the event.

"Go on," Mona says, shoving me forward again.

I try to get back in line, but Kate and Mona are holding hands. I feel the television cameras on us and don't want to make a scene. It looks like I've been pushed out of the crowd.

I hear somebody say, "It's Celestine."

I have one of those names that's easy to hear when others mention it, even behind my back, or quietly, thinking I can't hear. With its *s* sounds, I hear it move like a wave over the crowd until finally the whistling is more like hissing, and then there's silence.

I take a few steps more and face them. "My name is Celestine," I say, and my voice is so quiet Lennox starts shouting.

"Can't hear you, Celestine. Get up on the stage."

I throw him an angry look but everyone else backs him up. I expect the Whistleblowers to stop me but they're unsure what to do at this point and nobody seems to be in control, considering some of their own people have just joined ours and their leader has retreated to the castle. They just watch as I climb up to the podium. I clear my throat.

It feels like a nightmare: my facing thousands of people, wearing nothing but a tight slip—my body, my shape, all my flaws revealed. It should be demeaning, but it's not. What's that thing they tell people who are afraid of public speaking to do? Imagine that everybody is naked, or in their underwear. Well, they are. Everybody's flaws are revealed. Nobody before me is Perfect. I don't feel judged. If anything, I feel so empowered looking at these humans who are all so self-aware that the panic disappears immediately.

"My name is Celestine North," I say loudly, my voice traveling over the vast crowd.

What follows is a huge cheer that surprises me. It surprises the Whistleblowers, too, and they straighten their backs and ready themselves for whatever will come.

"I watched Judge Crevan's interview last night, and we've all heard what he had to say, now I hope he hears me. Now it's my turn."

A Whistleblower steps forward to stop me. "My right to freedom of speech has not been removed," I say. He looks to his superior, who gives him a nod, so he steps down.

I don't know where it comes from, but everything I felt while watching Crevan on TV last night slowly bubbles to the surface.

"Arrogance, greed, impatience, stubbornness, martyrdom, self-deprecation, self-destruction. These are the seven character flaws Judge Crevan placed on us. But Judge Crevan, there are two sides to every story. When you tell me that I have greed, I call it desire. Desire for a fair and equal society. When you call me arrogant, I call it pride, because my beliefs make me stand above those who oppress me.

"When you say I am impatient, I say that I am daring to question your judgments, which are not law but mere morality courts. You call me stubborn; I say I'm determined. You say I want to make myself a martyr; I say I'm showing selflessness. Self-deprecation? Humility. Self-destruction? What I did for Clayton Byrne on the bus was not a deliberate act to ruin my life but a decision based on the belief that what was happening was inhumane. What you see as flaws, Judge Crevan, I see as strengths.

"Mistakes are nothing to be ashamed of. Mistakes teach us to take responsibility. They teach us what works and what doesn't. We learn what we would do differently the next time, how we will be different, better, and wiser in the future. We are not just walking mistakes, we are human." My voice cracks and the crowd erupts into joyous applause.

"To err is human. You learn from your mistakes," I say to the hushed crowd. "The rest of the world uses these phrases. If this is true, and Judge Crevan and our current leaders have *never* made mistakes, then it is *us* who can teach them a thing or two, because I stand before you the most branded, the most Flawed person in the world. Today we drift away from the shadow of the Guild, this morality court, and we emerge as the leaders of the future."

Mona punches the air and lets out a roar, and the rest of the crowd quickly follows. I see Professor Lambert clapping his hands proudly. Lorcan and Fergus are high-fiving others.

It was worth it. It really was. Despite what happens next.

SIXTY-TWO

I DON'T FEEL any fear as the Whistleblowers take me away. Right now, I'm on a high after my speech. I don't know where the words came from, they all just came tumbling out when I needed them most. I just hope that my family heard them, and Carrick, wherever he is.

The Whistleblowers aren't gentle with me, either. As soon as we're out of the TV cameras' views, the Whistleblowers tighten their grips on my arms, pull me along as they quicken their pace. This isn't Tina anymore. I'm not some misunderstood seventeen-year-old, but that's okay— I don't feel like the same girl who passed through these halls five weeks ago, terrified, clinging to my relationship with Crevan as my way of getting out of here. Every sound scared me, the guards scared me; I was always looking around, always afraid.

I'm not afraid anymore. This time I know that I am right and they are wrong.

I'm taken through the castle, down the elevator to the basement. I'm processed through reception, and each guard who sees me lets me know what they think of me. When we enter the holding cells, the first person I see in a cell of his own is Raphael Angelo. He's sitting on a chair, feet up, crossed at the ankles, watching Flawed TV, his back to me.

I smile at his casualness. On TV is an image of the crowd-filled court-yard outside. The Flawed have all sat down on the cobblestones and are whistling. A sit-down protest. Members of the public are visible at the gates, whistling, too; the crowds have grown since Crevan announced the Reduction of the Flawed plan. Whistleblowers surround the Flawed with their riot gear, but the Flawed aren't giving them any trouble.

Raphael Angelo turns around, probably seeing our reflections in his glass cage. He smiles when he sees me, offers me a thumbs-up. I go to return the gesture, but the Whistleblowers act like I'm about to throw a grenade. They grab my hands and twist them behind my back. I shout out in pain, bend over as they contort my body into an unnatural position.

"Home, sweet home," one of the guards says as we stop before my old cell. It hasn't changed at all since the last time I was here. Apart from one thing. I step inside and see Granddad.

"Granddad!" I say, running into his open arms and hugging him tightly, as though my life depends on it. "Are you okay?" I pull away quickly and examine him, my hands on his face, turning his cheeks this way and that to get a good look at him, to make sure they haven't harmed him.

"I'm all right, I'm all right," he says, pulling me into a hug again, and I see tears in his eyes. "I thought I burned you alive," he says, whispering fearfully. "As long as I live I'll never forgive myself for what I did."

"You didn't burn me, though, did you?" I hold him tight. "I'm here."

"But I didn't know until the next day. I couldn't be sure . . . I keep seeing myself drop the flame on top of you. At night when I'm sleeping here, I hear your screams." He hugs me tighter.

"Granddad, I'm here. You didn't hurt me." I lower my voice so that the guards don't hear. "You saved me. Remember that. I wouldn't have escaped if it weren't for you."

He kisses me on the head, and I feel his body trembling.

"Tell me what's been going on," I say, trying to get him to focus. "Why have they kept you here? They can't hold you here without any reasons."

"Ah," he says tiredly. "Every day there is a new *reason* they're looking into."

"That's enough," the guard says roughly. "Time's up."

Granddad is immediately resigned to the order. He's been here four days, he knows it's not worth the fight.

"I want more time with my granddad," I say, but they ignore me.

The guards hold him firmly and take him to the cell beside Raphael's, diagonal to mine. Despite his defeated air, something I have never seen in him before, Granddad looks good, clean-shaven, healthy. The facilities here are excellent—he has been well cared for, just confined for longer than necessary. He has had too long with his thoughts, and my heart breaks at his broken spirit.

I finally look to the cell adjoining mine, having a sudden ridiculous romantic pining for the man I've fallen in love with. I know it's ridiculous to want Carrick to be here in captivity with me, because he's out in the real world, in relative freedom, but this is where we met, and I've never been in this room without him.

I blink, thinking my eyes are deceiving me. Showing me what I want instead of the reality. But the vision doesn't change.

Carrick is there. Standing at the glass, looking at me.

There's bruising around his right eye. I freeze, unable to believe it. Is it my imagination or is he really here?

"Sorry," he mouths, looking defeated.

"Took your boyfriend in this morning. Just like old times now, isn't it?" The guards laugh as they leave me and lock the door behind me.

I rush to the glass and put my hand on the pane.

We're back to where we started, only it's not good enough now. I know what his touch feels like, I know what his voice sounds like, I know how he smells. And this thing between us that separated us but linked us before is not good enough now.

He was supposed to be safe. This wasn't part of the plan.

I kick the glass and scream.

SIXTY-THREE

I'M NOT ALONE in my cell for long. Judge Crevan, Judge Sanchez, and Judge Jackson and a man in a crumpled white linen suit, with a gray goatee and a bad sunburn, enter. The judges are in their red cloaks, the Guild crests on their chests. *The Purveyors of Perfection* have all graced me with their presence.

They march toward me in single file, on a mission, like a little army, their folders under their arms. Judge Sanchez looks like she's going to be ill and looks at me with wide, alarmed eyes.

This should be interesting.

Immediately Carrick, Granddad, and Raphael all stand to watch. My backup even if they're separated by glass, but their presence guides me. The guard unlocks the door for the judges, they stream in, and then the guard stands in the corner.

"You can leave," Crevan instructs the guard, who looks a little put out at being dismissed.

"Sit, Celestine," Crevan says. He looks tired. Older. I've aged him and I'm glad.

"I'd rather stand."

"Jesus, Celestine." He slams his hand down, which makes the man with the bad tan jump.

I smile.

"Can you just do *one* thing you're told?"

" 'Stubbornness. Resisting change,' " I quote him.

He's so clearly on the edge, I'm enjoying this. Judge Sanchez looks at him nervously, at me nervously. Am I going to tell on her? She's probably wondering.

"I heard what you did to my sister, Juniper." I look him dead in the eye, both of us knowing it was me he captured on the top of the summit. "Do the other judges know, too?"

Jackson is clearly aware of this and looks at Crevan with annoyance. "It was an unfortunate misunderstanding, though I understand you and your sister have been mistaken for each other before."

"And what about Logan, Colleen, Gavin, and Natasha? Who did you mistake them for?"

Jackson looks at Crevan; maybe it's an answer he'd like to hear for himself.

Crevan is cool as anything. "They, and the guards, were helping me and a special team of Whistleblowers with my investigation into your whereabouts. We take evaders seriously in the Guild."

His coolness makes me fear he'll get away with what he's done, despite Mom arriving with a police officer, a lawyer, and a newspaper editor, despite them finding missing teenagers, my innocent sister, drugged guards, a journalist, and a lawyer. He could get away with it all over again.

"Perhaps I could speak with Celestine on my own for a moment," Sanchez says suddenly.

"Why?" Jackson asks.

"Woman-to-woman. I know that Judge Crevan and Celestine have a personal history that makes their communication difficult."

"All the same, I'd rather stay in the meeting," Jackson says. "And I'm sure Judge Crevan would, too. Perhaps if we agree to do the talking and, Judge, you can take a backseat on this one."

This request angers Crevan.

Judge Sanchez looks at me. "There are things that Celestine and I had the opportunity to talk about before, shortly after her branding, that I'm hoping still stand."

Our deal is back on? Me and her versus Crevan? But Sanchez double-crossed me once already—can I trust her, and do I want to try?

Granddad, Carrick, and Raphael are all pressed up against the glass of their cells, trying to decipher what's going on. Carrick is so close to us it's as though he's in the cell with me, but he can't hear a word of what is going on. Raphael motions at me. He wants to come in here.

My head pounds. I love mathematics because a problem always has a solution. Follow the theorem and you can always find the answer. Lately, I'm confused, there are no theorems, just people playing games with one another, changing the rules as they go along. But just because they change the rules doesn't mean that I have to.

"Who are you?" I ask the linen-suit man with the tan.

"This is Richard Willingham," Crevan replies, even though I didn't ask him. "He's here to discuss your case. You're legally required by Flawed rules to have a representative."

"I already have a representative."

Crevan puts his pen down. "Mr. Willingham has flown in from abroad, last-minute, to assist me here today."

"Sorry I disturbed your golf holiday," I say to the lawyer. "Seeing as my previous representative, Mr. Berry, is in a drug-induced state, I request to use my new counsel. We don't need any private jets to get him here. He's right over there. I won't talk to you a second longer until you bring him in."

They all look at Raphael. He waves.

"*Him?*" Willingham asks.

"I find that the people who've had to fight the hardest in their lives are the strongest. What have you ever had to fight for, Mr. Willingham? If you want my business, you'll have to sell yourself to me."

"No," Crevan says simply. "Mr. Willingham is your appointed lawyer."

Sanchez and Jackson look at Crevan because they know that's not right. I should be able to choose who I want.

"I think that Ms. North retains the right to choose her counsel," Judge Jackson says, overruling Crevan.

While Jackson, Crevan, and a hotheaded Willingham discuss the changes between them, Sanchez is busy texting on her phone. I wonder what she is up to.

"Mr. Willingham, thank you for your presence today. I'll make sure the Guild jet is at your disposal," Crevan says finally.

Mr. Willingham seems very unhappy and he lets it be known through a series of huffs and pants and stern looks, but that's as far as he goes: His hands are tied; the powers that be have spoken. He passes Raphael as he leaves, giving him a disgusted once-over.

Raphael is brought into my cell, sits down, crosses his legs. "Now, where were we?" he says.

"We're here to discuss Celestine's sentencing," Jackson begins. "This has been a very public disobedience and disrespect of the Guild, of Guild rules, and she must be punished accordingly. Though evading the Guild is nothing new, and there are sanctions in place for that, her case is unprecedented. We thought it best to gather and discuss it out of court."

Crevan and Sanchez sit quietly. They both have other plans.

"Indeed, Judge Jackson, we appreciate your settling it in this way," Raphael takes over. "It's best for everybody involved. So let's begin, the Guild is a morality court. What immoral acts has Celestine carried out recently? Making a speech at a gathering that you arranged? A very inspiring one by the way, Celestine. No, I believe the Guild has not yet removed freedom of speech. All Celestine has done to the Guild is evade her Whistleblower and missed her curfews, and if she is to be punished for that, we look to precedent. In the case of Angelina Tinder missing a curfew, you removed her children from her care for one week; in the case of Victoria Shannon, you arranged to have her work without pay for one week. For Daniel Schmidt it was one month; for Michael Auburn it was six months, until he missed his mortgage payments and his home was *almost* taken from him, until common sense prevailed in the form of the high court."

He rattles all these cases off the top of his head.

"But Celestine doesn't have a job, she doesn't have children, and she certainly doesn't have a home. If you punish her family, then I will take you to court for human rights violations. Families of Flawed cannot be punished for Flawed acts.

"But let's not forget the Guild incorrectly incarcerated her sister, Juniper, who did nothing wrong, and her grandfather, who you have yet to prove has done anything wrong."

"He aided an evader," Crevan says.

"But where is your proof? If you had any, then you would have charged him by now. These acts against Celestine's sister and grandfather were carried out in order to bring Celestine out of the woodwork. The Guild has done nothing but antagonize my client and fill her with fear so as to prevent her from finding her way back. Instead of discussing punishments, I say Celestine North deserves an act of mercy."

"Mr. Angelo, the court of the Guild doesn't sit to administer clemency," Judge Jackson politely says, denying the request.

"I agree. Nor does it sit to introduce a role for justice after a wrongful conviction. But the government can," Raphael explains. "A government without decency, a government without mercy, is a pretty harsh overlord. I intend to appeal to Prime Minister Percy on this issue."

"A wrongful conviction?" Judge Jackson frowns. "We're here to discuss Celestine's evasion. And with all due respect, Mr. Angelo, the election is tomorrow. You will be taking a risk—who knows who will be in government?"

"Indeed, it could very well be Prime Minister Sleepwell, and I'm sure she'll take a more favorable view."

"I hardly think that will be the situation," Crevan snorts.

Judge Jackson looks less sure and annoyed that Crevan keeps talking despite being told to take a backseat.

A guard interrupts our meeting. "Judge Jackson, there is an important phone call for you, in your office."

"Can't it wait?" Jackson asks, confused. "*This* is important."

"It's urgent, sir."

I look at Sanchez, who seems coy, and I realize whatever she was texting on her phone made sure that Jackson would have to leave the room. This disappoints me, as I think Raphael was getting through to Judge Jackson, or that at least he could be more fair.

When Jackson leaves, Raphael continues. "How do you wish to further punish my client? After all, you branded her already in the five areas."

"Well, we can always find more areas," Crevan says to me jokingly, with a twinkle in his eye.

He actually thinks that nobody knows. Sanchez regards him differently then. I can tell his arrogance has angered her.

"A spine, perhaps," Raphael says.

My heart drums manically. We're finally there. Raphael is going for it now.

Sanchez senses it, too, and sits up rigidly.

Crevan looks at Raphael coldly.

There's a long silence.

"Let's all be honest with one another now," Raphael says. "There is footage, Judge Crevan, that reveals you branding this young lady's spine yourself, without anesthetic."

Crevan's eye twitches. "This footage allegedly exists but it is rather elusive, as nobody can seem to find it. Personally I think it's an idle threat, one that doesn't exist."

"It exists," I say.

"I can assure you, Judge Sanchez, there is no such footage, and even if there is, I'm sure it's a cheap re-creation, along with everything else we can view on the Internet," he says to Sanchez.

He's trying to reel her in. She remains silent, keeping her cards close to her chest. I can't be certain whose side she's going to eventually take.

"I know that Celestine was in your home this morning," Crevan says, suspicious.

"Indeed, I called you personally to tell you, but the Whistleblowers got to her first."

"I called the Whistleblowers on myself," I interrupt their cat-and-mouse game, which is starting to bug me. No games. Just honesty. "Judge Sanchez wanted to hand me over to you herself. She wanted to give me to you for something in return. Do a little deal."

She looks at me, surprised, but must continue now that I've begun.

"You've made too many mistakes, Bosco," Sanchez says. "There is a private inquiry into your actions; it has asked me to comply. I'm going to have to answer honestly."

"What do you want from me?" Crevan asks her, and it's as if Raphael and I suddenly aren't in the room.

"I want you gone. I want to be head judge of the Guild."

Crevan laughs nervously. "You want me to step down?"

"I want control. Full control."

He stiffens, stands up. "You want to take my job in return for what? *Her?*" He points his finger at me. "I already have her."

I'm insulted that he can't even say my name. As is Raphael, who regards this all with disgust.

"*I* have the footage," Sanchez says, and I see the color drain from Crevan's face. "I saw you hold that iron in your hand and brand that seventeen-year-old girl. It was deplorable. Disgusting. This is not what the Guild was founded for."

He is momentarily shaken by this. "As I said, the footage was faked."

"I think people would be extremely doubtful about that."

He swallows.

"It puts the entire Guild in disrepute, Bosco, and I will make it public if I have to because they are *your* actions. Your remaining as head judge will bring about the end of the Guild. It's already happening. I can begin a new relationship with the new government. It will be like starting fresh, continuing on with what we set out to do."

Crevan isn't happy about this. The Guild is his baby; perhaps Erica Edelman is right about Crevan treating the country as if it were his child. When his wife died he fell to pieces; he started blaming everybody else for her loss, starting off by branding the doctor who missed the cancer, who misdiagnosed her. Then he got a taste for revenge, and that's when he came apart at the seams, becoming this monster.

"You can't do this." Crevan leans toward Sanchez threateningly. "The Guild was founded by my family. It has always been led by a Crevan."

"I can do this and I will," Sanchez says, standing.

Raphael and I look at each other. This isn't looking good for me. They're working out a deal and I'm not gaining anything.

"It is the right and best thing to do," she says. "You leave on your terms, at the start of a new government, a new era, a new beginning for the Guild. You go quietly, no questions asked, no video released."

"What about me?" I ask, breaking their long stare.

"I will grant you your freedom," she says. "Mr. Angelo is correct. The Guild is not above an act of decency and mercy."

"You will overrule me?" Crevan raises his voice.

"It's the only way."

"It is not," he yells. Carrick and Granddad are glued to their glass walls, trying to understand what is going on, just as much as Raphael and I, who are in the room.

Crevan marches to the door of my cell, tries to open it.

"It's locked," I say.

"For God's sake, open this door," he yells at the top of his voice.

"They can't hear you from here," I say calmly. "Soundproofed."

He turns to us, face red and trembling, his insides bubbling with rage, ready to explode. The guard comes just in time to unlock the cell and he catapults himself out of here as fast as he can, almost knocking over the guard.

SIXTY-FOUR

SANCHEZ EXHALES, a long shaky breath.

"So you're granting me my freedom. I'll no longer be Flawed."

"Yes."

"You'll let my granddad go, too?" I ask Sanchez.

"Yes."

"You'll let Mr. Angelo go?"

"Yes."

"My parents had to pay my legal costs."

"That will be refunded by the Guild."

"Marlena Ponta, she was my character witness at my trial. You will say that she didn't mislead the Guild. Publicly."

"Yes."

"Celestine's brands," Raphael says. "The Guild will cover the costs of their removal."

Sanchez is thoughtful. "Yes."

"This verdict overturn will be public knowledge?" Raphael asks.

"It will."

My heart pounds. This is everything I wanted. I want the world to know that Crevan made a mistake so that it will help shine a light on all his Flawed cases. If Crevan is Flawed, then so is the entire Guild. Then perhaps it will bring an end to the Flawed regime. I can't believe this is everything that I wanted. Though not quite everything.

Sanchez gathers her papers and, as if reading my mind, asks, "That's everything?"

I look over at Carrick. "And Carrick Vane. His verdict must be overturned, too."

She looks at me then, and I think I see a smile at the corner of her lips.

"No," she says.

SIXTY-FIVE

"BUT YOU HAVE to grant Carrick his freedom, too." I raise my voice.

"Carrick Vane isn't part of your case," Sanchez says. "He has nothing to do with this discussion."

"But he is being punished for being on the run with me."

"He is being punished for evading his Whistleblower. There will be no punishment for his colluding with you, if that's what you're worried about."

"But you have to let him go free," I say, voice shaky now.

"No," she says again firmly. She looks at Raphael. "Are we finished here? I'll draw up the paperwork."

"I need time to consult with my counsel," I say, to their absolute surprise. "I need time to think."

Raphael closes his eyes, with dread.

"How much time?" Sanchez asks.

I look at the clock. "I don't know. Tomorrow?"

"You have until the end of the day."

"But they've agreed to everything, Celestine," Raphael says. "You have your life back. *Take the deal.*"

"Listen to your counsel, Celestine," Sanchez says, gathering her papers. "My offer comes off the table at six PM today." She walks to the door and the guard opens it for her immediately.

"What's going on?" Raphael asks as soon as she's gone. "You should take the deal. This is exactly what you wanted. Your case *publicly* being overturned will raise questions about the entire Flawed system, which in turn will help everyone."

"And, realistically, how long will that take? I want Carrick to be free now."

"When you began this, you wanted to find Crevan Flawed. This is a step in that direction. Celestine, you have to stick to the plan. Don't be foolish. You can do a great deal more good for Carrick and for all of the Flawed after you've regained your freedom. Don't let Carrick sway your decision."

My heart pounds at the enormity of the choice facing me.

I glance up at the clock, watching the minutes pass.

"Look, you're young, I understand," continues Raphael. "When I was eighteen I was crazy about this girl, Marie. Christ, if you'd asked me to jump off a cliff for Marie, I would have. Celestine, don't give up your freedom at eighteen for somebody else. You have so much to learn. You have to think of yourself now. Take the deal."

I finally look at Carrick, who is so close to the glass he looks like he wants to punch through it if I don't tell him what's going on.

I sigh and pick up a pen and paper that Judge Sanchez mistakenly left behind, though nothing she does ever hints at being a mistake. I lift the page and show it to him.

They agreed to everything, except you.

He stares at it for a moment, allowing it to settle, and then he nods, in a *so what* way. He folds his arms and studies me intently, asking me, telling me, to let him know that I took the deal. I squirm under his gaze.

I shake my head.

He throws his hands up angrily, and though I can't hear him, I see him shouting at me. He wants me to be free. He wants me to take the deal.

I write again and push the paper flat against the glass.

I will never feel free if you're not.

This seems to break him. I know it touches him, but it breaks him more because he snaps. I know he's shouting my name but I can't hear a word from my soundproofed box. I shake my head and look away; I don't want to see any more protests. He can't argue with me when my back is turned, which I know will drive him demented, but I can't argue with him here, not like this. I've made my decision, and yet what Raphael has said stays with me. Am I being foolish?

"Sometimes you must be selfish for the greater good," Raphael says, shaking his head.

"Whatever decision I make, Raphael, you and Granddad will be okay. I wouldn't do that to both of you."

"I appreciate that," he says, almost sadly, for me.

But he doesn't realize, I *am* being selfish. I have grown to love my Flawed world. I love the friends I have made. I love Carrick. I know who I am. I feel like one of them. For that to be taken away would be to go through it all again, being ripped away from a world and people I know. I feel at home being Flawed, maybe more comfortable than ever; I feel at peace in my scarred skin. I don't want my brands removed. I don't want to go back to who I was, to the life that I had. I would never feel at home being perfect. It doesn't exist; it's all fake.

But I don't tell him any of this.

I look up at the clock.

Watching the time.

Waiting.

"Why do you keep looking at the clock?" Raphael asks, suddenly suspicious.

"No reason," I say.

He narrows his eyes. "Celestine, you're up to something, aren't you?" he says, watching me. "That's why you're not taking the deal."

"I'm not up to anything."

It's not a lie. I'm not up to anything now. I've already done it. Something is about to happen. Something I put into motion before I was even captured.

SIXTY-SIX

I GLANCE AT the guard, who's still in the room.

"I'm not up to anything," I repeat.

Granddad watches me, eyes narrowed, as though he's trying to figure me out. He knows me well; he, too, suspects something. Or perhaps he already knows. Carrick is now beyond angry with me. He picks up a chair and throws it against the far pane of glass. It just bounces back at him. I see his red face, the veins pulsating in his neck, the anger high.

"Uh-oh," Raphael says.

The guard in my cell jumps to attention.

"Leave him. He'll calm down," Raphael says.

"Back in your cell," she says to Raphael, opening the door.

"I'm not finished with my client," he protests.

But he doesn't get to say much more because he's strong-armed back into his cell by two guards who come racing in to settle the Carrick situation. I need Carrick to calm down—he can't lose it now. Carrick has his back to me, deliberately so, a sign of his anger. His back is heaving up and down as he tries to gather himself. I write quickly and slam the page against the window adjoining our cells.

He's going to ruin this if he doesn't realize what is about to happen.

Turn around, Carrick, turn around.

I bang on the glass but of course he can't hear me.

The guards open his door and I pray he doesn't attack them. He finally looks at me, but I've lowered the page. I can't risk the guards reading what I've written. I rip it up into a million pieces and throw it in the trash. The guards go to either side of him. They hold their hands out in front, like they're taming a wild horse. Carrick ignores them, turns around to look at me, eyes red like he's been crying. He thinks he's ruining my life, but he has no idea how much he has saved me. If he had just read my note, he'd understand everything.

The guards stay with him for some time, blocking my view. Then, when they leave, he stays where he is, and I stand at the glass willing him to look at me, but he doesn't.

I smile and shake my head. It's not going to work. He can't make me hate him.

And there is nothing he can do to stop what is about to happen.

SIXTY-SEVEN

THE GUARDS RETURN with our food and deliver a tray to each of us. As they do that, they remove the pen and paper from my cell and dump the Highland Castle uniform down on my bed, red scrub pants and a red T-shirt.

Raphael picks up a fork and pokes through the food with a look of disgust. Granddad leaps in, heaping the forkfuls into his mouth. Carrick keeps his back to me, ignoring the guards, ignoring the food, ignoring everybody and everything. He wants me to hate him, but it's not working.

I go to the small toilet in the holding cell to change out of the slip and into the uniform. When I return I smell the food and my stomach rumbles. There's soup, a beige color that could be anything from vegetable to chicken. For the main course there is meat and two vegetables. I try the smell and taste test that Carrick taught me as I try to figure out just what exactly this food is. There is a distinct smell of mint. Or the antiseptic. Perhaps the mint is coming from the meat, which maybe is lamb, but it looks more like dried beef than lamb. I lift the soup bowl to my nose and close my eyes and breathe in. That slight smell of mint. What could it be?

I can't figure it out, and I decide I'm not eating this food. That would be a kind of victory on their part. Crevan was right about one thing: My chief feature is definitely stubbornness.

I long to be back in the kitchen with Carrick, sitting before the open fridge, blindfolded, feeling the tips of his fingers on my lips as he feeds me.

Pea and mint soup, I wonder, but then it would be green, not beige.

To think that this dry, overcooked, bad cafeteria food was the last thing I tasted before I became Flawed. Maybe it's a good thing I can't taste it now, though it hasn't stopped Granddad from shoveling it into him and Raphael from picking at it. Granddad has worked his way through it and is even lying down for a snooze.

Carrick gets up from his bed and makes his way to the table, his hunger taking over, too. He sits down and dives into the soup, tasting it straightaway, unlike me, who has to figure it out.

My stomach rumbles and I sigh. Fine. Just get on with it.

But it's as I'm spooning it to my mouth, as the spoon rests on my bottom lip, that I stall. My memory flashes to Crevan on the summit, that antiseptic smell that I thought was chewing gum. It reminds me of the hospital I woke up in after he stuck the needle in my thigh. It reminds me of how I felt when dragging myself along the floor.

I open my eyes.

They've drugged our food.

Granddad is lying down on his bed, eyes closed.

Raphael is slumped in his chair, head on his chest.

Carrick has his back to me and is dunking crusty bread in his soup. I jump up and start banging on the window, screaming.

He can't hear me, of course, but I can't think of anything else and so I continue, crying as I watch him eat more and more of it, my voice hoarse and my throat burning, my hands and fists throbbing as I pound on the glass.

I look around for the pen and paper but they're gone, removed by the guards when they delivered the food.

Then I think of something. I need to cause a distraction. Make a scene. I pick up a chair and throw it. I pull the blankets from the bed and throw them on the floor. I topple the table of food. Anything I can pick up, I throw. I trash the room. Carrick must eventually feel vibrations or see the reflections in the glass because he turns suddenly and his eyes widen when he sees the state of my room. The guards open the door to the holding cells and grab their keys.

I run to the glass and mouth, "The food." I shake my head. "Don't eat the food." I wrap my hands around my neck in a strangling way.

His eyes widen, he looks to his food and then back to me, understanding. He stands up to make his way to me but he goes in a diagonal direction. He wobbles on his feet. He looks to Granddad, then Raphael, and teeters some more. He looks back at me and his eyes have glazed over.

He looks over my shoulder and I see the pain in his expression as the guards open the door and come for me. It's the last thing he sees before reaching out for a chair for support and falling to the floor.

"Carrick!" I yell.

My cell door opens and I fire whatever I can at the guards, over and over again.

"Grab her," a guard directs another, and two of them come after me, batons in hand.

"Leave her! Stop!" a voice shouts.

It's Art.

SIXTY-EIGHT

ART IS WEARING his Whistleblower uniform.

"Don't touch her," he says.

"You disgust me," I say, kicking a chair toward him.

"Whoa, whoa, Celestine, stop!" His voice is like thunder.

"You drugged them!" I yelled.

He looks around the cells and sees the others.

I pick up my bowl of soup and throw it at his feet. "I wasn't hungry."

They all run at me, but it's Art who reaches me first. He wraps his arms around me, and even though he's not Carrick, even though he's smaller, he's still bigger and stronger than me. He wraps his arms around me and squeezes, to stop me from lifting my arms. It's not so much his strength that stops me, it's his scent, and the familiar feel of his body so close to mine, and his arms wrapped around me. It feels wrong to struggle against him. Unnatural. It's Art. My Art.

I start to wriggle again.

"Celestine," he whispers in my ear. "If you stop, they will go away."

I freeze. It was the *they*. The hint that it's us against them. Is that what I'm supposed to think, is that what he wants me to think, or is that what I want to think?

"We're fine," Art says firmly. "Thank you, I'll take it from here."

They begrudgingly close the door.

"Christ, they don't trust me, you don't trust me—when can I get a break?" He keeps his arms wrapped around me.

They don't trust him? I don't blame them.

"I'm not going to throw anything," I snap. "You can let me go."

He looks at me, deep into my eyes. I have to look away, just seeing them confuses me too much. His grip weakens and I push away from him. I move to the far side of the cell, the farthest I can get from him.

"What did you do to them?" I say, gesturing to Carrick, Raphael, and Granddad.

"I didn't do anything," he replies, studying them. Carrick is lying on the floor, passed out.

"Tell me the truth."

"I am. He was throwing furniture around, maybe they needed to calm him down."

"They didn't, he was already calm," I say. "And my granddad wasn't doing anything, nor Raphael. Neither was I. I'm the only one who didn't eat it."

Art looks at Carrick, a look of hate, and then he looks at Granddad and I see his resolve weaken. Art liked that Granddad never watched what he said in front of him, in fact his conspiracy theories seemed to grow whenever he was in Art's company. It amused Art; he was always fond of Granddad. "The spawn of Satan," Granddad used to call him, which bizarrely made Art laugh. I think he found Granddad refreshing, when he felt everybody else around him was always nice to him because of who his dad is.

"How did you know Carrick threw a chair? Were you watching us?"

"Celestine, the room is covered in CCTV cameras."

I wonder if he saw the meeting with the judges. I doubt it. "Spying on me for Daddy, Art?"

"Shut up." He stands. "I'm trying to figure out what the hell is going on here."

"You know what's going—"

"With him," he shouts, pointing at Carrick. "Did it happen in here? While I was out of my mind with worry, you were in here, cozy with him? Did it happen then?"

"Cozy?" I ask, then laugh. "Yes, because you can see how cozy this is, how much human contact is completely possible in here," I say sarcastically. "And what exactly do you think could have happened between me and him when I was scared out of my wits after your dad locked me up?"

He paces back and forth.

I take a deep breath. Try to calm down. "It was after," I say quietly. "After I got out. You weren't there for me. I had to run away. He was the only person who would help me, the only person who understood—"

"I would have understood. I was your boyfriend!"

"You went into hiding, Art. I had no one."

"I needed to figure things out."

"You obviously did. Now that you're wearing that uniform, I can see you decided what and who was right and wrong."

"When I came back you were gone," he says, trying to make me understand.

"I had to go."

"To him?"

"Art, stop it. It's not just about Carrick. I had to get away from your dad. He was hunting me down."

"He wouldn't have if you hadn't run. Why do you keep making everything worse? And that speech today, why don't you just *stop*? Just do what you're told. Every time you do something it just makes it harder for . . ."

"What?"

"Nothing."

"Tell me."

"Harder for us to be together."

I'm stunned. For a long time I don't know what to say. I can tell he's hugely embarrassed and maybe even close to tears.

"You still want us to be together?"

He doesn't reply.

"You're a Whistleblower, I'm Flawed, and you still want me?"

No response.

"Art, you know that regardless of these brands, I'm still the same person. Whatever I do, whatever I say, I'm still me."

"No, you're not." He shakes his head.

"Just like when you put that uniform on, you completely change?"

His head snaps up so fast. "I don't."

I leave the silence. *Same thing.*

"I need some air," I say, putting my head in my hands, feeling faint, unable to deal with this bombshell. *Art still wants me?*

"Good idea," he says. "We can talk more openly outside in the courtyard."

He opens the cell using his key card and we walk down the corridor. It's the same walk I took for the first time when Funar pretended he was taking me and Carrick to get some air but then forced us to sit on the bench and witness the screams of the Flawed man being branded.

The second time I took this walk, Carrick was sitting on the bench in support of me as I was branded. *I'll find you.* His words comforted me for so long when I got home.

The bench sits empty now. My head whirls with everything that has happened and all that Art has said.

Suddenly I break away from Art. He just misses me as he tries to grab me. I run into the Branding Chamber and lock the door. He appears in the viewing room, angry. I can't hear what he's saying but he can hear me. He's going to have to listen to me now—he has no choice.

"The last time I was in here, do you know what your dad did to me?" He covers his face with his hands.

"They put me in this chair. They tied me down. Five brands, Art. For trying to help that old man. And in the end the brands weren't for helping him, they were for lying to the court about it, for embarrassing your dad, for making him look stupid. You might be wearing that uniform, but I know you don't believe that's right."

I open the drawers filled with tools. So many *F*'s of different sizes, for different parts of the body, depending on the size of the person. I hadn't realized that, I'd thought one size fit all.

"I kept my anklet on during it all. You'd just given it to me and I wanted to believe that you were still with me and that you still believed I was perfect. Bark let me keep it. It was him who made it, wasn't it?"

Carrick had told me somebody at the Castle had made it, and I remember the flicker of recognition in Bark's face as his eyes clamped on the ankle of the person he was about to brand as Flawed, as he battled with the hypocrisy, the irony, the fragility of life.

Art nods, tears welling in his eyes as I relive it.

"At the time I was glad you weren't in the chamber, but now I wish you had been." I run my finger along the pokers, which become hot branding tools for the Flawed.

I look at him. "The guards were worried about me. Five brands was a lot to take at once. They wanted to stop, but they needed permission. Somebody called for your dad. He came in here. Instead of stopping it, your dad took the iron and branded me for a sixth time. On my spine, without anesthetic."

He's shaking his head. *No, no, no.* He doesn't want to believe it.

"He'll probably tell you that I've made it up. That I'm spreading lies about him. They're not lies, Art. He told me to repent and I wouldn't, so he did this to me."

I turn around and lift my T-shirt to reveal my lower spine. "He told a doctor that I did it to myself, but how could I have?"

I hear Dr. Greene's voice in my head. *How could a girl do this to herself?*

Art is shaking his head, tears rolling down his cheeks.

I run my hand over the rods again, trying to find the right one, wondering if I could reach around my back, if I could have actually done it to myself, is that what they will try to prove? Will they make me stand up in court and show them that I could do it myself? My hand stops. It hovers over a shape that stands out from the others. The three interconnecting circles of the geometric harmony anklet that Bark made for me, the symbol of perfection, is filed alongside the Flawed *F*'s. I pick it up and click it into place on the rod.

"What kind of person could do this to herself?" I repeat the words of the doctor, to myself.

I fire up the flame on the burner.

Art bangs on the glass over and over.

I place the poker over the flame.

"If everyone thinks you are something, why not become it? Isn't that what you did, Art? Become a Whistleblower because everyone thought you were like your dad? You didn't want to fight it anymore, you wanted to see what it was like. You didn't have anything else to lose."

He's crying and banging on the window, trying to get me to stop.

"Judge Sanchez wants to make a deal with me, did you know that?"

He shakes his head, confused.

"Your dad is out. Sanchez is in. On further review, the Guild thinks they've made a mistake. They say they're going to take my brands away from me."

It's clear Art isn't aware of any of this.

"But I don't *want* them to take my brands away. These brands have given me more strength than I've ever had, and I can't pretend that none of this happened. But there needs to be a balance. I still wear the anklet for balance," I say, realizing it now. "You gave me the greatest gift, Art. You told me I was perfect and I've worn it every day since, like it had a special power that beat the brands. But it wasn't the anklet, it was because you told me, because you believed in me."

He smiles sadly at me.

"No one will ever be able to take your gift away from me, you understand, don't you?"

He nods.

I roll up the bottom of my T-shirt, revealing my stomach.

"Transversus abdominis," I say. "Remember we learned about this?"

He lays his hands flat against the window, his forehead against the pane, giving up the fight to stop me.

"It's located under the obliques; it is the deepest of the abdominal muscles and wraps around the spine for protection and stability. It's our center of gravity."

I hold the poker in the flame, my heart pounding. I'm not seeking perfection; I'm not seeking justice. I'm seeking balance.

I push the branding iron against my stomach. Branded Perfect forever.

Perfect and Flawed on the same body.

Now I'm balanced.

SIXTY-NINE

THE PAIN IS almost unbearable. I drop the branding stick and reach out to the chair in agony, dizzy, seeing black spots before my eyes. I try to catch my breath. I feel nauseous and breathe deeply. There's banging on the door and I unlock it. Art bursts in and I collapse into his arms.

We both slide to the floor.

"What did you do?" he asks between sobs, panicking. "What the hell did you do? We have to get you to the hospital."

"No," I protest, and cling to him tighter.

"Oh, Celestine," he cries out to me, but it's soft and gentle and I feel his warm breath on my neck as he buries his head into me.

"Now there's a part of you with me forever, no matter what you think of me."

He lifts my chin with his finger so that we're looking right at each other, inches apart. "I think you're the strongest, bravest, most courageous, stupidest person I've ever met."

I smile. "You do?"

"I was jealous," he admits, loosening his grip on me slightly, as if remembering we're not together. "Of you and him. I should have done what you and he did. Instead of running away on my own, I should have just taken you and run."

He looks at me with that familiar look that used to make me go all weak at the knees, and I await the stir within me, but it doesn't come. Nothing but fondness, affection . . . but nothing more. I can't help thinking of Carrick, Carrick holding me, Carrick watching me, how Carrick smells and tastes. Carrick, who is lying on the floor of his cell.

"So even though you two going on the run angered me more than you'll ever understand, I'm glad he was there for you, like I should have been."

"Thank you," I whisper. "And I do understand. I felt the same way when I saw you with Juniper. . . ."

"We were just trying to protect you."

"I realize that now."

He looks away, knows that he's finally lost me.

"I thought I could be closer to Dad this way." He looks down at his uniform. "It's not working. Before, I never saw the side of him that everybody else did: the judge. I mean, you and I made of fun of it, the bravado, the persona he took on, I could separate it all. But now . . . he's different."

I remain tight-lipped.

"Did he really hurt you like you said?" he whispers.

I nod.

He squeezes me tighter. "Who have I been living with?"

"He loves you," I say, the only positive thing I can think of.

He moves me gently aside so that he can stand. I wince at the pain in my stomach. Art opens the units lining the wall and comes back to me with bandages.

He lifts my T-shirt, a move that is so familiar, and he winces as he sees the scar I made on myself. It's clear as day, nothing like the mess on my spine. This scar wasn't done out of punishment, it was done out of pride. He cleans the wound, which I have to grit my teeth for and grunt, and then he places a cotton pad on the wound and wraps a bandage around my waist.

"If he loves me like you say, then he'll forgive me," he says. "I'm getting you out of here."

"No. You don't need to do that."

"Yes, I do."

"But . . ." I look in the direction of the cells. "My granddad, Raphael Angelo." I swallow. "Carrick."

He pulls down my T-shirt. "I'll get you all out of here," he says quietly. "I just need time to work out how."

"Thank you." I take his hand and he helps me to my feet.

"It's the least I can do," he says. "I don't want people to think I'm like him. Imagine, that's my worst fear. Being like my dad."

"Nobody will think you're like him when they find out that you wanted to let us go."

"My fear isn't of people thinking it, it's of actually *being* like him."

"You're nothing like him," I say, and I really mean it. "Art, there's something I have to tell you. . . ." I have to warn him what's about to happen, but I look up and see Crevan. He's sitting in the viewing chamber—I don't know how long he's been here. I don't know what he's heard. I hope he heard every single word that Art said. Our eyes meet, through the glass, and I know from the broken look on his face that he has heard every single word. He's wearing his cloak, and it seems too big for his defeated demeanor. He stands up and leaves the room.

Art goes to look behind him but I stop him.

Then the guards come rushing in, see us, and make for the chamber door.

We don't put up a fight.

SEVENTY

"EASY, EASY," Art says as I wince from the pain in my core when they grab me.

"What happened here?" a guard asks.

"We'll talk about it somewhere else," Art says authoritatively.

"You take her. I'll take him," the guard says.

"I was following my father's orders," Art says, and the guard throws him such a look of contempt and mutters, "Daddy's boy," before pulling me away with him.

Instead of being brought back to my cell, I'm marched up a winding staircase, away from the holding cells in the basement and up to the Guild offices in the castle.

I've never been in this part of the castle before; nobody gets to come here—it's private, for Guild employees only.

Each step I take hurts me, but I have no choice but to keep going. We reach the top floor and I'm taken to the turret room. There is a round table in the center of the room, bookshelves lining the walls, broken up only by windows that overlook the castle courtyard on one side and others that look out to all the sides of the city. Sanchez, I can tell, likes to see the world from a height, and this is where the decisions are made.

Sanchez and Jackson are sitting together, looking troubled. With Crevan's position ambiguous after Sanchez faced him down, leaving the two remaining judges to deal with the aftermath of the announcement of Crevan's sinister program, the Reduction of the Flawed, they are in the midst of a crisis. I should be the least of their worries, but I know I'm at the top of the pile.

"You weren't feeling hungry?" Sanchez asks, frustrated, and I stare at her in shock. It was she who arranged for the food to be drugged. But why? And then I realize. She never wanted me to sign the deal. She screwed me over again. She *wanted* me to miss the deadline. Of course she wouldn't want my ruling to be publicly overturned, for the same reason she wouldn't allow the footage to become public. It would be the Guild's downfall, the Guild she is now the head of. She got what she wanted; why would she help me?

Feeling less confident than I did before, now that my three backups, including my legal representative, have been knocked out many floors below, I slowly sit at the table, my wound aching. It's me versus the remaining committee of judges; my fate is in their hands.

Sanchez places a document on the table before me, and a pen. A Highland Castle pen, from the tourist shop.

"As we discussed, the end of business today is your final date to agree to a new deal."

"Shouldn't I have legal representation?"

"I was told he couldn't be stirred," Jackson says. "And you sent away Mr. Willingham." His patience with me has clearly come to an end.

"We discussed these terms with your representative already, and you had time to discuss them with him. Nothing has changed. You either sign the contract or not," Sanchez says quickly, trying to hurry it all along.

I remain silent, my heart drumming. I think I actually really hate this woman.

"These are the conditions," Sanchez begins. "Instead of a Flawed verdict, we believe the verdict should have been a six-month prison sentence in line with the 'aiding a Flawed' law. We withdrew the Flawed verdict; your grandfather and Mr. Angelo have immunity, as you were not Flawed; and you begin your prison sentence in Highland Women's Correctional Facility on Monday for a total of three months. We removed the three months' time served as Flawed from that sentence. You can expect to serve one month of your three-month sentence."

I look at her in shock. "This is your act of mercy?" I look at Judge Jackson. "You weren't there, but believe me, this wasn't the deal she promised me."

"I didn't *promise* you anything. This is our *offer*, Celestine," Sanchez says, pushing the pages closer to me.

Jackson has a gentler tone. "I know at your age prison seems like a terrifying ordeal, but it will be minimum security, for a period of no more than thirty days, and then you will be free to live your life as a regular citizen of Humming."

I look at the grandfather clock against the wall. "But what about Carrick?"

"I told you, Celestine," says Sanchez, "he goes unpunished for any involvement he had with you, but his Flawed branding remains in place. His case is not related to yours, there's nothing we can do."

"What's going to happen to Judge Crevan?" I ask. "No prison sentence for him for what he did to me? No Flawed brand for *his* unethical, immoral mistakes?" I don't let either of them respond. "You just wanted his job. You said it was about cleaning up the Guild, but really it was just about power. You wanted the power. You lose your son and gain a job all in one day. Is it really worth it?"

Sanchez closes her eyes and breathes deeply, as though trying to keep her patience with a petulant child.

Judge Jackson steps in, still calm. "Think about the opportunity you have been given. You have been given a gift by the Guild. An opportunity to see what life is like on the other side. A chance. Nobody gets that. Take what you have learned and go forward."

"You're absolutely right." I finally look at Judge Jackson. "I'd like to tell you about what I've learned, if I may?"

I look at the clock again.

"I've learned a great deal throughout this experience, and one of the most important things you've taught me is about trust. Who to trust, and who not to trust. Before the branding I don't think I'd ever been hurt by anyone, not in a real way. But *since* the branding, people have surprised me. It wasn't me who changed. You put a letter on my sleeve and these scars on my body, and suddenly the whole world shifted. I've had to learn to adapt to that. I've been forced to figure out who I am, more than ever.

"Judge Crevan was right in his interview when he said that punishment helps people become more self-aware. I think of myself more, and think more of myself; but mostly I'm aware of my *instincts* more than ever. They've become my guide.

"Judge Sanchez came to me nearly three weeks ago, after the trial, looking to help me. She was concerned at that stage that my Flawed verdict was an incorrect verdict."

Judge Jackson's head snaps around to her so fast.

Judge Sanchez raises her voice. "Now, I don't think that this is the time for more lies—"

"I'd like to hear this," Jackson says firmly. "It seems many of this girl's lies have turned out to be true." He glares at her, then returns his attention to me.

I continue. "I did everything Sanchez asked of me. I went to her this morning with evidence powerful enough to remove Crevan from his position. Except the evidence was powerful enough to take down not just Crevan but the entire Guild, and so she decided to threaten Crevan instead, to take his job, not to help me, or to see that justice was done."

Jackson looks at Sanchez nervously.

I look at Sanchez and smile. "Thank you for teaching me about trust."

Sanchez shifts uncomfortably in her seat, just wanting this to be over so she can get on with it, not at all touched, moved, or guilty. I'm glad. It makes what's going to happen next easier.

"The thing is, the Guild has trained me well. Did you think I didn't know that this was what would happen?"

Her eyes narrow.

"Did you think I didn't guess that you *wouldn't* use the footage against the Guild? Did you think I would come straight to you from Mary May's house and hand over all my copies to you? Did you actually believe me? Did you think that I wouldn't know that you'd double-cross me somehow?"

I smile.

She braces herself.

"I was one step ahead of you. The whole time. Judge Sanchez, I'm *Flawed. You* shouldn't have trusted *me*."

I look at the clock. It's 6:00 PM.

"I suggest you turn on the television," I say.

SEVENTY-ONE

16 HOURS EARLIER

WHEN I WAS a child, my mom was always obsessed with the sun. Not by the sunset that signaled the end of the day, but by the sunrise that brought about the miracle of the new day. I don't know if this is because she was an optimist, a joyful soul who celebrated every new day, or because as a pessimist she feared that every day could be the end.

She used to wake early, wake us all up and take us to the lake, where we would watch the sunrise together. As we got older we refused to get out of bed during the week, and then we just went on weekends. Then it was just Sunday mornings, and as we reached our teenage years and didn't want to go at all, she went alone.

Just to keep her happy she planned what she called her "sunrise days," days planned well in advance of when we would accompany her. But our company was begrudging. Sleeping on pillows in the car, sometimes refusing to even get out, which angered or hurt her depending on the day. I remember watching her from the car one day, all bundled up and feeling so frustrated that our weird mother had taken us from the comfort of our warm beds for this, but when I conjure that image of her now I feel guilty for not sharing it with her.

It also makes me smile. The picture in my head of her with the sun rising before her makes me feel calm, fills me with love for her.

She would send us photographs of the sunrise from all around the world, from wherever she was doing modeling shoots. The sun coming up over Milan Cathedral while she was at Milan Fashion Week, over the rooftops of Montmartre during Paris Fashion Week. Rising over the Manhattan skyline or at London's Camden Market. Dad would grumble that she was probably only on her way home.

She'd fill photo albums just with these photographs, try to get as many of us with the sun rising as she could, and she would study them, mainly at night by the fire, curled up in her pajamas while the rest of us watched TV. It must have lifted her soul. I don't think I ever asked her why. It seems such an obvious thing to ask her now, but ever since I've had to leave my family behind I think of a thousand things a day that I want to ask or tell them. Even Ewan, who's only eight. I realize there is so much about his little life that I don't know.

After Carrick and I get our hands on the snow globe in Mary May's house, we quietly sneak away, terrified that she'll catch us. We don't call Raphael Angelo yet to collect us, as we promised him. Instead, we send a text message to my mom to meet us at the lake.

There are a number of reasons why I contact Mom. First, I need to see her before she charges the Whistleblower training center that holds Juniper. Second, I need her to help me with the next part of my plan. But mostly it's because I miss her. I want my mom. I want to touch her, smell her, feel her. I want her to make everything okay just as she always has done for me, or at least make me feel like everything is *going* to be okay. Help me with that extra armor for the world. I know I'm old enough, but I need her. Just like Mary May needs hers. Just as Art cried every day when he lost his, and how Crevan fell to pieces when his son lost his. Just as Carrick risked his freedom to find his.

I want Carrick to meet my mom. I want this so much.

We wait on the sand. It's 2:00 AM. I'm sure she will be awake, with her duty of charging into the Whistleblower base to get Juniper only hours away. I've no doubt she is plotting and planning, rehearsing and running through it over and over again with Dad, who no doubt wants to be the one to do it, but it can't be him, it has to be Mom, the mother.

Thirty minutes later, headlights appear. We hide. She pulls into the parking lot; no one follows her. She makes her way down to the sand, wearing an oversized cardigan, carrying a blanket and bag in her hands. We come out of our hiding place and she sees me. Her face crumples before she even gets to me. She opens her arms wide and I'm lost in that oversized cashmere cardigan, feeling her body heat. I feel like I'm in a cocoon. I can finally breathe, relax, cry.

"Mom, this is Carrick." I sniff.

"Oh, Carrick." She lifts her wings again and bundles all six feet of him inside, and the two parts of my life come together.

"I brought food," she says. "Are you hungry?"

"Starving," we say in unison.

We wolf down the sandwiches, while she watches us.

"Can you taste yet?"

I shake my head but shovel the sandwiches into my mouth anyway.

"Look at you." She moves hair from my face. "You look so grown up."

"It's only been, like, three weeks." I laugh, then self-consciously share a look with Carrick.

She looks at him then, and as if realizing what has happened between me and him, she studies him in silence.

Carrick chews slowly, sensing her eyes on him. He looks up at her and then away quickly.

"You cut your hair," I say, taking in her cropped style.

"I always thought it was such a cliché when women cut their hair, thinking it was like some kind of brave and strong thing to do, as if the hair is of any importance at all. Well, I was wrong. I had to keep it long, for the hair-care contracts. Keep it long, keep it blond, keep it this, keep it that. Half the time it was extensions because that's what we wanted to project, healthy hair. That *beautiful* means lots of hair, that *perfect* means fuller hair. I got tired of it. So I shaved one side for the Candy Crevan housewarming."

"I remember."

"After you left I dip-dyed it pink, but I hated it. I looked like Barbie's grandmother. So I cut it. We're supposed to think that long hair is feminine. The perfect look for summer, beach hair. I told them all to suck it."

Carrick and I laugh.

"You sound like Juniper."

"Your dad doesn't know what to think." She smiles. "But he likes it."

My throat tightens and my heartbeat speeds up at the mention of Dad. I feel Carrick's eyes on me but I can't go there yet. Carrick senses we need some time alone and announces he's going for a walk.

"Why did you always come here for the sunrise, Mom?"

"Juniper had colic as a baby, she never slept, she was always in pain, screaming most of the day and always at night. I used to have to walk the house with her all night while your dad was on night shifts. Those hours were the loneliest, scariest moments I'd ever known. Everybody was asleep, the entire street—it felt like the whole world was asleep. The seconds felt like minutes, the minutes like hours, and those screams . . ." She shudders at the memory. "One night she wouldn't settle, and I just got in the car and drove. I had no idea where I was going but I wasn't staying home for a second longer. Sometimes she'd fall asleep in the car, sometimes not, but this time I ended up driving to the lake. I sat on the beach with Juniper while she howled, but it felt like the water and the breeze took away the edge, and suddenly the night began to disappear, as the sun rose, and as it did I felt the weight lift from me, the pressure and the fear all rose with the light. And Juniper, knocked out by the breeze, and maybe sensing my own contentment, finally slept.

"I came here every single sunrise after that, whether she was sleeping or not. It helped me more than her. And I tried to as much as possible when I had Ewan, though it was harder with the two of you. I would say good-bye to the day I had and hello to the next day—it felt like starting again. A blank canvas. Yesterday's problems were gone, hello to a new day and new beginnings."

I sit beside her on the sand, her arm over my shoulder, and I cuddle into her. I watch Carrick by the water, just standing there, hands in his pockets, head down, lost in thought.

"He's very handsome."

"He is." I smile.

"Well? Tell your mother. . . ."

"I don't think I need to tell my mother anything. You always know exactly what's going on."

She smiles, and I see the concern in her eyes.

"I know, I know. Be careful, be wise, etcetera."

"Good. He seems like a good person. He cares about you, I know that. He's risking a lot to help you."

"So are you," I say, feeling afraid for her. "So has Juniper." My eyes fill, thinking of my sister in that place right now. And of Granddad in his cell.

"I'm not afraid, and neither was Juniper," she says. "I can't wait to march into that place and demand for my daughter to be returned. It's everything I wanted to do when you were in Highland Castle but couldn't, so I get my chance to do it now."

"Thank you, Mom. I'm so sorry I've put you all in this situation."

She places her hands on my cheeks. "Don't you ever be sorry for what has happened. You tried to help a man. You were a bigger person than any of us could be."

I appreciate those words.

Silence falls between us. And now's the time.

"How is Dad?"

"He's okay."

"Is he still working at the station?"

"Yes, just about, and it's killing him to be there working for the Crevans, but . . ."

"You need the money."

"No," she says, which surprises me. "I mean, of course we need the money, but he can work anywhere. Your dad wants to know what's going on with you, and working at News 24 means he gets to find out what exactly they know about you. He's like a little spy." She laughs.

I smile, thinking of him there, guarding me. "I need his help."

She looks at me, intrigued.

"Carrick thinks I've arranged to meet you to discuss plans to get Juniper."

We both look at him standing at the water's edge, hands still in his pockets, looking out, the weight of the world on his shoulders.

"But I don't want him to know about this. Because if he knows, then it won't work."

I show her the USB. "It's footage of Crevan giving me a sixth brand."

She looks at it in shock. "*Crevan* branded you? Himself?"

I nod. I refused to ever discuss it with her before.

"Mr. Berry filmed it," I explain. "Now Mr. Berry has gone missing, as have all the guards. It's what Crevan has been looking for."

She takes it in her hand, squeezes it angrily, while it all sinks in. What this man has done to her daughter. I can tell she's looking forward to her invasion now. "This is what they've been searching the house for?"

"And why he's been hunting me. He doesn't want *me*. He wants *this*. I need you to give it to Dad. I need Dad to make copies. Then I need him to find Enya Sleepwell. She and I have made a plan. She'll know exactly what to do with it."

"Enya Sleepwell, the politician?"

"We can trust her."

"Okay. But I don't understand why Carrick can't know about this."

"Because this is a backup plan. The fewer people who know, the better chance it has of working, and I'm hoping I won't need to use it. I need you to take this laptop. Keep it safe somewhere. Carrick transferred the footage to this, too. I need to hold on to the original USB. I have a meeting with Judge Sanchez."

Her mouth falls open. "You what?"

"Plan A." I grin.

The sun appears on the horizon, and the new day begins.

SEVENTY-TWO

BACK IN THE turret room with Jackson and Sanchez, I look at the clock.

There's a plasma screen on the wall. Jackson presses the power button on the remote control.

My entire body tremors, from nerves, adrenaline, and the pain of my abdominal wound.

Sanchez's eyes widen as she watches the television. It looks like she's not breathing. The party political broadcast is on every channel.

"Hello, my name is Enya Sleepwell, and I'm leader of the Vital Party. We began five years ago with relatively small numbers but we are now the fastest-growing political party in the country. Since I became leader two months ago we have taken a look at our policies and reinvented ourselves. We are representing the real desires, hopes, and dreams of real people. We are the party that stands by our beliefs; we ask the difficult questions, find the solutions. We want to make this country strong again, undivided, working in harmony, leading and taking it forward using compassion and logic.

"We're also about lifting the veil on hypocrisy, revealing the truth about the leaders in our society. What you are about to see may be distressing to many. It is shocking and deeply disturbing. Our current government is fraught with danger; our current government allows *this* to happen."

The broadcast cuts from Enya to the footage of the Branding Chamber. Me, strapped in the chair. Judge Crevan stands before me in his bloodred robe shouting at me to repent. I refuse, and instead hold my tongue out, my first act of defiance against him. Bark places a clamp on my tongue and brands it with the hot weld. The sounds that come from me are like those of a wounded animal.

It's distressing, and I see Jackson hold his hand to his head. I doubt he's ever witnessed a branding in his life.

Then Judge Crevan shouts at me some more, accuses me of being Flawed to my very backbone. He orders the sixth branding and Jackson sits up, turns to Sanchez in shock, then back to the screen again. He can't believe what he's seeing.

I hear sounds from outside. The crowd. Restless.

I stand up and make my way to the window that overlooks the courtyard. Neither Sanchez nor Jackson stops me; they seem frozen by what is happening on the screen.

Outside, the thousands of Flawed who gathered earlier are now gone, but the courtyard has been opened up again to members of the public, who are always invited to come to the courtyard to watch as accused Flawed are taken from their holding cells in one building, across the courtyard to the courtroom on the other side.

Many of the people outside are dressed in red, but they aren't Flawed. They are members of the public, they are protesting against the Guild. I see them wearing T-shirts just like the ones Mom, Juniper, Ewan, and the students were wearing, reading ABOLISH THE GUILD. The courtyard is mixed with protestors and regular people, and they are letting out shouts of disgust. Boos.

And then I realize why.

They are all watching the footage of my brandings on the large screen

306

people watch trials on. Somebody has switched the station from Flawed TV to this. More and more people flood through the gates of the castle to watch, to see what all the fuss is about. I see them hold their hands to their mouths in shock as they witness Crevan in action.

Bark refuses to brand my spine. He says that there is no anesthetic.

I hear the people gasp, I see them grab the arms of the people next to them. They are starting to realize what they are about to see. These are not just protestors: There are other members of the public there, too, who came to witness a Flawed being brought to court. I sense them changing sides.

Crevan takes the searing hot rod in his hands. The guards are emotional and crying, trying to murmur words of support in my ears, trying to hold me still. Crevan brands my spine and my scream echoes and rebounds off the Highland Castle walls in the courtyard and out over the city.

The crowd howls in disgust. My body is trembling.

"No." Sanchez stands. She is visibly shaking, her red robe quaking around her body.

"What is this?" Jackson asks. "Is this real?" He looks to Sanchez and then to me. "Dear God."

After the harrowing footage, Enya Sleepwell returns. "I apologize for having to show you that. I apologize to Celestine North for what happened to her. We cannot let this happen to the innocent people of our great country. It is because of this that the Vital Party is one hundred percent behind abolishing the Guild. If the Guild itself is Flawed, how can it continue? We need to address it now. No more baby steps, it's time to take leaps and bounds, and bring this country forward.

"Vote the Vital Party, for fairness and justice, for strong leadership, bringing this country forward with compassion and logic."

There's silence in the room.

SEVENTY-THREE

GUARDS RUSH INTO the turret room.

"Rioting outside. We need to move you to safety."

Jackson stands up so quickly the chair topples backward and he doesn't bother picking it up. He looks at me, his face filled with utter shock, fear, and disgust.

"Dear girl," he whispers, apology all over his face. He struggles to find words. He looks at Judge Sanchez; his contempt for her is clear.

"Judge Jackson, you should come with me quickly," the Whistleblower interrupts Judge Jackson's thoughts. His red robe billows behind him as he exits to save himself.

"I guess the deal is off," I say to Sanchez.

She turns to me then and I almost think I see a look of admiration: I successfully managed to pull the wool over her eyes. But then she coldly turns and hurries out of the cell without a word, under guard.

I'm left alone, in the round room, without a word of explanation as to what will happen to me. I wonder about Carrick, Raphael, and Granddad, if they're still passed out. I pace the cell, heart hammering. I look outside and see the Whistleblowers back in their riot gear. More members of the public are streaming through the gates, and it's not to cheer on the Whistleblowers. They are punching their fists in the air, demanding answers, demanding change. I want to be down there, not trapped up here.

The door bursts open.

It's Art.

"I heard there was a damsel in distress in the tower," he says. "Princess, I'm here to rescue you," he adds dramatically, with an awkward laugh.

I roll my eyes; now is not the time for one of Art's jokes.

But before I say anything he adds, "I'm rescuing *all* of you."

"They're out cold," I tell him as I move as quickly as I can to the door, trying to ignore the pain in my stomach. "How will we get them out?"

"I have a van ready at a side exit—we just need to get them to it," he says, starting to run down the spiral staircase. On every level I can see staff members using the emergency exits to escape.

"The lawyer should be easy enough to lift. I'll take him, you get your Granddad," he says, and I shake my head at another of Art's jokes, his coping mechanism in times of stress.

As everybody floods out of the building, we head in the opposite direction, going down, down, down to the basement.

I stop running. "Come on, Art, stop, let's think. Seriously, how can we do this? We can't carry them on our own."

He stops rushing down the stairs and looks back up at me. "Maybe they'll be awake by now."

"Art, *focus*. Last time I was drugged, I was out for most of the day, and when I woke up I was paralyzed from the waist down."

"The last time you were *what*?"

"But that was an injection; this could be something else. Maybe they're just sleeping pills. We need to think of something else. We need more help. We need people from outside to help us."

He thinks it through. "The Flawed are rioting. Members of the public are charging the gates in protest. Some fool accidentally pressed a button to air the Vital Party's announcement around the courtyard. They want my dad's head on a plate."

"I'm sorry," I say quietly.

"It was me who did it," he says.

I look at him, stunned.

"Okay, so maybe the people outside can help. We should go out there and talk to them. Only . . ." He looks down at his uniform.

"It's not safe outside for you, Art. You stay here, make sure they're safe, unlock their cells. I'll get help from outside."

The role reversal is ironic.

"I can open their doors from here." Art enters a private staff-only room, filled with CCTV cameras showing the cells downstairs. I go inside with him and urgently scan the screens for signs of Granddad, Raphael, and Carrick. They're all still where they were when I left them, no sign of movement at all.

"Mary May!" Art suddenly says, and I turn around quickly.

Mary May stands at the door, watching us, back in her Mary Poppins Whistleblower uniform, and her face is a picture of anger, twisted up so tight it's as though if she unscrews it, her face will come flying at me like a catapult.

I instinctively leave the room, not wanting to be locked inside the windowless space. Art follows.

"I'm taking her out of here. She's innocent, Mary May," Art says, standing in front of me, blocking her way. "Did you see the broadcast? It's all over."

"I don't care about any broadcast," she says dismissively, as if she has no idea of what has gone on. "You were in my home," she says to me slowly. "You spoke to my mother. You were in her bedroom."

Art turns to look at me, and the look on his face would be comical under different circumstances, but not now, because when we both look at her, she has a gun in her hand.

SEVENTY-FOUR

"WHOA! MARY MAY, put that thing away!" Art shouts, hands out in front of him. "What the . . . where the hell did you get that thing?"

She ignores him, as though she can't hear or see him, as though it's just me and her in the room. She takes a few steps forward and I start to edge back. I think of the unlocked doors in the holding cells downstairs, and I hope they will realize it, that whenever they do come around, they'll be able to escape.

"You were in my home," she repeats. "You were in my mother's bedroom."

"You were in my home, too," I say, hearing the shake in my voice. "You took things from me, remember? I was just getting them back."

"What did you do to my mother?" she asks, as though she hasn't heard a word that I've said at all, like she's just listening to the voice inside her own head.

Her pace quickens and I continue to back away, feeling Art's hand on my elbow. I don't want to turn my back to her, I don't want to test whether she will shoot me. My legs feel weak and yet there's a delirious giddiness awakening inside me. A feeling that none of this can be real, that after all of this struggle, it ends like *this*, a psychotic episode at the hands of a sad, lonely woman.

"I didn't do anything to your mother," I say nervously.

"Keep walking," Art whispers, guiding me down a corridor. We walk backward, always keeping Mary May and her raised gun in our sight. As soon as we turn a corner and she's out of sight, we pivot and run.

Art runs to the exit door. He waves his security card over the panel beside it, but nothing happens. Everything has been locked up to prevent protestors from breaking in to the building.

"It needs a real key," I tell him, and he curses.

He takes out a ring of keys and with trembling hands starts to try the first key in the door.

Mary May appears, walking at the same speed; slow, deliberate steps, hand holding the gun extended out in front of her.

"She said you sat by her bedside," she continues as though in a trance. "She called you her angel." She cocks her head to the side. "Why would she say that, Celestine?"

"I don't, I can't . . ." I can barely formulate a thought as I stare at the gun pointed at me.

Art continues working his way through the key chain for the correct key. These doors are old and the keys are enormous. Art has only ever had to use the security system where he waves his card, and he's clearly unfamiliar with the locks. I'm backed up against Art, but Mary May continues to advance toward me.

"She said she wanted to see the others. I told her no. Alice doesn't deserve to see Mommy, not after what she did. None of them do. They all knew about him and her. Just before she went, Mommy said she forgave me. *Forgave me for what?*" Mary May asks. "Everybody gets what they deserve. I don't need her forgiveness. They all got what they deserved. Alice stole him from me and they all knew about it. All of them. I *spared* Mommy," she says. "I did her a *favor*. You were in my house. What did you do to my mother?"

"I told you I didn't do anything. I retrieved what was mine, the things you stole from my bedroom. I took them back. I found the footage you were searching for. We put it on TV. Everybody saw it. Everybody knows. It's all over." I try to bring her back to the here and now.

"She woke up this morning. Ten past eight. She wouldn't eat her eggs. Two boiled eggs and two asparagus is what she eats every morning. She wouldn't eat them. Odd."

Despite the situation, I snigger, nervously I suppose.

"I didn't do anything to stop her from eating eggs," I reply.

Art swears behind me as he tries another key in the door.

"Yes, you did. Because she's dead now."

SEVENTY-FIVE

"WHAT?" I WHISPER.

Art stops at the door and looks up at me.

"I didn't do anything," I say. "I swear. Open the door," I say desperately now, understanding her motivation. Her mother is dead; she blames me; she's holding a gun: This cannot end well.

"She didn't eat her eggs," she continues. "She always eats her eggs, so I knew something was up. She said an angel had come to her during the night and it was time for her to go to the Lord. I told her not to be silly. Said she was having ridiculous notions again, because sometimes she did. Things would come and go for her. She asked for a bath at lunchtime and I bathed her."

Art finally finds the correct key and pushes the door open. I smell the fresh air immediately, hear the sounds of shouting in the air. I breathe in the air and step outside, moving away from her as quickly as I can. However, it's a courtyard, it's wide, it's vast, a perfect square of cobblestones: There's nowhere to hide. I'm a sitting duck for Mary May.

It's a private courtyard, for staff, not open to the public. Through a locked barred gate I see mayhem in the main square. One small group of staff sees Mary May with her gun and screams and runs in the opposite direction. This isn't the help I need. Where are the authorities? I realize that no one will come to my aid. Despite the fact Mary May is holding a gun, which is not an authorized Whistleblower weapon, I am Flawed and she is a Whistleblower and nothing can be done to stop this. If anyone tried, they may be seen as aiding me. The only people who could come to my aid are the police, and my last run-in with one at the supermarket didn't end well.

"After her bath, Mommy said she was tired," Mary May continues as though we haven't scared away a bunch of suits and are now surrounded by mayhem as the Flawed and the public protest in the public courtyard next to us. She's in a world of her own. "She sometimes has a morning nap. So I put her to bed. That's when she told me about you. She called you her angel, but I realized it was you. She said that you visited her last night, that you helped her get water from the lake. I thought she was making it up. Then she said she forgave me. That she will speak for me when her time comes . . ." She doesn't finish the sentence, but a single tear runs down her cheek and her hand starts to tremor. "You killed her," she says.

"Hey, stop it," Art says, stepping in front of me. "Put the gun down, Mary May, this is crazy!"

"You killed my mommy," she says, ignoring Art.

The gate into the courtyard opens and I quickly glance in its direction to see people flooding in. Flawed and public, escaping the main courtyard. I think I see Carrick's brother, Rogan, leading the pack, but I'm not sure, I'm afraid to take my eyes off Mary May and that gun.

"There she is!" someone yells, and I assume it's Whistleblowers coming to get me, and for a moment I feel relief, I don't care who the rescue comes from as long as I'm not shot, but it's confusing as everyone is wearing red now, so it's difficult to distinguish the difference. It's as though we're all the same.

"Don't you tell me how to do my job," Mary May finally addresses Art. "Your father instructed me to look after this girl and I will follow his instructions. My job is my life. I gave up everything for this, to answer to your father. I gave him everything. And I have never not finished the job I started," she yells, clearly uncomfortable with the growing presence of others in the square. She's attracting attention, too. People are moving close. Calling out to her to put the gun down.

"Here! I told you she'd be here." I hear a familiar voice and I look to the left and see Rogan. It *is* him. He's with a small group and he's pointing at Mary May. "You should have taken me in when you had the chance," Rogan shouts at her. "Look who I brought to see you."

Mary May finally hears them and turns to her right. She looks at them and her face changes, mouth open, skin pale in utter shock and terror.

"You can't ignore your family now," a man yells.

"Remember us, sis?" the woman says, and I look at them in surprise. It's her sister, Alice, and her three brothers.

"We want to see Mommy," Alice says.

"What did you do to her?" a brother asks.

"Nothing. Nothing. It was her," she says weakly, the power all gone from her as the family she was responsible for branding Flawed gangs up on her. Her father is dead, and now her mother is, too.

Her power has disappeared and it's as though she suddenly realizes it. She glances at the madness around her. Flawed, Whistleblowers, and members of the public all running wild. The Whistleblowers are now the hunted; the Flawed and unflawed are together, the hunters.

She lowers her gun; I see the panic start to show in her eyes. She backs away and starts to run. But she doesn't get far, because a hand appears from inside the door that we came through. A hand that pulled its body along the cold, hard floor of the holding cell floors, and up the winding staircase.

Carrick appears, sweating, panting, exhausted, just in time, to wrap his hand around her ankle, stopping her from getting away.

She starts to fall to the ground, and as she does her hands instinctively go out to break her fall. Forgetting the gun is still in her hand, she squeezes the trigger.

The gun fires. The sound echoes around the courtyard.

Everybody, *everybody* drops to the ground.

SEVENTY-SIX

WITH EVERYONE DOWN on the ground I don't know if anyone has been shot. There's a shocked silence, as everybody stays down.

But the screaming that begins is a hint. It's high, hysterical, and out of control. It's panicked. It tells me somebody has been hit.

And when I try to focus on where it's coming from, I realize it's coming from me.

SEVENTY-SEVEN

ART IS ON top of me, guarding me like a shield. He's not moving.

SEVENTY-EIGHT

"ART!" I SCREECH.

"Celestine!" Carrick calls out.

"Carrick!" Rogan yells, and runs to his brother.

"Art!" I try to get up from the ground but he's so heavy and I don't want to hurt him further.

"It was an accident," Mary May says from the ground. "It was an . . . I didn't mean to. . . ."

Her family gets to their feet and surrounds her. Her brother takes the gun away from her.

Her sister leaves her brothers and runs toward us. "I'm a vet. Or I was." She feels his pulse.

"Is he alive?" I cry.

"Celestine!" Carrick calls. "Are you okay?"

I can't answer him—my focus is completely on Art.

Alice nods and moves Art. He groans, and I'm so relieved to hear his voice.

"Get your hands off him!" Judge Crevan booms. I look up and see him running across the courtyard toward us. "He's my son."

Alice looks at Crevan and down at Art, making a connection. For an awful moment I think she won't want to help him because of who his dad is. But she makes a decision. "Last I heard, there was no rule against a Flawed aiding a Whistleblower," she says.

"He's not a Whistleblower," I say. "He was helping me escape." I need as many people to hear this as possible for Art's sake. He wouldn't want to be thought of like his dad: That was his greatest fear.

"Celestine," Carrick calls again, and I look up. He's desperately trying to make his way toward me. Rogan is trying to help him to his feet. I'm torn. I don't want to ignore Carrick, but I can see that he has help now, and I need to concentrate on Art.

Art, Art, Art.

SEVENTY-NINE

ALICE TAKES OFF her cardigan and wraps it around the wound on Art's stomach, and she presses down.

He acted as a shield for me; he took the bullet square on. He saved my life.

"Ambulance is on its way," a Whistleblower calls.

Crevan falls to his knees. Art's head is in my lap. I cradle it, run my fingers through his curls with my trembling fingers. They're covered in blood.

Crevan sits on the other side, leaning over his son, showering his face in kisses. The two of us are crouched over, crying.

"He'll be okay?" He weeps. "Tell me he'll be okay. I can't lose him. He's all I have."

Art's eyes flicker open and closed again.

"Who did this?" Crevan asks angrily, looking at me.

"Her," I say, venom in my voice.

Crevan turns around and we see Mary May on her knees as though praying for forgiveness, guarded by her three Flawed brothers, who look like they want to put her in the ground at any moment. She is a shell of herself, like her spirit has died and her whole life has fallen apart.

"Sir. Judge Crevan." She swallows. "It was an . . . I didn't mean to . . . I was trying to . . . I wanted to . . . It was Celestine," she says, the anger for me growing within her again. "That girl. I was trying to get that girl for you."

"I said *monitor* her, not kill her," he yells. "Guide her on the right path, not become a damn murderer!"

"Please, forgive me. This job is everything. This is my life. I always have and always will be answerable to you."

"He won't forgive you now, Mary," one of her brothers says. "You've failed. It's over."

"There's nothing left of the Guild," Crevan shouts at her. "Look around you!" And as she does, she becomes smaller, she shrinks down into her heels.

I cling to Art as he comes and goes, eyes flickering, coughing and moaning.

"Celestine," Carrick calls out one final time. His voice is hoarse from shouting.

I look up and see him sitting by the door of the castle, the one we escaped from. Rogan is on the ground beside him. Our eyes meet. He looks sad, lost, hopeful. In those green eyes I know he's asking me a question.

And then the arrival of the ambulance breaks our look, ending the possibility of an answer, which is just as well, because right now I don't have one.

EIGHTY

I SIT BY Art's bedside at the hospital, in complete stillness, surrounded by stillness. It's a stark contrast to the hours leading up to this, and the journey in the ambulance to get here.

Art is stable. The irony is that he was lucky, the bullet missed his small intestine, colon, liver, and abdominal blood vessels. He is going to be okay. Physically anyway: What the scars of a gunshot to the stomach will do to his already wounded mind, we will have to wait and see.

My eyelids feel heavy, like life has given me a rest. Over the past three weeks I have felt that if I didn't keep moving, then I'd never move again, and yet life has stopped me dead in my tracks as if to say, *No more, Celestine, no more.* I don't even feel like moving now. I wouldn't know where to go if I did move. Here is the only place I need to be.

My skin carries brands; Art has a bullet wound. Our scars and imperfections all have stories. My scars give me strength, remind me how I can overcome the toughest times in my life; his wound will remind him that he protected me, that he did good, that he came to the aid of a Flawed. He redeemed himself and in so doing defended me in more ways than he could realize. He defended my actions, too. Every day we look at our bodies, we live in our skin, and we will never forget.

A nurse arrives, Judy, she's nice. She removes my cold and untouched green tea from the bedside unit and replaces it with what smells like berry tea.

"I'll keep trying," she says, good-humored. "This was sent from the castle for you." She hands me my backpack, the one that was taken from me when I was brought to the fish-gutting warehouse this morning. I'm grateful for it, desperate to get out of the detainment clothes I was given at the castle to replace the red slip, and not just because they're soaked in Art's blood.

"Mr. Crevan, there are some men here to see you," she says, the kindness gone from her voice.

Crevan lifts his head from the bed where he's had it buried beside Art ever since we arrived. His eyes are red-rimmed and bloodshot, his nose constantly streaming like his eyes. We have been sitting together, quite comfortably, in complete silence for hours now.

"Is it the police?" he asks, sniffing. "You can tell them to come in." He wipes his face with the sleeve of his shirt in preparation.

Two men in suits enter.

"Mr. Crevan, we'd like a word with you in private, please."

"It's okay." He stands, pulling his jeans up by the waist. "Celestine was there when it happened. She's a witness, too. We've already talked to your men, uniformed police, but I'm glad and appreciate you're taking this so seriously. You're detectives?"

They nod.

He makes his way over to them to shake their hands.

"Mr. Crevan, we're here regarding other matters. This is not about your son. Mary May has been arrested and taken into custody."

"Oh. Then what is this about?"

The two detectives look at me and my stomach churns. This is about me. About the footage that was aired.

"As we said, we think it's best if we talk to you in private." This is said more officially, but Crevan is not ready to go without a fight.

"If this is about the actions of the Guild, then I can tell you it's already been addressed. I no longer work for the Guild, I've been removed from my position. There will be an announcement made first thing in the morning at a press conference. I'm also told there's an inquiry into the Guild's rulings, so I'm sure you'll find this is all in hand, gentlemen, it is being dealt with internally. I suggest you talk to the head judge, Jennifer Sanchez, about any matters."

He is in judge mode, trying to control everything, trying to be above everyone and everything. But he lacks power now, gone is his vibrant red robe, his Purveyors of Perfection crest, replaced with a crumpled checked shirt and bloody jeans. This is off-duty Crevan trying to command control, cleaning-out-the-garage Crevan, wash-the-car Crevan, drive-Celestine-and-Art-to-the-local-farmers'-market Crevan. I never saw the monster in him.

"If it's about Celestine, then she has been granted her freedom. That, too, has been settled within the Guild. She was due to start a prison sentence, but I think that will be waived. In fact, I'm sure of it."

"This isn't about the actions of the Guild, it's about your actions against Celestine North, which are a criminal matter," the detective says.

The other pipes up, less sensitive than the first. "We're also investigating the claims of Pia Wang, Nathan Berry, five guards who were present during the Branding Chamber crime, and four teenagers from Grace O'Malley secondary school, among others."

Crime.

And there it is, the face that I wanted to see for so long. The look of shock, at being put in his place by people in authority, by the law, a realization that he was wrong, that he is not above everybody, that what he put me and so many others through was wrong. I see it flash in his eyes, the confusion, the self-doubt, the self-hate, the apology, the questions. The veil of self-assurance all falls down.

"We're told that your son is in stable condition. We did wait for this news before talking to you. We'd like you to accompany us to the station."

Crevan appears torn at the prospect of having to leave Art. I think of being dragged off the bus away from Juniper and Art, the whistles ringing in my ears. Paraded through the courtyard to a hissing crowd, the branding chamber, the pain of six sears on my body, in bed for a week, tied up and locked away by supposed friends, the supermarket riot, buried alive, paraded half-naked through the streets. The worst thing of all, having to run from my family. This was all at his hands.

I watch Crevan being taken away. Our eyes meet, and in that look I see everything I have felt over the past five weeks. And I know he is feeling it, too.

The question is, does it make me feel better?

EIGHTY-ONE

NO.

For someone to win, somebody else must lose. For that person to have won they must have lost something in the first place.

The irony of justice is that the feelings that precede it and those which fruit from it are never fair and balanced.

Not even justice itself is perfect.

EIGHTY-TWO

I WATCH ART for some time after his dad leaves. He looks like an angel, his face completely unharmed, his baby skin, the light shadow of facial hair emerging. I run my fingers over his hands; his skin is smooth, his fingers are long. I see them playing the guitar and singing about the giraffe that couldn't find a turtleneck to fit, the monkey that had vertigo, the lion that couldn't use a smart pad, the zebra that had polka dots. We all used to sit around crying with laughter as he entertained us, but I guess we never put it all together. He always sang about something that didn't fit in, someone who was left out, someone who was losing or missing something.

Art has been living with his own demons since his mother died, no wonder he joined the Whistleblowers. I can actually begin to understand him now, imagine I can even forgive him, such is the depth of my understanding. Compassion and logic are all that's ever needed. Can I forgive him? Yes, I can even do that.

I pull the curtain around his bed, for privacy, so I can change into my jeans and T-shirt. They're the clothes I was wearing with Carrick when he helped me escape from Crevan's secret hospital, when he helped me break into Mary May's home for the snow globe, when I was taken from Sanchez's apartment to the docklands, when I was stripped and dressed in the red slip for the parade through the town. I imagine they smell of Carrick. Do I ever want to wear these clothes again? Will it feel like I'm going backward?

I dig deeper in the bag for something else to wear and my hands brush against Carrick's notebooks. I recall the last time I saw him before seeing him again in the castle. I had said good-bye to Mom; he was going in the car with her to rescue Juniper from the dreaded skin graft operation. Carrick was going to guide her there. I was to wait at the lake for Raphael Angelo, who was going to drive me to see Sanchez to make our deal.

I remember as the car drove away wanting to shout after them that he'd forgotten his books, which he'd trusted me to carry, but I stopped myself. I selfishly wanted to keep them. Not because I wanted to read them—well, of course I wanted that—but I wouldn't betray his confidence; it was because if I had something of his, it meant that I would absolutely have to see him again. It would mean he would be safe. A deluded thought process, but that's where I was at the time. He'd have to come for me to get his books back, or I would have to find him to give them to him.

Now, for the first time since the whole episode occurred, I start to wonder why on earth Carrick was in the cells at all. How did he get there? If he and Mom had gone to get Juniper from the hospital, and Juniper and Mom were safe and well, and the others—Mona, Lennox, Fergus, and Lorcan—all said that he'd gotten away safe and sound, then how did he end up in Highland Castle?

I do a quick search on my phone and among the hundreds of changing news stories documenting what's happening in our country I see it in black-and-white. Carrick Vane, accused of being on the run with Celestine North and evading Whistleblowers and breaking Guild rules, handed himself in.

That's how he ended up back in the cell beside me. He wanted to be there.

And I left him.

I've been sitting here, trapped in time, in a kind of shock until now. My eyes fill with tears.

I take out his notebooks, feeling guilty but determined to know what's inside, and I let out a whimper when I see the first page.

I find young, childish writing, and I realize they're his institution diaries, the ones he admitted to writing for all those years and then hiding from his teachers.

Today we did a smell and taste test. They wanted to know what the smells reminded us of. Paul Cott started crying when he smelled lemon. He had to tell them why and when he did the teachers told him that that is a memory he needs to forget, that his parents were bad people.

Baby powder reminded me of baths. I think I had baths with Mommy. I must have because there's only showers here. I remember the bubbles that I could hide under. I remember that they tickled my skin. I remember putting them on my chin and pretending to have a beard like Granddad. Then I remembered Granddad and Grandma and I remembered so many other things. I remember Mommy laughing. I remember her wrapping me in a huge towel like a baby and carrying me to her bed. I remember kicking and shouting and pretending I didn't like it, but really I did. I remember a glass of chocolate milk while she dried my hair.

It must have been when I was five. Three years ago. But I remember.

She's not a good mom, they say. Unfit. Dad, too. They tell me I'm here for my own good, that Mommy and Daddy want me here, but I don't think that part is right. I remember them crying when the men took me. Screaming and crying. If she is so bad then why do I smile when I smell her perfume on Ms. Harris, who I will never tell wears the same as Mommy, and why does my tummy feel sick when I think of them?

The teachers are right. One smell leads to another. It helps to remember things and now I can't stop thinking and remembering. They are the ones who made me start remembering, it's not my fault. I'm not going to be like the others and tell them what I remember. Not the real things. Because I don't want them to take them away from me.

As tears fall from my eyes I skip toward the end of the last notebook. I don't have time to read it all; I need to find him and give them back to him.

We've been told we can come up with our own surname on our sixteenth birthday. They make them legal and we get a passport and then we can travel. We're not allowed to keep our mom and dad's names, but they took that from us a long time ago. I would have been Carrick Brightman. I still use it in my head. I never say it out loud, though. Here we just have a first name and a number for our surname.

I've finally decided my name and they've approved it. I had to sit before the board and explain why. I didn't tell them the truth, but I haven't been telling them the truth since I started writing this thing. I think writing this makes it easier to lie to them because I know that somewhere I'm telling the truth. If they ever find this, I'll be branded and I won't care.

I remember being out late at night with Dad. I was on his shoulders. It was pitch-black and we were running. I thought it was a game, but now I think we were running from the Whistleblowers and they were trying to pretend it was a game.

I think we were lost, or I thought we were lost, and that's when Dad taught me about the stars. He showed me the North Star and everything that leads from that.

He told me if I'm ever lost, to find that star. I know that when I leave here in 1,095 days that I will try to find them. Finding them is the worst thing we could do; we're told this every day. But I want to find the woman who wrapped me in the towel that smelled of baby powder and the man who taught me about the stars. The two people who made me feel safer and happier in the smallest memories that I have than anyone has ever done in here.

I don't know where they are, but I know one thing: I'll look north. The answers are north, and I'll let the wind take me.

And that is why my new surname is Vane.

Carrick Vane.

————————

I close the diary, hot tears dripping down my cheeks, with a sense of urgency within me. I quickly change my clothes into anything I can find, I no longer care. I can wear the clothes of yesterday and still move forward. My sock catches on my anklet and I sit down and take it off.

I leave it by Art's bedside.

"You'll always be with me," I whisper, kissing his lips. "Good-bye, Art."

I leave the hospital room expecting to be stopped when I get outside. Instead, the nurses and doctors part for me. There are Whistleblowers at the door at the end of the corridor, and my heart sinks. I'm being taken again. The kind nurse urges me on. I frown. Then one of the Whistleblowers sees me. He reaches for the door, and he opens it.

I start walking, and the hospital staff starts clapping, smiles on their faces, some of them crying. I keep walking, expecting for somebody to grab me at any moment, but nobody does. I walk straight through those open doors, into the unknown.

EIGHTY-THREE

2 MONTHS LATER

I'M ON GRANDDAD'S FARM. It's July. The sun is beating down on my skin. I'm wearing a sundress, with spaghetti straps tied on my shoulders, a pretty floral design that's confusing the bees.

I'm alone in the strawberry beds, eyes closed, face lifted to the sun. I am free, but even better than that, I feel free. I was free before, but I never knew it, now I feel it.

I hear laughter and the flow of conversation in the distance, the smell of burning wood as the food is lifted from the cooking pit for all of us to share. The farmworkers, my family, Pia Wang and her family, Raphael Angelo and his wife and their seven children, Carrick's family, too. My new friends, Mona, Lennox, Fergus, Lorcan, Lizzie, and Leonard, are here. Cordelia and Evelyn are traveling; Cordelia is showing her daughter, the big wide world that she'd been forced to hide her from since her birth. Lennox has been hovering exceptionally close to Juniper ever since he laid eyes on her. I think the feeling is mutual; Juniper hasn't stopped smiling.

Mr. Berry and Tina decided not to come. It's not as easy for everyone. It's not easy for anyone.

It has been one month since the Guild press conference that was to announce Sanchez's replacement of Crevan. Instead, that press conference announced something quite different: the dissolution of the Guild.

Appointed by the state, the Truth Commission will write up a report of their findings on the Guild. This while the private inquiry into Crevan's personal behavior still continues, alongside the legal investigation by police into his criminal activities. Everybody wants to be seen to be doing something, but there are no solutions and no punishments as of yet.

Enya Sleepwell, on the back of her dramatic broadcast on the eve of polling day, was voted into power and is our new prime minister. The Reduction of the Flawed proposal has very much been scrapped, no possibility of it ever coming to light, and Enya has commissioned a study, titled the Sleepwell Report, separate from the Truth Commission, into the Guild's proceedings, examining the roles of every politician, businessperson, and legal eagle who passed through its halls. How exactly they are to be held accountable, I don't know. The findings from the reports are eagerly anticipated.

Enya said that nothing could happen overnight, but it did. After weeks of debate, the government voted against the Flawed court and anti-Flawed decrees, and the Flawed system was abolished at midnight on the day of the vote. In a matter of hours, Flawed were declared to have the same rights as everybody else in the country, no longer second-class citizens. The people, Flawed and un-Flawed, gathered in Highland Castle courtyard to celebrate. I was among them.

The aftereffects of this decision have been enormous. Raphael Angelo's office grows steadily by the minute as he takes on case after case against the government for compensation for the damage done to the lives of people who were branded Flawed. A government compensation scheme totaling one hundred million has been set up, the Clayton Byrne fund, named after the old man who died on the bus, the man I tried to protect but failed to save. His death will not be in vain.

But the most valuable compensation of all was Enya Sleepwell's well-meaning public apology to all the victims of the Guild for the government's failure to intervene. An apology is perhaps all that many people will receive, but Raphael won't rest until every single branded person receives *at least* a personal apology, until their reputations are redressed, until the suffering of anyone who was ever hurt as a result of the Guild has been acknowledged.

The government announced that never again will this country allow such "a lapse in humanity to poison us and strip people of their basic human rights." Everybody looks back and wonders how we allowed it to happen in the first place. It all seems so simple now.

As for F.A.B. children, all those children who had been taken from their homes or torn from their mothers at birth, have the right to return to their rightful homes if they so wish. And as for those who grew up without their parents, those who are no longer children, whose parents are aged or no longer living, who were told and believed all their lives that their parents were monsters, or that they weren't loved or wanted, they face having to come to terms with the reality that their parents went to their graves without justice or apology for their suffering. Enya Sleepwell has appointed Alpha to the F.A.B. Rights Alliance to help assist with this enormous mess.

So what does all that really mean for any of us?

For Crevan, he still walks the streets a free man, awaiting trial for his part in my sixth branding, for which he will receive a short prison sentence, no doubt. His reputation has been tarnished: He will not lead a life of power as he did before. People recognize him on the streets: They stare; they shout abuse; they judge. I know what he faces on a daily basis, I've been there. Thousands of us have been there.

For Art, he moved away from this country to study, to set up a new life where he can escape the shadow of his father. He will study science at college in September as he planned. He promises to stay in touch, and even though our bond has dissolved, it doesn't mean it has disappeared, it is still there somewhere, probably for the rest of our lives, just not visible to the human eye, not in the same form as it was.

As for me, my future is more uncertain. I have been invited back to my school to complete the exams they would not let me sit for in their halls only months ago. I won't return, but I *will* study, I will finish my exams. Enya Sleepwell calls continuously for my involvement in the Vital Party, as do various media outlets for my opinion on every daily occurrence. Professor Lambert has a job with my name on it, he says.

For once, I won't plan, I won't have any expectations. I will take things step by step, save the leaps for the times of necessity. I will enjoy the sun on my skin, the wind on my face, the feel of Carrick against my body, the sound of my family's voices, and the effects of their love, and value the loyalty of my new friends. The simple things, some say, but that depends on where you live and what laws control you, because there was nothing simple about any of us achieving this.

I pick a strawberry and drop it into the pot, feeling like a child again. As I look down, I see a weed growing in the beds and automatically bend to pull it out. But I stop myself. I leave it there and smile conspiratorially. Just our little secret.

Before I make my way back to the others, I can't help it—the strawberries are too tempting and, just for old time's sake, for the memory of me and Juniper as children picking our own strawberries, I reach down into the bucket and place one in my mouth. I can smell its sweetness, and, as I'm used to happening this year, expect nothing more. But as I bite into it, my eyes pop open. My mouth doesn't know what to do with the sensation.

I scream, a high-pitched shriek. The talking and laughter stop immediately. I run from the strawberry beds.

When I reach my family and friends, they're all standing, watching out for me, alert, worried, ready to attack, looking for predators and intruders because we've had our fair share of them.

Carrick drops his shovel and marches away from the cooking pit that he's working on with Granddad, Dad, and Adam, and hurries toward me, eyes black.

"What's wrong?"

I drop the tin bucket of strawberries and run to him. I leap up and he catches me, my legs wrapped around his body, clinging to him, my hands on his stunned face.

I ignore the fact that everyone is looking, that Kelly is looking at us dreamily, that Juniper is whooping, that Dad is uncomfortable and Mom is laughing at him, that Ewan is pretending to vomit, that Raphael Angelo's kids have replicated the very same move and are now swinging out of one another, making smoochy kissing sounds, that Mona, Lennox, Fergus, and Lorcan are cheering us on. Granddad cheers, which annoys my dad even more, and Pia Wang giggles, with her husband and two children beside her.

Or at least I pretend to ignore them, but I feel them with me, every single molecule of their energy, with happiness.

I gaze into Carrick's eyes. Green as can be. I press my lips to his, and I finally *taste* his kiss.

EIGHTY-FOUR

THERE'S THE PERSON you think you should be and there's the person you really are. I'm not sure who I should be, but I now know who I am.

And that, I say, is the perfect place to start again.

ACKNOWLEDGMENTS

ENORMOUS THANKS TO Jean Feiwel, Anna Roberto, and Will Schwalbe. To Molly Brouillette and the epic Fierce Reads team who were a joy to travel with. Thanks to my agent Marianne Gunn O'Connor, my beautiful supportive family, and, most important of all, my dream team David, Robin, and Sonny.